ZacBox
And The Pearls of Pleiades

Also by John Wesley Anderson:

Ute Indian Prayer Trees of the Pikes Peak Region

Rankin Scott Kelly, First Sheriff, El Paso County,
Colorado Territory

Native American Prayer Trees of Colorado

R.S. Kelly, A Man of the Territory

ZacBox and the Pearls of Pleiades

Sherlock Holmes in Little London, 1896 the Missing Year

ZacBox
And The Pearls of Pleiades

John Wesley Anderson

Honoring the Past

Shaping the Future

CIRCLE STAR PUBLISHING

COLORADO SPRINGS, COLORADO

Published in the United States of America by
CIRCLE STAR PUBLISHING
P.O. Box 60144
Colorado Springs, Colorado 80960

Anderson, John Wesley
ZacBox and the Pearls of Pleiades / John Wesley Anderson
First printing: July 2020
Library of Congress Control Number: 2020938059

ISBN 978-1-943829-03-3

Publisher's Cataloging-in-Publication Data

Names: Anderson, John Wesley, 1954-
Title: ZacBox and the pearls of Pleiades / John Wesley Anderson.
Series: The ZacBox Saucer Series
Description: Colorado Springs, CO: Rhyolite Press LLC, 2020.
Identifiers: LCCN: 2020938059 | ISBN: 9781943829033
Subjects: LCSH Space flight--Fiction. | Solar system--Fiction. | Extraterrestrial beings--Fiction. | Human-alien encounters--Fiction. | Southern Ute Indian Tribe of the Southern Ute Reservation, Colorado--Fiction. | Colorado Springs (Colo.)--Fiction. | High school students--Fiction. | Science fiction. | BISAC YOUNG ADULT FICTION / Science Fiction / General
Classification: LCC PZ7.1.A5245 Zac 2020 | DDC [Fic]--dc23

PRINTED IN THE UNITED STATES OF AMERICA
Circle Star Publishing is an imprint of Rhyolite Press LLC

Book design/layout by Donald R. Kallaus
Cover photograph of The Pleiades, Credit: NASA/ESA/AURA/Caltech

To Dr. Lisa Grayshield of the Washo Tribal Nation and all the other children of the Star Nations who are among us—they are us—and we have traveled far, traveled far.

CONTENTS

 ## Frybread and a Stick Shift

June 21ˢᵗ 10:07 hours MDST Astradate 11062.1 Summer Solstice
Four Corners Area, Southern Colorado, USA Planet Earth

"What's wrong Bo?" Zac asked as he looked back to see why his six-month-old black lab had whimpered softly and laid down on the ground. Zachary Box had been halfway into his morning run up Sleeping Ute Mountain when suddenly the ground beneath the fifteen-year-old's feet began to shake. Zac fell to the ground as smaller rocks tumbled down the mountain beside him. Instinctively, Zac curled up in a ball and covered his head with his arms and waited for the earth to stop trembling.

The tremors stopped as suddenly as they had begun. Zac sat up and glanced to where he had last seen his puppy. Bo sprang to his feet and dashed through the dust to Zac's side where he began licking his face. "I'm okay buddy," Zac said as he checked his puppy over to make sure he wasn't hurt. Zac found Bo was not hurt, but both his knees and the palms of his hands were skinned up and bleeding. That's when he noticed the burning sensation. "Ouch!

That hurts!" Bo noticed the blood on Zac's knees and hands and began to lick Zac's wounds clean.

"I'm okay," Zac repeated, trying to convince himself as much as Bo. Zac picked a few pebbles from the open wounds and then stood up slowly to test the strength in his knees. "See Bo, nothing broken," Zac said as he looked up at the jagged ridgeline above him which, from a distance, resembled an Indian sleeping on his back. Zac had been five miles into his run when the earthquake struck. This was his favorite summer training route; a half marathon to the top of Sleeping Ute Mountain, the most prominent geographical feature on the Ute Mountain Ute Reservation. Zac's grandfather lived on the Ute Mountain Ute Reservation, located in the Four Corners area of southern Colorado. Zac considered turning back, but he could see his destination above, the saddle just below the highpoint known as the elbow.

"Come on Bo," Zac said encouragingly to his furry friend, "we can make it." Zac started off jogging slowly at first and then picked up the pace. Stopping at the top of the saddle, Zac patted Bo on the head and sat down to catch his breath and calm his nerves. He had never felt an earthquake before, but he was sure that must have been what he had felt. The cooler temperature this morning had been perfect for a run. The morning sky a vibrant blue. White billowy clouds were starting to gather to the southwest, over Arizona, and the views were absolutely stunning from this elevation.

After a few minutes Zac pointed off in the distance to the west. "See over there? Those are the Blue Mountains; they're in Utah," he explained as Bo sat next to him and cocked his head to listen to Zac's explanation. "Those two peaks, that's the Bear's Ears. That's a special place, you know," Zac said as if sharing a family secret. Then he stood and turned around to face the east. "Over there, that high plateau, that's Mesa Verde," Zac said as he finished pointing. "My great-grandfather's great-grandfather, Five Eagles Soaring, helped move the Sun Dance from over there to here, where it would be safe on the Reservation."

Zac turned to face the sun, allowing the warmth of the sun to wash over his face. He closed his eyes and thought of the two ceremonies the Ute Nation held annually. The Bear Dance in the spring, the Sun Dance in the fall. The Bear Dance recognized the awakening of the bear from its winter hibernation. This was the time of year when the Ute honored their loved ones who had passed away, or "walked on" as the Ute say, and welcomed the babies born over the winter months. The ceremony coincided with the Spring Equinox; the time of year when the length of the day and the night were equal. Since he was three years old, Zac's father had brought him almost every year to the annual Bear Dance.

Ever since Zac's mother Leilani had died, when he was just two years old, he came to the Ute Mountain Ute Reservation to spend the summer months with his great-grandfather, White Elk. Three years ago, when he was twelve, White Elk had given Zac his Indian name, Strong Bear Running. But most of Zac's friends at school called him ZacBox; the name he was called by his middle school track coach, Mr. Tuttle. There were five other boys named Zac in his high school and two of those also ran track. Zac's close friends thought ZacBox was a cool name because it reminded them of the Xbox consoles and video games they played. They called ZacBox a "Jedi Master" on the Xbox as he was nearly unbeatable at video games.

Some of the older high school football players called Mr. Tuttle "Mr. Turtle," behind his back because he couldn't run very fast. ZacBox didn't like it when the older boys made fun of his track coach. What ZacBox knew, that some of the older boys may not have known, was that Mr. Tuttle's legs had been injured when he was serving in the U.S. Army fighting in the Middle East. ZacBox's father told him Mr. Tuttle's wounds were caused by a roadside bomb. But Mr. Tuttle never complained or even let on that he had been injured. ZacBox's father was always reluctant to discuss the War in the Middle East because ZacBox's mother, a helicopter pilot in the U.S. Air Force, had been shot down and killed during a combat Pararescue mission.

Being raised by a single father, ZacBox and his father were particularly close. Ezekiel Box, known as Zeke to his family and friends, was a firefighter at the U.S. Air Force Academy in Colorado Springs. He was a certified trainer for an elite team of smoke-jumpers, firefighters who parachuted into remote areas to combat wildfires. Zeke Box was often deployed during the summer months somewhere across the country. The summer months were the busiest time of year for the firefighters at the Academy, so they hired college students during the summer to backfill Zeke's position. This summer Zeke was away from home fighting a wildland fire in California.

To keep in shape, Zeke lifted weights and enjoyed running long distances. ZacBox loved spending time with his dad and they often trained together. This summer, ZacBox was training to run his first Pikes Peak Marathon, a 26.2-mile footrace to the top of Pikes Peak and back to where the race began in the small town of Manitou Springs. Pikes Peak had been a culturally significant place for his Ute ancestors, as well as a handful of other Native American tribes, including the Cheyenne and Arapaho. These other American Indian tribes called the Ute the Mountain People. White Elk taught ZacBox his ancestors were, "Strong people, because they lived high in the Shining Mountains and living in the mountains made them strong."

White Elk had taught Zeke the oral history he had learned from his ancestors. Ute oral history claims they are star people. The Ute Creation Story tells how Creator brought his children, the Ute, to the Shining Mountains at the beginning of time from the Pleaides. Zeke passed their oral history and stories down to his son and showed him how to locate the Pleaides Star Cluster in the night sky. ZacBox grew up knowing that of all the Shining Mountains, Pikes Peak, known as Tava or Sun Mountain to the ancient Ute, was spiritually significant because Creator allowed the day to start there first. The new day was a gift from Creator, given at the moment the morning sun first touches the top of Tava. The Ute elders teach the children that no one is promised a new day so they must use each day, each of Creator's gifts wisely.

Like most Ute, ZacBox was shorter in height, only 5'4" and weighing just 120 pounds, too small for football despite his speed. However, like his father, ZacBox was very strong and could run like the wind. White Elk said his ability to run was a gift from Creator. Zeke Box had run the Pikes Peak Marathon a half dozen times and had even finished in the top ten one year, but he had never finished first. That was ZacBox's goal this year, not just to finish the race, but to honor his Ute ancestors by winning this race on his first attempt.

ZacBox's father tried to teach him that finishing first wasn't as important as learning from the journey to the summit of their sacred mountain. But Zeke knew there are some lessons in life which have to be learned from personal experience, not taught. Zeke told how for centuries Ute were encouraged to make a vision quest to the top of Tava, at least once in their lifetimes, to gain strength from the journey and seek enlightenment from Creator. The ancestral Ute made their vision quests in solitude and in prayer. They were told to leave an offering, often a sacred stone or something of value, for Creator. The elders taught that whenever you ask for something, you must leave something in return.

What the ancient Ute sought in making a vision quest, Zeke explained to his son, was wisdom from Creator. What was it that He intended for His children to do with their lives? Were they to be hunters, so they could sustain their tribe or warriors so they could defend their tribe? Or were they to become medicine men or medicine women to help heal the People? But all ZacBox could dream about, were cars, girls and winning the Pikes Peak Marathon or at least not finishing last and dishonoring his Ute family.

ZacBox accepted that he was only half-Ute, but in not knowing any of his mother's family, he was naturally closer to his father's and great-grandfather's culture. ZacBox's mother, Leilani, was half-Hawaiian on her mother's side and half-Japanese on her father's side. ZacBox had never been to Hawaii or Japan; however, he learned as much as he could about the Japanese and Hawaiian cultures from surfing the internet. One of his father's most cherished possessions was a Bonsai tree ZacBox's mother had been given by her Japanese grandfather when she graduated from the U.S. Air Force Academy.

Captain Leilani Box, a distinguished graduate of the U.S. Air Force Academy, had been buried at the cemetery on the Academy with full military honors. All ZacBox could remember about her funeral was the low flyover of the four Pave Hawk helicopters, flying in what he later learned was the missing man formation. Her funeral at the Academy was on the same day as the Bear Dance. Now that ZacBox was older, he wanted to know more about how his mother died, but talking about her death was painful for his father, so the topic was avoided.

ZacBox enjoyed dancing at the Bear Dance; however, it was The Sun Dance, held in the autumn to honor the gift of the sun from Creator, he looked forward to the most. The Ute were the only tribe in North America who held a Bear Dance but many other Indian tribes across the U.S. and Canada also held a Sun Dance. The sun was considered sacred for it gave forth light and warmth needed to sustain all life on Mother Earth. Standing at this place, atop Sleeping Ute Mountain, was where ZacBox felt closest to Creator. ZacBox said a quiet prayer, "Oh Creator of all there is here on Earth and in the stars above, please watch over my father and his crew as they battle the fires in California trying to protect your trees, birds, animals and the people who make their homes near the ocean. Give me strength and courage so I can bring honor to my people."

Learning the Ute culture was important to ZacBox. It was something he looked forward to in coming to the Reservation to spend part of the summer with his great-grandfather White Elk. Here he could learn about his father's ancestors and their history and their culture, his Ute culture. "Grandfather," as ZacBox and most of the other children on the Reservation referred to White Elk, always made sure he was taught "the old ways"—their tribal traditions— which involved hunting, toolmaking, art and music. Ute children learned through experiential learning. White Elk taught, "You have to be present and listen and watch to learn. Listen to the stories and listen to the beat of the drums."

ZacBox loved to hear the stories and listen to the Ute men sing and watch them dance. From the time he could walk, he loved moving with the rhythm of the dance. Dance is what bonded him to his tribal ancestors. It was what captured his heart. When he was in the 7th grade, ZacBox decided to give a class presentation at his school, Discovery Canyon Campus, in Colorado Springs. He wanted to share with his classmates the importance of the Sun Dance. ZacBox talked his father into letting him wear his cherished feathered regalia to school.

When ZacBox showed up at school wearing his traditional ceremonial clothing, many of his classmates rushed up to him excited to learn about the feathers, bells and other accessories. Two of his friends were Boy Scouts and belonged to their National Honor Society, called the Order of the Arrow.

When ZacBox walked into the school cafeteria at lunch, one of the senior boys, Erik, pointed at him and started laughing. Erik had just transferred from a school in Arkansas, but was already earning a reputation as a school bully. ZacBox tried to ignore Erik, but when the older boy started walking toward him with a smirk on his face, ZacBox knew he would have to stand up to him. To Erik's surprise, six Mormon high school girls saw what was happening and came up to stand between him and ZacBox. The girls scolded Erik and told them that bullying was not tolerated in their school. Erik sheepishly backed down and apologized to ZacBox.

On the Reservation, ZacBox was always encouraged to wear his regalia when he danced. White Elk had introduced him to other tribal dancers so he could learn different types of Native American dance. ZacBox loved all the dances, but what fascinated him most was fancy dancing. The Fancy Dance, sometimes called the Fancy Feather Dance, was based loosely on the Fancy War Dance. It was a fast-paced style of dance that incorporated feathered regalia and silver bells stitched to the leggings, from the ankles up to the waist. There were also two small arm bustles, with white fluffy feathers, and two larger bustles made of strings of eagle or hawk feathers attached to a backboard. Eagle and hawk feathers are spiritually important to many tribes. Only Native American people can lawfully possess an eagle feather.

Standing atop Sleeping Ute Mountain, with his eyes closed and relishing the warmth of the sun shining on his face, ZacBox opened up his heart and his ears and listened. The echo of ancient drum beats was soft at first, and then grew louder in his mind and in his heart. ZacBox nodded his head with the beat of the drum, bent his knees and slowly began to sway his body in keeping with the rhythm of the drums. He extended his arms and began to turn clockwise, keeping in step with the drums. With his eyes closed he could see his body in his mind, executing the moves of the dance, as if he were an eagle soaring overhead, circling and looking down.

Then he heard the screech of an eagle. He opened his eyes and looked up to see a huge bird of prey perched on the edge of a rock. "Hey, where did you come from?" ZacBox said to the eagle as it cocked its head to the side. It looked down at him and Bo, who crouched behind ZacBox's leg. ZacBox watched as the majestic bird took flight and soared off above the trees to the south. "That was so cool!" ZacBox wiped the sweat off his brow with his T-shirt and noticed his hands and knees were still bleeding. He wiped his hands on his running shirt and shorts. Then, said to Bo, "Come on boy, let's go find grandpa to see if he can patch me up."

ZacBox enjoyed the downhill run. He stayed on the narrow dirt road leading from the top of Sleeping Ute Mountain to the cluster of modest homes and scattered buildings in the little town of Towaoc below. When he and Bo reached the place in the bend in the road where the gravel road ended and the pavement began, ZacBox picked up their pace. Soon the two were nearing the outskirts of the small town where his great-grandfather lived.

As ZacBox rounded the next street corner, he saw White Elk spraying water from a garden hose onto his old black pickup truck parked in the driveway. "Come on Bo, I'll race you home," ZacBox said as they raced the last half block to White Elk's small house. "Mique Grandfather!" ZacBox said as White Elk looked up from rinsing soap off his old truck with the green garden hose. ZacBox admired how White Elk, even at age 84, rose every morning before dawn to say his prayers, in keeping with the old ways, then did his daily exercises. White Elk wore his long white hair in two braids draped over his shoulders and down his chest.

"Mique," White Elk replied, pleased to hear his great-grandson use the Ute word for, "hi, hello, how are you?" When White Elk turned toward ZacBox he noticed the blood on his dirty shirt and running shorts. "Strong Bear, are you hurt? It looks like you lost a tussle with a cougar; what has happened to you?"

"Ha! No, nothing as exciting as wrestling with a mountain lion," ZacBox said as White Elk handed him the hose and encouraged him to take a drink. White Elk smiled as ZacBox made sure to give Bo a drink first. Taking care of the needs of others, especially animals came as naturally to ZacBox as it did to his father, White Elk observed. ZacBox held up his hands and explained, "I fell down when the earthquake happened. Did you feel anything down here?"

"I felt a little tremor earlier," White Elk replied as he bent over to get a better look at ZacBox's bleeding knees. "Here," he said as he lowered the tailgate. "Sit up here and let me take a good look at your wounds."

ZacBox handed the hose back to White Elk, then turned his back to the pickup and hopped up onto the tailgate. As he sat down he held up his palms and said, "I tried to catch my fall, but it happened so fast." Bo laid down nearby in the shade of the pickup for a nap.

"Here," White Elk said as he handed the hose back to ZacBox to wash the blood off his hands. "Take off your shoes and socks; then rinse off your knees. I'll go inside and get something to put on your wounds so they won't get infected."

As ZacBox gingerly washed the blood off his knees, he noticed Bo cock his head to the side. Then he heard the loud thumping of rap music coming down the street. ZacBox watched as a shiny, metallic blue, 1966 Buick Electra two-door drove by the front of his great-grandfather's house. There were two Ute teenage boys sitting in the front seat, both wearing red bandanas on their heads. They slowed as they passed White Elk's house. The driver held up two fingers and then pointed them from his eyes toward ZacBox, giving the sign for "I'm watching you."

Bo got up from under the pickup and moved in front of ZacBox, positioning himself between ZacBox and the Buick, and growled softly, "Grrr." They watched as the metallic blue lowrider slowly passed by. White Elk stepped out of his house at the same moment and looked toward the street. When he heard the loud rap music blaring from the passing car, he asked, "Friends of yours?"

"Hardly," ZacBox replied, "but they've got a way cool car. It's called a deuce-and-a-quarter."

"I remember when the Electra 225 first came out; it was a head-turner alright, just like my '49 Chevy 5-window here was when it was new," White Elk said as he patted the weathered wooden bed. ZacBox noticed the back of his Grandfather's hands were nearly as weathered as the old wood on the floor of the bed of his pickup. They watched as the customized Buick drove slowly out of sight. "Your grandmother would sit next to me, one of the benefits of bench seats over those bucket seats of today. Your grandmother and I, we would drive real slow through town and listen to our music, but we must have had better hearing when we were young because we never had to play our music that loud," White Elk concluded with a smile.

White Elk set a small unmarked glass jar on the tailgate next to ZacBox's leg and then turned to face him for a moment, quietly in prayer. ZacBox noticed the jar contained a white lotion of some sort. He watched as White Elk clapped his hands together three times and whispered a soft chant. Then White Elk began moving his hands above ZacBox's skinned knees and hands without touching the skin.

Almost instantly ZacBox felt the burning sensation beginning to leave his body. "What are you doing Grandfather?"

"I am smoothing out your energy lines. Everything in the universe is made of energy. When a person goes through a traumatic event it can disrupt their energy lines," White Elk explained as he picked up the lotion he had mixed using the roots of a plant. He rubbed the medicine from the plant into the open wounds on ZacBox's knees. "I am asking this plant to use its energy to keep you from getting infected and to help you heal."

"Ouch!" ZacBox shouted as he jerked his knee away and looked down at the clear lotion his great-grandfather was trying to spread across the open wounds on his knees. "That burns! What is that stuff?"

"It is biscuitroot, a plant that will help you heal. Now hold still," White Elk said trying to spread the lotion on ZacBox's moving knees and hands. To distract his grandson from thinking about the pain, he asked, "Who were those two boys in the car?"

"That's Jimmy Suazo and his cousin Lenard. They are escorts for Alicia Many Horses. Whenever she and her official party leave the Reservation on tribal business they are supposed to be her escorts. Alicia was appointed by the Tribal Chairman this year to be part of the Ute Mountain Ute Royalty Council. It's her second year in a row."

"Is her father Clarence Many Horses, one of the tribal policemen?"

"He is, but I haven't met him yet."

"You like this Alicia?"

"I do," ZacBox said as a wide grin spread across his face, "and I think she might like me, but every time I start to ask her out one of her escorts seems to show up. They don't trust me 'cause I'm not one of them and I don't live here on the Reservation."

"We can't all live on the Reservation," White Elk said with a serious expression on his face, looking around their small town as if taking a survey. "I don't think there is enough room."

"You know what I mean Grandfather, I'm not like you or them. I'm not full-blooded Ute. I might look like them, but I'm just a quarter Ute, so I don't even qualify for an allotment or to live here on the Reservation if I weren't staying with you in your house. And I am not full-blooded Hawaiian or Japanese, so I might look like them too, but I wouldn't fit in there either. Some of the other kids at school take one look at me and see I look different from them. Some of the things they say make me feel like I don't fit in there either, even though I have lived right across the street since preschool! Did my mother feel like she fit in here on the Reservation?"

"She did, and like you, Leilani looked Ute, but I believe in her heart she always felt like she fit in here just as much as she did with her Hawaiian or her Japanese family."

"Sometimes, Grandfather, I don't feel like I fit in anywhere," ZacBox said as his chin dropped down to his chest.

"Fitting in, or not, may be more than just a person's skin color or what they look like," White Elk said as he sat down on the tailgate next to ZacBox and put his arm around his shoulder. "Don't you see the wonderful gift Creator has given you, Strong Bear Running? Just like your mother, Creator made you the way you are, so you can fit in anywhere."

A tear began to form in ZacBox's eye. "Why did he allow her to die Grandfather? Why does Creator allow bad things to happen to good people?"

"I have asked Creator that question many times, in prayer. When my son, your father's father died, when my wife died, when your mother died. The only answer I ever found is I guess they had fulfilled what it was they came here to do."

"Forgive me Grandfather, but sometimes I question if there is a Creator. Have you ever had doubts?"

"No. No doubts. I know He is real. Whenever I feel the wind on my face, I know it is the breath of our Creator. When I first held you in my arms, felt your breath on my cheek, looked into your eyes, you were just a newborn baby, not even two months old, I suppose. I saw the spirits of your mother and father, and the spirits of my mother and father, and their mothers and fathers looking back at me. That's when I know He is real. Whenever I see a hummingbird, like that one over there sipping nectar from that flower, or a butterfly slowly emerging from a cocoon, I know they are messengers to and from Creator. These things are gifts from Creator, from someone up there who knows you and loves you."

White Elk paused for a moment and pointed to the hummingbird as it darted past them on its way to another flower in his tiny garden. Then he continued, "When you look deep into Bo's eyes, don't you see a reflection of his spirit looking back at you? That is when you know there is a Creator. These things could not have all just evolved on their own. You, being here on Mother Earth, right now at this moment, you are a gift from Creator. I do not know why your mother had to leave while she was yet so young, but I do know this, were it not for her love, and that of a loving Creator, you would not be here sitting beside me."

ZacBox dried his eyes on his t-shirt and then remembered, "Grandfather, I forgot to tell you I saw an eagle!"

"Oh? Where was it?"

"At the top of Sleeping Ute Mountain, just below the Elbow," ZacBox said as he pointed to the west. "It was just after the earthquake knocked me to the ground. I got up and said a prayer to

Creator, thanking him I was not hurt any more than skinned knees and hands. When I opened my eyes I saw this huge eagle."

"Was it a bald eagle? They can have a wingspan of seven to eight feet," White Elk said.

"I don't think it was a bald eagle, it didn't have a white head."

"It could have been a young bald eagle; they don't get white feathers on their heads until they mature, when they're about five years old. What did this eagle do?"

"It looked at me and Bo for several minutes, then it spread its huge wings and jumped off the rock and flew off to the south, above the tall pine trees."

"It may have been carrying your prayer to Creator."

"What does all this mean Grandfather? The tremors on top of Sleeping Ute Mountain and me getting knocked down and seeing the eagle?"

"I do not know, but you better pay attention, today is the summer solstice. I think someone may be trying to tell you something."

"Grandfather, there is something I wish someone would tell me. I, I want to know more about how my mother died. But whenever I ask my father, I know how much it hurts him to talk about it, so we both just let it go. But I do want to know how she died and why she died. Did she suffer or did she die quickly? But more importantly was it worth it?" Then ZacBox's tears overflowed and ran down his cheeks. White Elk sat patiently as ZacBox dried his eyes. "I am embarrassed I cried, Grandfather. I never see you or my father cry. Or ever get scared."

"Ute men might get scared, or some might even cry," White Elk explained, "but we never let anyone see us. One day you too will learn these things; you will soon turn into a man."

"How will I learn what I am supposed to know to become a man, Grandfather?"

"You see that butterfly?" White Elk asked as he pointed to an orange and black butterfly floating past on the wind.

"Yes," ZacBox replied.

"Before he was a butterfly, he was first a caterpillar. When he was a caterpillar he may not have known he was supposed to turn into a butterfly, but that's what Creator had decided he would become. But first the caterpillar had to turn himself into a cocoon and when he emerged from his protective shell, his wings had to struggle mightily to free him from his cocoon. During his struggle, from what he used to be to what he was to become, that struggle he went through, is what built up the muscles in his wings, so he could fly. Had he not gone through that struggle, strengthening his wings, he would not have had the strength to fly. I guess maybe that's why we all have to struggle in life, to evolve from what we are to what we are to become. To gain the strength to fly."

"Thank you Grandfather; that story helped. Did your grandfather tell you that story or did you make it up?"

"That butterfly over there taught me this story," White Elk explained pointing to an orange and black butterfly floating from one flower blossom to another in White Elk's modest garden.

"It's beautiful. Is it a Monarch?"

"No, it is a Painted Lady. They look like the Monarch, only smaller. That one is a male."

"Do they migrate all the way to Mexico every winter like the Monarch?" ZacBox asked as the butterfly landed on the yellow blossom of a squash.

"Painted Ladies do migrate to Mexico in the winter, like the Monarch, but with this one important distinction; the Monarch might make it all the way to Mexico in one lifetime. The Painted Lady is too small and can't make the trip all in one lifetime; its journey will require two or more lifetimes."

"How does it know where it's supposed to be going if it cannot make it to its destination in one lifetime?"

"I do not know," White Elk said as he watched the butterfly float over his low white fence into his neighbor's yard. "Maybe there is something in the Earth they follow, like energy lines, or maybe there's something deep within them that gets passed down from one generation to the next. I do not know how they know where to go; maybe they just follow their instincts."

"Thank you Grandfather; I appreciate you always sharing your wisdom with me."

"When is the next time your father will be able to call you?" asked White Elk.

"They are supposed to reach the base camp tonight around 7pm California time; then after they shower and eat dinner, each of the crew will get five minutes on the satellite phone to call their families."

"Then tonight, before you hang up, tell him what you told me, that you want to learn how your mother died. He has been waiting for you to ask until you were old enough to ask the question and to understand the answer. You are now emerging from your cocoon of being a boy and learning to be a man. I think your time to learn these things is now, but sometimes you will just have to follow your instincts and trust whatever it is that has been passed down to you to help guide you in this struggle of life. When you talk to your father tonight, tell him you want to learn about how your mother died."

ZacBox dried the last of his tears on his t-shirt and sat quietly for a time, trying to decide how to ask his father the question he had been waiting twelve years to ask. Then, with his head still bowed, ZacBox said half-heartedly, "Can't I just text him?"

"No Zac," White Elk laughed, then turned serious again, "there are some things that must be said and not read."

"Okay, Grandfather, I will ask him tonight when he calls."

"Then you best be back home when he calls," White Elk said as he moved the garden hose to water a small strawberry patch.

"Well maybe I shouldn't ask Alicia out tonight after all," ZacBox said, beginning to lose his nerve.

"I think you have time to do both," Grandfather said patiently. "I see you texting your friends all the time; don't you text your friend Alicia?"

"Yes, all the time, well, like almost daily."

"Then text her, right now, and ask her out."

"It's not that simple. I don't have a car. I don't even have a driver's license."

"But you do have a learners permit," White Elk replied calmly as he handed ZacBox the last of the lotion to rub on his hands. "Don't focus on what it is you do not have, for that list is endlessly long and unimportant. Focus on what it is you do have; that is how you solve problems. Ask her out. You are fifteen and a half now and can drive as long as you have a licensed adult with you. I will ride in the back here with Bo. You and your friend Alicia can ride up front and listen to your music. Maybe if you are lucky, she will sit next to you. Go, text her."

"But what if she says no?"

"But what if she says yes? Is the reward not worth the risk?"

"Well yes, well maybe, sure but, and I mean no disrespect, Grandfather, but your old pickup is not nearly as cool as a deuce-and-a-quarter. Don't get me wrong, I love driving your old pickup truck, and I appreciate you using it to teach me how to drive, but Grandfather, it is really old and there are holes worn all the way down through the floorboards—you can see the pavement below when we drive down the street!"

"If she is the kind of girl who will not go out with you if you do not have a nice enough car, then she is not the kind of girl you want to be sitting next to you in the first place. Now, do you have money?"

"Yes, Dad gave me fifty dollars when he dropped me off last month, and I haven't been anywhere to spend it. But where will we go?" ZacBox said, realizing he had just about run out of excuses and was stalling while trying to gather up enough courage to ask Alicia out.

"One day you will learn the destination is often not as important as the journey."

"Thanks, Grandfather. I will text Alicia and ask her out tonight after dinner."

"But first help me finish washing the truck," White Elk said as he sprayed ZacBox teasingly with the hose. ZacBox laughed and wrestled to take the garden hose away from White Elk. Bo joined in, biting at the cold water streaming from Grandfather's green garden hose.

Fifteen minutes, and ten first draft texts later, ZacBox nervously hit send on his cellphone. His text read, "Hi Alicia, its ZacBox, would you like to go out tonight after dinner?"

Within minutes came Alicia's reply that made his heart beat faster, "Sure! I'd love 2, I have to ask my folks first, where r we going?"

"I thought I could drive us over to get ice cream at the truck stop in front of the casino, tell your parents Grandfather will be with us."

Two minutes later, "they said ok, they love your grandfather, what time?"

"Would 6:30 b ok with u?"

"Sure, c u then!"

After dinner ZacBox took a quick shower and threw on a clean t-shirt and a pair of gym shorts and stepped into the living room where White Elk sat reading a John Grisham novel he had checked out from the senior center.

"I'm ready," ZacBox announced as he emerged from his bedroom.

White Elk looked up from his book, saw what ZacBox was wearing and said, "I don't think so. You go back in there and put on that nice button-down plaid shirt I ironed and a clean pair of blue jeans."

"Oh, Grandfather," ZacBox said as he looked down at his shirt and shorts, "but this is what I always wear. It's comfortable."

"Well then you better learn to get comfortable in your plaid shirt and jeans."

"Okay," ZacBox moaned, as he turned reluctantly and headed back to the bedroom.

"And put on your new cowboy boots. The ones I bought you at the tractor supply store in Durango."

"Oh, Grandfather, do I have to wear those boots?"

"Do as I say, or you might find Bo and me sitting up front between you and Alicia."

White Elk insisted they leave the house 45 minutes early, explaining, "We need to get gas; you drive. I'll ride in the back to make sure Bo doesn't jump out."

When ZacBox started the old pickup, he looked down at the gas gauge and saw it was still three-quarters full. Alicia only lived a few blocks away. They had plenty of gas. ZacBox looked in the rear view mirror to where White Elk and Bo were sitting in the back of the truck. He understood this was his great-grandfather's way of letting him know he trusted him enough to drive up front alone. It was ZacBox's first solo flight. ZacBox appreciated White Elk giving him this practice run to drive to the gas station before picking up Alicia.

ZacBox felt butterflies in his stomach, from being a little nervous, and accidently ground the gears a couple times. But his confidence grew as he sat up front by himself and shifted the gears. Every time he looked in the rearview mirror, he saw the reflection of Grandfather sitting behind him. It was comforting knowing he was there.

When ZacBox pulled into the gas station, White Elk handed him his credit card, "Fill it up, but pay attention, listen to make sure the gas doesn't overflow onto the paint."

"Yes, Grandfather," ZacBox said as he pumped the gas and listened for the tank to fill. "Dad says gas pumps use satellites up in space to charge your credit card."

"We used to just go inside and write down how much we owed on a little card. Then once a month or so, we would just go in with cash or a check and pay it off. I think it was much better then, when people trusted you. Now nobody trusts nobody. That's no way to live."

After ZacBox finished pumping the gas, he drove to Alicia's house without once grinding the clutch. When he stopped the pickup in front of Alicia's home, he got out of the cab and stood by the bed of the truck for a moment.

White Elk said encouragingly, "Go ahead, go up the steps and knock on the front door. If her father answers the door, introduce yourself and ask if you can please see Alicia. If her father offers to shake hands do so firmly and look him square in the eye. If Alicia's mother answers the door, you introduce yourself politely and hand her this medicine bundle."

ZacBox held the medicine bundle in his left hand and practiced what he was supposed to say as he walked up to the front door and knocked. He was relieved when Alicia answered the door. But his relief was short-lived when she invited him inside to meet her parents. Her father was sitting in a worn tan leather chair in the living room, reading the local Cortez newspaper.

"Father," Alicia said, "I want to introduce you." ZacBox watched as Alicia's father glanced slowly over the top of the newspaper, looking him over carefully from head to toe. His visual inspection concluded when he noticed ZacBox's shiny black cowboy boots. ZacBox glanced down and saw Mr. Many Horses was also wearing black cowboy boots. Mr. Many Horses set his newspaper aside, stood up and walked over to ZacBox with his hand outstretched. ZacBox was thankful White Elk made him change into a clean shirt and jeans and wear his boots. Alicia continued, "Father, I want you to meet Zac Box. Zac this is my father, Clarence Many Horses."

ZacBox did as White Elk had instructed and shook hands firmly while looking Alicia's father squarely in the eye. Wearing his cowboy boots, ZacBox stood almost an inch taller, but was still two inches shorter than Mr. Many Horses. ZacBox saw he was wearing his tribal policeman's badge pinned to his black leather vest and was relieved he wasn't wearing a gun.

"I am pleased to meet you, Sir," ZacBox said as they shook hands.

"I understand you are Zeke Box's son."

"Yes, you know my father?"

"Yes, we ran track together in high school. Is he away fighting forest fires again this summer?"

"Yes, sir, he's in California."

"You tell him hello for me next time you talk with him."

"Yes, sir, I will."

"Is White Elk with you?"

"Yes, sir, he's waiting in the pickup with Bo."

"Bo?"

"Mr. Bojangles, he's my puppy."

"Oh. I better go pay my respects to your grandfather and Mr.

Bojangles," Mr. Many Horses said with a smile as he retrieved a white straw cowboy hat from a hat rack on the wall near the front door. The hat rack was made from horse shoes welded together. Mr. Many Horses opened the front door, put his hat on his head and said, "Nice meeting you, Zac."

Alicia took ZacBox by the arm and said, "Come. I want you to meet my mother; she's in the kitchen making fry bread." ZacBox had smelled the fry bread as soon as he walked through the front door. It smelled delicious, but he had forgotten all about it when he met Alicia's father. It seemed like all his senses had shut down all at once, except for his eyesight, which seemed to catch every detail. He could still visualize the smallest details of Alicia's father, including the stitching on the toes of his black cowboy boots. But ZacBox's thoughts melted away as soon as he entered the kitchen and met Alicia's mother. She was very pretty, just like Alicia, especially when she smiled. She handed him a piece of warm fry bread.

"Thank you," ZacBox said as he handed her the medicine bundle, "This is from Grandfather."

Alicia's mother fussed over the gift and then held the small medicine bundle up to her nose and inhaled deeply. "Osha," she said smiling. "We Ute call it bear root. Look Alicia, it's tied with strands of purple mountain sage. Did White Elk grow these in his garden?"

"He did," ZacBox said proudly, struggling not to talk with his mouth full.

"I like my fry bread with honey on it," Alicia said as she squeezed honey on a small piece of fry bread and handed it to him.

Her mother smiled at the two of them as they sat at the kitchen table and talked. She instructed Alicia to thank ZacBox's Grandfather for the medicine bundle. Alicia's mother then asked him a few questions, mostly small talk, such as how his summer was going and inquired about his father being away in California. Then she said, "Alicia tells me you plan on going to the Air Force Academy when you graduate high school?"

Her question caught ZacBox off guard; he remembered mentioning his plans to Alicia several summers ago, but he was surprised she had mentioned his plans to her mother. "Yes, if they'll accept me. I know it's very competitive to get in, but I've been keeping my grades up and I hope to do well enough in track to give myself an edge."

Alicia's mom smiled, as if she knew something he did not. Soon ZacBox and Alicia were walking out the front door, headed toward where White Elk and Bo were waiting in the back of the pickup. As they approached the street, ZacBox noticed the metallic blue Buick deuce-and-a-quarter parked a half block away, under the shade of a cottonwood tree. He was pretty sure Alicia saw it too, but she put her arm around his and pretended not to notice. When they arrived at the passenger door, ZacBox did as White Elk had instructed and opened the passenger door for Alicia and waited patiently.

"Good evening, Grandfather," Alicia said respectfully as she stopped at the bed of the pickup and petted Bo on the head.

"Good evening," White Elk replied.

"My mother thanks you for the medicine bundle."

Grandfather smiled and nodded.

"Wouldn't you be more comfortable up front here with Zac and me?"

"I am fine back here with Bo, I have my warmer blanket if it gets cold," White Elk said as he held up the folded Indian blanket.

Alicia got in the passenger side of the pickup. ZacBox closed the door and then walked around behind the pickup truck, glanced up at White Elk as he scratched Bo on the chest. When ZacBox settled in behind the steering wheel, he was pleased to see Alicia slide across the bench seat to sit close beside him. He started the pickup, pushed in the clutch, slipped the stick shift into first gear, and slowly let out the clutch so he didn't kill the engine.

"I've never driven a stick shift," Alicia said, admiring how ZacBox seemed at ease operating the pickup.

"I hadn't either," ZacBox explained, "My dad's truck is an automatic. Grandfather had to teach me how to operate a clutch. Shifting is pretty easy, once you get started, but the hardest part is when you have to stop on a hill." ZacBox shifted into second gear and nodded his head toward the blue Buick parked under the cottonwood tree. Grandfather waved at the two boys wearing the red bandanas, as they peered over the dashboard.

Later that evening, ZacBox sat anxiously in his Grandfather's kitchen holding his cellphone waiting for his father to call. The call from "out of the area" finally came through at 8:15pm.

"Hello," ZacBox said, and then smiled at his Grandfather when he heard his father's voice.

"Hi Zac, how are you and Bo getting along?"

"Hi Dad, we're doing great! It's nice to hear your voice."

"What have you two been up to?"

"Oh, usual stuff, running, learning to drive, helping Grandfather with the dishes, going on a date," ZacBox said shooting a grin toward White Elk, who was putting the dishes away.

"A date? Tell me about it. Who was she; this was your first date wasn't it?"

"Yes, and Grandfather let me drive while he sat in the back with Bo."

"How are you getting along learning to drive Grandfather's old pickup?"

"I really like driving it. I like driving a stick shift, especially when you're downshifting. That's my favorite part. I'm not grinding the gears anymore, when I downshift. Grandfather taught me I have to come to a full stop to shift into first, but I forgot, and the transmission made a really loud grinding noise."

"I had to learn the same way Zac, so don't feel bad."

ZacBox then told his dad about Alicia, and passed along how her father had said to tell him hello. ZacBox asked how things were coming along fighting the fire in California and inquired if he knew how long he was going to be deployed. Before they knew it, their five minutes on the satellite phone had flown by.

"I better go Zac, let someone else use the sat phone. We're about to get this fire contained, maybe in the next few days. I should be home in a week or so, and then we'll talk more about this date of yours," Zeke said.

"Okay. Dad?"

"Yes, Son?"

"Dad…" ZacBox repeated.

"I'm still here, Zac. What is it?"

"I want to know about mom, about how she died. I know it's not going to be easy, but when you get home can we make time to talk?"

"Yes, Son, we will. I have some vacation time coming around the 4th of July. I have been waiting until you were old enough to talk about this…I think maybe the time has come for you to meet Saint Michael."

 ## Whole Lotta Shakin' Going On

June 21ˢᵗ 20:19 hours MDST Astradate 11062.1 Summer Solstice
USGS Geologic Hazards Science Center, Golden, CO USA
Planet Earth

The tremors were thought minor, at first.

"How deep are they?" Ted Shotwell, the 59-year-old supervisor asked of his 19-year-old intern Arjun Basu.

"They began 3.1 miles deep within the earth," Arjun replied, then added, "but this is normally a stable fault line. That's what first caught my attention, and it's surprisingly localized," the geophysics intern said to his supervisor, as they huddled around the Earthquake Information terminal in Golden, Colorado.

What puzzled Arjun and his white-haired supervisor the most wasn't the tremors' severity, averaging 4.3 magnitude, but their frequency occurring in such an small area, about the size of a football field, and of course, the last tremor's GPS location. This second earthquake had struck just a mile east of the U.S. Air Force Academy, in Colorado Springs, Colorado.

"What's even more astonishing," Arjun said as his supervisor continued to stand behind him scratching the whiskers on his chin, "these tremors seemed to have an occurrence rate calibrated to a binary logarithm. Sir, I think they might be computer generated!"

"Come on Arjun, that's crazy talk."

"Sir, I know it sounds crazy, but it seems almost like...what if we're being conditioned to ignore these tremors.

"Arjun, you've been at this since 10:15 this morning. It's after eight now; I think we need to wrap this up for the night."

"But sir," Arjun said in desperation, pointing his slender index finger at the spikes on the monitor as he traced both readouts, "these tremors are happening in the precise same location and rate as the previous quakes last month! Okay, the tremor in the Four Corners area seemed like it might have been natural or from fracking, I'll admit, but this second quake happened on a fault line running north to south along the Front Range of the Rocky Mountains that has been stable for at least forty million years! This shouldn't be happening!"

"Arjun, we spoke about this last time," Ted explained, "I've been doing this a long time and unexplained anomalies happen. Just write it up in your report, like I told you to do. When the director returns from DC next week, I'll make sure he reads your notes in the report, but I'm not requesting another visual ground site inspection. That last request you talked me into gained us absolutely nothing. The folks there on the ground in Colorado Springs are gonna stop taking our requests seriously."

Arjun leaned back in his chair, frustrated, and released a heavy sigh.

"While I admire your youthful enthusiasm, Mr. Basu, what you interns need to learn is when to let it go," Mr. Shotwell said as he picked up his coffee cup, leaving a ring on Arjun's computer console, "Just write it up."

Arjun Basu watched as his supervisor returned to his office and closed the door. The message was clear; he was not to be bothered again. Arjun stood up, decided he needed a break and walked down the hall to the men's room. He checked the floor beneath the stall doors to confirm he was alone. Then he carefully removed his pagri, the headdress worn by men in India as a symbol of honor and respect. The color he wore was white, a symbol of peace.

Arjun splashed cold water on his face and then wiped it dry with a paper towel. He stood looking at himself in the mirror for a minute and then, with his best Sean Connery imitation, repeated Mr. Shotwell's words of admonishment, "While I admire your youthful enthusiasm Mr. Basu," he said carefully rewrapping his pagri and squaring it back on his head. "What you interns need to learn is when to let it go."

Arjun was accustomed to not being taken seriously. At thirteen he had already graduated high school in India and by the time he was fifteen he was completing his undergraduate degree in geology at the Abu Dhabi University in the UAE. When he was seventeen, he graduated with a Master's Degree in geology from Oxford University in England, and two years later he was here in Golden, Colorado, where he hoped to obtain a Ph.D. at the School of Mines. Arjun felt comfortable wearing his pagri while studying in the UAE, just as he did in his homeland of India, but he often felt people here in the U.S. were staring at him and had profiled him as a terrorist because he was wearing a turban. Of course he could choose not to wear his pagri, but that would not be respectful of his Hindu faith, himself or his beloved parents.

Arjun's father, Daksha, an Indian name meaning "earth," and his mother, Bodhi, also an Indian name, meaning "enlightenment," had both been born in India, as was Arjun. His name was taken from the Mahabharata and was ancient Sanskrit meaning "honor, bright and courageous." Both Arjun's parents held doctorate degrees in science. Their family's last name, Basu, was a Bengali surname and also Sanskrit. It meant 'wealth, gem and radiance', which likely influenced Arjun's passion for collecting rocks and studying minerals as a young boy. His parents were proud of Arjun for pursuing a doctorate degree in the States. For his part, being away from home for long periods of time often made him lonely. But with his parents now living in the UAE instead of India where he was born, Arjun wasn't sure where home was anymore.

When Arjun was fourteen, his parents moved their small family to the UAE. Their family consisted of himself and a younger sister, named Indu, which translates to, "like the moon" and is meant as "a thing of beauty" in India. Indu always had a fascination with space. She had read countless science fiction books and had seen most of the science fiction movies filmed in the last twenty years.

Their father was employed as a scientist by the Abu Dhabi Oil Refining Company, which was owned by the Al Nahyan, the ruling royal family of Abu Dhabi. The royal family awarded Arjun a full-ride scholarship to attend Oxford University in England and a second scholarship to attend the Colorado School of Mines in America. Unfortunately, his scholarship could only be applied toward tuition and books. Therefore, Arjun was most grateful for this part-time work as an intern at the USGS Geologic Hazards Science Center; without this work he couldn't afford his small apartment, food and other expenses, including the often-needed repairs to his 1995 blue Subaru SVX with enough miles to have traveled ten times around the Earth at its equator.

Nodding at his reflection in the mirror, Arjun said in his normal voice, "Excuse me Dr. Jones," acknowledging the acting role

Sir Thomas Sean Connery, a Scottish actor, played as the archeologist father of Indiana Jones, "I have a report to write up." With that, Arjun's short break was over, and he returned to his workstation, all the while running the mathematical calculations over and over in his mind. Although he did not to mention it to his supervisor, Arjun was very aware that today's tremors coincided with the precise timing of the summer solstice, a date of religious importance in his homeland of India. After running another series of earthquake computer simulations, Arjun was more convinced than ever that he knew when—and more importantly where—the next earthquake would occur—and he vowed to himself he would be there when it happened.

Astradate 11062.1 Earth's Summer Solstice
Europa, sixth-closest Moon to Jupiter

Three hundred ninety million miles from planet Earth, Europa, the smallest of all the 79 known moons of Jupiter, held a total population of one. Standing at 8'2" tall, in Earth terms, Jorvik Eriksson was big, even for a Pleiadian. Like most humanoid extraterrestrials from the Pleiades Star Cluster, Jorvik had long blonde hair and blue eyes, and resembled the Nordic-Scandinavians. Unlike most other Pleiadians, Jorvik Eriksson had been born on planet Earth. Standing in his spacesuit, beside his downed spacecraft, Jorvik looked up from the barren icy surface of Europa at the stars above, where he hoped to one day return.

The most notable feature above the bleak surface of Europa was the huge gas ball planet Jupiter. The swirling gas giant consisted of layers of colors, ranging from tan to yellow to rust, accentuated by the "Great Red Spot" which looked more orange through the face shield of Jorvik's helmet. With a mass two-and-a-half times larger than all the other planets in the Solar System combined, Jupiter was the third brightest object in the night sky when viewed from planet Earth. Jorvik wondered if his father could be looking up at Jupiter right now. Thinking of his father always gave Jorvik hope of being rescued one day. Jorvik knew as long as his father was alive he would spend every day of his life trying to find a way to rescue his only child.

It had been 400 years since Galileo Galilei first gazed through his telescope and observed Europa, along with Jupiter's three larger moons, Io, Ganymede and Calisto. Galileo's discovery rocked the common belief at the time that Earth was the center of the universe. Jorvik had been stranded on Europa for over 150 years. Although Europa is roughly the same size as Earth's moon, its oceans below the icy surface may contain twice as much water as planet Earth. It was this presence of water that kept Jorvik alive, that and his overwhelming desire to avenge the death of his crew and complete his mission to return to the Pleaides.

 A Jump Drive Like No Other

July 4th 09:15 hours MDST Astradate 11070.4
Air Force Academy Chapel, Colorado Springs, CO USA,
Planet Earth

"Dad, is Saint Michael a priest?" ZacBox asked his father as they ascended the wide white steps leading to the impressive entrance of the U.S. Air Force Academy Chapel.

"No," his father explained, as they stopped before the huge double doors. "He was the last man to see your mother alive and lived to tell about it."

Zeke Box opened the heavy door on the right and held it open for his only child to enter. ZacBox walked anxiously into the vast expanse of the Air Force Academy Chapel.

As his eyes adjusted to the interior light, ZacBox saw the Chapel was empty, except for one lone airman, kneeling at the altar. ZacBox and his father walked partway down the center aisle, waiting patiently for the man in uniform to finish his silent prayer.

"The last time I walked down this isle," Zeke whispered so as to not disturb the man kneeling at the altar, "was sixteen years ago, the day Chaplain Vaughn married your mother and me. It was the second happiest day of my life."

Curiously, ZacBox turned his head and looked at his father standing beside him, "If marrying mom was the second happiest day of your life, what was the first?"

"The day you were born."

ZacBox turned his head back to face the front of the chapel, noticing the man kneeling at the altar had some difficulty standing. Leaning heavily on the marble alter as he rose; the serviceman in uniform turned to greet them; ZacBox saw he walked with a slight limp. The senior airman was wearing a dress uniform, his chest decorated with medals. He wore white gloves and carried a small black box in his left hand. He tucked his blue uniform beret carefully under his left arm and extended his right hand.

ZacBox's father stepped forward, and the two men shook hands and embraced one another. Their deep respect for each other was self-evident. They spoke quietly to one another for a moment; then Zeke stepped to one side and nodded his head for his son to step forward. "Zac, this is Chief Master Sergeant Michael Sandoval. Chief Sandoval, this is my and Leilani's son Zachary Box."

"It's an honor to meet you, Zac," the Sergeant said as he shook hands with the young man. "You look so much like your mother."

"I'll leave you two to talk," Zeke said. "Zac, I have to pull a training day at the fire station, but I'll be home around 5 and maybe we can talk more this evening if you want. Chief Sandoval will make sure you get home when you are finished here."

ZacBox watched as his father nodded respectfully at Chief Sandoval, and then his father turned and walked back down the aisle. ZacBox tried to imagine what a happy day that must have been for his father and his mother, their wedding day. He had often studied their wedding photo that hung in the living room of their three-bedroom condo in Flying Horse, just east of the Air Force Academy. The wedding photo, in the silver frame, showed his mother wearing a long white wedding dress and his father wearing his dress firefighters' uniform. Along one side of the aisle were six Air Force Academy graduates in their dress uniforms, with drawn sabers held high. On the other side of the isle were six firefighters in dress uniform, with chrome fire axes raised to touch the tip of the swords, forming an arch over the heads of the smiling newlyweds as they departed the chapel. ZacBox realized this was the exact spot where his parents were married as he stood next to the last man to see his mother alive.

"Shall we sit down?" Chief Sandoval asked, gesturing toward the front pew. "My name is Michael Sandoval, but most of my friends call me Saint Michael. You can call me whatever you like, as long as it's not sir, I am not an officer, not like your mother was."

Saint Michael sat to the left of ZacBox; they looked up at the huge silver wing-like structure hanging from the ceiling in the shape of a Christian cross. ZacBox thought it looked like a sword.

ZacBox spoke first, "Why do they call you Saint Michael?"

"Saint Michael is the patron saint of paratroopers and first responders. I was raised Catholic and always wore a Saint Michael's medallion around my neck, ever since I was your age. When I enlisted in the Air Force most everyone had a call sign or a nickname and if you didn't have one, someone was going to give you one. When I began flying with the PJs, the Guardian Angels, I gave a Saint Michael's medallion to each of my crewmembers to wear on a chain around their necks, next to their dog tags, so Saint Michael would watch over and protect each of them and us as a crew."

ZacBox nodded his head and then remained silent, as he wondered to himself where the patron Saint Michael was the day his mother and her two crewmates died.

"Your father tells me you have some questions?" Saint Michael finally asked.

"I want to know..." ZacBox began, and then choked back the words stuck in his throat. He swallowed, cleared his throat and tried again, "I want to know how my mother died."

"I cannot tell you how she died, I wasn't there, but I can tell you why she died."

That was not what ZacBox was expecting to hear and he looked quizzically at the man sitting next to him.

"Your mother died, Zac, so that others might live. She was a true hero and one of the most skilled pilots and bravest officers I ever had the privilege of serving with during my 26 years in uniform. We were assigned together with the 31st Rescue Squadron, U.S. Air Combat Command 18th Wing, stationed out of Kadena Air Base, Okinawa, Japan. The fighting during the War in the Middle East was very intense at the time. Our crew had flown 42 rescue missions—Flight 43 would be our last. Are you familiar with the mission of the Air Force Pararescue units? They're called PJs or Guardian Angels?"

"No," ZacBox commented, "this is all new to me."

"Our mission was to do whatever is required to deny the enemy a victory and bring our warriors home to fight another day. Whenever any of us took on any PJ mission, we swore to leave no airman, marine, soldier or sailor behind. That, Zac, is why your mother died. Do you want to hear more details about our last flight together, Mission 43?"

"Yes, please go on."

"Mission 43 started off as usual; your mother, Captain Leilani Box, was the pilot, sitting in the right seat; Captain Dave Kelly was her co-pilot, sitting in the left seat. On fixed-wing aircraft it's reversed, because on a helicopter the hoist is on the right side and you always want your most experienced pilot over the boom. I was left door gunner and Pararescue medic. Master Sergeant Neil Taylor was our right door gunner. Neil was African-American and I am Mexican-American, but that never mattered to us; he was my brother and I still miss him every day. Our crew, Neil and your mother and Captain Kelly, we were all family. Like most PJs, our squadron flew the HH-60 Pave Hawk helicopter. A more righteous bird never flew; she could take a punch and keep on fightin'. She got us home every time, even though she was more often than not all shot up, but she always brought us home…every time; every time but one—Mission 43." Sergeant Sandoval grew quiet, in solemn reflection of their last flight. ZacBox waited patiently in silence.

Finally, Sergeant Sandoval took a deep breath and began again, "It was fourteen hundred hours when we got the call, a dozen Army Rangers had come under attack, most had been wounded, five KIAs. We knew we'd be going into a hot LZ. Two clicks out they launched a SAM; I heard the tone and looked out my door and saw it coming, headed right at us. We hadn't descended yet, but had begun our approach. Captain Kelly tossed chaff while your mother fought for a little more altitude, and then at the last second, dove straight down into this clockwise barrel roll she had perfected, completely inverted. She took us down in two 360s to shake off the SAM. SAMs are radar-guided surface-to-air missiles and very deadly. Dropping straight down and rotating in a tight spiral like she did shook off the SAM. Other Pave Hawk pilots, and even the chopper's manufacturer, said that maneuver can't be done. But she had saved our butts more than once with those downward 360s. Taylor and I named the maneuver after your mother; "hang on, here comes another 'Leilani Loop', we'd shout to one another, knowing we better grab hold of our harnesses and hang on."

ZacBox watched as the airman closed his eyes and clutched

both hands over his chest. "We'd just hang on tight to our harnesses in the backseat and enjoyed the ride. It was a real rush! When we came out of that second loop Captain Kelly spotted the LZ directly below and to the right. I couldn't see it out my door, but your mom did, and I heard Neil shout into his headset that it looked like the Rangers were about to be overrun. Musta been over a hundred of 'em attacking what was left of that twelve-man Ranger team, dead and wounded all huddled together on this barren rocky outcropping. God, it was hot that day—well over a hundred and fifteen degrees in the shade, and as the saying goes, no shade."

"Altitude, temperature, humidity, windage, remaining fuel, a lot of things for a good Pararescue helicopter pilot like your mother to take into consideration, especially when deciding how many passengers and crew they can carry to safety. Goin' in I remember suckin' water out of my camelback like there was no tomorrow; for most of the Rangers on the ground and the rest of my crew in the air, there wouldn't be a tomorrow. I've felt guilty every day since, wonderin' why I lived, and they all had to die. I would've traded places with any one of them in an instant, without a second thought, especially your mom or Captain Kelly, who had two kids. Neal and I were both single. I glanced over and saw Sergeant Taylor cock his fifty cal and heard him shout something like, "This must have been what Custer felt like. Then he opened fire."

An Air Force chaplain walked past the pew on his way to the front of the chapel. He was carrying a beautiful red, white and blue floral arrangement and placed it prominently upon the white marble alter next to the Bible. Then ZacBox remembered today was the Fourth of July and wondered how many men and women serving in uniform had also died fighting for freedom since that first Independence Day in 1776. As the chaplain started walking back up the aisle, he nodded at Sergeant Sandoval as he passed, taking notice of his uniform shoulder patch with three chevrons up and five rockers below on his dress uniform and rows of medals on his chest.

Noticing the chaplain looking at them Sergeant Sandoval asked respectfully, "Sir, are we holding up anything being here?"

"No, my son," the Chaplain replied as he looked at his wristwatch, "we don't have another service until noon. Please take your time, Chief."

Saint Michael waited until the Chaplain was gone before he continued, "Your mother's voice came over the comms, ordering a low-level strafing run, to soften up the LZ before we landed. One of the Rangers popped smoke, so she could better judge her windage, as she balanced the bird and hovered steadily above the rocky outcropping. The bad guys had stopped firing after the strafing run, grabbing whatever cover they could, so Neil and I both jumped to the ground and started loading the five worst of the wounded into the back. It's a hard thing, trying to decide in an instant who might have a chance to live and who is probably already too far gone. You try to rely on your training, but when the bullets are flying and people are dying, mostly you have to just rely on your gut. Your mother held the helicopter just above the rocks, and then just as we loaded the fifth injured Ranger up into the chopper, the shooting started all over again."

"'Leave the dead,' Captain Kelly shouted into his headset to me and Neil on the ground, 'we'll have to come back, can't carry everyone out on this first flight!' Your mother had already requested a second Sandy—that's the PJ's call sign, our call sign was Sand Box One. The other Sandy, Sandy One Two, was flying in off a carrier out in the Med; everyone knew this firefight would be long over by the time they arrived. I was loading the fifth wounded Ranger into the back of the chopper when I was hit. Felt like my leg had been smashed with a sledge hammer. Knocked me to the ground. Bullets whizzing past overhead. Sounded like a bunch of mad bees. I tried to get up but Neil jumped on top of me to shield me with his body and tried to stop the bleeding. I helped him strap a tourniquet around my leg, and then he lifted me into the chopper, almost with one arm."

Sandoval, paused for a moment, then rubbed his left leg subconsciously before he began again, "Neil was an incredibly strong dude, played college football for Penn State, lifted weights all the time. I'm not a small man, as you can see, but he tossed me into the back of that Pave Hawk like I was a rag doll or somethin'. Then he smiled at me with that big goofy grin of his and said he'd catch me later and keyed his mic to tell your mom he would wait for Sandy One Two. He gave up his seat for a wounded Ranger. As we lifted off I tossed Neil my spare magazine for my handgun. He caught it midair, tapped it against his Kevlar helmet and waived farewell. We flew away. I never saw my friend again; well, until his funeral at Arlington.

The Ranger's commanding officer, who I later learned was a highly decorated Iron Major, along with their Command Sergeant Major, were both on their third tour of duty together in the Middle East. They fought alongside Neil with small arms as long as they could. By the time your mother got to them the fighting was pretty much hand-to-hand. But she wouldn't leave them, even when they tried to wave her off. I attended all seven of the Rangers' funerals. The Rangers watch over their honored dead 24/7, until the last of their fellow soldiers is lowered gently into the ground. I stood by them at the funerals, representing the Guardian Angels."

"Those had to be difficult funerals for you to attend," ZacBox said.

"Those, Dave Kelly's and Neil's at Arlington and your mother's here at the Academy, those were the toughest ones for me. It's especially hard when there are kids left behind; Dave had two young children; twins, about your age, a boy, Jason, and a girl, Jordan."

"You were here then, at my mom's funeral?" ZacBox asked, looking at the airman sitting on the pew next to him.

"Yes, I was here; I saw you that day, sitting right here, in the front pew, with your father and his family from the Reservation. White Elk wore a headdress; you kept playing with the eagle feathers."

"I don't remember much about my mother's funeral," ZacBox said, feeling guilty he couldn't remember more. "I do remember the helicopters flying overhead in the missing man formation, and taps. The twenty-one-gun salute made me jump, even though my dad warned me it was coming. Please Saint Michael, go on, what happened next, I mean with your last mission with my mom."

"Well, she knew Sandy One Two would not be able to reach Neil and the Rangers in time for a rescue. So, she made the decision to put me and the five wounded Rangers down on the ground closer to the coast for Sandy One Two to pick us up. Then she and Captain Kelly would go back inland for the second load of survivors. She gave Sandy One Two our GPS coordinates and then landed us on a flat rooftop of a building on the outskirts of a small village believed to be under our control. It looked defensible, and three of the wounded Rangers confirmed they were still in the fight. Captain Kelly helped me offload the five wounded Rangers onto the rooftop and handed me my rifle and first aid equipment. Then your mom, Sand Box 1, lifted off for a second rescue run. Back at the first LZ, when we left Neil with the other Rangers on the ground, his call sign became Sand Box 2, and when they dropped me on that rooftop, I became Sand Box 3, not knowing I would be the only survivor of Mission 43."

ZacBox looked over at the battle-hardened war veteran sitting next to him and saw a tear roll down his cheek. They both sat in silence for another minute before Saint Michael continued.

"I went about tending to the five injured, best I could with my busted-up leg, and listened through my headset. Sand Box 2's—Neil's—last transmission reported he and the last two Rangers had all been wounded and were running low on ammo. Neil called in their coordinates for an airstrike, knowing they were about to be overrun, but then Sand Box 1, your mom, came over the radio to report Captain Kelly had been killed from ground fire, but she was still inbound and would be landing at Sand Box 2's location in 10 seconds. 'Hang in there, Sand Box 2! I'm coming in hot on your six…' was the last thing she said.

"Then all we could hear over the radio was intense gunfire and the sound of the helicopter taking multiple hits from incoming rounds and coming apart, then nothin'. Next radio transmission was from a drone operator from Nellis Air Force Base, outside of Las Vegas, Nevada, two minutes later, reporting Sand Box 1 was down, laying on its side, on fire. Thermal images from the drone, a Global Hawk UAV, reported no survivors aboard or anywhere on the ground. Sandy One Two arrived at my location fifteen minutes after your mom's last transmission. The five injured Rangers with me all survived."

ZacBox swallowed hard, then said, "Thank you for sharing your story with me, I won't forget it."

"Here," Saint Michael said, handing the small black velvet box to ZacBox. "It's the Distinguished Flying Cross, the medal awarded to any officer or enlisted member of the U.S. Armed Forces who distinguishes themselves in support of operations by heroism or extraordinary achievement while participating in an aerial flight. Your father asked me to hold on to your mother's medal until you were old enough to accept it; this medal was awarded to your mother posthumously."

"I understand," ZacBox said, as he opened the box and stroked the small ornate propeller blades on the bronze medal affixed below the red, white and blue ribbon.

"The smaller service ribbon is worn on the duty uniform, the larger campaign medal is worn on the dress uniform."

ZacBox glanced over at the rows of medals on Saint Michael's dress uniform. "Do you have one of these?"

"No, I was awarded one of these instead," Saint Michael replied, pointing to a small gold and purple heart-shaped medal with three tiny gold stars. "It's the Purple Heart; it's awarded to those service men or women wounded or killed while serving with the U.S. military. This was my third Purple Heart; that's what the tiny gold stars are for; this will be my last medal."

"Why's that?" ZacBox asked, looking at the square-jawed service man sitting next to him who appeared ready for combat at any time or anywhere.

Saint Michael lifted his pant leg to where ZacBox could see the titanium metal tube of the prosthesis where his left leg had once been. ZacBox now understood why he walked with a limp.

"The Air Force allowed me to stay in the military, providing training for other PJs mostly, until today, the Fourth of July. Today is Independence Day, my retirement day. I've never had time to marry or have a family, like your mother did, so my brothers and sisters in uniform are my family, and serving in the military has been the greatest honor of my life. I'd do it all over again in a heartbeat. Service alongside your mother and all the other Guardian Angels has been my life. I'd gladly give my other leg for just one more Sandy Pararescue flight, one more chance to fly with the PJs, a chance to bring one more warrior home to fight another day. But with only one good leg, I would be an impediment now. It's my time to go. Time to retire."

"But what will you do now?"

"I've been offered a job with one of the big defense contractors, Lockheed Martin; I think it might be a good fit. They have an office across the Interstate there," Chief Sandoval said, "off Interquest Parkway west of Voyager."

"I know where that is; Interquest is along my morning training route," ZacBox said in acknowledgement.

"Please know, Zac, that if you ever need anything, anything at all, I wrote my contact information on the inside of that box you are holding. Just reach out and I'll be there, always."

"Thank you for that and for sharing your story with me," ZacBox said as he closed the black velvet box and scooted forward in the pew preparing to leave. "I think Mr. Bojangles and I need a long run."

"Mr. Bojangles?"

"Yes, that's what I named by dog; I call him Bo."

"That song, Mr. Bojangles, was your mother's ring tone on her cellphone, whenever your father called."

ZacBox smiled, clutching his mother's Distinguished Flying Cross in his hands. "The last video my dad shot of me and my mom was her holding me in her arms as we danced to that song. That's why it was always special to her and Dad and me."

"Come," Saint Michael said as he struggled to stand, "let me drive you home." Then the two of them stood, turned around and began to walk toward the back of the chapel.

For the first time ZacBox noticed hundreds of Air Force Cadets had quietly slipped into the chapel, since his father had left, and had filled the back several pews. The cadets stood in unison as they waited for Saint Michael and ZacBox to walk past, "Where did all these cadets come from; I don't understand, why are they here?"

"They are here to honor the memory of your mother; she was

a distinguished graduate of the Academy and a recipient of the Distinguished Flying Cross. They also stand in recognition of the service and sacrifice of all the PJs around the world."

"How did they know we were here?"

"That chaplain with the flowers must have told someone we were here; he may have been the one who gave her funeral service; I don't remember his name. Many of these young men and women will go on to become pilots. They know if they were ever to be shot down behind enemy lines, their best hope of survival will be themselves, applying the skills they learn here at the Academy. But they know their best hope of a rescue will be a Pararescue in the form of a Guardian Angel flying in from above, a Sandy."

July 4th 11:15 hours MDST Astradate 11070.4
Flying Horse, East of USAFA, Colorado Springs, CO USA
Planet Earth

Saint Michael drove ZacBox home in his new blue Chevy Camaro. They exited through the north gate of the Academy, then headed east on Northgate Blvd past Voyager Parkway.

"Take the next right," ZacBox said, "What a cool car! Z28 sixth-generation isn't it?"

"It is, I'm impressed—you know your cars," Saint Michael said approvingly. "Let me know when you get your license. I'll let you drive the Z and be your wingman."

"Oh wow! That would be awesome! Turn right up here, then my house is the second set of townhomes in the cul-de-sac there on the right," ZacBox said pointing to the tan stucco, one-level, rancher patio homes with the terracotta tile roofs and attached two-car garages.

When Saint Michael dropped ZacBox off in front of his house, he asked about ZacBox's favorite video game, Return to Pleiades. "It's a lot of fun," ZacBox said. "You'll have to drop by sometime, and I'll challenge you to a game."

"I don't know," Saint Michael said, as ZacBox stepped out of the sleek new sports car, "Your dad tells be you are the champ and no one on this planet can beat you!"

"I don't know about that; you'll see it's just a lot of fun. See you later," ZacBox said as he closed the car door and watched Saint Michael exit the cul-de-sac. As Saint Michael drove away in his shiny Z28 Camaro ZacBox waved goodbye and took special notice of his personalized license plates; "STMIKES."

"Wow, someday I'm going to have a cool car just like that," ZacBox said to himself, as he walked up the driveway. He punched the security code into the key pad next to the garage door; it opened and he went inside. They rarely used the front door, except for packages or guests.

ZacBox thought briefly about going in and playing a video game on his Xbox. He laughed thinking about how his dad told all his firefighter friends at the Academy that they were doing advanced modeling and simulations. But ZacBox knew they were just playing video games and having fun. ZacBox had become very good at playing space video games and almost always beat his dad and most of the cadets he played against. But Return to Pleiades was his all-time favorite video game, and he loved the challenges of space flight. The maneuverability of the flying saucers had become almost second nature to him, and he even found himself waking up in the mornings realizing he had been flying the saucer and shooting down alien spacecraft in his sleep.

Once inside the house, Bo greeted him instantly. "Hi boy, you ready for a run?" ZacBox asked as he gave Bo a hug before letting him outside in the backyard for a few minutes. Then he changed into his running gear and texted his dad, "Hi Dad, thanks for arranging for me to meet Saint Michael. He's an awesome guy. Bo and I are going for a run."

Within seconds came his father's text reply, "Ok. Thanks for letting me know, which route you taking?"

ZacBox texted back to his dad, "Northgate, then south to Interquest, east of I-25 and we might stop by Fibonacci's Diner to say hi to Professor Fibonacci."

"Ok, but don't eat too much. We've been invited to her condo this evening for a BBQ with Reggie, and then watch the fireworks over the Academy with her and some of her cadets."

"Sounds like fun, Luv you dad, ZB1."

"Luv u 2 ZB2. B careful."

ZacBox's parents had picked out their dream home in Flying Horse partly because it was close to the Air Force Academy, where ZacBox's father still works as a firefighter, when he isn't away training smokejumpers how to fighting forest fires. But what was most important for his parents was that Flying Horse was across the street from Discovery Canyon Campus, DCC, one of the top schools in Colorado Springs. ZacBox had gone to school at DCC ever since kindergarten. He was excited about starting the 10th grade after the summer break and couldn't wait for track to start back up again. DCC was K-12 grades, all on one campus, and although there were three separate schools, elementary, middle and high school, they were designed to be interconnected.

The month after ZacBox's mother passed away, one of her former physics teachers from the Academy, Professor Lisa Fibonacci, bought the patio home next door. Professor Fibonacci often babysat ZacBox when he was little. Professor Fibonacci retired from teaching at the Academy before ZacBox started kindergarten and he often stayed overnight with her when his father was working his regular 24-hour shift at the Academy's fire station. Although Professor Lisa Fibonacci wasn't teaching physics fulltime at the U.S. Air Force Academy anymore, she remained connected to the Academy from having been granted the distinguished title of Professor Emeritus, which gave her access to the Academy resources and cadets. Soon after she retired from the Academy Professor Fibonacci built a diner just north of Interquest Parkway, where ZacBox always knew he could stop for a good meal. There were always lots of cadets around Fibonacci's Diner, and she also sponsored cadets in her home next door, giving them a home away from home and ZacBox a constant set of young men and women to hang around with or play video games.

ZacBox and his father's condo had been built with three bedrooms, but since there were only the two of them, his dad converted the smaller bedroom into an office, where ZacBox could do his school homework and play video games. It seemed ZacBox had almost an endless pipeline for the latest video games, from the cadets next door or from Professor Fibonacci, who was always giving him a new game to play on his Xbox. ZacBox and his father loved the video games that had anything to do with flying in combat or travelling in space the most. His father told him he had inherited his mother's flying skills, which gave him an unfair competitive advantage over him and most of the cadets since flying was in his DNA.

Since middle school, it was not unusual for ZacBox to receive two or three new video games a month and he often kept notes to give to Professor Fibonacci on ways he thought the games could be improved. When ZacBox started high school last year, two engineers from a government organization with a funny sounding name, like DARPA or something, met him in a building on the backside of the Academy and asked him a bunch of questions about what he liked best or least about some of the video games; even though they wore business suits, he knew they were working for the military. ZacBox's dad wasn't there that time, but Professor Fibonacci was, and she was always interested in asking his opinion on various things. He especially liked it when she asked him to taste many of the wonderful new recipes she was always making in her gourmet kitchen next door or at her diner.

ZacBox even got to meet two engineers from NASA visiting the Academy, and one time, Professor Fibonacci arranged for three of the engineers from one of the video gaming companies to meet with him and his dad over dinner at her diner, to discuss his detailed notes and frequent suggestions. Last month Professor Fibonacci dropped by ZacBox's house and handed him a new video game to play. It was called Return to Pleiades. When she handed ZacBox the game, he recognized it was different from any video game he had ever seen. This game was on a thumbdrive, about an inch and a half in diameter, and shaped like a flying saucer with a USB dongle. The file size was so big the game couldn't be downloaded, so ZacBox had to play it while it was plugged into his laptop computer. Almost overnight, ZacBox lost interest in all his other video games; they just didn't seem as realistic or fun to play anymore.

ZacBox wasn't very familiar with Pleiades before he started playing this video game, but it had quickly become his favorite. He played it all the time and got to a level where he could easily beat his dad. Whenever a player logged on, the top ten scores appeared on the screen. ZacBox used the call sign ZacBox1 whenever he logged in, and his scores usually appeared in the top five. Last month Professor Fibonacci arranged for a group of cadets to challenge ZacBox virtually, and eventually he beat all of them too.

ZacBox took the flying saucer USB game with him that summer, to plug into his laptop, to play while he was staying with his grandfather. Three weeks before ZacBox was to return home, Professor Fibonacci brought two aerospace engineers from Lockheed Martin to the Ute Mountain Ute Reservation Casino Hotel to ask him more questions.

ZacBox understood they wanted to ask him more about how he was able to master the controls of the flying saucer, even though he had not been given an instruction manual. Then one of the engineers handed him a thin case, about twice the size of his smartphone. When he flipped open the lid, he saw an elaborate looking joystick, shaped like a figure eight lying on its side, and the inside of the lid was a tinted glass screen. At the center of the yoke-shaped control was a round disc, also about one and a half inches in diameter, shaped like a flying saucer.

"They're calling this game Battle Stations Taurus," Professor Fibonacci explained to ZacBox. Then after looking around them at the other booths in the restaurant to make sure no one was listening in on their conversation, she continued, "You can pull the center saucer-shaped disc out and plug it into your laptop or you can play it in the case. It has a much more advanced weapons and navigation system. Push down on the top and turn it a quarter turn clockwise." Professor Fibonacci demonstrated how to remove the disc from the control yoke and handed it to ZacBox. "It's like a docking station."

ZacBox did as instructed and noticed the top and bottom of the saucer separated about an eighth of an inch, exposing what looked like dark-tinted glass encircling all the way around the saucer, just inside the rim, and the USB stick came out of the bottom. Then he turned the two halves counterclockwise, and the USB stick retracted back into the disc as the top and the bottom of the saucer came back together to form a tight seal. Then he plugged it back into the control yoke and closed the lid.

"That's so cool!" ZacBox said, "I can't wait to get to Grandfather's house to play it!"

"We only have seven of these, so be careful you don't lose it," Professor Fibonacci cautioned. "And don't let anyone else play with it, at least for now. Your dad knows about it, but we're trying to keep it a secret until we understand more of what this technology can do. When you get home they'll need to get this one back, but we are all very interested to hear what you think of it. Please be careful with it."

"I'll be careful. Why did you call it Battle Stations Taurus?"

"The Pleiades Star Cluster is located in the Taurus Constellation," Dr. Stella Lockwood, the younger of the two engineers explained. "Two thousand years ago, when the ancient Greeks were studying the planets and the stars, they thought this constellation looked like a bull and named it Taurus. The Pleiades is where the eye of the bull would be located. The game, we think, simulates the flying saucer defending the Eye of Taurus from a fleet of alien invading spacecraft. The disc is like a $1/20^{th}$ scale model, so if it were a real life-size flying saucer, it would measure approximately 21 meters in diameter and 8 meters in height."

"Fibonacci numbers," ZacBox said as he examined the disc.

"What was that?" Dr. Lockwood asked.

"They're Fibonacci numbers, you know, the Fibonacci Sequence: 5, 8, 13, 21, 33, 54, only the number 13 is left out."

"Guess I never thought of that," Dr. Lockwood said. "As you will see, the game is very realistic, and I will be very interested in hearing your comments. But before we leave there's one question I wanted to ask you now Zac."

"Sure, what is it Dr. Lockwood?"

"Well, how do you know how to fly the saucer so well in the video game? You were never shown how to fly it. You were never given an instruction manual. And yet, you were able to fly further and advance faster than any of our gamers at Lockheed Martin's Center for Innovation or all the cadets at the Air Force Academy. How do you think you have done so well?"

ZacBox had replied at the time, "You can't think about flying it, you just have to fly it."

Beep, Beep, Beep!

July 4th 11:57 hours MDST Astradate 11070.4
Field East of U.S. Air Force Academy, Colorado Springs, CO
USA Planet Earth

ZacBox had been halfway into his ten-mile run when the ground beneath his feet began to shake. "There it is again!" ZacBox said to Bo as he spread his feet apart, balancing himself as he stood waiting for the last of the tremors to subside. After a few seconds had elapsed, ZacBox said, "At least it wasn't as bad as last time." He took several steps forward, tested his footing. He looked at the ground ahead leading to what appeared to be an old trail ahead off to his right.

"Funny, I didn't know this trail was back here," ZacBox said to Bo, the curious puppy at his side. Just then Bo took off running and barking down the winding trail to the right. "Bo! Come back here!" ZacBox yelled as he started running down the trail after Bo.

Within a few hundred meters, the trail zigzagged downhill, crossed a creek, and then weaved between two taller Ponderosa pine trees and vanished out of sight behind some scrub oak.

ZacBox followed the narrow single-track trail as Bo ran ahead and continued on out of sight. ZacBox could still hear Bo barking and knew he was close behind. ZacBox came to an old barbed wire fence that crossed the trail. He knew this was private property but didn't see any No Trespassing signs. He crawled over the top wire and followed the sound of Bo's barking. Then the barking stopped. ZacBox raced down the trail beneath the canopy of cottonwood trees. Then he saw the trail was leading up to a small hill thirty meters ahead, and he saw Bo was sitting near the trail staring up into the trees.

"Bo," ZacBox scolded, "don't do that again!" ZacBox stopped next to Bo and bent over to catch his breath. "I was worried about you," ZacBox said letting his heartrate and breathing return to normal. ZacBox noticed Bo had his head cocked to the side and was still looking up into the trees. When ZacBox looked up to where Bo was staring, he thought he caught sight of a small multicolored orb of some kind hovering about ten feet above the trail in front of him in the trees. The orb was smaller than a soccer ball, but bigger than a softball. ZacBox thought at first it might have been a weather balloon that drifted across the Interstate from the Air Force Academy.

As he approached the orb to see if it had any markings, it moved slowly back along the trail almost as if it were beckoning them to follow. "That's no weather balloon," ZacBox said as he turned to Bo. "Come on boy, let's see where it's going." ZacBox jogged ahead slowly but kept looking down the trail and into the surrounding trees thinking they might come across some cadets out searching for a wayward science project or an experimental drone or something. Running at a faster pace now, to keep the orb in sight, the pair of adventure seekers followed the narrow foot trail as it began winding up a slight rise leading to the small mound where the trail seemed to come to an end.

ZacBox slowed to a fast walk as he approached several larger rocks that appeared to have been arranged upright in a circular arc slightly wider than his house. What he saw at the center of the stone enclosure stopped him dead in his tracks. Jutting up between several layers of broken sedimentary rock was a three-foot-tall metallic rod attached to an upright piece of metal of some sort, kind of resembling the nosecone of a jetfighter pointing skyward. The orb was hovering three feet above the rod sticking up out of the ground.

At first ZacBox thought maybe he had come across a plane crash, thinking back to how his mother had died, but there was no debris scattered about the area. Looking around, ZacBox believed he was not on the Air Force Academy property, but still half expected to see an Air Force K-9 team emerge from the trees lining a creek bed a hundred meters to the north. As he cautiously approached the metal rod, the small orb began hovering six inches above what he thought might be an antenna atop a structure buried under the raised ground where he was standing. He heard the faint whirling sound of the orb spinning. When it was within reach, ZacBox held out his hand to touch it. Suddenly, the orb was sucked down the metallic rod, which had expanded its diameter to allow the orb to travel down the length of the hollow rod making a "thumpth" sound, as if someone had sucked a big grape down a straw.

ZacBox grasped the metal rod in his hand, noticing it was cool to the touch, but it was very strong, and he could not bend it. When he held it in his hand, the rod seemed to turn into a semi-liquid state, which was how the orb passed down into whatever it was that he was standing on. He felt a slight vibration of the rod and the ground seemed to raise four or five inches beneath his feet. Then he heard what he thought sounded like the zapping sound of an arc welder coming from below ground. ZacBox continued to clutch the rod in his hand as he walked all the way around inspecting the ground, half expecting at any moment to hear the shout of the Air Force Security police shouting, "Hey, you, kid! What do you think you're doing there!" This rod must lead to a secret underground government base he finally concluded. He released his grip and slowly began backing away from the metallic rod.

Not wanting to get into trouble, or do anything that might jeopardize his dream of someday attending the Air Force Academy. ZacBox looked around one last time before turning to Bo, "Come on boy, I don't think we're supposed to be here." As they started jogging toward Fibonacci's Diner, about two hundred meters from where they had found the metal rod sticking up out of the ground, ZacBox heard the sound of a car starting. It must have been parked up ahead where the trail crossed a gravel road he concluded. ZacBox sprinted to where he could see the road below and watched as an older blue Subaru drove away.

July 25th 12:15 hours MDST Astradate 11070.4
Fibonacci's Diner, Colorado Springs, CO USA Planet Earth

It had been nearly two weeks since ZacBox first discovered the metal rod poking out of the ground, but he still hadn't told anyone. He was concerned he might have been trespassing when he followed the shiny orb down the trail to the small mound. This all sounded so crazy, he was sure no one would believe him, but then there was another concern that he might be disclosing the location of a secret underground government facility he wasn't supposed to know about. If this were a top secret military base he'd stumbled across while trespassing, he questioned if he might have jeopardized his being accepted to the Air Force Academy or worse, jeopardized his father's career as a firefighter at the Academy.

Eventually, ZacBox decided he had to tell someone and texted Professor Fibonacci to see if she could talk with him at the diner after lunch. He knew she was still connected to the Academy and hoped she wouldn't think he was crazy.

The day was hot and there was not a cloud in the blue sky as ZacBox rode his mountain bike out of his Flying Horse neighborhood and west along Northgate Blvd. The long-sleeve, button-down shirt he wore over his white t-shirt flapped in the wind as he steered his bike west toward the north entrance of the Air Force Academy. At Voyager Parkway he turned left, and then in a few miles made a right turn headed to Fibonacci's Diner. When he guided his bike into the parking lot, there were only five cars parked in front of the diner. Two of those were newer black Chevy Suburbans with dark tinted windows. He assumed those were military vehicles. Then there was a UPS delivery van and Dr. Fibonacci's green Subaru Forester SUV. But the fifth car was an older blue Subaru, similar to the one he had seen driving away from where he had felt the last tremors on the Fourth of July.

ZacBox steered his mountain bike casually behind the blue Subaru so he could get a look at the license plates. Colorado license plates, nothing noteworthy there, but on the back bumper he spotted a School of Mines parking sticker and next to it a bumper sticker which read, My Other Car is a Starship. "Gotta be a story there," ZacBox thought to himself as he rode his bike around to the back of the diner and dismounted next to an expensive road racing bike. ZacBox opened the back door and waved at the African American cook with a shaved head and legs as big around and solid as tree trunks cooking in the kitchen. "Hi Reggie. What's good for lunch?"

"Hi Champ!" Reggie said with a smile, "I believe the Professor has a new spaghetti and vegetarian meatballs recipe she wants you to try. Where's Bo?"

"Oh, I left him in the kennel," ZacBox said as he accepted a piece of garlic toast Reggie handed him on a paper towel, blew on top to cool it off and then took a bite. "Thanks, hot out of the oven! The melted provolone cheese and the dab of marina sauce on top is a nice touch. Awesome! As Professor Fibonacci would say, 'my compliments to the Chef!'" ZacBox said as he stuffed the rest of the toast in his mouth and wiped his lips with the paper towel. Reggie mentioned he was training for the Bolder Boulder, a popular 10K footrace in Boulder, Colorado that ZacBox had run once with his father.

ZacBox said, "I saw your bike out back, you doing legs today?"

"Yeah, you?" Reggie replied as he plated a serving of spaghetti.

"Me too, but right now I'm starved!" ZacBox said as he left the kitchen and headed into the main area of the diner. He was curious to see if he could spot who might be driving the older blue Subaru parked out front. ZacBox looked around, noticing two tables were filled with a half dozen airmen wearing flight suits. At another long table there were seven or eight cadets having lunch while speaking with Professor Fibonacci. In one corner booth sat two UPS drivers drinking coffee, neither appearing to be in any particular hurry to go back to work. ZacBox had noticed how popular Fibonacci's had become with UPS drivers over the past few months; but who could blame them, the food here was awesome, even if the diner was somewhat off the beaten path.

As ZacBox took a seat in a booth near the window, he took note of two men and a woman wearing white lab coats at another table. Just as he looked up, they were joined by another woman with long brown hair and thick framed glasses, returning from the restrooms located toward the back of the diner. When she sat down, it looked like the others were talking to her about him and he saw her turn her head toward him and smile. ZacBox buried his head in his menu and decided he was just being paranoid. When he looked up again, she was gone. He guessed she was in her mid-twenties and very attractive. He looked out the window to see if she was getting into one of the five cars parked out front, but she was nowhere to be seen.

The interior of Fibonacci's Diner was decorated with beautifully framed photos of various examples of the Fibonacci Spiral found in the nautilus shell, waves in the ocean, big sunflowers, pine cones and the spiral galaxies in deep space. Professor Fibonacci was a direct descendent of Leonardo Fibonacci, the most famous Western mathematician of the Middle Ages. He had been born in the 12th Century, in Pisa, Italy and brought the Arabic numerals, including the use of the zero, into the Latin world. But the Fibonacci sequence of numbers, where each number is the sum of the previous two numbers, is what most fascinated Professor Fibonacci.

Out of all the beautiful images illustrating the Fibonacci spiral, Professor Fibonacci had selected the colorful Fibonacci 49 cent U.S. Postage Stamp as the logo for her diner. This image appeared on her menu and on the modest-size sign that hung in front of her diner. She had taught ZacBox to count since he was three years old, using the Fibonacci sequence: 0, 1, 1, 2, 3, 5, 8, etc. Sometimes, when she was babysitting him at night, she would have him repeat the Fibonacci sequence as high as he could go to help him fall to sleep instead of counting sheep. Most nights by the time he got to 55 he was fast asleep, but his record was one night when he made it to 233.

There were not very many other businesses around Fibonacci's Diner, so whoever was at the diner came for the food. Reggie was a world-class chef. ZacBox had often admired Reggie's bio highlighted on the back of the menu; Chef Reginald Barnhill and his twin brother Marcus had been professionally trained at some of the finest restaurants in Italy and New York City. Marcus became a famous celebrity chef on TV, and Reggie accepted the position as sous-chef de cuisine at the famed five-star Broadmoor Hotel here in Colorado Springs.

Three years ago Chef Reggie became the executive chef at Fibonacci's Diner, a bit of a demotion most people would assume. When ZacBox asked Reggie why he left the Broadmoor he said Fibonacci's gave him more freedom to pursue recipes that one day would be out of this world. ZacBox envied how Reggie had traveled all around the world. The only place ZacBox had ever been, besides his Grandfather's Reservation, was the one trip when Professor Fibonacci had taken him to Santa Fe, New Mexico, four summers ago. She wanted him to see the Miraculous Staircase, at the Loretto Chapel.

When ZacBox and Professor Fibonacci arrived at the chapel the only other person inside at the time was an older priest. Professor Fibonacci talked to the priest, and handed him a cash donation, then the priest smiled and left the chapel. ZacBox remembered he and Professor Fibonacci lying on the floor, scooting on their backs until they were directly under the winding staircase, looking straight up at the center of the wonderess spiral from the floor.

"This is why we're here Zac," Professor Fibonacci said, "I want you to always remember what the Miraculous Staircase looks like staring up into the heavens." ZacBox thought it looked pretty cool at the time, but the thing that made the biggest impression on him was the hotel swimming pool where they stayed next door to the chapel. Professor Fibonacci had given ZacBox swimming lessons several summers at the Academy and he really loved the water.

The only other buildings located near Fibonacci's Diner were a couple of older structures located a few hundred meters to the northwest, surrounded by a high fence, topped with barbed wire and posted with no trespassing signs. The buildings were rather run down, and ZacBox thought they may have at one time been for some sort of a salvage business. Once when riding his bike, ZacBox spotted the hulk of an old car beside a shed. He had stopped his bike and tried to look through the fence to see if he could identify the make or model of the old car.

ZacBox and his dad were always on the lookout for an old car they could buy and fix up for him to drive when he turned sixteen. When you're fifteen and a half, waiting six months until you finally get your driver's license in Colorado can seem like an eternity. ZacBox couldn't get a good look at the old car because a guard dog, a German Shepard, came rushing up to the fence barking at him. He backed away quickly, rode away on his bike and never stopped there again.

Once in a while ZacBox would see construction workers sitting in the diner eating lunch. He wondered if they might work at the salvage yard, but most of the customers were in military uniform or well-dressed business people. ZacBox looked around the diner as he pretended to be studying the menu—which he knew by heart —hoping to see who was driving the blue Subaru parked out front. This was the first time he realized there were far more people inside the diner eating than there were cars in the parking lot. "Oh well," he told himself, "maybe they just carpool."

Then ZacBox spotted him, sitting alone in a corner booth, a slender dark-complected younger man, not much older than he was, wearing a white pagri, the traditional headdress of men in India. ZacBox guessed he might be a college student, thinking back to the School of Mines parking sticker on the Subaru. ZacBox also noticed his headdress was similar to one worn by a visiting scientist from India that he had met during one of the meetings Professor Fibonacci arranged for him on the Academy.

Trying not to get caught staring, ZacBox watched the young man as he finished his lunch and gathered his things to leave. ZacBox thought he looked very smart. "You'd have to be smart to be going to the School of Mines," ZacBox reminded himself. But judging from the bumper sticker, about his other car being a starship, and now seeing him now, ZacBox concluded he was probably just a nerd. It was obvious to ZacBox that here was a guy trying and failing, to blend in with the crowd. ZacBox noticed the young man had also caught the attention of the two UPS delivery men in their brown uniforms. One of the UPS men was texting on his smartphone and for an instant ZacBox thought he saw him snap a picture of the young man wearing the pagri as he was leaving.

"Try this," Reggie said as he set ZacBox's plate of spaghetti and meatballs down in front of him, along with another piece of garlic toast with melted cheese on top.

"It smells wonderful," ZacBox said as he inhaled deeply.

"What'll you have to drink, sport?" Reggie asked.

"Water's fine, thanks Reg. Hey, any idea who's that guy leaving the corner booth over there, the one wearin' the pagri?"

Reggie glanced over to see the young man stand up, reach into his billfold to leave some cash on the table, and then head toward the front door. "He's been in a couple times in the last two weeks or so. I haven't met him but he seems friendly enough. He's vegetarian and Professor Fibonacci told me he loves our spaghetti and vegetarian meatballs, so obviously he's an excellent judge of fine cuisine. Hey, maybe he's an international food critic and he'll give us a five-star review!"

ZacBox laughed as Reggie headed back to the kitchen and watched as the young man walked outside and got into the blue

Subaru and drove away. One of the UPS drivers also walked outside, climbed into the brown delivery van, and drove off in the same direction as the blue Subaru. The other UPS man signed a credit card receipt on the table, picked up a clipboard and headed toward the restrooms. ZacBox looked outside and noticed now there were only three cars in the small parking lot in front of the diner, and one of those was Professor Fibonacci's car. Strangely enough, the diner still had more than a dozen people inside, including the second UPS delivery man who had yet to return from the restroom. "That's odd," ZacBox thought to himself, "maybe he had another delivery van parked out back I missed when I rode up."

After ZacBox started in on a second plate of spaghetti, Professor Fibonacci, finally was able to take a break from serving her customers seated at the counter and the other tables. She sat down in the booth across from him, looked down at his nearly empty plate and smiled. "My mother's recipe, she was full-blooded Italian. Mama would have enjoyed watching you eat."

ZacBox wiped his mouth on the back of his shirt sleeve and said, "I'd like you to think I'm carbo-loading, but the truth is I just love your and Reggie's spaghetti and vegetarian meatballs! I think everything on your menu is good, especially your cheese pizza, but your eggplant lasagna and this spaghetti are outta this world." Turning serious for a moment, he asked, "Professor Fibonacci, can I ask you something?"

"Sure dear, what is it?"

"Have you ever felt any tremors here at the diner? The other day one nearly knocked me down again. Just like when I was on Grandfather's Reservation. It's weird but it kind of feels like the last time it happened, it was on the Fourth of July, well it felt like the tremors were right beneath us, like coming up right here from underground."

Professor Fibonacci smiled, "I have felt them too; would you like any dessert dear?"

"No, thank you, I'm stuffed, I can't even finish my last two bites, but there is something else I have wanted to talk with you about, if you have a few minutes."

"Of course, dear. Our lunch rush is over, Reggie can handle things from here. What is it Zac? You look worried. Something troubling you, dear?"

"Well, besides these tremors seeming to be happening wherever I'm at, on Sleeping Ute Mountain or here at home, I keep worrying about when the next one will hit and if it might be worse. You know, like those quakes you hear about that killed all those thousands of people overseas. I keep wondering, are we in any danger? And now, well, I'm beginning to think people are staring, or talking about me, and well, besides being paranoid or thinking I'm going to die, I…I think I'm beginning to see things…"

"What kinds of things dear?"

"Well, I know this sounds crazy, and I haven't told dad yet, he's got enough to worry about with this fire season and all, but two weeks ago, when I was running with Bo, he started barking and ran off down this trail chasing this shiny round ball of some kind floating in the air. I thought it was a weather balloon or a drone or something from the Academy, at first, and here's the really weird part, and please don't laugh at me…"

"I'm not laughing Zac, do go on."

"Well, it…this floating shining ball, it seemed like, well, I think it wanted me to follow it, so, I did. I might have been trespassing on someone's property, I don't know for sure. It was just like halfway between the diner here and that old salvage yard or whatever it is over there. Then this shiny ball stopped in midair and hovered over this long metal rod sticking out of the ground. It seemed like this orb was trying to communicate, so I reached out to touch it and thumpth, it got sucked down this metal rod. Then I'm thinking this might be like a secret military project of some kind." ZacBox lowered his voice so he wouldn't be overhead and then asked, "Have you ever seen anything like that around here or maybe over at the Academy?"

Thinking for a moment, Professor Fibonacci finally replied, "Zac, come with me, I think maybe it's time for you to meet Olaf Eriksson, he's the proprietor of CAT^2."

"What's CAT^2?"

"It stands for the Center for the Advancement of Talent and Technology. A few friends and I have been helping Mr. Eriksson get his idea off the ground. The concept is based on the premise that talent and technology will flourish most when they are clustered tightly together around an important mission. You'll understand more in a moment Zac."

ZacBox had a dozen questions, but held them as Professor Fibonacci slid out of the booth and started toward the back of the diner. ZacBox followed behind her through the diner toward the restrooms. From the interior of the diner you couldn't actually see the restrooms, just the sign pointing the way, but having used the men's room countless times, ZacBox knew there were only three doors leading off this hallway. The door on the left went to the men's restroom, the one on the right to the women's restroom, and then there was a third door a short distance ahead of them at the end of the hallway. It was marked with a nondescript sign that read "Janitor's Closet." Professor Fibonacci opened and held the door as ZacBox walked inside the small closet. They turned around to face the front, like they were getting on an elevator. Professor Fibonacci smiled at ZacBox as she closed the door behind them.

"Uh, perhaps you haven't noticed Professor, but we're in your broom closet," ZacBox said in a low voice, with a puzzled look on his face.

Professor Fibonacci continued to smile and then replied, "Not everything is always as it seems."

Standing quietly inside the dimly lit broom closet in Professor Fibonacci's diner, ZacBox looked up above the door at a small brass sign engraved with a quote from Neil DeGrasse Tyson, "We are stardust brought to life, then empowered by the universe to figure itself out—and we have only just begun."

Then Professor Fibonacci smiled again and suggested, "You might want to hold on to something dear." ZacBox reached up to grab hold of a coat rack as she pushed the mop handle forward. The floor beneath their feet dropped suddenly. It felt to ZacBox like he was riding an elevator descending rapidly to a basement. ZacBox felt the broom closet slow down and come softly to a stop. He didn't know how many floors below ground they were, but thought they had traveled down at least three floors. He watched as Professor Fibonacci released her grip on the mop handle and pushed a button beneath a shelf which opened the doors. She nodded to ZacBox to step out of the closet into the dark. ZacBox trusted Professor Fibonacci completely, but this was really weird.

As they stepped forward into the darkness, a soft bluish-colored light came on overhead, illuminating the way ahead. ZacBox realized they were walking through a small cavern, much smaller than the diner above their heads. The rock walls and roof overhead showed signs of being carved by hand a long time ago and reminded him of a school field trip his fifth-grade class had taken to the Mining Museum located a few miles west of his school near the Interstate. ZacBox had to walk quickly to keep up with Professor Fibonacci. He guessed she had to be in her late sixties, but it was hard to tell because she had always kept herself in such great physical condition, no doubt from all those years teaching yoga and swimming classes to her cadets.

As they walked deeper into the cavern, the lights ahead of them blinked on one at a time and the lights behind them flicked off. ZacBox noticed two things that were different about the lighting: the lights were now located along both sides of what seemed to be a long tunnel, and as they continued walking forward, the darker bluish-colored light became a lighter color blue.

Professor Fibonacci slowed and then stopped as they approached what seemed to be an intersection of a street circling around from their left to their right, with tiny yellow lights in the floor that reminded him of the track lighting in the floor of a movie theater. Then ZacBox's jaw dropped as another overhead light came on to their left, and he saw a two car garage; right in the middle of the garage was a gleaming red Tesla convertible sports car.

"Holy smokes!" ZacBox said aloud as he walked over and stroked the edge of the hood with his fingertip to make sure it was real. ZacBox walked slowly around the car, admiring its aerodynamic design and black interior. "This looks just like the one Alan Trask launched into space. Cool!" When he reached the rear of the car he looked down and saw a personalized license plate, SPIRAL2. "Wow! Is this yours?"

"Yes," Professor Fibonacci said with a smile, "Alan saved it for me; he said it was the next one off the assembly line behind the one he launched into space. Alan said I might need something to run a few errands. It's electric, gasoline engines don't do very well down here underground as you can imagine."

"You know Alan Trask?"

"Well, he's been here a few times."

ZacBox stared at the red convertible sports car and then looked up at Professor Fibonacci, a woman he had known all of his life. But now he was starting to question if he really knew her at all. ZacBox saw the lights on the tunnel off to their left flicker on, then off again, rhythmically as someone on a two-wheeled Segway approached. "Come dear, I want you to meet Julian."

The Segway glided quietly to a stop. It was a man wearing a UPS delivery uniform, like the two he had seen upstairs in the diner, only this man had an MP5 automatic submachine gun slung over his shoulder. He stepped off the Segway and walked up to Professor Fibonacci. "Zac this is Julian Piccard. He was with the Swiss Guard responsible for the safety of the Pope at the Vatican in Rome. Julian is now the chief of security here at CAT^2."

"Master Box," Julian said with a slight bow, "tis an honor to finally meet you."

"Ah, you too," ZacBox said, "I guess. Is this CAT^2?" ZacBox looked down the dark tunnel and wondered what was underground here that needed such high security.

"Yes. CAT^2," Professor Fibonacci explained, "is an acronym for the Center for the Advancement of Talent and Technology as I mentioned. T^2 is T squared. Come, let us see if we can find Mr. Eriksson. I think he might be able to answer your questions better than I."

Julian pointed toward the center tunnel and said, "I believe you will locate Mr. Eriksson off there a bit, towards the Electra's launch apparatus. Pleasure to make your acquaintance Master Box." ZacBox watched as Julian mounted the electric-powered Segway and continued quietly down the underground street leading off to the right.

The lights ahead of Julian turned on, then off, one at a time as he passed slowly down the tunnel that curved off to the left. In his mind ZacBox began to realize this underground street must form a large circle, like his bicycle wheel laid on its side, only much bigger. They were facing straight ahead, like they were standing on one of the spokes looking ahead at where the axle would be located at the center of a concentric circle.

"Come, dear, Mr. Eriksson has been looking forward to meeting you," Professor Fibonacci said as she walked forward towards the center of this underground complex.

"How does he know who I am?" ZacBox asked, noticing how the color of the light was slowly fading from light blue to green, then to yellow. He held out his arms and noticed the changing light on his shirt sleeves and said, "It feels like we're walking through a rainbow."

"Very good, Zac. Yes, these lights are arranged in the color sequence of a rainbow or a prism. Tell me what color will be next?"

"Red?" ZacBox guessed.

"Almost; orange will follow yellow, then comes red," she explained patiently without missing a step. "To answer your question, Mr. Eriksson, your father, some other friends and I have discussed you several times recently, mostly about how smart you are and all."

ZacBox wanted to ask more questions, but as they were walking, he noticed two large stone columns off the cavern on their right, supporting the weight of the ground overhead. Then they came to an opening between them the columns leading into another cavern. Inside he noticed several cadets talking with a scientist wearing a white lab coat. ZacBox recognized her as one of the two engineers Professor Fibonacci had introduced him to, the one who had given him the second disc with the advanced video game. She looked up and walked toward them.

"Dr. Stella Lockwood," she said as she reintroduced herself and shook ZacBox's hand, "We met on the Ute Mountain Ute Reservation. It's a pleasure to see you here ZacBox."

ZacBox shook her hand and glanced around, realizing there was clearly a connection between the Return to Pleiades and Battle Stations Taurus video games and this mysterious underground complex. Another of the scientists looked up from a workbench and then waved at Professor Fibonacci. It was the pretty young lady he had seen upstairs, with the long, brown, wavy hair and the thick framed glasses.

"Hi Wendy, have you seen Olaf?" Professor Fibonacci inquired. The interior of this cavern sort of reminded ZacBox of the Disney movie Indiana Jones and the Temple of Doom.

"You'll find him just off over there welding on something or other," she said with a nod toward ZacBox. She removed her glasses and said with a smile, "Welcome ZacBox. I am Dr. Wendy Hubble, Chief Mission Officer." She shook hands with ZacBox as his eyes took in these unfamiliar surroundings, trying to unravel the mystery behind this strange place.

ZacBox was at a complete loss as to what they were doing here in this underground complex. The only thing he knew for sure was that Wendy was very pretty, and he liked the touch of her hand. ZacBox smiled back shyly, wishing he had enough confidence to ask an intelligent question about their mission. But no words formed in his throat. Then he realized he had to hurry to catch up with Professor Fibonacci and said to Wendy, "I better go!" When he caught up to Professor Fibonacci he asked her, "How does everyone seem to know me?"

"Well, you're a bit of a celebrity around here I suppose, ZacBox1," the Professor said, nodding at two cadets who had stopped what they were working on and watched ZacBox as he passed by. "You used ZacBox1 as your call sign when you logged into all the Xbox video game competitions and you were virtually the only person to come even close to mastering the Return to Pleiades video game." Then the Professor gestured toward a man welding on a large metal framework stretched across the ground and said, "Oh, there he is; now don't let Mr. Eriksson's appearance startle you dear."

ZacBox wondered what that warning was all about, as he followed Professor Fibonacci to where the man in the dimly lit shaft was welding on the metal apparatus. ZacBox recognized the noise the welder made for it was the same sound he had heard when he first saw the metal rod or tubing sticking up out of the ground. It was fairly dark where the man was welding. He knew from working with his father in their garage at home not to look directly into the bright light of the welder. As he looked away, he could hear his father's voice cautioning, "You don't want to burn the retinas in your eyes." ZacBox's dad taught him to make sure he always wore protective glasses before he started welding.

Whatever it was this man was welding seemed to be a large support structure of some kind running along a channel toward the center of the underground complex. ZacBox guessed the center must be a few yards down the tunnel from where they stood. Now he was sure this had to be a secret underground military complex; maybe it was an underground tunnel connecting the Academy to Cheyenne Mountain or possibly connecting all the Air Force bases in the region.

ZacBox thought that maybe this tunnel could have been built for an underground high-speed maglev train, like the Shanghai Maglev Train he studied in his science class. He remembered reading how the maglev train uses two sets of magnets, one to repel and one to push the train up and hold it off the tracks to achieve levitation. ZacBox's mind raced as he thought that maybe this high-speed maglev train ran under his grandfather's Reservation to Dulce, NM. ZacBox wondered if these underground tunnels connected to other military bases across the country, or to Area 51 in Nevada or Area 52 in Utah, just like he'd seen on "Ancient Aliens."

The Professor and ZacBox stood patiently behind the man waiting for him to stop welding whatever it was he was working on. This gave ZacBox an opportunity for his eyes to adjust to the dim orangish-colored light. As he waited, he noticed the man was not much taller than he was, but he had exceptionally wide shoulders. The welding torch made a distinctive "pop" sound, as the man turned it off, and then flipped up his face-shield. The man turned around and started to stand up. ZacBox was stunned to see the man had been kneeling. As the man stood up ZacBox realized that he was absolutely huge; he had to be at least seven or perhaps eight feet tall. ZacBox, at 5-4, was small compared to most adults, but now he felt like a child. The man had a bushy reddish-brown beard, accented with streaks of gray. ZacBox couldn't even begin to guess his age, but he looked really old. The man removed his thick leather gloves.

"Olaf Eriksson," Professor Fibonacci said, "may I introduce Zachary Box, great-grand son of White Elk, Ute Mountain Ute Tribal Elder." Then she turned to ZacBox, "Zachary Box, this is Olaf Eriksson, grandson of Viking Leif Eriksson and one of the first Norse Explorers to discover North America."

"I have been looking forward to meeting you, Strong Bear Running. Your grandfather has told me much about you," he said as he shook ZacBox's hand.

It felt to ZacBox like he was shaking hands with a giant, one wearing a leather catcher's mitt, "You know my grandfather?" ZacBox asked nervously.

"Well, yes. White Elk and I have known each other since he was your age, maybe longer."

"You've been to his Reservation?"

"Yes, many times. What you know as Sleeping Ute Mountain is a very special place to your people and my people alike. Whenever White Elk ran away from the Whiteman's boarding school he would hide in the caves beneath Sleeping Ute Mountain. That's where we met. When White Elk got hungry or missed his family, he would emerge from the caves and allow a tribal policeman to catch him and take him back to Towaoc. The tribal policeman always made him ride on the back of his horse."

"That sounds like Grandfather, but I don't understand. How can you be Leif Eriksson's grandson? Didn't he die like 1,000 years ago or something?"

"Yes, he did, during the earth year 1020 A.D. to be precise. His father was Erik Thorvaldsson, who was more commonly known as Erik the Red. By your earth years, I am 650-years-old. You see my people can live a long time by your standards, for many centuries."

"Who are your people?"

"We are Pleiadians, we come from the Star Cluster Pleiades, the same Star Cluster your Ute ancestors came from."

"I remember Grandfather telling me the Ute Creation Story, how Creator brought them here to the Shining Mountains at the beginning of time, but I thought it was just a legend."

"Most legends or myths have some element of truth. Come, I want to show you something."

Mr. Eriksson placed his huge arm around ZacBox's shoulders and led him toward what ZacBox assumed had to be the center of this underground complex. They entered what looked like the Bat Cave in the Batman movies. The interior of the central cavern was slightly smaller than his high school gym. The cavern was backlit with a soft reddish-colored light. ZacBox's eyes followed the metal support to see a large disc-shaped object. To get a better look, ZacBox stepped closer to the object. Then he stopped in his tracks;

there before him was a flying saucer! It was a life-size version of the flying saucer thumbdrive for the video game Battle Stations Taurus.

"Is this real?" ZacBox asked, hardly believing what he was seeing.

"It is. This is a real flying saucer," Mr. Eriksson said as he walked underneath the space craft and rapped his knuckles on the solid metallic hull overhead. "This is the starship Electra. Beautiful, isn't she? She has been awaiting her captain and crew."

"When do they arrive?"

"The crew will be along shortly; her captain just now arrived."

ZacBox looked around the vast cavern to see if he could spot the starship's captain. He saw several airmen and cadets in their flight suits, Julian and two uniformed Air Force Security police, one held the leash to a German Shepherd wearing a vest marked K9. ZacBox saw a few engineers in their suits and several scientists wearing white lab coats, including Dr. Lockwood and Wendy Hubble. Then ZacBox realized everyone had stopped working and was looking at him.

"What? Wait!" ZacBox said as he took a step back toward Professor Fibonacci. "There's been some kind of a mistake—I'm no starship captain! I'm only fifteen! I don't even have a driver's license!" Everyone smiled; a few even laughed and nodded their heads in amazement.

"Want to take her for a spin?" ZacBox heard a familiar voice say and turned around to see Saint Michael standing near one of the three upright supports looking up at the saucer. Saint Michael was growing a beard. Although he was no longer wearing an Air Force uniform, he still looked "spit and polished" or at least that is how ZacBox's father would have described his appearance. Instead of his blue uniform Saint Michael was wearing a tan long sleeve shirt with a button-down collar, black cargo pants, black belt and highly polished black boots. On the shirt ZacBox noticed the Lockheed

Martin logo with a star, embroidered above the pocket.

Staring up in disbelief, ZacBox traced the outline of the space-craft, and then realized it was sitting atop a launch apparatus. It looked as if it were positioned to be forced up through the ground by the metal apparatus Mr. Ericksson had been repairing. ZacBox walked over and touched the leg of the support holding the fly-ing saucer. It vibrated, as if recognizing his touch, and began to come to life. The saucer rose up another three inches toward the ceiling. ZacBox jerked his hand back and the vibration stopped. He stepped out from underneath the saucer and glanced up at the stone ceiling above the saucer. It had been carved out to resem-ble the shape of the Miraculous Staircase he had seen in Santa Fe. ZacBox walked all the way around the flying saucer, admiring the outer hull of the sturdy spacecraft. Mr. Eriksson was right, she was stunningly beautiful. The disc-shaped flying saucer was sleek and elegant in its design.

Beneath the saucer a soft bluish light filtered downward through an open hatchway. ZacBox felt instinctively drawn to the soft light and walked underneath the hatchway. Then he heard it, a faint "beep" followed by another "beep" then a little lower, "BeeBot." The noise wasn't coming from above him but from behind him. He looked around and saw a short, three-foot-tall blue figure step out of the darkness toward him. It took another three quick steps for-ward and then stopped again. He saw the blue figure had two big almond shaped eyes and two small protruding ears, but no nose or mouth. Its small size and the way it walked it reminded him of the extraterrestrial from the movie ET.

ZacBox stared in disbelief, as the chubby little blue figure re-peated, "BeeBot." Then it began hopping excitedly from one foot to another, holding its protruding stomach. It looked like it was made of blue Play Dough, like what ZacBox played with growing up. This three-foot-tall creature had two fingers and one thumb on each hand and clearly wanted to communicate. Whatever it was, the little blue figure seamed really excited to see him and in a big hurry to tell him something.

"What is it?" ZacBox said as he bent closer to the curious blue figure in front of him.

The little blue creature took three more quick steps toward him, then stopped. It reached with both hands into a pouch in his stomach. The pouch reminded ZacBox of how a kangaroo mother carried her babies. Then the blue figure said softly, "Bee," as it pulled out a shiny pearl colored orb, just like the one ZacBox had followed with Bo.

"That's it!" ZacBox said as he turned his head toward Professor Fibonacci. "That's what I saw in the field on the Fourth of July!" ZacBox turned back to see the shimmering orb lift off from the blue figure's hands and float in the air toward him. ZacBox saw it was spinning around horizontally as it moved forward. Then it stopped and hovered just a few feet in front of him at eye level. "That's what it was doing when I first saw it," he said as he turned to face Mr. Eriksson. "What does it want?"

"It wants you," said Mr. Eriksson, "It has chosen you."

"Chosen me? For what?" ZacBox said as he turned back to face the orb.

"To be captain. It has chosen you to be the captain of the Starship Electra."

"Me! But I don't know how to fly a starship," ZacBox said in desperation, looking at the familiar-shaped spacecraft resting atop the large three-pronged launch apparatus beside him.

"You remember all those video games I brought you, don't you, dear?" Professor Fibonacci said patiently, "and those engineers you met over the past three months at the Academy and there on the

Reservation? Well, they and a growing team of experts and I have been studying how the Electra and her sister ships fly."

"Sister ships," ZacBox said as he climbed up the launch apparatus a few feet to where he could touch the hull of the saucer ten feet above him, "how many of these are there?"

"Originally," Mr. Eriksson explained, "there were seven saucers, but so far we've only discovered the whereabouts of three ships."

"Where are the other two?" he asked.

Dr. Wendy Hubble stepped forward and said, "The three confirmed locations are or were here in Colorado. The Celaeno, we believe, is in a similar cavern such as this, hidden somewhere beneath Sleeping Ute Mountain. The Electra is here, being readied to launch. The Sterope was launched some years ago from beneath the Pine Ridge Forest west of Denver."

"When was it launched?" ZacBox asked.

"1842," Mr. Eriksson answered.

"1842! Who was that starship's Captain?" ZacBox inquired as he peered up into the open hatchway leading inside.

"The Captain of Starship Sterope was Jorvik Eriksson, my son." Mr. Eriksson replied, as he watched ZacBox staring up into the open hatch underneath the spacecraft. "It's okay; you can go up if you want."

ZacBox excitedly bound up the footholds, like it was a ladder up to a treehouse or a piece of familiar playground equipment he might have played on in elementary school. When he entered the spacecraft, a soft golden light came on from above welcoming him onto the open bridge. He felt like he had been here before, like he had always been here, he thought as he touched the back of the captain's seat facing forward. This sensation wasn't just from playing the video game; it was almost as if the ship was part of him and he was part of the ship.

ZacBox glanced around the bridge, nodding knowingly as if he knew exactly where everything was positioned. Two conformal crew seats were arranged below, to the left and right of the captain's seat. Two other seats were positioned to the right and left of the captain's. ZacBox's eyes were drawn to the instrument clusters and multiple view screens surrounding the five crew seats. Each terminal had a familiar feel. He intuitively understood what was required for navigation, communication, life support, weapons and engineering—everything the crew would need for deep space exploration was here at their fingertips. Evidently, whoever designed those video games made them much more realistic than he ever could have imagined.

"I can't believe this is happening," ZacBox said as he walked to his left and entered the crew quarters. "This is awesome! Here's the captain's quarters," he said as he walked by and pointed into the cabin on his right. Going further down the curved hallway, "Here's where two crew members bunk." Turning to his left, "this is the galley, where the crew makes their meals. Over there, that room, that's for exercising. This is so cool! Back here is the engine room and down the hallway here is where the other two crew members bunk." Continuing down the curved hallway he walked past the second crew quarters then returned to the front of the ship where he sat down in the captain's seat. He looked around the cockpit with a nod of his head, "It feels like I've been here before, like maybe in a dream or something."

Professor Fibonacci, Mr. Eriksson and Wendy had followed him patiently around the interior of the spacecraft. Wendy made several notes on the clipboard she carried, writing down his movement and comments with a mechanical pencil. Once they returned to the bridge, Dr. Lockwood and Saint Michael entered the bridge and sat down in two of the crew seats. ZacBox watched as Mr. Ericksson and Professor Fibonacci settled into the other two seats meant for the ship's crew.

Without thinking, ZacBox's hands reached up and grabbed the yoke on the steering column shaped like a figure eight lying on its side, just like the one in the video game Dr. Lockwood had given him on the Reservation. His fingers began tracing over every inch of the controls and instrument cluster within his reach. As ZacBox touched the dashboard, the lights came on and the interior of the spacecraft came to life. Wendy stood behind him and wrote additional notes on her clipboard. ZacBox's thumb flipped a switch with his thumb and the weapons display appeared on the main screen.

"This is the first time this has happened. How did you do that?" Wendy asked.

"I don't know. I just touched it."

"Maybe it has a biometric scanner," Dr. Lockwood suggested. "It could be reading ZacBox's fingerprints or palm prints."

"Possibly," Wendy said as she wrote a quick note on her clipboard and then continued, "Or it could be reading his DNA extracted from his palm or fingerprints. The center knob there, where a horn button would be on a car, you can push it in or pull it out, and you can turn it two clicks to the right or left, but we haven't been able to figure out what it does."

"It took me a few minutes to figure it out too," ZacBox said as he pushed down on the disc-shaped button that looked exactly like the saucer-shaped USB for the video game. "In the Battlestations Taurus video game, when you turn the center button to the left," he said as he demonstrated, "the first position is for the maglev, then the second position is for the hydrogen drive; but it won't work now because we're docked. It's like a four-speed stick-shift manual transmission on a car. When you switch back to the center position, it's like in neutral, but when you push down you go to battle stations. Then the top of the saucer comes down and seals the spacecraft. Oh, and you can't use the airlock when you're in battle stations mode."

"What happens when you turn the knob to the right?" Wendy asked.

"The first position to the right is the quark-jump drive; that's really cool, and the second position to the right is for when you want to go to ZPE drive." ZacBox watched as Wendy wrote something on her clipboard and then erased it. "It was kind of hard for me to remember at first," ZacBox said as he took her clipboard and drew a circle representing the center control knob of the yoke. Above the circle, at the 12 o'clock position, he wrote the letter N, then to the left he wrote an M at the 11 o'clock, and next to it an H at 10 o'clock. To the right he wrote a Q at 1 o'clock, then a Z at 2 o'clock. "The N is for neutral, M for maglev drive, H for hydrogen drive, Q for quark-jump drive and Z for ZPE drive, that stands for Zero Point Energy. I don't understand how any of this works, but it's way cool!"

Then ZacBox noticed the only people who these seats seemed to fit were him and Mr. Eriksson. He felt how his seat had been adjusted somehow to perfectly fit his smaller frame. He stroked the black padded arm rests and allowed his hands to form naturally around the steering yoke on the steering column, moving it naturally in all directions. It felt exactly like the one with the video game Dr. Lockwood had left with him on the Reservation, but this yoke was a little larger and felt tailored to fit his smaller hands. Without looking, his thumbs traced the familiar touch of the weapons system he had used countless times to blast attacking alien spaceships to pieces on his computer screen. The button on top of the steering yoke to the right operated the ion cannons, the button on top to the left fired the neutrino torpedoes.

"What does this series of numbers suggest to you?" Wendy asked as she pointed with her pencil to the green digital numbers to the right of a chrome shaped T-handle on the console built into the cockpit immediately to the right of the captain's seat.

ZacBox read the numbers aloud, "0, 1, 1, 2, 3, 5, 8, 13…those are the Fibonacci numbers. That's the Fibonacci sequence," ZacBox said as Professor Fibonacci smiled.

"What do you think they mean?" Wendy asked, as she made another note on her clipboard.

"Oh, they're used here like the speedometer on a car," ZacBox said as he gripped the chrome handle on the console with his right hand. "The video game tracks speed for acceleration by F numbers; Fibonacci numbers. When you want to slow down it's like downshifting a manual transmission, because you don't have any brakes in space, except for the hydrogen or maglev, which really are more for very slow turns in space or those close to the ground. When you want to slow down, you downshift from eighth gear, to third, then to third, then to second-first, then first-first, and then into neutral, which is the only time you can dock with another saucer or land."

"Why did they build it with two first gears?" Wendy asked, looking at the number next to what must be a throttle. The numbers were arranged in a line and read higher as the T-handle is pushed forward.

"You can't downshift from second to first while you are in motion, you'll grind the gears," ZacBox said with a smile.

"I guess that must be a universal law," Saint Michael said as everyone laughed.

ZacBox continued, "In the second video game, the more advanced one you call Battle Stations Taurus, if you want to come to a complete stop you have to down shift to the second first gear, then come to a full stop before shifting into the first gear, then to zero or neutral."

ZacBox looked around at the faces of Wendy, Mr. Ericksson, Professor Fibonacci, Dr. Lockwood, Saint Michael and the blue BeeBot. He noticed they were all smiling and nodding their heads in agreement. Without any doubt ZacBox definitely knew how to fly this flying saucer better than any other person they had talked to over the past several months.

"Wait a minute!" ZacBox said as he shot up out of the captain's seat, "Just because I'm good at video games doesn't mean I can fly a starship!" ZacBox turned toward Mr. Eriksson and said, "Hey, I know, why don't you get your son to fly this one?"

"He can't," Mr. Eriksson replied, "Jorvik has been stranded on Europa, one of the distant moons of Jupiter." ZacBox watched as Mr. Eriksson's head drooped to his chin, obviously missing his son. ZacBox knew his father would be missing him as well, if their roles were reversed. ZacBox heard the now familiar "BeeBot" as the little blue figure climbed up and sat on Wendy's lap. The shining orb floated overhead hovering near ZacBox's right shoulder.

"You see," Mr. Eriksson continued, "Jorvik and his crew launched from the base beneath the Pine Ridge Forest and was shot down while on orbit around Europa in 1843. I have been working since to try to get the Electra ready for a rescue mission before it is too late. Too late for Jorvik that is, unfortunately it is already too late for his crew. All four of Jorvik's crewmembers were earthlings, like you. The last one passed away in 1932. Jorvik has been stranded alone on Europa for nearly a century. We think Electra here is about ready to launch, and we've been working to select her crew, but no one we've brought here seems compatible with the spacecraft. Apparently, we can select the crew but only the Electra selects who she wants for her captain."

ZacBox turned to the blue figure sitting on Wendy's lap beside him and asked, "But why me?"

"Don't ask him," Wendy said with a smile, "he's just an AI."

The blue figure shrugged his shoulders and emitted a short, "Bot," pointed to his chest, then added, "Bee" as it pointed to the pearl colored orb.

ZacBox didn't know what to say. Wendy went on, "Our little Blueman here is just a bot, you know, a robot, artificial intelligence, an AI," then she pointed the eraser end of her pencil toward the pearl colored orb floating beside ZacBox's shoulder, "Ask Bee, we think he's probably who picked you, he, or should I say, *it* is a sentient being."

"Sentient being?" ZacBox inquired as he continued to look at something that resembled a floating soccer ball only slightly smaller.

"Yes," Professor Fibonacci explained, "Sentient beings are beings with a consciousness—spiritual entities that are technically made up of the five aggregates skandhas: matter, sensation, perception, mental formations and consciousness. Like you and all of us," she said as she pointed to everyone present except for the little blue figure on Wendy's lap.

"You mean this orb here has a spirit, yet that cute little blue guy over there doesn't? How's that fair?"

"Well," Professor Fibonacci went on to explain, "He was made by an intelligent being that was a sentient being. However, only the Creator, only God if you will, can create a sentient being, someone or something with a spirit, like Mr. Bojangles."

"Why does it get to make the decision on who is to be the captain?" ZacBox asked, pointing his thumb at the orb.

"Because it's going with you," Wendy explained, "its presence is mission critical. He or it is the only known Bee on the planet. We believe it may come from the Pleiades Star Cluster. The BeeBot and the Electra are apparently critical for space travel, but there has to be a human or humanlike physical presence aboard as well. Jorvik and even his father were born on earth. He, or *it*," Wendy explained, "is the only spiritual entity who may know the way back."

"That's the other half of your mission," Saint Michael explained, "Rescue Jorvik, complete the return to the Pleiades and then return safely back to earth."

"Wait a minute now," ZacBox said shaking his head from side to side, "I'm not going anywhere, except to high school in two months. BeeBot might be mission critical, but I'm not."

"Zac," Professor Fibonacci explained, "no one knows why it picked you, but it did. Your great-grandfather knew this day was coming, based in part on a vision he had shortly after your mother died."

"This is way over my head," ZacBox explained as he scratched his head and tried to imagine how his world had changed from just an hour ago when he parked his bicycle behind Fibonacci's Diner. "I can't do this, this...this is a rescue mission, you all need someone like who my mom was. You need an experienced captain with a couple of PJs, like you, Saint Michael! You should be flying this mission. Not me! I am only in the 10th Grade!"

"Wish I could go Zac; I'd give an arm and my one remaining leg to go," Saint Michael said as he got up, left the bridge and dropped down the hatchway.

"He knows he might be a liability to the rest of the four crew-members," Wendy explained. "We don't know space travel well enough to understand the effects of spacetime, but we believe you were selected in part because of your age. The other four crew-members we have been interviewing are also in their mid-to-late teens. When you return from deep space travel, all of us here on

Earth will have aged more than the crew. We don't know how long your mission will require, so there's a distinct advantage to having a younger crew. There's also a remote possibility that when you return all of us may have already grown old and some passed on.

The bridge remained silent for several minutes. Mr. Eriksson finally spoke softly, "Maybe White Elk's vision was clouded and in error. Maybe this isn't your destiny."

"What was his vision?" ZacBox asked quietly, as he stood up and leaned against the back of the captain's seat.

Mr. Eriksson explained, "White Elk told me long before you were born, that one day the sleeping Ute warrior on top of Sleeping Ute Mountain would be awakened. This would be a time when his people needed him most. White Elk told me in his vision he saw a strong bear running down from the top of Sleeping Ute Mountain. In his dream he saw the bear had been transformed from the Ute warrior, into a strong bear. That's why he named you Strong Bear Running. He knew one day you would be born into this world, at a time when his people needed you most. Like the ancient Ute warrior asleep on the sacred mountain, White Elk predicted you would be made of the stardust required for a perilous journey. He saw this as your destiny."

ZacBox's shoulders slumped, he felt sick to his stomach and his mind slowly closed down.

"I'm sorry about your son Mr. Eriksson," ZacBox said as he turned and started for the open hatchway. Then he heard a whimper and turned back to see the blue figure sitting on Wendy's lap had a tear rolling down its face. He looked from Wendy, to Mr. Eriksson, Professor Fibonacci and Dr. Lockwood and lastly at the shiny orb, "I'm sorry, there's been some kind of a mistake. White Elk's vision must be meant for someone else. I'm not a starship captain."

ZacBox slipped effortlessly down the hatch, almost as if he had done it a thousand times before, and started walking slowly down the long corridor back toward Professor Fibonacci's broom closet. Along the way he could feel the eyes of the cadets, the scientists and engineers following him as he walked away. As he approached the bluish colored light, announcing the end of the underground corridor, he saw Julian standing off to the side of the elevator.

"Hey Julian," ZacBox said as he stopped in front of the elevator doors. Without looking at him, ZacBox said softly to Julian, "It was nice meeting you, can you please show me how this thing works?"

Julian placed the palm of his hand against a glass panel on the side of the door, "Perhaps the gentleman inside can show you how to operate the lift."

As the double elevator doors swished open ZacBox looked up to see Saint Michael standing in the elevator. "Going up?" Saint Michael asked.

"No, probably not," ZacBox said as he stepped inside and turned around to see the double doors swish closed. "I'm afraid I let a lot of people down back there Saint Michael. I think at this point in my life I might be going anywhere but up."

As they reached the ground level, the elevator doors opened, and Saint Michael handed ZacBox a piece of paper, "Professor Fibonacci asked me to give this to you."

ZacBox stepped out of the elevator/broom closet and turned to face Saint Michael, "I wish I was as strong as you," then lowered his head in shame. "I wish I were as brave as my mother."

"I wish I were half as brave as your mother," Saint Michael said, then added, "Unless I miss my mark, I suspect her courage runs through your blood and doing what is right is imprinted throughout your DNA."

ZacBox watched as the doors closed. Then he walked down the

short hallway and turned to the right into the men's room. He was alone and stared at his sad reflection in the mirror for several seconds before opening the note Saint Michael had handed him. He suspected Professor Fibonacci had to have written the note and given it to Saint Michel before she introduced him to Mr. Eriksson. That meant she must have anticipated he would refuse this calling, that he would not have the courage to do what was expected. ZacBox blinked back the tears forming in his eyes and recognized Professor Fibonacci's graceful cursive handwriting. The note read, "Seek Dr. Therkel Brondsted, you will find him deep in the Pine Ridge Forest, at the GPS coordinates below, tell him Lisa sent you."

 **Rust Bucket Classic**

"Here you go Bo," ZacBox said as he opened the kitchen door to let his puppy out into the back yard. ZacBox watched as Bo lifted his hind leg to pee on the fake red fire hydrant his father had installed by the dog run. After Bo finished his business ZacBox watched as he ran next door to the adjoining patio home where Professor Fibonacci had lived since before he was in kindergarten. Having two adjoining backyards provided a big fenced yard for Bo to run and ample space for the frequent volleyball games during visits by the Air Force Academy cadets to Professor Fibonacci's home. Bo scratched on her kitchen door and ZacBox heard her screen door slide open, letting Bo inside. ZacBox knew anytime he showed up at her door she welcomed him with a big hug, always assuring him everything would be okay.

But ZacBox knew that's not what he needed, not today anyway. Unfortunately, he wasn't at all sure what he needed. Whatever it was, ZacBox knew he wasn't going to find it here at his home in Flying Horse. The answer to his problem has to lie out there, ZacBox knew as he walked to his bedroom and picked up Professor Fibonacci's note from his nightstand. He stuffed her note, along with his wallet and smartphone into the pocket of his sweatpants, and headed to the attached garage. ZacBox's father was at work, so was his black Chevy pickup—not that ZacBox was thinking of taking it—the way his luck was running he'd be pulled over within the first half mile from home and given a ticket for not having a driver's license. Then he wouldn't be able to get his license until he was eighteen. ZacBox rolled his only means of transportation, his 18-speed mountain bike, outside, closed the garage door and hopped on his bike, and peddled off having absolutely no idea where he was going.

ZacBox was still trying to process everything he had seen yesterday, under Fibonacci's Diner. He had slept little, agonizing over the fact he had let so many people down. When he finally dozed off he dreamt he was flying the starship. By the time his father's alarm clock went off at 5:30 am, ZacBox was wide awake. He had thought about getting up and talking to his dad some more, but he knew his dad was expected at work by 7am. White Elk had taught ZacBox that Ute men were never late and always kept their word. Besides, ZacBox and his dad had talked well past ten o'clock last night and all his father could say was that things usually work out the way they were supposed to; unfortunately, ZacBox found this advice of not much comfort. ZacBox rode his bike past his school, hoping maybe to spot Mr. Tuttle's car parked in the teacher parking lot. But he saw only two cars and they belonged to four senior girls playing tennis. "Even they have cars," ZacBox mused to himself as he peddled west on Northgate Blvd.

As ZacBox approached Voyager Parkway, he gave a fleeting thought of turning left to tell Olaf Eriksson he had changed his mind. He tried to imagine how the huge Pleiadian would react if he told him he would go rescue his son stranded on that distant moon of Jupiter, whatever its name was. But ZacBox knew deep down that today he was the same scared and confused fifteen-year-old boy that he was yesterday. So, he kept peddling west toward the Air Force Academy. He thought about visiting his mother's gravesite, taking her some flowers, but no, that would just make him feel all the more sorry for himself. He rode his bike underneath the two bridges for I-25, past the double roundabouts, and turned right into the parking lot for the Santa Fe Trailhead to think.

Staring at the map for the trailhead, ZacBox realized he was at a crossroads. He got off his bike and looked around. He could go south toward Colorado Springs or north toward Palmer Lake, and then he remembered the GPS coordinates at the bottom of Professor Fibonacci's note, directing him to find a Dr. Brondsted. But ZacBox had no idea how far away these GPS readings were or how he would even get there. Then he saw it—an older blue Subaru parked in the back row of the trailhead parking lot. ZacBox slowly rode over and spotted the School of Mines parking sticker on the back bumper. It was the same Subaru he saw parked at the diner yesterday, and on the Fourth of July.

The older teenage boy, wearing the white pagri, was sitting in the driver's seat studying a map of the Academy. ZacBox rode his bike over behind the Subaru, dismounted and leaned his mountain bike against the wooden split rail fence. Then he walked up to the driver's door. The driver's window was rolled down, but the driver hadn't seen him yet, "Who are you and why are you following me?" ZacBox demanded as the young man behind the steering wheel jumped.

"Geez, don't do that—you startled me!" the older teenager said as he grabbed his chest with the palm of his hand. "I thought you were base security again."

"You tell me who you are and what you're doing, or I will tell them you're here," ZacBox demanded.

"Very well, but you go first," the older teenager said as he got out of the car and looked ZacBox in the eye. "Who are you and why are you following me?"

When he stood up ZacBox saw the older teenager was several inches taller than he was, but rather than argue, he thought what he needed now were answers so he decided it was probably best for him to go first.

"My name is Zachary Box, but my friends call me ZacBox. I go to Discovery Canyon High School, further down Northgate here and I'm not following you…" ZacBox paused and thought about the other two occasions when and where he had seen this other boy. "I guess we might be just on the same trail, at the same time, so maybe we're searching for the same thing. Okay, your turn, who are you and what are you doing here?"

"My name is Arjun Basu; I go to the School of Mines, in Golden, and I am, well I guess I am, well . . . I think I might be here searching for an earthquake or something?"

"That's so lame," ZacBox said as he leaned back against the dirty front fender of Arjun's old Subaru and rubbed his forehead.

"Hey, watch the paint!"

"Paint?" ZacBox said as he stood up and looked at the only clean spot on the fender, the one he had just wiped clean with the seat of his sweatpants. ZacBox brushed off his butt with his hand, "When was the last time you washed this rust bucket?"

"Rust bucket? Don't you know nothing about cars? This is a vintage 1995 Subaru SVX; it's a classic!"

"I know a lot about cars," ZacBox said wishing for the hundredth time this month he had a car, any car. "And I suppose your other car is a starship."

"Well, at least I have a car—is that a girl's bike you're riding?"

ZacBox laughed, "No, but I'll bet you've never even seen a starship, have you?"

"No, have you?" Arjun said not expecting an answer.

"Well," ZacBox said, not really sure what to say, thinking back to the one he saw yesterday. ZacBox stuck his hand in his pockets and found the note Professor Fibonacci had written him. He pulled the note out, unfolded it and pointed to the GPS coordinates written on the bottom, "If you're so smart, do you know how to read GPS coordinates?"

"Of course, since like the second grade."

"Then where's this?"

Arjun glanced at the bottom of the note for a second, and then looked up toward the northwest, pointing with his long slender index finger, "Up there, in the mountains west of Denver. About seventy-five miles from here, I'm guessing." He handed the note back to ZacBox and nodded at the mountain bike leaning up against the split rail fence. "A bit of a ride from here, don't you think?"

"That'd take me two days," ZacBox said.

"Or two hours by car, if you don't mind riding in a rust bucket and all."

"I'm sorry, Arjun," ZacBox said, "I didn't mean it. I guess I'm just not myself and maybe feeling a bit jealous."

"Come on," Arjun said, as he laid the back seats down and popped open the trunk, "toss your bike in back here; you'll have to take the front tire off, but it should fit okay."

"You mean it?" ZacBox asked, "You'll take me up there?"

"Yes, but I'm not sure why." Arjun said as he looked around the north entrance to the Air Force Academy. "Nothing seems to be happening around here."

"Well," said ZacBox, as he loaded his bike carefully into the trunk of Arjun's Subaru, "sometimes things aren't always as they seem."

"True enough, I suppose," Arjun said as they headed north on I-25.

The two boys made small talk as they became acquainted. They found they had much in common—in music, sports, especially football and hockey. The Denver Broncos and the Avalanche were their two favorite teams. Then the conversation lagged for several miles. ZacBox was the first to break the silence.

"Why were you there," ZacBox asked, "on that dirt road on the Fourth of July and then at the diner yesterday?"

"Well," Arjun began, "I'm interning this summer at the USGS Geologic Hazards Science Center in Golden and I had run a series of computer simulations for the Earthquake Information Watch Center. I predicted when and where that quake would hit on the Fourth of July. But no one, including my supervisor, believed me. I wrote a report about what would happen, but it must have fallen into a black hole because no one above my immediate boss even commented on it. I predicted it would not be a major quake, probably wouldn't even cause any real damage, but it was isolated to one spot, just north of that diner so I scheduled time off from my job to be there, to see what happened. I was right! But, I know there has to be more to the story; those tremors are just the tip of the iceberg."

"You got that right; those tremors are just the tip of something…" ZacBox replied, and then changed the subject. "How many miles you got on this?"

"Nearly 250,000. Why?" Arjun asked.

"I'm just calculating our odds of us picking up any girls in this classic car of yours," ZacBox said teasingly.

"Better odds than us picking up any girls on your bike," Arjun teased back with a smile.

"I'll bet you haven't even been on a date with a girl yet," ZacBox teased back.

"Yes, I have, have you?"

"Sure, I was on a date just last month."

"Were not," Arjun challenged.

"Were too."

"Were not."

"Were too!"

"Okay, what was her name?" Arjun inquired, suspecting he had trapped the younger boy in an untruth.

"Alicia. We went for ice cream," ZacBox said defensively, "Where did you go on your supposed date or was it somewhere in your mind?"

"We went to the movies, so there!"

"Oh yeah, what was the movie?"

"We watched an IMAX rerun of the Martian, directed by Ridley Scott and starring Matt Damon, best movie ever!" Arjun said and then added softly, "But…my mom insisted my little sister go with us."

Both boys laughed, then ZacBox confessed, "Well, don't feel too bad, my great-grandfather and Mr. Bojangles, my dog, rode in the back of my great-grandfather's old '49 Chevy pickup truck, and no one knows how many miles it has on it cause the odometer broke back in the '70s."

The boys laughed easily with one another, and the more they talked the more they realized just how alike they were; they both enjoyed running, liked much of the same music, shared the same interest in video games, Xbox and sci-fi books and movies and neither had any particularly close friends. In almost no time, they were beginning to like, and more importantly, trust one another.

"Hey, Arjun," ZacBox said, "Have you ever heard of a Pleiadian?"

"No, but I'm guessing that might be someone from the Pleiades."

"So, you know about the Pleiades?"

"Sort of; I know it's the nearest star cluster to Earth." Arjun pointed down to the Subaru emblem at the center of his steering wheel. "The Japanese name for Pleiades is Subaru."

Glancing over at the emblem ZacBox counted the stars, "I only count six stars on the Subaru logo."

"Correct. The seventh star, Merope, is the hardest to see without a telescope. In India, where my family is from, the Pleiades Star Cluster is called the Star of Fire." Arjun glanced down at the digital map on his smartphone plugged into the cigarette lighter, "We exit 470 up ahead, at the Morrison exit. What do you hope to find once we get to these coordinates?"

ZacBox looked out the passenger window for a moment and replied quietly, "Answers."

July 26ᵗʰ 12:26 hours MDST Astradate 11072.6
Pine Ridge Forest, Bailey, CO USA Planet Earth

"Are you sure you want to go in there alone?" Arjun asked ZacBox as they stared at the locked metal gate with the large NO TRES-PASSING sign wired to the top rail.

"I've come this far; I can't turn back now," ZacBox said as he slowly opened the passenger door and stuffed his cellphone into the pocket of his sweatpants.

"I'll come with you," Arjun offered.

"No, thanks, I think this is something I'm supposed to do by myself," ZacBox said as he read again the name on Professor Fi-bonacci's note—Dr. Therkel Brondsted.

"I don't know ZacBox; this place doesn't look very inviting," Arjun said as he peered through the pitted windshield of his old Subaru. "Listen, if I don't get a text from you by 1 o'clock, telling me you're okay, I'm dialing 911 and then me and Boson are gonna lead the cavalry in there on a rescue."

"Boson?" ZacBox asked.

"Boson," Arjun said as he patted the dash of his Subaru.

"You named your car Boson?"

"Yes, in honor of the Indian scientist Satyendra Nath Bose."

"Now I know we're in trouble."

"Why?"

"We're never going to pick up any girls in a Japanese car named after an Indian scientist," ZacBox said slowly shaking his head from side to side as he got out of the car.

"Probably not, but I'll tell you one thing for certain," Arjun said with a laugh.

"What's that," ZacBox said stalling for time as he looked over his shoulder at the fence posted with the intimidating no trespassing sign.

"If we do pick up any girls…" pausing for effect.

"Yes?" ZacBox said prompting a reply.

"They are bound to be smart ones," Arjun said with another laugh before adding, "Remember, you text me or I'll text you at thirteen hundred hours, letting me know you're okay and when you will be ready for me to pick you up."

"Thirteen hundred hours?"

"Yes, its military time, measured in twenty-four hours, you just add twelve hours to the time if it's in the afternoon."

"What are you going to do while you're waiting?"

"There's a rock shop in Pine Junction I found on the internet I've been dying to check out; its only ten minutes away. I'll check it out for a while then meet you here at the gate unless you text me differently."

"Okay, thanks Arjun," ZacBox said as he watched his new friend drive away down the narrow dirt road. "I'll bet there are a lot of girls hanging around that rock shop in Pine Junction this afternoon," ZacBox said to himself as he inspected the lock on the gate. Finding it secured he tested the barbed wire fence that trailed off for as far as he could see in both directions beneath the tall pine trees. Deciding there was no better way, ZacBox climbed over the metal gate and began walking up the driveway. Before he had walked ten steps on the other side of the gate, a man's voice shouted out, "HEY! Where do you think you're going?" The voice was accentuated by the snarling growl of an unseen guard dog in the background.

"Ah, I'm here looking for a Dr. Therkel Brondsted," ZacBox replied, trying to control his fear while trying to decide where he should be directing his answer.

"GO AWAY!"

"I am here to see Dr. Brondsted," ZacBox said as he looked around to see if he could spot a security camera hidden in the trees.

"What makes you think Dr. Brondsted wants to see you?" the voice inquired with growing impatience. "Answer quickly boy or I'll release the hounds!"

"Professor Fibonacci sent me," ZacBox replied as he caught the movement of a camera lens concealed in a plain wooden birdhouse attached to the trunk of a tall Ponderosa pine to the right of the dirt driveway.

The voice was quiet for nearly a minute, and then said more softly, "Step over here."

ZacBox walked over to the birdhouse and stopped a few feet away as he looked toward the round opening.

"You don't look old enough to be one of her cadets; how old are you?" demanded the voice.

"I'm not a cadet, Sir; I'm only fifteen and a half," ZacBox replied, with an emphasis on the half.

"Why are you here?"

"I…I don't honestly know. Her note said to tell you Lisa sent me."

The man waited another minute before he replied, "I'll send Persephone to get you."

While ZacBox waited by the wooden birdhouse, on the narrow drive into the pine forest, his mind raced, searching for any clue of who or what Persephone might be. He felt the outline of his smartphone in his pocket. He pulled it out and was surprised to see he had four bars. He Googled how he guessed Persephone might be spelled. Then he read, "In Greek mythology, Persephone, also called Kore, is the daughter of Zeus and Demeter, and is the queen of the underworld. Homer described Persephone as the formidable, venerable majestic princess, who carries into effect the curses of men upon the souls of the dead."

ZacBox felt his heart beat quicken, and he tried to control his fear as he looked back at the locked gate. He calculated how many steps it would take him to reach it and rehearsed in his mind the best way for him to clear the gate on the run. When he looked back up the trail, he saw her racing down the hill coming directly toward him and wagging her tail—Persephone was a small, tan-colored Cocker Spaniel.

The little dog leaped into ZacBox's arms and began licking his face. As ZacBox laughed, she wiggled out of his arms and began barking and leading him up the narrow driveway between the trees. At the end of the driveway ZacBox saw two small, tin-covered buildings, one was an old garage built into the hillside. Persephone wagged her tail excitedly as she led him through a partially open garage door and past an older orange Range Rover SUV.

ZacBox noticed a number of tools scattered along the long dusty workbench, some of which he recognized, but many were not like any of the tools in his father's garage at home. Persephone barked to get his attention and then she walked behind a heavy wooden door that led into a dark tunnel.

The tunnel looked like an abandoned mine shaft, with a few antique looking picks and shovels strewn about. Then ZacBox realized the light had a familiar bluish tint. As he looked into the tunnel it led deeper beneath the mountain. He could see Persephone running ahead. The lights in the tunnel came on as she ran. The tunnel was similar to the cavern beneath Fibonacci's Diner. To keep up, ZacBox started running behind her, through the green and into the yellow light bands of the prism light. He increased his pace as he passed through the orange light and into the red, sensing the center of the tunnel must be directly ahead. Off to his right he saw two large stone columns. He watched as Persephone turned right and darted inside a cavern.

ZacBox started to walk as he entered the cavern. He saw an older man with a short gray beard sitting behind a large wooden desk. A fire burned in a big stone fireplace behind him, illuminating a wall lined with built-in bookshelves overflowing with books.

The older distinguished-looking man stood up, walked around the desk and approached ZacBox, "You are not whom I was expecting."

"Who were you expecting?" ZacBox asked.

"I don't know, an experienced astronaut, or maybe an accomplished fighter pilot, or at least an upper-class cadet."

"Sorry to disappoint you," ZacBox said, lowering his head. "I seem to do that a lot anymore."

"I'm not disappointed, just a little surprised is all," the man said in a grandfatherly kind of way.

"You're surprised!" ZacBox said. "I'm supposed to be going into the 10th grade, not off to some distant moon of Jupiter to rescue a Pleiadian!" Dr. Brondsted reminded ZacBox of the actor Sean Connery, who played 007 in the James Bond and Indiana Jones's father in the movies; the only thing Dr. Brondsted needed was a fedora. In the firelight, ZacBox noticed the man was dressed like a college professor, wearing a bowtie and tweed jacket with leather patches on the elbows. His face and hands had the weathered appearance of a seasoned archeologist, although ZacBox questioned if he wasn't being overly influenced by his recent conversations with Arjun. During their two-hour car ride Arjun made ZacBox laugh with his Sean Connery imitations.

The distinguished-looking man said, "Tell me, how is Lisa?"

"Professor Fibonacci? She's fine, I guess," ZacBox said, realizing he had never heard anyone call her by her first name. Then he noticed a smile on Dr. Brondsted's face and a twinkle in his eyes when he mentioned her name. ZacBox began to wonder just how well these two professors may have known one another back in their younger days.

"Come, sit down," Dr. Brondsted said, pointing toward two red leather chairs near the fireplace, a coffee table positioned between them held two tea cups on saucers. ZacBox sat down in one of the large comfortable chairs and watched as Dr. Brondsted lifted a pot of hot water, "Tea?" he asked.

"No, but thank you," ZacBox said as he watched Dr. Brondsted pour hot water into his teacup, set the pot of water down on the coffee table. ZacBox recalled a video he had come across on the internet from the best-selling author Stephen Coonts talking about his book called "Saucer." ZacBox reached over and picked up the teacup sitting in front of him. He removed the cup from the saucer in front of him, sat it aside, and then picked up Dr. Brondsted's teacup saucer. He turned one of the saucers upside down and mated the two saucers together, forming the shape of a flying saucer.

Dr. Brondsted watched with a smile on his face and patiently stirred his tea. ZacBox sat across from him in the overstuffed chair, while looking around the cavern. The room felt like a large college den room or a study hall at the Academy. Then he spotted it on the fireplace mantel, a well-worn brown fedora sitting on the head of a white marble bust of some Greek mythical god. ZacBox looked back at Dr. Brondsted, imagining what he would look like wearing the fedora.

"Are you an archeologist?" ZacBox asked.

"I am," Dr. Brondsted replied.

ZacBox examined the two tea cup saucers he held together for a few minutes and then resumed his quest for answers.

"Why is he there?" ZacBox asked.

"Who?" Dr. Brondsted asked as he sipped his tea.

"Jorvik," ZacBox said as he replaced the tea cup saucers on the table. "Jorvik Eriksson. This Pleiadian who's supposedly stranded on one of Jupiter's moons? Why is he there?"

"Jorvik and his crew of the starship Sterope were shot down while on a mission to harvest a handful of crystals from an underground cave on Europa. These crystals are among the densest crystals in the known universe. These particular crystals are absolutely essential to fueling the dual-propulsion system of Jorvik's starship. For Jorvik and his four crew members to reach the Pleiades, and return in our lifetime, they must travel faster than light, or FTL."

"How much faster?"

"Faster than light calculated using the Fibonacci sequential numeral 21, or FTL x F21."

"Who shot them down?"

"The Centaurians."

"Who are they?"

"One of our not-so-friendly neighbors in the Milky Way; they are from the Omega Centauri Star Cluster, identified as NGC 5139."

ZacBox heard his cellphone ring, pulled it from his pocket and looked at the screen to see who was calling him. "Oops, I forgot," ZacBox said as he answered Arjun's frantic phone call.

"Why are you not answering my texts?" Arjun asked in an excited voice. "Are you okay?"

"Sorry, Arjun," ZacBox said apologetically. "I've been searching for answers and now they're coming at me in waves and I just forget to check the time."

"How do I know you're not under duress?"

"I'm fine, thanks for checking."

"I need a code word, otherwise I'm calling the Jefferson County Sheriff's Office," Arjun insisted.

"What code word? We didn't settle on any code word."

"What's the name of my car?"

"Please don't make me repeat that," ZacBox pleaded seeing Dr. Brondsted watching him with a smile on his face. "Not now, I'm kind of in the middle of something."

"Say it or I'm dialing 911," Arjun demanded.

"Boson," ZacBox said softly as Dr. Brondsted smiled.

"Okay, text me when you're ready for me to pick you up," Arjun said then hung up.

"Sorry," ZacBox said to Dr. Brondsted as he put his smartphone back in his pocket.

"Boson?" Dr. Brondsted inquired.

"Yes, my friend named his car Boson."

"After Satyendra Nath Bose, the famous Indian scientist?"

"Evidently," ZacBox said as he looked sheepishly at the floor.

"I'll bet you two boys don't pick up many girls in that car, do you?"

"Not yet," ZacBox said and then added with a smile, "but if we ever do, I'll bet they're going to be smart ones!"

Dr. Brondsted and ZacBox shared a laugh, "I'm surprised my cellphone rang down here underground," ZacBox said, "You must have a good Wi-Fi system."

"I do here underground, and there are a handful of transponders scattered around outdoors hidden in the trees," Dr. Brondsted said, impressed with how ZacBox questioned the problem and figured out the solution all on his own. Then the archeologist returned to the business at hand, "Where were we, with your questions?"

"Why Pleiades?" ZacBox asked seriously.

"Ah, now that, my boy, is *the* question," Dr. Brondsted set his teacup on the coffee table, stood up from his chair and walked over to the fireplace. "Come over here," he said as he pointed to the large framed color photograph. As ZacBox approached the photo, he saw it looked like an ancient cave painting of a red-colored hand with a series of red dots around it. "I took this picture when I was about your age. This rock art is believed to be at least 44,000 years old. It was discovered in a cave on an island off the west coast of Great Britain. For thousands of years ancient man has gazed up into the stars and dreamt of returning to Pleiades."

"Who's this?" ZacBox asked, pointing to the white marble bust, wearing the fedora.

"This is Hafiz, the Persian Poet," Dr. Brondsted said, as he walked over to the white bust of a man's head positioned below the photo on the fireplace mantel. "He lived from 1315 to 1390 AD. Many of his poems still survive today, but perhaps his best-known quote was one he gave as a compliment to another poet saying, 'To thy poems Heaven affixes the Pearl Rosette of the Pleiades as a seal of immortality.'"

"What's a rosette?"

"It's a rose-shaped decoration, like the center of a blue ribbon, usually awarded for winning first place in a contest."

ZacBox nodded his head knowingly, thinking of the many blue ribbons hanging in his bedroom that he had won in track. "Is the Pearl Rosette of the Pleiades real or just a myth?"

"It's real. The Pendant of Pleiades, as it is sometimes known, was discovered in the late 18th Century in a cavern much like this one, beneath Sleeping Ute Mountain. It was found by a Ute named Five Eagles Soaring, a distant relative of yours I'm told. He recognized the seven pearls at the center of the rosette, representing each of the seven stars of the Pleiades Star Cluster. The Pleiades, as your great-grandfather may have told you, is where your Ute ancestors claim to have come from, as well as many other people from around the world. According to Ute oral history, their creation story teaches the Nuche, the Ute, that Creator brought the People to the Shining Mountains at the beginning of time from Pleiades. For the Ute, time began when they arrived here, in the Shining Mountains."

"Where is the Pearl Rosette of the Pleiades now?"

"Last anyone knew, Jorvik was wearing it around his neck when he climbed aboard the Sterope. It launched in 1842 from right here," Dr. Brondsted said. "Jorvik's mission was to place it in the hands of the reigning monarch on the ruling planet in the Star Cluster Pleiades. It was to prove that mankind, here on earth anyway, had crossed the cultural and technological threshold to where they were ready to join the Pleiadians and other peaceful universal star travelers."

"What's this?" ZacBox asked as he pointed to a bluish-green-colored bronze disk the size of a small dinner plate resting on a wooden stand on the right side of the fireplace mantel.

"This is the Newport Sky Disc," Professor Brondsted said as he lifted the sky disc from its stand and handed it to ZacBox. "This is one of a pair of bronze sky discs that date back to the beginning of the Bronze Age, roughly 1,600 BC. The Nebra Sky Disc was unearthed by two treasure-hunters illegally metal detecting on a small mound in Saxony-Anhalt, Germany. These seven gold inlaid circles here," Professor Brondsted said pointing to a cluster of seven dots near the point of what resembled a crescent moon, "are believed to represent the Pleiades. The disc was resting on the chest of the large man who was buried inside the tomb. Apparently, he was going somewhere in the afterlife and the Nebra Sky Disc was to show him the way."

"Where is it now?" ZacBox asked.

"Inside the Sky Disc Visitors Center near Nebra, Saxony-Anhalt, in Germany," Dr. Brondsted replied. "It is thought to be the oldest known depiction of the cosmos and has been termed one of the most important archaeological finds of the twentieth century. Professor Fibonacci and I unearthed this one together on an archaeological dig near the Newport Tower in Newport, Rhode Island. That's where we met, our first year out of college. I graduated from Colorado College and she from Yale. Lisa went on for her PhD, at MIT, and I went to Oxford. From there I studied at Stonehenge in England and the Goseck Circle in Germany, near where the Nebra Sky Disc was unearthed. I went on to study the pyramids in South America. I spent twelve years at Tikal in Maya, where the seven main pyramids were built in the configuration of the Pleiades. Lisa went on to teach at the U.S. Air Force Academy. I moved to Colorado, so we could be closer to one another, but then I met Olaf Eriksson, and he led me here to the Pine Ridge Forest. This is where he had last seen his son, Captain Jorvik, when he climbed aboard the starship Sterope with his four crewmembers. That was in 1842."

"This would be impossible to believe, had I not met Mr. Eriksson yesterday," ZacBox said as he turned the Newport Sky Disc over to inspect the back. He read aloud a small engraved plaque attached to the back, "To Therkel Brondsted, PhD., Danish Archaeologist & World Traveler. With deep appreciation, The Explorers Club."

"What's The Explorer's Club?"

"The Explorer's Club is an international multidisciplinary professional society intended to promote scientific exploration and field study. It was founded in 1905 in New York City. I am a Past-President. Famous honorary members include President Theodore Roosevelt, journalist Walter Cronkite, HRH Prince Phillip, HRH Duke of Edinburgh, HRH Albert I, Prince of Monaco and Colonel John Glenn."

"John Glenn, the astronaut?"

"Yes, and one of the most famous exploratory firsts accomplished by our members was when Neil Armstrong and Buzz Aldrin became the first men to walk on the moon. Do you know what their first radio transmission was when they landed?"

"I don't," ZacBox said, wishing he had paid more attention in history class.

"The Eagle has landed. Those four words were the first to be transmitted from the lunar surface," Professor Brondsted said as he replaced the bronze disc carefully back on the fireplace mantel. Then he retrieved the fedora off the bust of Hafiz, the Persian poet, and plopped it on his head. "Come, ZacBox," Professor Brondsted said. "I will show you what Leif Eriksson was searching for when he led the Vikings to discover Greenland and what we know today as America, about 400 years before Christopher Columbus supposedly discovered America."

ZacBox watched as Professor Brondsted tipped a well-worn book away from a bookshelf, opening a secret chamber. He followed the professor behind the bookshelf, which led to a small compartment behind the fireplace. As they walked down the narrow corridor, ZacBox realized they were leaving the tunnel and walking toward the daylight beyond.

Professor Brondsted continued as if he were giving a lecture to a hall full of students at Oxford University in England, but here, as they emerged from the tunnel beneath the Pine Ridge Forest, ZacBox was alone with what he thought might be one of the world's most accomplished archeologists and one of the most interesting men he had ever met. "The Vikings traveled down the 3000-mile long intracoastal waterway, where they encountered many Native American tribes, most notably the Cherokee, one of the five civilized tribes of North America. Legends within the Cherokee Nation still persist today, telling of a battle long ago between the Cherokee and a race of tall red-bearded men who were fierce warriors and had arrived in longboats. The Cherokee eventually defeated these fierce warriors; however, a few of the wounded men and a handful of women survived and eventually intermarried. Olaf Eriksson's wife died during childbirth; however, their young son, Jorvik, survived. During modern-day Cherokee powwows or reunions, when the Cherokee families gather, there are some Cherokee who are notably very tall and some have beards and red hair. They are the descendants of these Norsemen, a few of whom, if not all, were thought to have been Pleiadians."

"How many of the original Pleiadians are still here on earth?"

"As far as we know, just one," Dr. Brondsted said, as they walked past an unusually bent pine tree with a distorted twist to the trunk. "Olaf Eriksson is likely the last Pleiadian on earth."

ZacBox's smartphone rang and he saw it was Professor Fibonacci's cellphone number. "Hello? Yes, I'm standing right next to him. Okay, sure. It's for you; it's Professor Fibonacci," ZacBox said as he handed his cellphone to Dr. Brondsted.

"Hello Lisa," Dr. Brondsted said in a warm tone. "Yes, it's been too long. Yes, he is. I hope so. I see. No, that wouldn't do. Yes, I would imagine time is of the essence. Indeed. I will. I promise. Good-bye." Dr. Brondsted then handed ZacBox's cellphone back to him. "Dr. Fibonacci—just making sure the two of us were getting along."

"She checks in on me a lot," ZacBox said, "but I'm still not certain why I'm here."

"Over there," Dr. Brondsted said, pointing down the hill toward a circle of white stones in the shape of a wheel. "These rocks are milky white quartz crystals. The tall center stone there is over three feet tall and must weigh several hundred pounds. Around the circle are four large stones, each aligned precisely with the four cardinal directions: true north, at 0 degrees; south, at 180 degrees; east, at 90 degrees; and west, at 270 degrees. Based upon the lichen, the greenish-colored growth on some of the stones, this medicine wheel is thought to be over 300 years old, which seems to correspond with the age of the majority of the Culturally Modified Trees in the vicinity, like the one we passed back there on the ridge with the bent trunk. There are four other prominent rocks situated here along the outer row of rocks and while the precise meaning of these stones remains a mystery, they do appear to have been aligned with the winter and summer solstice and spring and summer equinox."

"They were used as a calendar then, like Stonehenge?" ZacBox asked.

"Yes, but not necessarily to tell them the day or month of the year. More than likely they were to indicate the season and let the ancient Ute know when they had reached the longest day and shortest night of the year, or the shortest day and longest night of the year, mid-summer or mid-winter. Then they would know where they were supposed to be during annual migratory routes and at what elevation. We are at about 8,000 feet above sea level here in the Pine Ridge Forest. According to the Ute, that makes us closer to Creator, and as such, our prayers are thought to be closer to Creator, so they would have less distance to travel to reach Him."

"Wow, over three hundred years old. This medicine wheel predates the founding of America then," ZacBox said in amazement. "I wish my great-grandfather could see this."

"He has," Dr. Brondsted replied, "several times. This stone feature is believed to be a very sacred place and it helped White Elk see his vision more clearly. There, just beyond the circle," Dr. Brondsted said, pointing to the northeast, "three shimmering lights, spirits wearing feathered headdresses, came to White Elk during his prayers and told him how a brave warrior will rise up from his people to stand to defend Mother Earth and her children, to protect them, and all animals and the forest from the invaders from the stars. This is why you are here ZacBox."

As ZacBox stood behind the west stone, he watched a hummingbird fly between him and Dr. Brondsted and perch on a log stump a few feet behind the south stone. "Grandfather told me the hummingbird, the eagle and the butterfly are messengers from Creator."

"He shared that with me as well, he thought this might be a spiritual portal of some sort," Dr. Brondsted replied. "When he was here the last time, sixteen years ago, a bald eagle flew overhead and White Elk offered a prayer to Creator and asked the eagle to deliver it."

"I wonder if it made it," ZacBox said.

"I'd like to think so; I understand you were born nine months later." Dr. Brondsted replied. Then he pointed to an orange and black butterfly floating gently on the wind and into the stone enclosure.

"It's a Painted Lady," ZacBox said as they watched, the butterfly landed on the center stone, flapped its wings a few times. Then it flew over and landed on ZacBox's hand.

"It has chosen you," Dr. Brondsted said, nodding his head. Then as the butterfly flew away, he added, "Come, we haven't much time to prepare; they are on their way."

"Who?"

"The Centaurians, the aliens I mentioned from the Omega Centauri Star Cluster. Lisa told me on the phone that SETI, the Search for Extraterrestrial Intelligence, intercepted a message from deep space. One of the alien spacecraft is to remain on orbit around Jupiter until it can be joined by fourteen other starships. It won't be long before they begin their attack."

"On who?" ZacBox asked.

"On us."

"What do they want?"

"Our mineral wealth, starting with all our oil and gas, we suppose," Dr. Brondsted said as he stood and looked towards the sky. "We suspect they will likely kill everyone who opposes them and force the rest of us into slave labor. If that doesn't work, they may simply exterminate us. Come, we only have a couple weeks to prepare you and your crew before you launch."

"My crew, I don't have a crew," ZacBox protested as he stood up and watched two more butterflies fly over the center stone and head downhill.

"I understand the crew are now being assembled. Professor Fibonacci is giving a tour of CAT² this afternoon for John Paul von Braun; he's the great-great-grandson of Werhner von Braun," Dr. Brondsted explained, "He will be your chief engineer."

"But I'm only fifteen. How old is he?"

"He's also fifteen," Dr. Brondsted replied as he led ZacBox back up the hillside. "Do you know a man named Julian? Apparently he's into security or something along that line of work."

"Yes, why?"

"According to what Lisa told me to tell you, this Julian just landed in Japan; he's there to interview your security officer."

"How old is he?"

"She is also fifteen," Dr. Brondsted said as he led ZacBox past the workbench and back into the interior of the underground complex.

"She?" ZacBox asked.

"If I understood Lisa correctly, she comes from a long line of female samurai warriors."

"I didn't know the samurai had female warriors."

"Oh yes, fearless warriors from what I've read. Come," Dr. Brondsted said. "It would be good for you to understand how the universal docking stations, the UDS, work. As they neared the center of the underground tunnels, ZacBox spotted the familiar-looking metal launch support structure, exactly like what he observed beneath Fibonacci's Diner, only the flying saucer on the top was missing. "After the saucer launches, the three legs of the support system retract and remain underground. I'm told the saucer can dock with another Pleiades class starship in space."

"How long will this launch mechanism remain retracted underground?"

"Until the flying saucer returns, I suppose. No one knows for certain since there's only been the one launch from here, over a century and a half ago, and as you know, that starship never returned," Dr. Brondsted explained as they walked around the launch apparatus and inspected the three claws used to connect the starship into the docking station. "Do you know a man named Saint Michael?"

"Yes, he was a Pararescue medic. He flew several missions in the Middle East with my mother," ZacBox said as he followed Dr. Brondsted around the dimly lit cavern. "Why?"

"He's evidently on a plane headed to South America. He's meeting with your medical doctor and her parents on an ancient Mayan pyramid ruin near Tikal."

"Don't tell me, she's also fifteen?" ZacBox asked somewhat incredulously.

"No. Evidently, she's an older woman," Dr. Brondsted said with a sly smile.

"How much older?"

"She's sixteen."

"What? Why are we all so young?"

"I don't know really. I suspect it has something to do with how long it takes for deep space travel. No one from earth has ever done this before, but there's some reasonable expectation that deep space travel may require several years, even if you were to surpass the speed of light. Some speculate if we were to launch an older crew the mission may exceed their natural life expectancy. Plus, the rigors that will be placed upon your bodies traveling near light speed will be enormous. Therefore, this space mission calls for a well-conditioned younger crew whose members possess the intellect to learn on the job, so to speak. Each crew member is to be assigned a mentor, and it appears, according to Lisa, that I am to be your mentor, ZacBox. If you agree that is," Dr. Brondsted concluded as they returned to his den. He plopped his fedora down on the marble bust on the fireplace mantel and sat down in one of the overstuffed chairs.

"I would be honored Dr. Brondsted," ZacBox replied as he sat down in the other chair, "Right now I feel a bit overwhelmed. If I'm going anywhere I think I'm going to need a good mentor." Persephone jumped up into his lap and licked his face again.

"Sorry," Dr. Brondsted replied, "we don't get much company up here; apparently she's taken a fancy to you."

"That's okay, Dr. Brondsted, she reminds me of my dog, Bo."

"The only unfilled slot on your crew is your science officer. Evidently Dr. Hubble has been interviewing candidates since yesterday, but she's having some difficulty locating someone with an indepth knowledge of geology and a passion for physics."

"Well," ZacBox said with a smile, "I happen to know of a nineteen-year-old, working on his PhD in geology from the School of Mines. He is sitting in a rock shop just a few miles from here studying rocks and minerals."

"Does he have a strong understanding of physics?"

"He named his car Boson," ZacBox replied with a laugh.

"Well then," Dr. Brondsted summarized, "I will let Lisa know the Electra and her crew are set. The launch is in twenty-one days with or without you at the helm."

"I'll go…" ZacBox replied, and then added softly, "but, Dr. Brondsted I have to confess I'm more than a little scared."

"Scared of what ZacBox?"

"Scared I might fail, scared I might die, but mostly I'm just scared I might let my family and Dr. Fibonacci, and now you, down."

"Do you suppose your mother or your father were ever scared before a mission?"

"I don't know that my father was ever scared of anything in his life; he's Ute and pretty much fearless I'd say, but I imagine there were times when my mother was probably scared to death," ZacBox replied. "Where do I find their kind of courage?"

Dr. Brondsted stood, walked over to the bookshelf, selected a well-worn book and read, "John Wayne, the famous American actor, once said, 'Courage is being scared to death and saddling up anyway.'"

6 The von Braun Kilt

August 31st, 06:54 hours MDST Astradate 11083.1
Starship Electra Launchpad, Colorado Springs, CO Planet
Earth

"Saddle up," ZacBox said to his First Officer Arjun Basu.

"Aye, aye Captain," Arjun replied back excitedly. The crew of the Electra did not salute their captain; theirs was a rescue mission, not a military operation. Besides, none of them were in the military; well not yet anyway. Arjun looked to where hundreds of people were gathered to the west of the launch tower. The crowd stood beyond a ring of white quartz rocks, resembling a medicine wheel, with four interconnecting spokes. The stones had been placed around the launch apparatus over the past two weeks. The Ops Center was underground, beneath the stone feature.

The Electra flying saucer had broken through the ground two weeks ago and began inching skyward more every day. It finally leveled off at its present height of 144 feet. Every day more and more curious people came to stare up at the technological wonder sitting atop the tower. Arjun pointed toward the people standing by the largest upright white rock in the west and asked ZacBox, "Is that your father over there with Mr. Bojangles, Professor Fibonacci and Julian?"

"It is," ZacBox said proudly, "and I'm glad some of dad's Fire Department friends were able to be here too, but I wish my great-grandfather White Elk could have made it this morning. I think he would have enjoyed seeing his vision come to reality."

To honor his Ute family, ZacBox wore his Fancy Dance regalia with twin bustles adorned with brightly colored feathers, leggings with silver jingle bells below the knees and elk hide moccasins his great-grandfather had made. Last night ZacBox had asked his father to help him shave his head for a Mohawk, leaving just a two-inch strip of his jet-black hair running over the top of his head to just above the back of his neck. He also wore a beaded headband and cuffs in the traditional colors of the Ute Nation: white, black, red and yellow, which represent the four primary colors of all The People who live on Mother Earth. White Elk had also added blue beads, to honor Father Sky and green beads to honor the trees.

"Where is Dr. Brondsted?" Arjun asked ZacBox as he scanned the faces of the crowd assembled around the outer ring of white stones.

"Below ground, with Mr. Eriksson," ZacBox replied, pointing beneath their feet to the underground complex. "They're manning the Ops Center. I'll check in with Dr. Brondsted on our individual crew comms system just before we launch. We will all get a few minutes to have a final talk with our mentors before we disconnect from the launch tower. As you know, for security purposes, once we disconnect from the launch tower, we'll sever all communications. I think Mr. Ericksson is right; we must assume the Centaurians will be able to intercept our digital communications since we are able to intercept theirs. When you get settled in, could you please welcome the crew aboard and ask them to stow their personal belongings in their cabins and then change into their flight suits? I want us to be underway at the earliest opportunity."

"I'll see to it," Arjun replied. He was dressed in a Sherwani, recognized in India as the traditional clothing for an adult male. It consisted of a long white jacket with exposed buttons running down the length of the garment. Today he was wearing a beautiful deep purple pagri with a matching silk scarf tucked into his jacket's breast pocket. ZacBox watched as Arjun hoisted his tote bag over his left shoulder and waved goodbye to his parents and sister, Indu, who were standing with dozens of other observers in the east. ZacBox also waved at Arjun's family, and then turned his attention to Dr. Cadence Bahar, the next crew member walking toward him up the stone-lined walkway from the south.

As he waited for her, he glanced over her right shoulder to where he could see Reggie, wearing his chef's uniform, standing near the rear of Fibonacci's Diner. The Diner had become very popular in the last few weeks, and while the restaurant had always been open for breakfast, lunch and dinner, now they were open 24/7, requiring Professor Fibonacci to hire additional staff. Reggie told ZacBox he had talked with his famous brother, Marcus, about coming to join him at Fibonacci's, but no decisions had been made. ZacBox was looking forward to tasting more of Reggie's recipes once they reached deep space.

The sixteen-year-old doctor from South America stopped in front of the fifteen-year-old starship captain and said, "Captain ZacBox, Cadence Bahar, Medical Officer, reporting for duty."

"Welcome aboard; Dr. Bahar, we are delighted you could join us," ZacBox said as he glanced back to where her family was standing. "Where is Saint Michael? I thought he would be here to see us off."

"Oh, I think we'll be seeing him shortly," Cadence said with a knowing nod of her head above the Air Force Academy to the west of Interstate 25. ZacBox looked across the Interstate but didn't see anything. When he looked back, he noticed Cadence's fingernails were painted to match the purple sash she wore around her beautiful ivory-colored Aztec blouse, called huipilli. She was wearing open-toe sandals and her toenails had been painted purple to match her fingernails. She held out her long skirt, which she explained has been referred to as enredo in more recent times. She and ZacBox discussed one another's cultural clothing while waiting for the next crew member.

In keeping with Aztec traditions for both men and women, Cadence wore gold jewelry, including bangles, earrings and necklaces, adorned with seashells, bone, and wood, along with stones of various types, including green jade, blue topaz and black obsidian. Her headgear was laced with jaguar and crocodile teeth, jaguar claws and brilliant blue-green feathers. She carried her crew tote bag in her left hand, and in her right hand, she held a beautiful medical bag made from crocodile hide. She and ZacBox saw their next crewmate approaching as Cadence entered the tower elevator to carry her up to the awaiting Electra. Before the doors closed she turned back toward ZacBox and said, "I am honored to be representing my people on this voyage."

"We are honored to have you accompanying us," ZacBox replied sincerely. Then he turned to face the north to welcome Electra's Chief Engineer John Paul von Braun, the great-grandson of Wernher von Braun, the leading figure in developing rocket technology in Nazi Germany during WWII. Dr. Brondsted had told ZacBox that as the war was drawing to an end, Wernher von Braun was secretly moved to the United States, along with about 1,600 other German engineers, scientists, and technicians, as part of what was called 'Operation Paperclip.'

ZacBox learned later it was John Paul's great-grandfather who helped develop the rockets that launched Explorer, America's first space satellite, and later, the Saturn V heavy-lift rockets used to launch the Apollo spacecraft to the moon. Professor Fibonacci told ZacBox that Wernher von Braun's mother was a direct descendant of Philip III of France, Valdemar I of Denmark, Edward III of England, as well as Robert III of Scotland.

To honor his Scottish heritage, John Paul had chosen to wear a modern kilt, made of woolen cloth in a red, blue and green tartan pattern. He was tall, six-foot-two, with short-cropped blonde hair. He wore a dark blue cap, a matching short jacket, and a tartan vest, with a white shirt, navy blue bow tie and white woolen knee-high stockings. A black-handled dirk, in a black leather sheath, was tucked into his knee-high stocking. John Paul sat his black Electra crew tote bag down and transferred a well-worn burgundy leather briefcase to his left hand. "It belonged to my great-grandfather I use it to carry my personal laptop," John Paul explained, seeing ZacBox looking at the briefcase. Then asked, "Permission to come aboard Captain."

"Permission granted," ZacBox replied warmly as he shook hands with the fifteen-year-old engineering prodigy. ZacBox watched as John Paul turned back to wave at Dr. Wendy Hubble and his family. Then said, staring up at the Electra, "She's quite a ship, isn't she Captain Box?"

"That she is, Mr. von Braun," ZacBox replied proudly. The title, Captain Box, was used by his mother and the honorable English ship captain, Captain Godfrey Box, who his Ute family had been named after. For just a moment ZacBox wondered if the excitement he was feeling now had been shared by those two captains as they welcomed their crews aboard their vessels at the beginning of their missions. "That she is," ZacBox repeated, as he looked up admiringly at the sleek saucer-shaped craft above them, accented by a row of rotating colored lights encircling the outer rim of the ship. "I'm looking forward to us seeing what she can do out there."

"I don't think she will disappoint us, Captain," the Electra's Chief Engineer said confidently.

"Agreed. I look forward to sharing this adventure with you, John Paul, and the rest of the crew. Welcome aboard," ZacBox said as John Paul stepped into the elevator shaft and pushed the up button. Captain ZacBox turned to greet the last of Electra's five-member crew, fifteen-year-old Anzu Gozen. Although ZacBox would never admit it, he questioned to himself why Julian Piccard had selected a fifteen-year-old Japanese girl to serve as Electra's Chief of Security. ZacBox figured that when Julian worked security with the Swiss Guards he must have worked with the finest security officers in the world while protecting the Pope on international travel.

ZacBox was looking forward to getting to know Anzu and the rest of the crew better, once they were underway. Their training time as a crew had been less than three weeks and much of that time had been spent with their mentors preparing them for their individual positions. Most of their advanced STEM—Science, Technology, Engineering, and Math—educational components would have to be learned in-flight; followed by an endless array of computer modeling, simulations and analysis exercises. The ground crew had worked diligently to help prepare Electra's young crew to face the many challenges that lay ahead, but they knew once they had reached deep space, they would be on their own.

There wasn't much known about their final destination, the Pleiades Star Cluster, but Mr. Ericksson shared what he could about the mission to return to Pleiades. But first they had to rescue Jorvik, stranded on Europa, one of the distant moons of Jupiter. If that weren't challenging enough, ZacBox had shared privately with his mentor, Dr. Brondsted, the aliens who had shot down Sterope, were out there somewhere, waiting for reinforcements. "Oh, and don't forget," ZacBox said to Dr. Brondsted, "when Captain Jorvik was shot down, he was at the helm of an identical spacecraft to ours, and he couldn't have been a less experienced pilot then me."

ZacBox knew too that they would have to depend on the skill and training of their Chief of Security if they had any chance of accomplishing their mission or ever returning home and seeing their families again. ZacBox wished Julian could have found an experienced warrior, like Saint Michael, someone to protect them, or maybe another huge Pleiadian, like Olaf Eriksson, or maybe a fierce Viking with a battle scar across his face, with a fitting name like Erik the Red. But no, ZacBox had confided privately to Dr. Brondsted; Julian Piccard had picked a fifteen-year-old girl, shorter than he was by several inches, to protect the very lives of him and his crew.

"What was Julian thinking?" ZacBox whispered one morning to Dr. Brondsted.

"I don't know," Dr. Brondsted replied. "The Pope trusted Julian with his life; shouldn't you?"

"I should, but..."

"So I imagine you can trust her with your life," Dr. Brondsted said before adding, "By the way, she might be shorter than you, but if I were you, I wouldn't challenge her to fight. She looks like she can handle herself."

Today ZacBox saw Anzu for the first time dressed in the traditional clothing of a Bushi Class Samurai warrior. Until three weeks ago he didn't even know there were female Samurai warriors. But now he was going into space with one. She walked toward him from the east, a female Samurai warrior, descendant of Japanese nobility, whose family bloodline had for centuries engaged in battle alongside Samurai men. These women, Julian explained to ZacBox, were trained in all manner of weapons to protect their household, family and honor in times of war. Although these Japanese female warriors were predominantly trained to use the traditional Samurai weapons, including the sword and crossbow, the naginata, a long pole weapon with a single-edged curved blade on the end, was their preferred weapon of choice. Anzu was wearing black and red Samurai armor, including a fierce-looking helmet with a half-face mask, and in her right hand she carried a six-foot long naginata. Her Electra crew tote bag was in her left hand.

Anzu stopped in front of ZacBox, removed her helmet and came to attention. She tapped the end of her naginata on the ground twice, as if knocking on a door. Then she looked ZacBox in the eye as she said, "Security Chief Gozen requests permission to board, Captain."

"Granted," ZacBox replied. "We are honored to have you as a member of our crew."

"Julian Piccard wishes you safe travel, Captain ZacBox," she added lowering her naginata toward the man wearing the dress uniform of the Swiss Guard standing in the west.

"Thank you. I noticed there are three other Swiss Guards here this morning. One is positioned opposite Julian, over there in the east, another one is in the north and one in the south. I am told the Pope himself sent them from the Vatican yesterday."

"Is one of our crew Catholic?" Anzu asked.

"No, I asked Julian the same question. Julian explained the Vatican views our mission as a unique opportunity to unite the people from around the world. He told me the Vatican has an interest in space exploration and operates some of the world's most advanced observatories for viewing stars. The Pope sent the Swiss Guards as a universal show of support for our mission."

ZacBox waved at Julian, and then turned to Anzu, "I wish he were coming with us, there can never be enough Piccards' in space."

"Agreed," Anzu said as she set her duffle bag on the ground. "I am sure he wishes he were coming with us as well, as do most of the others," she said as she nodded her head toward the hundreds of Air Force cadets wearing their flight suits standing behind Julian. ZacBox watched Anzu place her Samurai helmet back on her head and walk fifteen meters toward Julian and the cadets. Then she raised her naginata above her head and let out a fierce roar "URRAH!" Her spirited demonstration caused the cadets to shout "URRAH!" and pump their fists in the air. The rest of the crowd joined enthusiastically in the loud cheer as Anzu walked the entire inner circle around the Electra, energizing the crowd with each thrust of her naginata above her head, generating three more loud roars of "URRAH.".

"She has spirit," ZacBox thought to himself. "I'll give her that." Then he watched as Anzu returned to where she started, picked up her tote bag, slung it over her shoulder and assumed a position at her captain's side.

"Let us make them proud," ZacBox said as he and Anzu stepped forward into the elevator shaft and pushed the up button together so that they could join the rest of their crew already onboard the starship Electra.

As they stepped off the elevator and into the starship's main cockpit, Arjun came to attention and tapped the round Electra insignia on the left side of his collar to activate the ship's intercom system. "Ten-HUT! Officer on deck!" Each collar insignia carried the rank or position that person held on Electra's crew. It was also equipped with a tracking device as well as an internal comms system.

ZacBox watched as John Paul stood alongside his crew seat,

below and to the right of the captain's chair. John Paul smiled at ZacBox and nodded his head toward the complex instrument cluster located on the dashboard in front of his Chief Engineer's seat. "THIS is going to be an adventure!" John Paul said as a wide smile spread across his face showing that he was eager to return to exploring this engineering marvel. A forward hatch cover popped open and BeeBot jumped out, coming to attention while he patted his protruding tummy where the pearl colored orb was safely tucked away.

"BeeBot," ZacBox said in acknowledgement. It still was not clear to anyone what his role might be, but they assumed from what they had been told, BeeBot's presence was "mission critical" and would be proven soon enough.

ZacBox wondered if each of the other six Electra-class spacecraft had its own AI, or if this little blue BeeBot was unique just to their ship. He tried to imagine the Sterope on Europa, and visualize the starships Merope, Alcyone, Mia, Taygeta and Celaeno, each named after one of the sister stars of the Pleiades Star Cluster. Will they ever know what happened to the missing one, Merope, the lost Pleiades? Will they ever return to this launch tower, and if so, what will be different? Will anything ever be the same? All good questions, which would not be answered tethered to the ground.

Cadence joined them from the women's crew quarters located behind the bridge to the right of the hallway. She, like Arjun and John Paul, had already changed into one of the matching flight suits. Dr. Wendy Hubble and her team of cadets had designed the Electra's flight suits, which were intentionally manufactured to be as comfortable as pajamas for long space missions. To keep the interior of the Electra clean, they wore socks instead of shoes or went barefoot, which allowed them to feel the slight vibrations of the saucer beneath their feet.

ZacBox and his crew had carefully selected Electra's crew logo, designed in the shape of the Tree of Life. Their logo embodied the Pleiadians' wish for universal "love, peace and spirituality," as explained to them by Mr. Eriksson. He shared how he was certain his son Jorvik was still alive, having communicated telepathically dozens of times over the years. He told them Jorvik's crew of earthlings had all perished. Two were killed as they were shot down, one in battle with something called a Puckster, and the last died of old age in 1932 at the age of 92.

Mr. Eriksson had explained the Pleiadians had evolved genetically to where they had eliminated most common diseases responsible for the deaths of most earthlings every year, which helped explain their longevity as a people. They had also eliminated nearly all violence or any need for currency, having reached the capacity to provide for the essential needs of every Pleiadian. Their people had also evolved to where no one had to compete over scarce resources, which is what he believed motivated the Centaurians to come to their solar system, having depleted their own fossil fuels. Mr. Eriksson believed the Centaurians were intending to first invade Europa, kill or capture Jorvik so he could be tortured and interrogated, and then strip Sterope so they could better understand how to defeat her weapons systems. He shared how he was certain Jorvik wouldn't allow himself to be taken alive by the Centaurians.

Mr. Eriksson, along with all of the crew mentors, had recorded various training modules to be absorbed by the crew, collectively and individually, according to their specific assignments or duties during their long flight. Mr. Tuttle, ZacBox's high school track coach and history teacher, had worked with the staff from DCC to allow ZacBox and Anzu to complete their high school educational requirements so they could graduate, after passing their GED, when they returned to earth, if they returned to earth. Arjun, John

Paul and Cadence had already graduated high school and all three were working on or had already earned doctorate degrees; John Paul in engineering, Cadence in medicine and Arjun in geology.

"What are your orders?" Arjun inquired as the Electra's crew stood by to receive their captain's launch instructions.

"Cadence, please assist Anzu in stowing her gear and changing into her flight suit. I will change into my flight suit in my cabin," ZacBox replied. Then he looked around as the cockpit seemed to come to life, his eyes coming to rest on the digital clock displaying the Astradate calibrated to the Rocky Mountain Time Zone in Colorado Springs, Colorado. "Mr. Basu, please complete our preflight checklist. I'd like us to be underway by 07:30 hours."

"Aye, aye Captain," Arjun acknowledged as the crew went about their assigned prelaunch duties.

Upon entering the captain's quarters, ZacBox began to change from his Fancy Dance feathered regalia into his flight suit. He spotted a twelve-inch square black box sitting on his desk that hadn't been there earlier when he unpacked his tote bag. He picked up the box, felt there was something inside, and read the small card tied to the box with a thin yucca cord, "To Strong Bear Running, From White Elk." ZacBox smiled and stashed the box in his bottom desk drawer until later when he could concentrate on whatever gift his great-grandfather had chosen to send with him on this mission.

ZacBox stowed his regalia in his small closet, put on his flight suit, and checked himself in his bathroom mirror. He thought how fortunate starship captains were to have their own private cabins and bathrooms while other crewmembers bunked together, the two men sharing one cabin with a bathroom, and the two women sharing a separate cabin with a bathroom.

The Electra's galley, dining area, exercise room, and library, which doubled as a small five-person theater, were co-ed of course;

however, they were designed for the much larger-bodied Pleiadians, which provided more than ample room for a crew of five teenage earthlings. As the crew assumed their positions on the bridge, ZacBox climbed into his Captain's seat and buckled his shoulder straps. Then he took a moment to look at the faces of his four intrepid crewmates. Each had given their families and loved ones their most heartfelt goodbyes, except of course for Captain ZacBox. In keeping with Ute tradition, ZacBox hugged his dad, then hugged Professor Fibonacci, lastly gave Bo a pat on the head, and simply walked away—the Ute have no word for goodbye. Like his Ute ancestors, ZacBox accepted he would see all of them again, in this life or the next.

Each crewmember donned their headset and was given one last communication with their mentors. ZacBox keyed his mic, "ZacBox1 to Dr. Brondsted, are you there, sir?"

"I am here Zac," Brondsted replied.

"Ship and crew are ready to launch, but I'm still a little fuzzy on one thing," ZacBox said softly so that he could not be overheard.

"What is it Zac?"

"When exactly did I agree to be a starship captain?"

"I don't know for certain, but from talking with White Elk I think it may have been the moment you were born into this world, son, the moment you were born."

ZacBox took a deep breath, held it for a moment, and then let the air out slowly as he keyed his all-comms button, "All systems go for launch?"

"All systems green for go here Captain," John Paul replied as he made one last visual scan of the Electra's intricate dashboard.

"All systems green for launch here in the Ops Center," Chief Mission Officer Wendy Hubble acknowledged.

"Decouple docking station," ZacBox said to John Paul, as he and the crew watched on the large flat panel color display in front as the three-pronged launch apparatus released the hull of the flying saucer. The crew felt the familiar floating sensation of their craft hovering above the launch tower. They had tested the decoupling maneuver yesterday during a brief training session. However, yesterday they had only allowed the spacecraft to rise slowly and hover a few feet above the launch apparatus while testing the Electra's electrogravitics system.

The Electra, and presumably her six sister ships, were designed and built using a dual-propulsion system: electrogravitics for interplanetary travel and Zero Point Energy or ZPE for interstellar travel. Electrogravitics uses an anti-gravity force field created by leveraging an electric field's effect on a mass. Electra's electrogravitics force field was like trying to push two negative or positive magnets together. Opposites attract, while negative or positive ends resist one another. The alien technology uses the earth's gravity, or the gravity of any heavenly body, such as a moon, planet or a star, as an electronic force field. The underside of the outer hull of the Electra-class spacecraft, being much smaller than any heavenly body, could be pulled or repelled similar to the negative or positive ends of a powerful magnet.

Just inside the inner hull and beneath the crew quarters lay a coil of circular metal tubing, similar to an air-conditioning unit; however, these tubes were filled with liquid mercury. When mercury is super cooled, it will create a magnetic field causing lift, like the maglev trains ZacBox had read about in science class. Some parts of space can be very hot, but the temperature in space can drop to as low as minus 270.5 degrees Celsius, equivalent to minus 455 degrees Fahrenheit. Space provides a natural environment for super-cooling almost anything, including mercury, and it is sustainable and free, once you get there.

"Electrogravitics will help you reach space, but ZPE can take you wherever it is you want to go in the universe," Wendy Hubble told them during their 30-second test flight.

The crew learned ZPE is based on quantum theory using what scientists call the "quantum vacuum," which is technically not a vacuum at all since it contains tiny electromagnetic fields that continuously fluctuate in space around their "zero-baseline" values. The theory of ZPE can be traced back to the 1920's, but the first experiment, in 1948, is attributed to H.G.B. Casimir, a Dutch researcher, and today this theory is known as the "Casimir effect." Casimir, like a handful of other visionaries, such as Leonardo da Vinci, Nikola Tesla and Albert Einstein, was known for going off on retreats for weeks or months at a time where he would meet privately with other brilliant likeminded people. Rare sightings, chiefly from hotel staff who were occasionally known to gossip, described one man as being huge, perhaps measuring as much as seven or eight feet tall. Rumors persist to this day that not all those likeminded people were from planet earth.

During their training, Dr. Hubble had referred to an article in the March 2004 issue of Aviation Week & Space Technology, written by William B. Scott, from Austin, Texas. His article, titled, "To the Stars" related how, "Zero point energy emerges from science fiction, may be key to deep-space travel." In the article, Wendy pointed out, "Mr. Scott predicted that zero point energy could be the next breakthrough in aerospace vehicle propulsion. He theorized ZPE-driven powerplants would enable fighter jets to travel at Mach 4 and 1,200-seat hypersonic airliners to travel to the moon in 12.6-hours."

Dr. Lockwood explained, "The problems associated with ZPE research for space travel today are centered on the issues of radiation, generation and quantification. How can we protect a spacecraft, along with its crew or cargo, from the harmful effects of radiation produced by ZPE? Secondly, assuming you could you generate sufficient qualities of ZPE, how would you quantify or measure this energy, let alone control what appears to be a series of continuously random zero-baseline value fluctuations. The Electra-class spacecraft solves the first two problems with an advanced radiation shield, or ARS, built into its titanium hull. The metal of the outer hull has blended composite layers of several other elements from the Periodic Table of Elements, including one of the new elements called 'ununpentium.' Electra's power plant uses vibrations, emitted by the excitement of onboard crystals, to produce sound waves to power the flying saucer during interplanetary travel."

Dr. Hubble said, "The spacecraft is both pushed and pulled through this vacuum in space. The faster the spacecraft travels, the more the space vacuum becomes extended or is elongated further out in front and behind the vessel." Hearing Wendy explain the General Relativity Theory of Warp Drive, attributed to Migel Alcubierre in 1994, reminded ZacBox of how the metal rod expanded as he watched the pearl orb get sucked down into the saucer underground. Dr. Hubble explained further, "Using Einstein's spacetime as a mathematical model that fuses the three dimensions of space, while bending the fourth dimension of time, creates a space vacuum tunnel with two ends. Each end of the tunnel is connected to separate points or specific places in spacetime. This tunnel, commonly referred to as a wormhole, can connect extremely long distances measured in billions of light years, or shorter distances; such as a few meters. Theoretically, a wormhole could achieve connectivity between two different universes at the same point in time."

"Overcoming the challenges of conducting precise measurements using the Casimir effect," Wendy explained, "had been the basis of Professor Fibonacci's opus in physics spanning nearly a half-century." She explained how Professor Fibonacci's research in quantum physics proved that zero-baseline value fluctuations of ZPE are not fluctuations at all; they follow a precise mathematical model: the Fibonacci Spiral found everywhere in nature from the depths of earth's oceans to the deepest recesses of outer space.

"Professor Lisa Fibonacci," Wendy explained during the first week of the crew's training, "is a direct descendent of the twelfth century, Italian-born mathematician from Pisa, Leonardo Fibonacci, who first popularized the Fibonacci Sequence. Theoretically, as a spacecraft is propelled through the vacuum of space, it can be guided by shifting the weight of the mass and controlling its speed calibrated relative to the Fibonacci numbers of 0, 1, 1, 2, 3, 5, 8, 13, 21, 34, 55, 89, 144 and on to infinity. Since the first two baseline numbers are 0 and 1, Fibonacci numbers are binary meaning they can be used digitally to write software for advanced computers and computer-based devices."

"Another extraordinary feature of the Electra," John Paul added excitedly to his crewmates during one of their previous training sessions, "is the Environmental Control Unit, or ECU, which creates a force field around the ship to shield it from meteoroids as small as a grain of sand, which are deflected off the force field. However, I think we should steer around asteroids larger than a Volkswagen," he added in all seriousness. "Plus, the ECU can create artificial gravity onboard the craft, which can be modulated across the gravitational continuum to mimic the gravity we grew up with on earth, or the lesser gravity we might encounter on the lunar surface, like what we might encounter on Europa. Using spectral analysis, the ECU can also recreate most environmental conditions for any planets or moons before we visit them so that our bodies can become somewhat acclimated, if there's time; otherwise, we'll have to wear our space suits."

During the last 48 hours of training, the diverse interests and passions of the crew became more apparent. They had come to trust one another and understand how they might leverage one another's strengths. Cadence wanted to know how to use the ECU to minimize the effects of zero gravity on the crew to prevent muscle atrophy. Arjun wanted to know what caused the crystals to become excited. Anzu wanted to better understand the Electra's weapons systems. John Paul wanted to know how the Electra flies. ZacBox just wanted to fly.

Now, the moment ZacBox had been waiting for had arrived. He pulled back lightly on the steering yoke, and then turned the saucer slightly to the left as it lifted off the launch tower. The crowd watched as the Electra began a slow ascent in a counterclockwise direction. He widened the spiral slightly as he tipped the edge of the saucer toward the ground, allowing the crew to peer out the left side windows as the spectators waved enthusiastically from the ground below.

While operating as a maglev spacecraft, the Electra was perfectly quiet and left no trace of exhaust. ZacBox steadily gained another fifty feet in altitude as he expanded the spiral to where he was now flying over his house and banked slightly to the left above his school. Continuing in a steady counterclockwise spiral, ZacBox gained another hundred feet in altitude, banked again to the left, to where he was now flying toward the Air Force Academy. They were coming in from the north, for an approved low-level fly-over above the Academy football stadium.

Interest in the mission of the Electra, and her international crew of teenagers, had drawn so much attention from around the world that the expected crowd on the morning of the launch was estimated to be in the tens of thousands. But as word spread through social media, fueled by nearly round-the-clock news coverage of the Pleiadians, coupled with a possibility of seeing an actual flying saucer, the crowd below had swollen to over a hundred thousand people. People wanted to know more about Pleiadians, including the one stranded on a moon of Jupiter.

The rescue mission of the Electra and her teenage crew dominated most conversations around the world. Then the SETI communication intercept was leaked by an anonymous source inside the Air Force Academy. Governments around the world began broadcasting warnings of an invading alien force potentially headed toward earth. The last 48-hours had seen a flood of delegations from India, Japan, Europe, and North and South America, all gathering in Colorado Springs and in the Denver metro region to the north.

News media outlets assigned teams of reporters to cover every aspect of this global story. People demanded to know more about these five teenagers who were now aboard this flying marvel headed to a distant moon of Jupiter. What were they supposed to do once they reached this star cluster most people had never heard of until the last ten days? Speculation grew about the abilities of this young crew asked to carry out such an important mission. Fifteen-year-old John Paul von Braun and sixteen-year-old Dr. Cadence Bahar were both viewed as teenage prodigies within their respective communities and countries.

When nineteen-year-old Arjun Basu or fifteen-year-old Anzu Gozen, were put under the microscope by the international media, they had to be accepted as not simply your ordinary teenagers with interests in rock collecting and martial arts. But when ZacBox was examined closely, and what he had humbly said all along was evidently correct, he was simply a fifteen-year-old boy with dreams of one day attending the U.S. Air Force Academy. The harsh reality was that the fate of humankind on earth rested in the hands of this Captain ZacBox who wasn't even old enough to get a driver's license in Colorado.

ZacBox leveled the Electra off at 500 feet above ground level, or AGL, and looked out to see the early morning sunlight shimmering off the windshields and roofs of the tens of thousands of cars packed tightly around the Air Force Academy football stadium. He had received a text two days ago from Alicia letting him know she and her parents and representatives from all three Ute Reservations would be in the stadium. Her text said that she would be waiting for him when he returned to earth. Thoughts of sharing his adventures with Alicia, upon his return, excited ZacBox, yet he couldn't help but wonder if Jimmy Suazo and his cousin were down there in the crowd right now serving as Alicia's official tribal escorts. ZacBox cleared his mind of Alicia and concentrated on his mission, directing his attention to the four blips on the radar screen ahead.

ZacBox saw the four blips were slow flying aircraft that had also leveled off at 500 feet AGL and were also headed south. Then he recognized the "finger-four" formation; helicopters flying in the missing man formation. He thought of his mother's grave, located directly below and to the right of his spacecraft. "That might be where her body was laid to rest," ZacBox thought to himself as they flew over the cemetery, "but I know her spirit is with me now."

"They're HH-60 Pave Hawks!" John Paul shouted, pointing to his computer display which had rapidly matched the aircraft to images extracted electronically from Jane's Information Group. "The second slot from the right has been left open; you suppose that's for us?"

"Yep. They're PJ's," ZacBox said to his crew as he slipped the Electra into the formation.

"There's Saint Michael," Cadence said as she pointed to the nearest helicopter to their left. ZacBox watched as the helicopter side door opened and the helmeted crewman with a beard stepped out onto the left skid rail with his good leg and then held his thumb up in salute as they flew over the crowded football stadium. "The Guardian Angels wanted to make sure we had a fitting sendoff," Cadence replied as she waved at the helicopter crews through the thick glass of the saucer.

ZacBox jiggled the flying saucer slightly from side to side, acknowledging Saint Michael's thumbs-up signal. Once they were south of the stadium he slowly eased the yoke back to gain altitude, breaking formation and then banked the spacecraft to the west. "There's the Garden of the Gods," ZacBox said as he watched the image on the Electra's main display screen tracing the earth's energy field. "We'll follow that ley line running along the front of the red rocks, then head west over the town of Manitou Springs and begin a spiral ascent around Pikes Peak."

"Look at that!" John Paul said as he pointed to the electromagnetic field that enshrouded Pikes Peak. "No wonder Tesla came here to conduct his experiments."

"It is made of granite," Arjun commented, as he absorbed the view.

ZacBox continued to gradually gain altitude above 15,000 feet to where he could fly over the glistening Summit House atop Pikes Peak. He saw the four-lane ribbon of silver pavement below. Highway 24 went up and over Ute Pass toward the high meadows of South Park where his ancient great-grandfather's Ute ancestors once hunted food for survival. White Elk had told ZacBox stories about the many battles the Ute had with the Cheyenne, Arapaho, and Comanche tribes over the Ute's sacred hunting grounds. He wondered how many warriors had been killed in this age-old competition over scarce resources. He questioned if he could kill to defend his tribe; his answer would come soon enough.

A pair of F-22 Raptors flew up beside them; the pilots gave their spacecraft a visual inspection, followed by the universal hand signal for okay. They wished them well with a farewell salute of respect. ZacBox continued south-southwest, toward the Four Corners of Colorado. He accelerated the flying saucer above the Shining Mountains, heading toward where his great-grandfather lived on the Reservation south of Cortez, Colorado. As they neared the small town of Towaoc, ZacBox slowed the Electra and dropped in altitude to where he was flying just 300 feet above the tree tops, following the nape of the earth. He could see White Elk's small blue house in his modest neighborhood, as he banked the flying saucer to the right, so he could see out the windows. The driveway was empty. ZacBox turned the saucer further to the right, gained altitude, and aimed at the saddle just below the elbow of Sleeping Ute Mountain.

"There he is," ZacBox said as he spotted White Elk's old black pick-up truck parked along the dirt road at the top of the ridgeline. White Elk knew this was ZacBox's mid-point during his training runs. Now ZacBox was close enough to the ground that he could see his great-grandfather; a large bird of prey was sitting on his shoulder. It was a young eagle. As the Electra approached, ZacBox watched as the young eagle leaped into the air, flapped its wings, and flew off to the west toward the Blue Mountains in Utah, the sacred Bear's Ears.

ZacBox smiled and pulled back on the yoke, accelerating and climbed effortlessly above 83,000 feet, before leveling off to where they could see the curvature of the earth. Now came their next visual inspection, in the form of a Lockheed Martin RQ-3 DarkStar. At 45,000 feet the sleek reconnaissance unmanned aerial vehicle, or UAV, pulled up beside them for one last look before the Electra headed into near-earth orbit. The RQ-3A jiggled her wings and then dropped away back toward planet Earth. The Electra's crew leaned back in their seats as ZacBox accelerated faster and tilted their spacecraft toward the heavens.

Within two and a half minutes the Electra had reached low Earth orbit or LEO, where ZacBox leveled off at an altitude of 807 miles above the Earth.

"There they are Captain," Anzu reported, "dead ahead."

"I see them," ZacBox acknowledged. "John Paul, you'll take the first shot, target the one in the lead. I'll take the second shot, at the middle one. Anzu, you take the third shot on the last one and clean up any John Paul and I may have missed. Three-round bursts. On my command. Fire!"

All three of John Paul's shots missed the aging Chinese communications satellite. The Chinese government had three older communications satellites they planned to decommission and offered them up for the Electra's crew to live-fire their weapons systems in space. Knowing this might be the one and only time the crew had to test their weapons, Dr. Hubble had jumped at the opportunity. She had coordinated a date, time and precise location in space for the three comms satellites to drop out of geostationary orbit or GEO, at about 22,236 miles above the Earth's rotation, where they would hopefully burn up entering the Earth's atmosphere. Whatever debris remained was aimed toward the center of the Pacific Ocean. Most of the debris was likely to be incinerated if the satellites were broken up prior to plunging into the Earth's atmosphere.

"You have to lead them more," Anzu instructed so ZacBox could adjust his aim.

ZacBox fired the external-mounted ion canon as the crew watched two of his three rounds slammed into the second Chinese communications satellite. The satellite burst apart, but there was no fireball or explosion. The remaining fuel on board had already been bled off as it was deorbiting, and with no oxygen, there was no fire.

"Switching select-fire to singleshot," Anzu said as she glanced toward Captain ZacBox for approval.

"Go," he replied.

Anzu's first shot hit her target dead center; then she rotated her external gun port toward the first satellite dropping rapidly out of range. The crew could feel a slight bump with each shot of the ion cannon and now recognized the familiar "boom" sound as the round left the muzzle of the cannon. They watched as her shot impacted the satellite, and thousands of metal pieces from the three aging satellites began to ignite as they rained down into the Earth's atmosphere below.

"Nice shooting," ZacBox said, complimenting his security officer.

"Let's hope that's the last time the ion cannons need to be fired on this mission," Arjun said as he contemplated the dangers of their mission and tried to visualize the faces of their alien enemies out there somewhere in the dark.

"Next stop the ISS," ZacBox said, as he directed the Electra upward toward the stars.

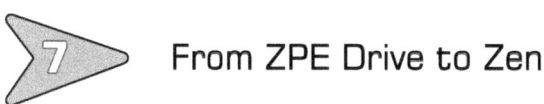

7 From ZPE Drive to Zen

It had been a busy morning, ZacBox thought to himself, as Electra's crew scanned the horizon for a visual on their next planned stop-over—the International Space Station, the ISS. This short stop was the final stage of the Electra's training for the crew and shakedown flight for the spacecraft. After ZacBox and his crew departed from the ISS, there would be no turning back. Their flight plan called for a rendezvous in space, at the ISS's apogee of 853.8 miles, the furthest distance it reaches beyond the Earth's rotation. While the two spacecraft were tethered together in orbit, traveling at a speed of 17,150 miles per hour, two members of the Electra would don their space suits for a spacewalk to the ISS, while two members of the ISS crew, one Russian and one American, would put on their space suits to come aboard the Electra.

Unfortunately, the docking stations for the Electra and the ISS were not compatible, but taking precise measurements of Electra's docking port to accommodate future dockings with other Electra-class spacecraft was one of the objectives of this impromptu space visit. Another objective today was simply to deliver the mail. Eventually, the international space teams hoped to write the specifications for a universal docking station, a UDS, but for now the two spacecraft would have to be maneuvered to within fifty meters of one another and then sync up in parallel orbits. Once they were tied together, their two selected crew members could follow a thin steel tether connecting their spacecraft. At that speed and altitude, every rotation around the Earth would take only 92 minutes before returning to their starting point in space, which had been previously selected by the ground crew as an ideal site for the Electra's journey into deep space.

Two orbital rotations, 184 minutes, was all the time Dr. Hubble said could be spared from the Electra's rescue mission. Captain ZacBox would have to have his two crew members back onboard, disconnect the two spacecraft, and be ready to launch into outer space at the top of the apogee in 3 hours and 4 minutes. The digital clock on his cockpit display monitor was counting down. Not wanting to risk any radio communications being intercepted by the Centaurians, it was predetermined there would be no electronic transmissions exchanged between the ISS and the Electra.

As the ISS extended her long white robotic arm outward toward the Electra, the red Canadian maple leaf became visible against the gleaming white apparatus. ZacBox could see the hook at the end of the tether was being brought over by one of the ISS spacewalkers to be attached to his spacecraft. The crew of the Electra watched as two ISS astronauts in their white spacesuits floated out of an open hatch beneath the ISS. One astronaut stayed at the end of the fully extended robotic arm, now only 20 meters from the Electra, while the other clutched the tether hook and fired a small jetpack on his suit propelling him toward the Electra.

ZacBox had decided he would remain aboard the Electra to welcome the two astronauts aboard for a short visit. As captain he had asked Arjun and Cadence to pay his respects to the ISS commander and deliver a care package sent up from Earth, including some special gifts from Reggie. John Paul and Anzu remained on the Electra with ZacBox to welcome her two space visitors from the ISS, flight engineer Sergey Noviskiy and science officer Brian James. ZacBox watched out the window as Arjun and Cadence, wearing their space suits, were guided by the tether attached to the robotic arm to the open hatch of the ISS.

"If you start to feel sick, don't look down; look away from the Earth's surface," Cadence said to Arjun over the secure comms system embedded in their helmets.

"I can't help myself," Arjun said back. "It's so beautiful, it's mesmerizing! It doesn't feel like we're traveling over 17,000 miles per hour; it feels just like being back onboard the Electra, like we're barely moving at all." He was right. The effects of flying thousands of miles per hour in space felt like you were riding in a car other than being pushed back in your seat when you accelerate or leaning to the side when you are turning. Sitting inside a car feels like you are not moving even though your car may be traveling at 75 miles per hour down a highway.

John Paul monitored the ECU to pressurize the internal chamber of the docking station. He gave a thumbs up signal to the two space visitors letting them know it was okay to remove their space suits. Anzu stepped inside the docking chamber to help Sergey and Brian with their space suits. ZacBox watched their progress on his forward monitor screen and glanced at the countdown clock: 132 minutes and counting. When ZacBox saw they were ready to enter the bridge, he stood up from his captain's seat and met them as the cockpit doors spread apart. Both astronauts stepped forward on unsteady legs.

"It's nice to feel gravity again, even if it is artificial gravity," Brian said as he extended his hand toward ZacBox. "Captain ZacBox, my shipmate and I request permission to come aboard."

"Permission granted," ZacBox said as he shook hands with the two ISS astronauts.

"Thank you for having us aboard, Captain ZacBox," Sergey, a Russian cosmonaut, said with passably good English as he observed the saucer's interior. "What a marvelous vessel."

"Come," ZacBox said as he led the two guests toward the galley, "your families sent each of you a care package, and Chef Reggie Barnhill prepared a special lunch for us to enjoy."

On the way to the galley, ZacBox gave Sergey and Brian a short tour of the Electra. This wouldn't take long since the crew compartments were all on one level. Then he led them into the galley where he invited them to take a seat in the booth. Anzu, John Paul and ZacBox served their guests first, and then sat down next to them in the booth.

ZacBox explained what Chef Reggie had prepared: "Honey glazed salmon with angel hair pasta, fresh asparagus spears, tossed green salad with Italian dressing and strawberry cheesecake for dessert." ZacBox watched the two astronauts as they stared at the fresh food. "I understand Reggie polled each of your mothers to get a consensus on what we should serve today."

"This is quite a feast for us," Brian said, without taking a bite.

"Actually, anything not squeezed out of a tube is a delicacy," Sergey added with a laugh.

ZacBox noticed neither man were eating and kept looking down at their plates. "Would you like to say grace?"

"No," Brian replied, "it's not that, we all do that privately, each in our own way."

ZacBox watched as the astronauts glanced toward where their

crewmates remained aboard the ISS.

"Don't worry," ZacBox said. "Reggie sent up plenty for them as well. If I'm not mistaken your crewmates are probably enjoying lunch with Arjun and Cadence now, and I'm sure Chef Reggie sent plenty for leftovers. Please dig in."

With a nod of gratitude, both men hungrily dug into their salads, salmon and the wonderful angel hair pasta.

"Anyone want my radishes?" Arjun asked.

"Sure," Brian replied as he picked them off the top of Arjun's salad.

"You should eat them; they're good for you," Sergey said with a smile.

"Eat your vegetables; you sound like my mother," Arjun teased back.

Over lunch the two crews of the ISS and the Electra talked about their families, their backgrounds, and where they went to school, but they avoided talking about their mission. As John Paul served the cheesecake, Sergey and Brian decided they couldn't wait to open their care packages sent up from their families on Earth.

Sergey went first. "Caviar!" he shouted. "Beluga Sturgeon, my favorite!" he said as he held up the small blue tin with the gold lettering. "And crackers, and here's a photo of my daughter, Alexie; she just turned two, and here," Sergey said as he held up a scented notecard to his nose, "well here's a note from my wife; I'll save this for later. You go now Brian, what you get?"

The tough marine colonel unwrapped the small black 10-inch square box, lifted the lid and removed an urn. He read the notecard attached to the top silently and placed the urn back in the box, replaced the lid and wiped a tear from the corner of his eye. "These are the ashes of my grandfather, Naval Commander Jackson James. He was an Annapolis graduate. He died three months ago in hospice, while I was stationed up here. I wasn't able to attend his funeral services back home in Tennessee. He always dreamed of going to space. Grandpa encouraged me to apply to Annapolis when I was in high school and wrote countless letters of recommendation for me to get into the astronaut program. Now, thanks to all of you, he's here in space with me. I can't thank you enough for this. Thank you."

"We are honored we could help him fulfill his dream," ZacBox said.

BeeBot waddled into the galley and leaned his head against Brian's shoulder. "Who's this little guy?" Brian asked.

"This is BeeBot, he's part of our crew," ZacBox explained.

"What does he do?" Sergey asked.

"Well," ZacBox said with a laugh, "we're not exactly sure. But whatever it is we think it might be important."

"Here you are," John Paul said, placing the cheesecake on the table in front of their guests. "Now, who wants fresh strawberries and whipped cream on top?"

After dessert, Brian James asked ZacBox if he could speak to him privately. ZacBox agreed and asked John Paul to show flight engineer Sergey Noviskiy what they had learned about the Electra's docking station. Anzu offered to clean up their dishes, one of the many chores the Electra's crew, including her captain, rotated daily.

ZacBox had been briefed that Brian was a Lieutenant Colonel in the U.S. Marines and led him to the captain's quarters. Then he pushed the button that closed and sealed the cabin's doors behind them, "It's soundproof," ZacBox said, noticing the marine looking around the interior of the cabin.

"Very well," Brian said, satisfied their conversation would not be overheard. "Captain ZacBox, after you launched this morning I received an encrypted top-secret message. While I cannot disclose our methods or sources, since you do not hold the proper security clearances, I have been directed by my commanding officer to inform you, as captain of the Starship Electra, that the alien ship on orbit around Neptune broke out of orbit early this morning and appears to be headed toward the planet Jupiter."

"They must be going after Jorvik."

"One more thing you should know, the analysts with the unnamed intelligence agency who deciphered this message intercepted from space, believe the name of the alien who gave that order translates to something like Zhorban the Merciless. I wish I and a few of my Marine buddies were going with you, Captain; we'd like to meet this Zhorban."

"I wish you were coming along too, but I'll bet this Zhorban the Merciless never tangled with a Samurai before," ZacBox said. Then he asked the Colonel, "Is the ISS armed?"

"It is not," Brian replied. "Ours is a humanitarian mission; weapons are prohibited. The crew of the ISS will remain here on board and on orbit, providing an early visual warning to alert all nations of any unwelcomed or hostile enemy spacecraft approaching Earth. You are the only manned spacecraft between the aliens and us. After you and your crew, we are the only manned spacecraft to stand in the way of these invading aliens and planet Earth."

"What do you think they want?"

"Best guess is after they take out our spacebased assets, they will try to kill off all of us who will resist. Everyone else will be forced into slave labor, possibly to harvest gas and oil."

"That seems consistent with what we've been told," ZacBox said shaking his head in agreement. "The spectral analysis of the alien spacecraft's exhaust trail suggests it is driven by fossil fuel, which can't last forever on any planet."

"Captain, we are aware that you are armed, and we monitored

your weapons system test closely this morning. Downing three satellites in less than seven seconds is pretty impressive shooting in my book, Captain ZacBox. But you may be going up against a formidable adversary. As marines, we are trained in a variety of weapons systems, and although I am not personally familiar with the weapons onboard your ship, I may be of some assistance to your Chief of Security. With your permission, Captain, I would like to discuss your defensive and offensive weapons capabilities with Anzu Gozen, Electra's Chief of Security."

"Permission granted," ZacBox said. "We are all in this together, and any advice you can share with us would be greatly appreciated."

ZacBox pushed the button to open the door and returned to the galley where Anzu was nearly finished cleaning up the dishes. "I can finish up here Anzu, would you please show the Colonel our weapons systems?"

"Very well," Anzu said as she led the Colonel to the front of the ship and sat down in her crew seat. Colonel James stood behind her and watched as she explained her dashboard. "We do have a force field that offers us some protection from smaller meteors but we don't have any idea how well it will hold up against enemy fire. Actually, we don't even know what they will be firing at us. This is the ion cannon, the weapon we used this morning to down the three Chinese satellites. It can be operated from here or by the Captain seated behind me or by the Chief Engineer seated to my right." Anzu nodded her head toward John Paul as he took his seat beside her in front of the captain's seat.

"How does it work?" Brian asked.

"John Paul?" Anzu asked, deferring the Colonel's question to the Chief Engineer.

"From what we have been able to determine, the main guns consist of four externally-mounted ion cannons, one on each side of the ship, one forward-mounted and one rear-mounted. They are rechargeable." To get a closer look, Brian walked over and stood behind John Paul's seat as he rotated view screens to each of the four firing positions. Crosshairs appeared on the large hi-res screens obviously intended for targeting. Brian noticed John Paul had his briefcase open on his console and recognized the Presidential Seal embossed on a small cream-colored envelop attached to a divider in the top of the briefcase with a gold paperclip.

"That envelope came from the Oval Office," Brian commented. John Paul removed the envelope and handed it to the astronaut. He opened the envelope, removed a small note card and read the handwritten note aloud, "To Wernher von Braun, with great appreciation. John F. Kennedy." He replaced the notecard back into the envelope and handed it back to the fifteen-year-old engineering prodigy. "You are related to that von Braun?"

"Yes," John Paul said modestly, "he was my great-grandfather. This was his briefcase; my family presented it to me when I was selected to be part of this crew."

"What's the story with the gold paperclip?" Brain asked.

"When my great-grandfather was trying to arrange for his surrender and that of his team of engineers and technicians to the Americans, near the end of WWII, he met secretly in his office in Germany with representatives of the U.S. military. Had Adolph Hitler discovered my great-grandfather and his team of rocket scientists, technicians and engineers were trying to defect and take whatever technical drawings, blueprints and other plans they could carry with them, he would have had them executed or placed in concentration camps. They had already decided they didn't want to be taken prisoners by the Russian army, no offense Sergey," John Paul said looking at the Russian astronaut.

"None taken," Sergey replied.

John Paul continued, "They needed a code word for their secret operation, which was intended to transport his team of scientists, technicians and their immediate families out of Germany and sneak them into Argentina where they would be turned over to the Americans. My great-grandfather reached over and picked up that paperclip off his desk and suggested the code name 'Operation Paperclip.' When John F. Kennedy was President, he met many times with my great-grandfather while planning the mission …"

Brian interrupted and finished John Paul's sentence, "To land a man on the Moon and return him safely to Earth? So, it's true, Wernher von Braun was instrumental in helping guide President Kennedy in creating your space program?"

"Yes," John Paul said, "my great-grandfather was there in 1961 when JFK addressed a Joint Session of Congress. After the President delivered his speech my great-grandfather presented him with this paperclip. The President had it gold-plated and returned it to him in this envelope with this handwritten notecard. It's been here in his briefcase ever since."

Brain said, "Many credit Wernher von Braun as being the father of the American space program."

"He died before I was born, but I know he would be proud of what we are doing here today. When my grandfather handed me this briefcase he said we stand on the shoulders of many giants in the space program and challenged me to make them proud," John Paul said and turned back to his workstation. John Paul touched his monitor screen to flick an image depicting a cross-section of the ion cannon onto the main view screen in front of the cockpit. John Paul stood and walked over to point at the image on the large hi-res view screen as he continued, "Each cannon has 18 chambers designed to revolve around, and run parallel to, the base of an 8-foot barrel. The interior of each cannon barrel appears to have been grooved internally to cause the ion shots to spiral as they go downrange, kind of like throwing a football in a spiral to improve accuracy, much like most firearms on Earth use today. The ions are trapped, cooled and then housed inside each of these 18 chambers. The rounds are ignited electronically and emit a sound similar to the electrical zapping noise of an arc welder, followed by a boom once they are fired."

Anzu stood and walked over to the other side of the forward view screen, "Each cannon can be fired in single shot, three-round bursts or fully automatic mode," she said pointing to an enlarged view of the cross-section of the ion cannon. "Each cannon has one central mounted laser, but it appears to be intended more for range-finding than to be used as an auxiliary weapon."

"If the laser is held long enough in one place, could it be used to cut through the hull of a spacecraft or a space suit?" Sergey asked as he joined the conversation, having completed a detailed inspection of the docking station with Captain ZacBox.

"I don't know," Anzu acknowledged as she studied her visual color-coded dashboard. "There does appear to be a dial here to boost the gain on the laser. It might cut through a space suit but probably not the hull of a ship, at least not one as thick as the Electra's. The ISS might be a softer target."

"Well, we still have to live aboard the ISS, so let's hold off on trying that experiment out for the time being!" Sergey joked,

The crew laughed together as ZacBox took note of the time remaining on the countdown clock; 58 minutes.

"I might advise caution when firing the forward mounted cannon," Brian said as he examined the view screen. "I don't see anywhere where you can monitor shot velocity or terminal distance, but you don't want to fire a shot then accelerate so fast that your ship overtakes the speed of your round."

"Good advice, Colonel," ZacBox said, "Thank you. I would not have thought of that—anything else?"

"Yes, one other thought. How long does it take for the ion cannons to recharge?" Colonel James asked, seeing ZacBox looking at the countdown clock.

"Three seconds per chamber," Anzu said, adding, "If all 18 rounds are fired at once, it may require up to 54 seconds before the ion cannon is reloaded and ready to fire again."

"Captain, if you get caught waiting for your ion cannons to recharge, you may want to consider rolling your ship out and coming about sharply, in an inverted figure eight," the Marine Colonel suggested, demonstrating with his hands. "The old sea captains would sail alongside an enemy warship to fire their first broadside. They would then come about as quickly as they could and fire a second barrage from their other side when they sailed past the enemy ship a second time, while the first rank of cannon was being reloaded."

"Good suggestion, thank you, Colonel," ZacBox said as he tucked this new battle tactic away in the back of his mind. "We better start wrapping this up, but before you go, Anzu, you might mention the torpedoes."

"Yes, Sir," Anzu agreed as she brought up another visual display on her monitor, "We haven't tested them yet, but it looks like we have a full complement of 18 neutrino torpedoes. Nine are preset to explode upon impact, six are set to detonate upon demand by pushing this button here and three appear to be configured with a timer for detonation, which we theorize could be used for laying a minefield."

"That brings up a question, Colonel," ZacBox said, "Would using torpedoes in space to mine the entrance or exit of a wormhole be considered to be illegal or immoral?"

"That's a legitimate question, Captain ZacBox," Colonel James acknowledged as he stood up, looked at the fifteen-year-old Captain and reframed the question. "Is mining a wormhole against the Geneva Convention? I doubt anyone ever thought of that before, but my gut tells me the Geneva Convention's intergalactic counterpart is one day going to have to grapple with that and many other ethical issues. My experience as a warfighter tells me there are often a lot of unintended causalities associated with a minefield, including allies and civilians. I'm not sure what to advise you there, I guess you'll have to follow your gut instincts. I think Sergey and I had best get off your ship. If I'm not mistaken, you have a stranded Pleiadian to rescue."

"It's been a pleasure to have you aboard, Brian and Sergey," ZacBox said as he escorted the American astronaut and Russian cosmonaut to Electra's air lock in the docking station where their space suits were waiting.

"If you're ever in the neighborhood please drop by again," Sergey said with a laugh.

As ZacBox watched the astronauts depart the Electra, he saw Arjun and Cadence were already making their way back from the ISS. He glanced at the countdown clock: 39 minutes to apogee.

Arjun and Cadence were excited to tell all the things they had learned from their short visit aboard the ISS. They shared how appreciative the ISS crew members were to receive the packages from their families and how they enjoyed the wonderful meal Reggie had prepared. ZacBox wanted to hear all the details, but nodded toward the countdown clock, "3 minutes to apogee. We best ready the ship for launch and then take our seats."

Anzu did a visual inspection out the portside window to make sure the robotic arm of the ISS had retracted the tether cable and waved at the other spacecraft as the Electra began to slowly float away. "Cleared to launch Captain," Anzu acknowledged as she buckled herself tightly into her seat. ZacBox glanced around at the faces of his four crewmembers, as they looked to him for any last minute orders.

"Next stop Jupiter," ZacBox said as he slowly pulled back on the yoke with his left hand and accelerated by pushing the throttle forward with his right, guiding the Electra toward the stars.

September 1st, 15:05 hours Astradate 11090.1
Approaching the darkside of Earth's Moon

The flight path of the Electra called for leveraging the centripetal force of the moon's gravity to accelerate the flying saucer and slingshot the starship into deep space. Once they were well away from the moon's gravitational force, ZacBox would need to incrementally increase their speed using the Electra's ZPE propulsion system. Professor Fibonacci had given the Electra's crew a crash course on Einstein's Theory of Relativity, but no one really knew how or if this was all going to work using an alien-built starship.

"To understand Einstein's concept of spacetime," she had begun her instructions saying, "think about a jet aircraft traveling at 500 mph; it could cross the continental U.S. in 4 hours, well below the speed of sound. Many people, including some very bright scientists, predicted at the time that man would never break the speed of sound. They thought that when they hit the sound barrier, their aircraft would break apart. Then, in 1947, U.S. Air Force ace, Chuck Yeager, proved the skeptics wrong by becoming the first pilot confirmed to have exceeded the speed of sound in level flight across the ground. To put things in perspective, the speed of sound is 741 mph; however, the speed of light is 186,000 miles per second—per second, not miles per hour. Traveling at light-speed you could circumnavigate Earth's equator 7.5 times in one second."

"Will we have to travel faster than the speed of light to rescue Jorvik in time?" ZacBox had asked during their training.

"Yes," Dr. Hubble had answered, "while we do not know for certain the speeds the aliens' spacecraft can travel, we must assume for them to have traveled the great distances between the stars, they almost certainly had to have traveled faster than light or FTL."

"But," Arjun said raising his hand in class, "how do we know for certain the Electra won't break apart when we reach FTL?"

"We don't," Dr. Hubble said.

"Here's the good news," John Paul said. "Traveling that fast we'll never know until it's over and if we were wrong, we won't feel a thing."

Professor Fibonacci said, "You should know there are many skeptics today, including one of my personal heroes, Dr. Neil de Grasse Tyson, who wrote in his wonderful little book, Astrophysics for People in a Hurry, that 'The Speed of Light: It's Not Just a Good Idea. It's the Law' and many people consider him to be one of the most gifted physicists of our time. I have consulted with several notable physicists, including the preeminent Dr. Richard J. Cook, another retired physics professor from the U.S. Air Force Academy, who also holds the distinction of professor emeritus. Dr. Cook agrees with my research findings—FTL is theoretically possible."

"To reach Jorvik in time," Dr. Hubble reiterated, "and to have the best chance of going on from there to the Pleiades Star Cluster and back in our lifetimes, you will need to exceed FTL."

"You should also know," Professor Fibonacci continued, "Einstein's Theory of Special Relativity includes what is referred to as time dilation. As you travel through space, then your time slows down. However, time on Earth continues at the same rate. When you return to Earth, you may have aged only three months, while everyone on Earth will have aged three years. 'Time is relative,' Einstein taught us. Therefore, spacetime, as he called it, is relative to whatever time it is at that place in space. This will be the most historic journey in the history of mankind."

"It is a mission to save mankind," Dr. Hubble added, "at least mankind as we know it."

ZacBox recalled in his mind that moment back on Earth when his courageous crew committed to their mission.

"I'm in," Anzu said as she stood up.

"Me too," Cadence said as she also stood.

"Count me in," Arjun said and stood.

John Paul stood to join Anzu, Cadence and Arjun, saying "I wouldn't miss this ride for the world!"

ZacBox remembered when he too stood up, and said, "I'm in," as he looked into the faces of his four crewmembers, adding, "I just hope I don't let you down if we have to do battle against these aliens."

Anzu stepped forward, looked into the eyes of her shipmates and said confidently, "Ever since I was a little girl, I have been instructed in The Art of War, written by Sun Tzu. He taught 'Be positive at all times. If you expect to fail, you will. Before the battle begins, make sure you expect to win—then there will be no battle, for you will have won before it starts.'"

ZacBox remembered admitting that he didn't question any of their abilities, only his own.

He recalled how Cadence stepped forward next and placed her hand gently on his shoulder, saying, "It is only natural to question if we are the best people for such an important mission. I question if I possess all the medical skills necessary should one of you become sick or injured. All I can do is promise you I will do the very best I can every waking moment of our journey, whether our journey be long or short."

ZacBox recalled Anzu's words of strength and Cadence's words of comfort often. It was reassuring to him knowing he was in the company of such a talented and dedicated crew. He gained confidence knowing they were beside him and soon realized there wasn't another young person anywhere on planet Earth he would rather be leading on this mission to do what many people thought was impossible. John Paul had calculated that even traveling FTL they would not reach Europa for two months, three weeks, one day, seven hours and eleven minutes.

But first they needed to see if Electra's ZPE-driven powerplant was capable of achieving F3, and even at that speed their flight would require 12.6 hours to reach Earth's moon. The five crewmates buckled themselves into their seats. ZacBox looked out the forward row of windows at the tiny crescent-shaped white moon off in the distance. He thought of the first radio transmission from the lunar surface, "The Eagle has landed." That mission took extraordinary courage. "So will this one," he thought as he looked at the stoic faces of his four crewmembers. The distance to Earth's moon paled in comparison to the distance to Jupiter. But as White Elk taught him, "Each journey begins with a single step."

"Prepare to engage ZPE thrusters," Captain ZacBox said to his crew. ZacBox noticed BeeBot had buckled himself into the harness of a jumpseat located to the left of Arjun. When he looked at the AI, it patted its protruding belly where the crystal orb had been safely tucked away during their flight. "Engage," ZacBox announced as he pushed the throttle forward to accelerate from F1 to F2. But nothing happened. ZacBox pushed the throttle to F3 and still nothing happened. "What the heck?" He said, and then looked toward John Paul. "What am I missing here?"

"I don't know, Captain," John Paul said as he went through his preflight checklist another time.

"Disengage the ECU," he told John Paul, "Maybe zero-point-energy only works in zero gravity."

"Good thought," John Paul said as he deactivated the ECU's artificial gravity capability.

The crew felt their bodies becoming weightless for the first time and watched as a pen John Paul had been writing with began to float across the cabin.

ZacBox caught the pen, floated it back toward John Paul, and then asked his crew, "Other thoughts please? This is going to be a long flight to the moon, and we'll never reach Jorvik if we don't get this ZPE thing figured out."

Cadence and Anzu both shook their heads from side to side.

"Maybe whatever it is that excites the crystals has not engaged," Arjun suggested.

"What is it that excites the crystals then, do we know?" ZacBox said.

"I don't know; it might be dark energy, a companion to dark matter, but we don't know enough about any of this," Arjun said as he unbuckled his seatbelt and started toward the engine room located in the back of the ship between the captain's and crew's quarters. "I'll look again, but I don't know what I'm looking for."

"I'll go with you," John Paul said as he unbuckled his seatbelt, used the back of his seat for a springboard and started floating toward the rear of the ship.

"We'll all go," ZacBox said as he, Anzu and Cadence unbuckled their seatbelts and floated across the cabin toward the engine room. Even BeeBot unbuckled his harness and floated with the rest of the crew toward the back of the ship.

"There," Arjun said as he pushed the blue diamond-shaped button that opened a chamber surrounded by the beautiful colored crystals. They heard a hissing sound as air escaped from the chamber. "When the crystals vibrate they would need air to emit vibrations, but I think there must be something missing. It looks like something should fit into this void area in the center."

"But what could it be?" ZacBox said as he looked around at the empty faces of the crew.

BeeBot tugged on his pant leg, "Not now BeeBot," ZacBox said impatiently. "We're kind of busy here."

BeeBot tugged again on ZacBox's pant leg, and then pointed at his protruding belly, "Bee. Bee!"

The crew watched as the pearl colored orb floated freely from the pouch in the front of BeeBot's belly and began spinning slowly as it floated toward the open chamber lined with various colored crystals. The orb began rotating horizontally and then lowered itself gently into the chamber. The orb fit like a glove. As the orb rotated, the crystals in the chamber began vibrating and coming to life. As the jiggling intensified, the crystals began to emit the colors of the rainbow, filling the chamber with brilliant prism light. The collective vibrations of the beautiful crystals inside the drawer began to produce a soft hmmm, as the spacecraft itself began to also hum and come to life around them. The floor of the saucer below them and the ceiling above them compressed together with a slight hissing sound, as the row of windows retracted into the hull.

"That's it," Arjun said. "The vibration of the orb spinning is what excites the crystals! The crystals must somehow come into harmony with the universe when they're excited."

John Paul pushed the diamond-shaped blue button on the drawer again, causing it to retract back into the chamber. "I think we're in business!"

"Let's give it another go," ZacBox said as the crew floated back toward the forward cockpit area. Each crewmember delighted in experiencing zero gravity, as their blue Bot showed how to do a summersault as he floated into the jumpseat next to Arjun. ZacBox remembered Dr. Hubble telling them that a nuclear-powered submarine, with its inches-thick dual-hulls, was the closest vessel man had ever built to what would be required for deep space travel. Although ZacBox had never been aboard a submarine, he imagined this was what it must feel like.

With the upper and lower hulls clamped together, the crew could no longer look out the windows to see what was around them, but the monitors in front of each of them gave them a clear 360-degree view around, below and above the saucer. As the crew buckled themselves back into their safety harnesses, they felt their seats recline further back. Footrests extended out of the floor, and they braced their feet naturally on the footrests and pushed their bodies back against their seatbacks. They knew they were in for a ride.

ZacBox pushed down on the saucer-shaped button on the center of his steering yoke and turned the knob two slots to the right, just like the center button on the video game the Eye of Taurus. Then he said, "Engaging ZPE thrusters!" as he pushed the throttle forward. Instantly the crew was pushed back into their seats and felt the rush of great acceleration.

"F2," John Paul announced, watching the numbers on the digital gauge climb, "F3!"

Although they understood they would not hear a sonic boom in space, the crew knew they had just surpassed the speed of sound and would eventually reach the speed of light.

"Alright!" Arjun shouted as he rammed his fist into the air.

ZacBox glanced over at Arjun, "Sorry, Captain," Arjun said with a sheepish grin, "I couldn't help myself."

"That's alright, First Officer Basu," ZacBox said, "I couldn't have said it better myself." ZacBox felt the Electra was solid as a rock, and then pushed the throttle forward past F3.

"F5," John Paul continued to read aloud, "leveling out at F5, Captain."

The crew could no longer feel any acceleration, but after-half-an hour they knew they were making great progress as they watched the image of the lunar surface slowly coming toward them on the large view screen in front of the cockpit. As they flew toward the moon, ZacBox guided the Electra through a series of graceful maneuvers, culminating in a double barrel roll.

"Now that's what I'm talking about!" Arjun shouted.

"Better than any ride at Disneyland," Cadence said.

"And no lines!" Anzu added, as the excited crew rejoiced in laughter.

Then the crew grew silent for several minutes simply enjoying their ride in space.

John Paul was the first to break the silence, "Anyone hungry for cheese pizza?"

"Sounds good to me," Arjun said, "but, delivery doesn't seem to be an option."

The crew laughed together until tears came to their eyes.

"Give me fifteen minutes," John Paul said as he reactivated the ECU's artificial gravity. "Reggie gave me his famous recipe for marinara sauce."

The Mano Machine, being developed on Earth through reverse engineering, was one of Electra's advanced technologies the cadets at the Academy were most excited about. This onboard food-producing device was cable of growing a sufficient amount of protein daily to sustain a crew of five indefinitely during deep space travel. The Electra's powerplant also burned hydrogen, H, which helped steer the spacecraft in the vacuum of space. When hydrogen, H, is burned, it produces oxygen, O^2. When H and O^2 are burned together they can produce water, H^2O. The oxygen is medical-grade and the water comes out as pure filtered water. O^2 and H^2O, when coupled with the protein produced by the Mano Machine, are what the Electra's crew would need to feed and sustain them during deep space travel to the Pleiades and back again.

One challenge Electra's crew would have to address during their mission was that the Mano Machine was programmed to take itself offline to conduct an internal self-cleaning, which Wendy calculated would require 24 hours to complete. However, the machine was programmed to produce twice the quantity of protein on the sixth day before it went into its 7th-day self-cleaning cycle. The other problem was that the protein, in its raw form, tasted not just bland but simply awful. But that problem is what Chef Reggie and some of Professor Fibonacci's cadets had been working on the past several months at Fibonacci's Diner. The most popular food, at least to the cadets, was cheese pizza, which John Paul improved with Reggie's famous marinara sauce. Many cadets preferred to eat leftover pizza cold for breakfast or reheated it in the microwave for lunch.

As the crew unbuckled their safety harnesses and started toward the galley in the rear of the ship, ZacBox turned toward the little blue AI watching them from the jumpseat, "You got the helm Bot." ZacBox said after he had set the controls on autopilot. The crew could monitor the ship's progress from the galley or anywhere else onboard. Bot, being asked to fill in for Captain ZacBox, was thrilled as he leaped from his seat with great enthusiasm and settled into the captain's seat. Since Bot didn't need any water or protein to function, and Bee seemed to be rightfully positioned in the engine compartment where it served like the beating heart of the Electra's powerplant, ZacBox felt they were now in very capable hands.

As the five human crewmembers gathered around the booth in

the galley, John Paul served slices of cheese pizza and their flavored carbonated waters. Each of the crewmembers enjoyed rotating the cooking and kept up with their daily chores to keep the interior of the saucer clean and orderly while in space. The advantage of doing the cooking was that you got to fix whatever it is you liked to eat, and if another crewmember wanted something else they were welcome to fix that for themselves. However, they didn't get to opt out of the cooking and cleaning responsibilities. Cadence had encouraged them to eat together whenever possible, rather than to eat at their duty stations or in their cabins. This kept the crew on a healthy dietary schedule of three regular meals per day while creating three daily opportunities for team bonding.

During their brief training time together on Earth, Dr. Wendy Hubble taught them the meaning of the acronym SWAP; standing for size, weight and power. The size and weight of the spacecraft had a direct impact on the power required to launch the craft into space. Once they were in space, the Electra's power could continue moving her forward indefinitely. The maglev was intended to help the saucer lift off from a planet or moon's surface, and the external hydrogen ports positioned around the exterior of the craft were intended to help steer the saucer while they were in deep space.

Another game Professor Fibonacci had taught the crew was similar to Four Square, only instead of a square, she painted a circle on the ground divided into four equal pieces, like a pie. She used a red rubber ball, similar to what they played with in elementary school, that she called the conversation ball. The idea was to keep the conversation ball moving by bouncing the ball from one space to another by using the acronym FORM, which stood for "family, organizations, recreation and message." She taught them to keep the conversation flowing, using FORM and to make sure no one is left out of the conversation. She reminded them, "No one likes a ball hog."

"Cadence," Arjun asked, tossing the imaginary conversation ball into Cadence's square, "what are you going to be working on for the next two and a half months?"

"Well, with all of your permissions, I would like to access your medical records and monitor your physical conditions throughout our trip. As we all learned from Wendy, muscle atrophy is one of the greatest challenges for human beings during deep space travel. With the Electra's ECU, we have a wonderful opportunity to not only mitigate the risk of muscle atrophy but also to reverse that tendency. Wendy hosted a telecom for me with the Cleveland Clinic in the UAE. Several of the medical staff, engineers and former astronauts from the ISS participated. We believe by calibrating the ECU to mimic the gravity and environment conditions on Earth, you can maintain or possibly improve your physical condition for when we return to Earth."

"That will be very helpful," Anzu said. "Cadence, could you please pass me a napkin?"

"Certainly," Cadence said as she handed Anzu a cloth napkin. "Theoretically, it may be possible to conduct a spectral analysis from space of the planet or moon we plan to visit so that when we arrive, your bodies will be better adjusted to the gravity and atmospheric conditions you will encounter. Depending on the length of our mission, it may be possible to slowly improve your physical conditioning to exceed normal parameters."

"Could you give us an example?" Arjun asked.

"Sure," Cadence said as she picked up her glass and held it an inch above the table. "As you know, on Earth you can jump only so high, let's just say a foot. Since the gravity on Earth's moon is less, you might be able to jump 2 feet. While we don't know the precise gravitational pull on Europa, if it is less than half of the Earth's moon, you might be able to jump 4 feet off the ground. However, if John Paul can conduct a spectral analysis of the surface and atmosphere of Europa at a distance and continues to refine the results as we get closer, we might be able to exceed Europa's lunar conditions so that your endurance and strength might allow you to jump maybe eight feet off the ground and run several miles without getting tired."

"You mean when we return to Earth, I might finally be able to dunk a basketball?" ZacBox said as everyone laughed.

"It's certainly possible," Cadence replied, and then continued, "I recommend we schedule sleep into our daily routines, maintain a healthy diet and get sufficient exercise to improve our strength and conditioning, while minimizing stress. Further, if you are all in agreement, I will work with John Paul to slowly adjust the ECU to exceed the gravitational thresholds and atmospheric conditions of Europa in an attempt to improve our overall strength and endurance."

The crew enthusiastically agreed to participate in Cadence's study; after all, who doesn't want to improve their physical condition, especially if it can be done while you sleep?

"To help with sleep," Cadence continued, "I recommend we stay synchronized with our normal daily routines we all grew up with on Earth. If you need any help falling asleep I have brought several natural herbal teas and can program the ECU to play relaxing music in your cabins. I might also recommend trying aroma therapy if you still have trouble falling asleep. There is no reason why our overall health and physical conditioning can't be better when we return to Earth than when we left. One more thing we should prepare for, as you know if our round trip turns out to be, say for example nine months long, then we will have aged nine months. However, as you are aware, our friends and families back on Earth will have aged three years. Time everywhere is relevant to something. We will have some adjustments to make mentally as well as physically."

"You mean everyone I went to school with last year will have already graduated by the time we get back home?" ZacBox asked.

"Yep."

"And Mr. Bojangles, my six-month-old black lab puppy will be three years old?"

"Yep, and in dog years he'll be 21."

"Swell, even my dog will be older than me," ZacBox said.

"Well, look at the bright side," Arjun joked, "at least you'll finally be sixteen and old enough to get your drivers' license."

"Finally," ZacBox said as everyone laughed.

"How about you John Paul, what are your plans?" Cadence asked, tossing the conversation ball back into his court.

"I plan to write a white paper on the feasibility of providing free wireless electricity around the world, just like Tesla suggested over a century ago, and suggesting how we might be able to burn hydrogen to produce clean water and oxygen. Can you imagine if we eliminated our dependence on fossil fuels, improved our air quality and produced clean water and sufficient food to feed everyone on Earth, while minimizing fishing and farming? The implications are staggering! The political and technical challenges will shift from a competition over scarce resources to a fair distribution of abundant resources. We'll have to ensure the global business communities are financially incentivized to ensure a fair exploitation of the technical innovations the Electra offers. Jobs worldwide will need to shift from fishing, farming, mining, gas and oil to exploiting the advanced technologies that are sure to evolve from our mission, including AI."

The crew looked around to see where their little blue Bot was, and then laughed as they remembered he was flying the spacecraft.

John Paul continued, "Another challenge in the corporate sector will be to promote the advancement of these advanced technologies while protecting Intellectual Property, or IP. Turns out one of the reasons Saint Michael accepted a position with the Lockheed Martin Corporation is to help facilitate the exploitation of these emerging technologies. Saint Michael joined a division of Lockheed Martin that's firewalled off, or isolated physically and contractually, from other parts of the corporation, headed up by Billy Graham, a retired U.S. Navy Admiral."

"Sounds like a real evangelist," Arjun commented.

"Well, he's not related to that Billy Graham," John Paul replied, "but I understand he has a very loyal following within his business sector, called the SI. The SI has been contracted by the U.S. Government, for a 5-year period of performance, to help manage the transference of advanced technologies from the Electra to the corporate world and then into the not-for-profit sectors worldwide. After this 5-year period is up, the next best corporate athlete will have their chance at bat. Corporations will also be asked to pave the way for a fundamental shift in the global work force. Pay, benefits and retirement packages will all need to be improved, while the average work week will be reduced from 40 hours in the U.S., to 32 hours or less. The economic net effect will be more free time for things like entertainment and pleasure, creating more jobs and opportunities in those sectors. Music, dance and all the arts will flourish. How about you, Anzu, how are you going to spend the next couple of months?"

Anzu replied softly, "I study Japanese Zen, which gives insight into one's true nature, to perfect my abilities as a Samurai, and I will strive to paint a perfect butterfly."

"Oh," John Paul replied respectfully, "neither of those thoughts occurred to me." The crew laughed, and then John Paul tossed the imaginary conversation ball to Arjun. "How about you Arjun?"

"I will begin my research project for the capstone for my doctorate degree in geology, starting with the interaction between the light emitted from those beautiful colored crystals in the ZPE chamber and the pearl orb that together somehow create the vibrations to power this amazing spacecraft. Pearls, at least on Earth, start with some tiny grain of sand that finds its way into an oyster shell. The oyster naturally encases the foreign body in a thin layer of material that hardens over time. Each year the oyster adds another layer, just like a tree adds an annual growth ring every year. I believe Electra's pearl would have required thousands, maybe tens of thousands of years to be created and it appears to be perfectly round. To be perfectly round, I think it had to have been spaceborne. If I can prove how the orb excites the crystals, how the orb was created, and where to find more crystals, well perhaps our international space program might be positioned to help humankind make a quantum leap forward in technology."

"Geez, listen to all of you," ZacBox said with a half laugh. "I just want to pass the 10th Grade!"

After everyone stopped laughing, Arjun offered to help tutor ZacBox with his studies and monitor his and Anzu's GED examinations. Arjun liked to teach and he was really good at it. ZacBox and Arjun had met twice with Mr. Tuttle at DCC and together developed an academic strategy for the next three months for ZacBox to finish high school and pass his GED. If everything went well there was a possibility that when they returned to Earth, ZacBox might be able to fulfill his dream of attending the U.S. Air Force Academy.

"When we come out of ZPE drive," ZacBox said—no longer feeling compelled to add, "if"—in two months and three weeks from now, we need to be prepared to do battle and defeat the Centaurian ship before we can rescue Jorvik. I would like all of your initial inputs, but Anzu, I would like us to start our preliminary planning, with you as our Chief of Security."

Anzu pushed her plate away and folded her hands on the table before her, reflective in thought for a moment, and then began, "Sun Tzu taught, 'bring down your opponents by any means. Bring him down by deception, by craft, through uncertainty, through insecurity—better to bring him down than to bring you down.' Sun Tzu taught, 'Know your enemy. Know yourself.' We do not know this enemy. We must attack with great speed, daring and unpredictability."

"Thank you," ZacBox said turning to his First Officer who had raised his hand, "Arjun?"

"I advise starting with diplomacy Captain," Arjun said, intentionally not referring to ZacBox by his first name, even though ZacBox had become his closest friend over the past few months. "Try to engage the captain of the alien ship in conversation; ask him to state his intentions. If his intentions are hostile, then we destroy their ship. If they are not, we invite them under no uncertain terms to leave our solar system at once."

"I respectfully disagree, Captain," Anzu stated, "From their intercepted communications, we can only assume their intentions are hostile, and if they do leave, which would take critical time away from our rescue mission, there is nothing to prevent them from returning when we are most vulnerable on the surface of Europa. The risk is too great. We have the element of surprise on our side and must attack at the moment of first contact, when they are most vulnerable."

"John Paul?" ZacBox said turning to his Chief Engineer.

"I agree with Arjun; my spacetime computations suggest the

Centaurians will arrive approximately 18.6 hours prior to us coming out of ZPE, assuming an orbit around Europa. I calculate they will make at least one full rotation around Europa before they know where to land on the surface. They shouldn't be expecting another spacecraft anywhere in the vicinity. Best case scenario we come in from behind, on their six, but there are simply too many variables to predict where we will make first contact. I suggest you prepare for the worst; they will come at us head-on. If I were them, I'd want to know who we are and take the time to conduct a rapid SWOT Analysis, assessing our strengths and weaknesses, while probing for opportunities and threats. If you can engage them in communications, even for a few seconds, it will buy me a little time to scan their ship and probe them for weaknesses. You and Anzu should have your weapons locked and loaded, but try to wait before firing as long as possible."

"I will try to buy you as much time as possible," ZacBox said, turning to Arjun before adding, "while striving for a diplomatic resolution." Then turning to Anzu said, "As soon as we make contact with the alien ship you will target the enemy, and be prepared to fire, but we will hold our fire until we are fired upon. Thank you for your inputs; fortunately we'll have plenty of time to refine our battle strategy and diplomacy before we reach Jupiter," ZacBox said. "For now I suggest we all try to get some sleep. Bot can alert us to any problems. John Paul, let's deactivate the ECU's artificial gravity for tonight. In the interest of science I think we can afford the luxury of zero gravity for tonight, don't you Dr. Bahar?"

"I think zero gravity might help all of us fall to sleep tonight," Cadence said and then added with a smile, "Let's just not make it a habit."

As ZacBox prepared to float into his bunk, he remembered the package White Elk had delivered to his cabin before they left Earth.

He floated down and removed the black square box from where it had been tucked away in his bottom desk drawer. He pushed himself away from the desk with his toes and floated over to his bunk. He secured the web netting around his Pleiadian-sized bed to keep him from floating around his cabin while he slept.

ZacBox removed the lid of the box and a beautiful 10-inch handcrafted drum floated out of the box. It was made from a small hollowed-out tree trunk covered with a tan animal hide he suspected was elk. ZacBox ran his fingers over the leather stitching that White Elk had used to stretch the animal hide tightly across the top of the drum. ZacBox had no doubt every stitch had been carefully threaded by his great-grandfather during prayer. He turned the drum over and looked inside. Inscribed around the inside of the drum was his great-grandfathers handwriting using a wood burning tool. ZacBox read White Elk's words: "May you forever feel the beat of the drums and let your spirit dance in the wind." He read the words again, spoken as his great-grandfather would have said them aloud, cherishing the acceptance of the wind as the breath of Creator. ZacBox closed his eyes and thanked White Elk for this precious gift.

Then ZacBox looked inside the box and saw a drumstick and two small packages floating inside. ZacBox removed and opened the first small box. As he lifted the lid a beautiful gold St. Michael medallion on a chain floated free from the box. Now he understood it was Saint Michael who had placed the box in his cabin earlier that morning. ZacBox caught the medallion floating in front of his face and turned it over to read the inscription on the back, "These Things We Do, That Others May Live."

"Thank you Saint Michael," ZacBox whispered in gratitude as he slipped the glimmering gold chain around his neck. There was also a small notecard with an embossed logo of the U.S. Air Force

Pararescue Unit where his mother had been assigned when she died. The note card explained the design of the Pararescue emblem, "The angel holding the globe is emblematic of protection and rescue from danger. The red robe is significant of the valor with which the Air Rescue Service carries on its humanitarian mission. The blue shield is indicative of the sky which is the field of operations, and the golden light represents a ray of hope for those in need of the Air Rescue Service."

On the back of this notecard, ZacBox read a handwritten message, "Zac, you and your team are the golden light that offers humanity a ray of hope for those in need. Make us proud. Michael J. Sandoval." ZacBox closed his eyes again and whispered, "Thank you Saint Michael."

Then ZacBox opened the last box. He felt the black velvet box and opened it to find his mother's Distinguished Flying Cross inside. He fought back tears, thinking of his mother as a guardian angel watching over him and his crew. He closed the box and tucked it under his pillow held in place by Velcro strips on the back. He wouldn't need a pillow tonight, but knowing her medal was within reach comforted him. He clutched the St. Michael medallion around his neck and toyed with his drum watching it spin above his head.

While ZacBox drifted weightlessly above his bunk, he reviewed in his mind his crew's accomplishments for the day: they were the first documented humans to launch a flying saucer into space, and they shot down three aging Chinese communications satellites, had lunch with the crew of the ISS and surpassed the speed of sound on the way to the moon. But tomorrow, after they accelerated around the moon to gather sufficient speed, they had to achieve something no person on Earth had ever done—something many smart people say can't be done—they must travel faster than the speed of light.

As a crew they may never know if they had failed, but if they were successful, they would soon find themselves in orbit around Europa, two and a half months later, prepared to defeat an alien spacecraft and its crew while searching for the captain of Electra's downed sister ship Sterope.

8 ▷ Get your OODA Loop on

November 15th 07:43 hours UTC Astradate 11111.5
Starship Electra, Approaching Europa, Distant Moon of Jupiter

After two and a half months of planning and running computer simulations Captain ZacBox had to accept he and his crew were as ready as they would ever be to do battle with the Centaurian spacecraft standing between them and the rescue phase of their Return to Pleiades Mission. He had also accepted that given the odds of success, they were at a perilous disadvantage. ZacBox had studied the three components of warfare—the crew, the ship and the environment—from every angle he could conceive. The crew of the alien ship was far more experienced, this environment was unfamiliar to him and his crew, and the full capabilities of the Electra were as yet unknown. As captain, ZacBox would have to rely on his instincts to survive.

"Battle stations," Captain ZacBox ordered as he downshifted the Electra out of ZPE drive and entered orbit around Europa, the bluish ice-covered Moon of Jupiter.

"Enemy vessel dead ahead, Captain," Anzu announced as they came around the curvature of the giant gas ball planet known on Earth as Jupiter. "Markings on the hull indicate it is from the Omega NGC5139 Star Cluster; it is a Centaurian warbird."

"They are hailing us Captain," Cadence said as the crew watched the alien spacecraft break out of orbit and accelerate toward them rapidly.

"Put them on the main screen," ZacBox said to John Paul. The bridge of the enemy vessel appeared on the large hi-res screen in front of the crew. The captain of the enemy vessel was speaking to the Electra; however, the translation would take several iterative cycles before the Electra's automated communication system could lock on to a common language.

"Heave to and prepare to be boarded," the captain of the alien ship commanded.

"I'm afraid that won't be possible," ZacBox replied. "This is Captain ZacBox; we are on a humanitarian rescue mission and mean you no harm. To whom am I speaking?"

"I am Coda, captain of this starship, and if you do not surrender your ship this instant, you will be fired upon."

"Well, Captain Coda, that's not very friendly terms," ZacBox replied as he stalled, watching John Paul tap commands into his keyboard, trying to learn as much as he could about the Centaurians' capacities by remotely scanning the alien ship. The interior of the enemy spacecraft was dark and the captain was wearing a black helmet with a dark shield covering his face. There was a red emblem of some sort on his chest, reminding ZacBox of the red hour-glass shape on the underside of a black widow spider.

"Why," Captain Coda said, as he leaned forward menacingly in the captain's seat trying to get a closer look at the Electra's crew appearing on his monitor. "Why, you are just children! Where's the one who calls himself Jorvik? Perhaps he didn't survive the last time I shot down your puny spacecraft? I demand you put whoever is in charge of your flimsy little vessel on screen now!"

"Well, again, that would still be me; I am Captain ZacBox," ZacBox replied calmly, and then muted his mic and looked at Anzu. "Are your weapon systems locked on?"

"Affirmative Captain," Anzu said, "but the alien ship is closing fast. I advise we fire now or take evasive maneuvers."

"Stand by to fire, Chief Gozen, but only fire if we are fired upon," ZacBox directed. "John Paul, prepare the quark-jump drive for the three evasive leap maneuvers we practiced, 100 meters to port, just like our battle plan called for, but jump only if we are fired upon. If possible, John Paul, wait for Anzu to fire her three-round burst before you activate the three quark jumps. Arjun you know what to do," ZacBox said and then unmuted his mic and spoke directly to the enemy vessel closing fast, "Captain Coda, for the safety of your ship and crew we ask you to stand down from your hostile confrontations."

"HOSTILE CONFRONTATIONS! HA, HA, HA!" Captain Coda shouted and laughed menacingly. "I'll show you hostile confrontations, you insubordinate little Pejorative! FIRE!"

Arjun instantly switched off their camera projecting the interior of the Electra and shifted their main view screen to an exterior view of the alien vessel. Two fireballs shot out from under the enemy vessel and headed straight toward the bow of the Electra. Anzu fired a three-round burst from her ion cannon. Boom! Boom! Boom! As soon as the third round was away John Paul activated the quark jump drive. The Electra immediately jumped from where she had been, 100 meters to her portside. Quark jumps had only been thought theoretically possible for several decades, although some early experiments on Earth successfully had demonstrated particles could travel from one location, Point A, to another location, Point B, instantaneously. But only in the vacuum of space could a flying saucer travel from Point A to Point B without traveling the distance between these two points. Now the Electra would make another quark jump from Point B to Point C.

The Electra's crew watched anxiously as the two fireballs passed through where they had been a split second ago, at Point A, and then the alien warheads raced off into deep space. The Electra crew continued to watch as the enemy vessel performed exactly as Anzu had predicted and fired their next round of salvos at Point D, where their enemy had calculated the Electra saucer would be in space. During the last two weeks, the Electra's crew had carefully rehearsed this exact battle plan, leaning on Anzu's Art of War lessons from the writings of Sun Tzu; "Be mysterious rather than obvious. Pretend to be here when you are there. Be close when he thinks you're far, and far when he thinks you are close. Be unpredictable. Be frightening. Be daring."

In an unpredictable and daring maneuver, Captain ZacBox accelerated to F3 and aimed the nose of their flying saucer straight down toward the giant gas ball planet below them—Jupiter. "Anzu, could you see where your shots went?" ZacBox asked as he picked up more speed as Electra entered Jupiter's gravitational force field.

"I could not, Captain; I may have missed," Anzu replied, beginning to question her shooting abilities as she watched the undamaged alien vessel pursuing them on their rearview screen.

"You didn't miss," Cadence replied. "I watched all three of your shots bounce off their hull."

"That can't be good," Arjun said grimly, and then switched their main view screen to a split screen showing the view in front of them on the left screen and the rear view behind them on the right screen.

"Well, now we know where not to aim," ZacBox said calmly as he began a wide spiral Leilani Loop down and to the right, just like what Saint Michael had told him his mother used in the Middle East to avoid enemy ground fire. ZacBox dropped the Electra into the pinkish red and brown gas cloud enshrouding the planet Jupiter. Their hi-res color monitors went blank as they dropped into the thick layers of maroon colored haze. "John Paul, did you learn anything from your scan of their vessel and their maneuverability?"

"Beyond the obvious, that they're trying to kill us," John Paul began as he pointed excitedly to a green 3D illustration of the enemy vessel now closing on them from behind, "the front hull of their ship is super thick, nearly twice as thick as the hull along her sides, top or bottom. She might be a little top heavy as we get closer to the surface. She is approximately 3.7 times as large as the Electra, which suggests her turning radius is probably wider. I predict her most vulnerable structural component, as with almost every vessel ever built, will be her stern. Since we're no longer in the vacuum of space, I don't know how our quark-jump drive would work in all this soup. I think quark jumps are off the table. My only suggestion captain, as you well know, is that you are going to have to get inside this captain's OODA loop."

The OODA loop had been explained to them by Dr. Hubble during their training. Wendy said, "The OODA loop is the decision cycle of observe, orient, decide and act, developed by U.S. Air Force Colonel John Boyd, a fighter pilot and Pentagon consultant in the late 20th century on Earth. Colonel Boyd had flown multiple combat missions in World War II, the Korean War and the Vietnam War. The OODA loop theory states, 'Time is the dominant parameter.' The pilot who goes through the OODA cycle in the shortest time period prevails because his opponent is caught responding to situations that have already changed."

By invoking the series of three quark jumps, Captain ZacBox had now forced Captain Coda to shift from being the aggressor to having to respond to his adversary's actions. Colonel Boyd's combat lessons taught, "Observation: the collection of data by means of the senses. Orientation: the analysis of data to form one's current mental perspective. Decision: the determination of a course of action based on one's current mental perspective. And Action: the physical playing-out of the decisions. Get inside your opponent's OODA loop and the victory is yours."

Captain ZacBox had taken this lesson to heart. Unless conditions changed, unless he or Captain Coda disengaged and flew away, Captain ZacBox was now inside Captain Coda's OODA loop. It was only a matter of time before the Electra gained a firing advantage.

"They are gaining on us," John Paul said nervously. "The Centaurians are trying to take a shot at our stern Captain!"

"Good, let's slow down a little, bring them in closer," ZacBox replied, slowly pulling back on the chrome T-shaped throttle.

"What!" John Paul said as he turned to look at ZacBox sitting in the captain's seat behind him.

"Is that advisable Captain?" Arjun whispered to his friend sitting to his right.

"Let them think they're eventually going to overtake us," ZacBox replied as he continued in his downward spiral and bled off a little more speed by feathering the edges of the saucer. With each revolution of their downward spiral the distance between the ships tightened. Then it happened; in the deadly game of space chicken, Captain Coda blinked. As the alien ship captain followed the Electra racing toward the surface of Jupiter, he discovered his ship was not capable of turning tighter than his adversary. The Centaurian lost his nerve and pulled up out of the downward spiral. That was the break Captain ZacBox was looking for—their adversary was disengaging from the ever-tightening spiral and pulling up out of the gas cloud above Jupiter. When Captain Coda popped his spacecraft up above the gas cloudbank he glanced into his rearview monitor to find his adversary was right on his tail.

"Gozen, you may fire your neutrino torpedo when you are ready," Captain ZacBox ordered.

Anzu skillfully lined up her crosshairs between the three stern thrusters of the alien ship as it tried desperately to get away. Security Officer Gozen deftly squeezed off her fatal shot. "Torpedo away, Captain."

Captain ZacBox pulled the Electra up sharply to the right, so they wouldn't fly through the debris. The crew watched as the neutrino torpedo impacted the rear of the enemy spacecraft, precisely where Anzu had aimed.

KABOOM!!!

The Electra's hi-res monitors flashed white, before slowly reacquiring the image of the alien spacecraft. All the Electra's crew could see were three larger pieces of the spacecraft tumbling through space, being trailed by hundreds of smaller pieces of the ship in her wake.

"YES!" John Paul shouted as he unbuckled his shoulder harness and jumped up out of his seat with his hand raised high in the air to high-5 Anzu. "Nice shooting! Right up the wazoo!"

Anzu stared straight ahead at her monitor, ignoring John Paul's celebration.

"What?" John Paul questioned as he turned from Anzu's rebuke and looked into the somber faces of the three senior crew members seated behind him on the bridge. "What?" John Paul repeated as he shrugged his shoulders and said, "Hey, Anzu saved our butts! They got what was coming to them; if the roles had been reversed, they would be celebrating our deaths right now!"

"John Paul, it's not a video game," Cadence said patiently as she looked down toward their Chief of Security who had fired the fatal shot.

The crew grew quiet; John Paul looked from Anzu to the monitor in front of them as the pieces of the enemy ship continued to tumble out of sight. He stood there in silence not sure what to say or do, and then asked, "I don't understand. What am I missing?"

Arjun was the first to break the awkward silence, "John Paul, when you scanned the enemy vessel, did you count how many life forms were aboard?"

"Yes, seven."

"How many life forms are there now?" Cadence asked solemnly.

"Well, none," John Paul said as he glanced back at his monitor briefly to confirm and then looked back at his crewmates. "There are no survivors." John Paul nodded his head and sat down heavily in his seat to reflect on what they had just done.

Anzu bowed her head in silent prayer. When she finished, she explained softly, "I was taught to honor your adversary, both in life and in death. It is the way of the Samurai."

"John Paul," ZacBox said softly, as he unbuckled his shoulder harness and leaned forward to place his right hand on John Paul's shoulder, "combat and killing is new to all of us. We are each experiencing a range of mixed emotions. Like you, we're all extremely thankful to be alive, but taking seven lives doesn't feel like anything to celebrate, even if they 'had it coming' or even if they would have celebrated our deaths. Let us hope our actions in victory rise above what our enemy's behavior may have been in our defeat. Let us hope our actions in battle, and in victory, bring honor to our families and pride in the eyes of our honorable peers."

"I'm sorry everyone," John Paul said in a heartfelt apology. "On the screen it looked just like a video game. I guess I got carried away in the adrenaline rush. It won't happen again."

Anzu nodded her head toward John Paul, silently letting him know his apology was accepted.

"Now," ZacBox said, as he turned the Electra back toward Europa, "let's go find Jorvik."

November 15th 09:53 hours MDST Astradate 1111.5
Starship Electra, Approaching Jorvik's Landing, Europa, Moon of Jupiter

"He's more to the right," Cadence said.

"How can you tell?" asked Arjun.

"I feel him," Cadence answered. "Mr. Eriksson told us the Pleiadians communicate telepathically. He showed me how it had been done for thousands of years. I feel I am in communication with a higher life form now, coming from down there, on the surface of Europa. The feeling grows weaker or stronger as we get closer. He's more to the left now, beyond that hill."

"I have a possible bogie," John Paul said excitedly as he watched the image on his scanner come into view.

"Main screen," ZacBox said as the crew watched the image on the icy surface of Europa growing larger as they dropped closer. Following an energy line, ZacBox slowed, switched off the ZPE and engaged the maglev propulsion system. The top half of their flying saucer extended upwards 18 inches so that they could now see Europa's whitish-blue surface through the ship's 2-inch-thick windows. "We should start seeing a debris field, if the Sterope came in from this angle."

"No debris field, Captain," John Paul said as he scooted forward in his seat to get a closer look at his screen. "There! It's an Electra-class flying saucer! The ship seems to be relatively intact, and look, there is a single life form exiting the ship!"

"That's gotta be Jorvik," Arjun said.

"It is Jorvik," Cadence said as she opened her eyes. "We found him and he's grateful."

"I am surprised the Centaurians were not able to locate the downed saucer with their scanners before we got here," said Anzu.

"They either had just arrived on orbit," John Paul said, "or they didn't know what they were looking for on the surface. I entered the exact dimensions of the Electra spacecraft into our surface radar and directed our scanners to search for anything with similar measurements to the Electra that was emitting a heat signature. That's why we found it so quickly. It would have taken us much longer if the Sterope had broken up when it impacted the surface.

ZacBox set the Electra down within fifty feet of the Sterope and then turned to Cadence, "It looks cold out there; I would imagine we will need our space suits?"

"Yes, it is very cold on the surface, so you will need your space suits for warmth, air and protection; the icy crystals are razor sharp. However, I don't think your space suits will be needed below the surface. Scientists have predicted that below Europa's icy surface lies an ocean of liquid water capable of sustaining life. Electra's ECU has conditioned our bodies sufficiently to where we can maneuver below ground without our space suits, but shout out if you start feeling lightheaded or experience anything out of the ordinary. I will stay behind and monitor your progress; let me know if you need anything."

"I will stay with you," Arjun volunteered.

"Very well," ZacBox said. "Come, Anzu and John Paul, let's go meet Olaf's son."

Anzu retrieved her six-foot long naginata from her cabin and assumed her position behind and to the right of her captain. After putting on their space suits, Captain ZacBox, Security Officer Gozen and Chief Engineer von Braun climbed down from Electra's airlock and became the first Earthlings to walk on the surface of Europa in nearly a century. Thanks to Cadence's gradual manipulation of Electra's artificial gravity, the three crewmembers found the gravitational effect of Europa to be far less than they were used to aboard Electra. They easily bounced ten inches above the surface as they walked toward Electra's sister ship, Sterope, parked off their port side.

Upon approaching the Sterope, the three crew members of the Electra stopped to watch a large male figure descend out from under the flying saucer, also wearing a space suit. When the Pleiadian stepped out from under the ship, he stood up to his full height and waved with both hands above his head. From his huge size, ZacBox estimated Jorvik must be at least eight feet tall and was even broader-shouldered than Mr. Eriksson. They moved to greet one another.

ZacBox extended his gloved right hand in greeting, then said through their radio comms, "I am Captain ZacBox, commander of the Starship Electra. This is my Chief of Security Anzu Gozen and Chief Engineer John Paul von Braun. We are delighted to meet you!"

"I am Jorvik Eriksson, Captain of the Starship Sterope, descendent of Erik the Red, proud son of Olaf Eriksson," the Pleiadian said and then bent down and looked each crewmember in the eye, through their face shields, as he shook their smaller hands, beginning with ZacBox.

"Your father sends his best wishes," ZacBox said.

"My father is well then?"

"He is," ZacBox continued. "He helped train us for this mission."

"What is your mission?" Jorvik said as he stood up and cocked his head to the side waiting for the reply he was hoping to hear.

"To rescue you and return to the Pleiades Star Cluster as ambassadors of the people of Planet Earth." ZacBox said proudly.

The message was slightly distorted over their comms system, but it was what Jorvik had been waiting almost a century and a half to hear. "Wonderful! And did I hear you say your last name is Box?" Jorvik asked.

"It is."

"Are you also known as Strong Bear Running?"

"I am, a name given me by my great-grandfather."

"Then you are Ute and a descendent of White Elk," Jorvik said with a knowing nod.

"You know my great-grandfather?" ZacBox asked.

"I never met him, he and my father know one another, but I did know Five Eagles Soaring," Jorvik said then turned toward John Paul. "Could you be Wernher von Braun's grandson?"

"Great-grandson," John Paul replied.

"I never met your great-grandfather either," Jorvik said in recognition. "He and President Kennedy met with my father several times in Colorado Springs. I know my father spoke often with other senior advisors about America's space program. But I was here when the Eagle Landed," Jorvik said, and then turned to face Anzu. "I do not know the name Gozen," Jorvik said, "but long ago I had the honor of fighting alongside two Samurai women from Japan who, like you, carried the naginata with Pleiades engravings on the blade identical to yours. You are a descendent of nobility in your country then—are you Bushi Class?"

Anzu nodded her head in acknowledgement.

"I am honored to meet you, Anzu Gozen. Thank you, thank all of you, for coming to my rescue," Jorvik said as he bowed his head in gratitude to Anzu and her captain and their Chief Engineer. "My family and I will forever be in your debt."

Coming from behind, the crew of the Electra watched their orb spinning overhead as it flew toward the front of the Sterope. An identical pearl-colored orb dropped out of the Sterope's airlock and joined with the Electra's orb in an excited aerial dance, like two butterflies flying gracefully above their heads. Then the pearl-colored orbs disappeared out of sight, whizzing off toward the ice-covered hillside in the distance behind the Electra.

"Come," ZacBox said as he motioned toward the Electra, "we will be able to talk better out of these space suits. Besides we have two other crewmates who are also excited to meet you, Jorvik."

Once aboard the Electra they took off their space suits, and ZacBox looked through the interior window of the Electra's airlock as Cadence gave a thumbs-up, letting him know she had completed her medical screen. This was standard protocol to ensure they were not bringing any possible viruses or contaminants into the interior of the flying saucer.

As Jorvik stepped into the Electra's cockpit, Bot ran up, grabbed his leg and jumped up and down with excitement. Jorvik picked him up and gave him a big hug, "Hello there, little Bot. It's nice to see you again." Then he placed the blue AI down and stepped further onto the bridge.

"Captain Jorvik," ZacBox said as he gestured toward Cadence, "this is Dr. Cadence Bahar, Chief Medical Officer."

Jorvik bent forward and extended his hand toward Cadence. Instead of shaking his hand she reached up and embraced the huge Pleiadian around the neck and kissed him on the cheek. Jorvik returned the embrace and patted Cadence gently on the back.

ZacBox waited a moment, and then turned toward Arjun. "Jorvik, this is my First Officer Arjun Basu."

Jorvik took note of the light-blue-colored pagri Arjun wore. Then instead of shaking hands he placed the palms of his hands together in front of his chest and bent forward at the waist, as a sign of peace in Arjun's culture.

Arjun repeated the gesture, and wondered if this greeting might also be a sign of respect and peace in Jorvik's culture as well.

"You wear a blue pagri, not the traditional white?" Jorvik asked.

"You are well versed in the traditions of India, I see," Arjun said, and then explained. "The men in my culture wear a white pagri as a symbol of peace; however, we will occasionally wear a blue pagri to remind ourselves and others that while we prefer peace, we are prepared for war.

"A wise precaution in your solar system," Jorvik acknowledged, "perhaps in any solar system."

"Come," ZacBox said, "let us gather in our galley; there is much to discuss. In my Ute culture, we like to enjoy a meal together and then sit around a campfire and tell stories. I imagine you must have many stories to tell, Jorvik?"

"Indeed," Jorvik said as he led the way toward the Electra's galley. ZacBox noticed that with Jorvik aboard, the interior of the Electra no longer seemed as spacious. As ZacBox passed by his cabin, he imagined that with a crew of five Pleiadians aboard, the interior of their saucer would probably feel rather cramped.

When the five Earthlings and the one Pleiadian gathered around the u-shaped booth, Jorvik said, "It is comforting to be in the company of you Earthlings again. My crewmates aboard the Sterope were all Earthlings. They were honorable people. I have missed each member of my crew every day. It was a privilege for me to serve with them. Three of them are buried not far from here. They too enjoyed gathering around the booth in Sterope's galley, and telling stories, but I must confess none of us were particularly good cooks," Jorvik concluded with a laugh.

"Well the Mano Machine makes for a poor pizza oven," ZacBox said jokingly, and then added, "Except we have a secret advantage."

"What's that?" Jorvik said.

"Not what but who," ZacBox explained as he expertly rolled out two large cheese pizzas on the counter, dropped them in the convection oven and set the timer for fifteen seconds. "Chef Reggie! You've never tasted any pizza on Earth better than you are about to taste with Reggie's marinara sauce—which, I might add, is now officially out of this world."

"Well," Jorvik said, laughing at the enthusiasm ZacBox showed in preparing their lunch. "I'll have to take your word for it ZacBox. You see, us Pleiadians lost our sense of smell several generations ago, and therefore, our sense of taste has been genetically diminished." ZacBox served everyone hot slices of pizza and their favorite flavored carbonated waters, before sitting down next to Jorvik. Jorvik picked up his glass for a toast, "To all our fallen comrades."

"Hear, hear," the Electra crewmembers said somberly as they raised their glasses toward the sky in salute. ZacBox added a silent prayer of remembrance for his mother.

"We expected your ship would have been more badly broken up when you crashed," John Paul said to Jorvik as they ate.

"I was fortunate not to have a dead stick," Jorvik explained. "When the Sterope was hit, all our propulsion systems blew, except for the hydrogen thrusters. I glided us in magnetically along an energy line and aimed for a heat vent protruding up through the ice. The shot from the Centaurians, followed by the impact of our crash landing, still killed two of my crew, but it could have been worse. The ECU remained intact; however, we were never able to bring our main propulsion systems back on line. I still burn a little hydrogen from time to time, to produce small amounts of filtered water and oxygen, but the tiny solar panels embedded in the saucer's outer hull still generate sufficient electricity to keep us warm and recharge our primary batteries."

"I thought those tiny sensors in the hull might be solar panels; ingenious," John Paul commented reflectively.

"The Sterope and her sister ships are extraordinary achievements of advanced Pleiadian technology," Jorvik commented.

"There's one thing I haven't been able to figure out," ZacBox said to Jorvik.

"What's that?"

"I was expecting our bodies to have to deal with the g-forces associated with the extreme acceleration of ZPE or the sudden changes of direction during a quark jump. When we used the maglev or the hydrogen propulsion, our bodies could feel the effects by being pushed back in our seats during acceleration, or pushed to the side when we turned, but when we accelerated to ZPE or did a quark jump, we couldn't feel anything."

"One of my crewmembers, Captain Richard Morgan, was a brilliant physicist, and he theorized the saucer's Environment Control Unit overcame gravitational force accelerations or quark jumps by shifting all life forms and everything else contained within the ECU to another dimension, a parallel universe, for just a nanosecond. Then the ECU brought everything back inside the spacecraft after the rapid acceleration or quark jump was completed. Did you try to accelerate beyond light speed before securing the upper and lower hulls of the saucer together?" Jorvik asked.

"We did," ZacBox said, "it didn't work. BeeBot showed us how to close the upper and lower halves of the Electra flying saucer together, like when we went to battle stations."

"Exactly," Jorvik continued, cupping his hands to demonstrate how the upper half of the saucer clamped down on the lower half and made a slight turn to lock it in place. "When the upper portion of the outer hull retracts and locks into the lower portion, the ECU is completely sealed. The thick glass of the saucer's windows is no longer exposed, and the airlock is secured. Everything sealed within the ECU's inner hull is temporarily parked in another dimension for just a fraction of a nanosecond, while the acceleration or quark jump is made, and then returned inside the ECU wherever the saucers had been moved. This interdimensional shift happens so quickly our bodies don't feel the shifts in speed or direction, because they are not inside the ship when it happens."

"That's brilliant," John Paul commented. "How many dimensions are there?"

"I don't know," Jorvik said, "but Richard theorized this parallel universe was very close, spatially, to the fourth dimension of time or spacetime, he referred to it as the Fifth Dimension. I remember once he said he thought there may be as many as twelve dimensions, maybe more. I wish he had lived longer; I am sure he would have taught us much more about the universe."

"We are all looking forward to learning as much as we can from you Jorvik," ZacBox said, "but if we are finished with our lunch I would like us to concentrate on the problems at hand. John Paul, worst case scenario, how much time do you calculate we may have before Captain Coda's buddies reach Jupiter?

"CAPTAIN CODA!?" Jorvik blurted out, slamming his fist on the table. "He's the bloody Centurion who shot us down, killing Captain Morgan and another of my crew. That Centurion is a coward and not to be trusted! He feigned that his ship was in distress, and drew us in, then fired on us once we were within range."

"Well," ZacBox said, "he won't pull that stunt ever again."

"You—you killed him?" Jorvik asked.

"They attacked us; we defended ourselves; their ship had no survivors," Anzu explained, "We took no joy in killing Captain Coda and his crew, but we have been trained to do whatever is required to deny the enemy a victory and to bring our warrior home to fight another day."

"It was the only way," Arjun said. "You are our warrior, and we are proud to be able to bring you home to fight another day."

"Thank you," Jorvik said once again.

"We must assume their battle actions were monitored by this Centaurian who calls himself Zhorban the Merciless," said ZacBox as he stood to help Cadence clear the dishes.

"The interstellar radio transmissions between Coda and Zhorban were being monitored on Earth," John Paul explained. "We believe these Centaurians have their sights set on Earth's gas and oil reserves. Captain Coda and his crew were evidently advance scouts sent to gather intelligence before the Centaurians' main battle force invades our solar system."

"We believe Zhorban's intentions are to capture you," Arjun explained. "We suspect you would have been subjected to torture and the Sterope stripped so they could better understand how to defeat us in space."

"Let's head back up to the bridge," ZacBox said, as he and the other four crewmembers followed Jorvik back to the front of the saucer.

"How much time do we have before this Zhorban reaches this solar system?" Jorvik asked.

"It's hard to say for certain," John Paul replied, as he sat down at his engineering console and brought up a view of the solar system on the main screen in front of them. "I estimate we might have between 48 and 72 hours before they reach Jupiter; that's assuming they come here first instead of going straight to Earth."

"They will come here first," Anzu replied confidently.

"How can you be so certain?" John Paul asked.

"That is what I would do," Anzu answered. "No military leader would leave an adversary in his rear, especially one who has already demonstrated their ability to destroy one of their starships and defeat one of their most capable starship commanders. Zhorban would not send his least capable captain on such an important reconnaissance mission; he would send one of his best. His pride will seek vengeance. He will come here, to where Captain Coda's ship was destroyed. He will be seeking revenge, but may also want to ensure Coda's ship was destroyed sufficiently so we could not reverse engineer their spacecraft to assess their vulnerabilities. As soon as Zhorban and his fleet reach our solar system, they will come immediately here to Jupiter."

"To finish us off," said Arjun.

"Then we will be waiting for them," said ZacBox confidently.

"We would have a better chance if we had two flying saucers waiting for them instead of just one," Jorvik said with a twinkle in his eye.

"Sterope is space-worthy?" ZacBox asked.

"Almost," Jorvik said nodding his head. "From the moment we crash-landed, my crew and I have worked every day but three, to repair the damages."

"Which three days did you not work?" Cadence asked.

"Those were funeral days," Jorvik said, and he lowered his head in remembrance of his crew. "In trying to repair the damages, we immediately realized we had hit two major obstacles. Come," Jorvik said as he turned toward the hatch, "it will be easier to show you, rather than tell you. Let's go over to Sterope."

As the five Electra crewmembers put on their space suits and departed their ship, they were followed by their blue bot, who did not need a space suit. ZacBox noticed Anzu had brought her naginata, Cadence had retrieved her medical bag from her cabin, and John Paul had brought his laptop, which he carried in his great-grandfather's briefcase. As the Electra's crew made their way across to the Sterope, they were rejoined by the two pearl orbs returning from their excursion to the nearby mountain.

"I named it Olaf Peak," Jorvik explained, adding "in honor of my father."

ZacBox, Arjun, John Paul, Anzu and Cadence followed Jorvik up Sterope's ladder and through the open airlock. Once inside, they got out of their space suits and found the interior of Sterope to be identical to Electra's, although it was obvious she hadn't been flown in years. The interior was mostly clean, but it was apparent that many of the repairs were makeshift, which was to be expected. The ship had been operating on life-support for over a century, and had a musty smell, but it was still warm and comfortable.

With everyone aboard, Jorvik said, "Please take a seat; there's something I want to show you; I keep it locked in my captain's quarters." Within two minutes Jorvik returned holding a small one-and-a-half-by-one-inch rectangular blue pendant attached to a silver chain. He held the pendant up to the light and said, "This is the Pendant of Pleiades. It belonged to my father's sister, Sophia. Like my father, Sophia was born on Earth, but unlike my father, her parents decided to return to Pleiades when she was just a child."

Jorvik handed the pendant to Cadence to examine and pass around the rest of the crew. Cadence held it up to the light and said, "It's beautiful. It looks like a string of pearls floating in a deep blue ocean." Then Cadence handed the pendant to Anzu.

"I count seven pearls," Anzu said, passing the pendant to Arjun. "Do they represent the location of the Seven Sisters, the seven brightest stars that make up the Pleiades Star Cluster?"

"Yes, and if you look closely you will see a small, red heart-shaped diamond near Merope, the star toward the bottom of the Pendant. The name of the heart-shaped diamond is Cumorah, also known as Inspiration Point. It identifies the location of the third planet in orbit around Merope, similar to Earth being the third planet from your yellow sun. There is an ancient pyramid on this planet, known as Pyramid Cumorah, which served as a tomb for many of the greatest leaders the Pleiadians have ever known. It also serves as a vault for many of the greatest treasures ever discovered in the Milky Way, along with the most advanced technologies ever invented."

"I hope it's well-defended," John Paul said, as he handed the pendant back to Jorvik.

"I do not know," Jorvik said. "From what my father told me, Pyramid Cumorah was to be our distination once we reached the Pleiades Star Cluster. If anything should happen to me, I ask that one of you place the Pendant of Pleiades around the neck of my Aunt Sophia. If she is no longer alive, hand it to the ruling monarch of Pleiades. It will prove humankind has accomplished their mission, to return to Pleiades. Now, if you will follow me to the engine compartment I will show you the mechanical issues we must overcome for the starship Sterope to reach Pleiades."

As they walked toward the rear of the ship, the Electra crew noticed the two empty cabins with the four empty bunks, reminding them of the dangers they face and the price that had already been paid in mankind's journey to return to Pleiades.

"Down there," Jorvik said as he opened the hatch leading down to the maglev propulsion engine, "is our first challenge. When we crash-landed, one of the metal coils for the mercury cooling system cracked, and the liquid mercury leaked out and pooled on the bottom there," he said and pointed. The Electra crew and their blue bot gathered around Jorvik and peered down into the dark hatchway.

"As you may know, mercury is highly toxic, and I haven't been able to construct a noncorrosive container to pump the mercury into while making the repairs. To complicate things, while the mercury onboard is no longer super-cooled, it's still so cold that when it comes in contact with almost any surface it freezes instantly. That's how I lost my blue bot."

Everyone looked at Jorvik, including the Electra's blue bot, who cocked his head to the side and emitted a quiet chirping sound, "Bot?"

Jorvik nodded his head and reverently retrieved a blue plastic tub from an overhead cabinet and placed it on the floor. As he removed the lid, they saw it contained a dozen or more small blue pieces of what was left of the Sterope's blue bot. Jorvik explained, "We tried to repair the cracked coil without pumping the mercury out, but when Bot accidentally came in contact with the mercury, he froze solid. When I lifted him up out of the hatch, and he came in contact with the air inside the ship, shriveled up, and cracked and then broke apart."

Everyone watched as the Electra's blue bot knelt beside the plastic tub, leaned over the broken pieces of his counterpart and began to sob. It was heartbreaking to watch their small blue companion suffering with such grief. The two pearl orbs hovered near him, as if to console him. Slowly he picked up each piece out of the tub and held it up briefly between the two orbs. As the two orbs hovered around the piece of the broken blue bot, a small yellow energy beam of light shot between the two orbs and into the piece of the departed bot. The energy beam only lasted a split second, reminding the Electra's medical officer of her training on an Automated External Defibrillator, or AED, used to shock a patient to reactivate their heart.

"I don't think it's working," Cadence whispered as they watched their blue bot tuck the small blue pieces into the pouch in the front of his stomach, repeating the process for each of the other pieces in the plastic bin. One at a time, Bot held each piece up reverently as the two spinning orbs emitted a brief flash of yellow light into the broken bot. After the broken pieces were tucked carefully into the Electra's blue bot's stomach pouch, it looked carefully into the plastic bin to make sure no pieces had been missed.

The crew watched as their blue bot held his protruding stomach, let out a sorrowful moan and waddled slowly toward the front of the ship, followed by the two pearl-colored orbs.

"That's so sad," said Cadence.

"Are they going to bury him?" John Paul asked.

"I don't know, I was going to bury him, alongside my four crew-members," Jorvik said, "but I wasn't aware of what the proper protocol was for an AI, so I put him in this bin where he's been for one hundred and fifty of your Earth years."

"I think we should let them have some privacy; they appear to know what to do," ZacBox suggested. "I think we need to turn our attention back to the challenges at hand. What's next Jorvik?"

Jorvik pushed a blue diamond-shaped button on the front of the cabinet containing the colored crystals. When the drawer slid open, they saw it contained several multicolored crystals, just like on the Electra. "As you can see, the crystals are probably dimmer than those on the Electra, and this large purple one here in the center is cracked. We spent over a hundred of your years exploring Europa's subsurface caverns and finally discovered a cave beneath Olaf Peak containing this type of purple crystal. That's where I lost Major Steve Martinez, the third member of my crew to die," Jorvik said as he grew quiet thinking of his lost companion.

"How did it happen?" ZacBox asked. "Maybe we can pick up where Major Martinez left off."

"I can draw you a map to the entrance of the heat vent beneath Olaf Peak. You enter what looks like a long tunnel, which turns to the right and into this large cavernous opening; from there on you won't need your space suits. The vent begins to narrow the further back you go. In about 150 meters, there's an underground river you will have to swim across; it's only about ten meters wide and five meters deep. The current is not overly swift, so the crossing is manageable for good swimmers, which I am not. Once you cross the river, the cavern narrows dramatically over the next fifty meters. There you'll find the opening to the innermost cave, where the purple crystals are located. There are many other multicolored crystals, diamonds and various gemstones embedded in the walls and on the ceiling of this inner cave. The purple crystals are at the very back of a narrow shaft. I couldn't fit inside myself, because I'm too big, so Steve crawled in on his stomach and handed them out to me. Martinez was a little bigger than any of you, so you should be able to reach the crystals without much difficulty, but one of you will need to stand guard. That's where we went wrong, that's where I went wrong. I let down my guard. That's when he attacked us."

"Who?" Anzu asked, "Who attacked you?"

"It was a giant white Puckster," Jorvik answered.

"Describe him," Anzu asked, intent on learning everything she could about her adversary.

"He was huge, twice as big as I am. This one must have been sixteen or eighteen feet tall and had to have weighed five, maybe six hundred pounds. He was covered with shaggy white hair, and they all have enormous, extremely sharp teeth and claws. When Pucksters are newborns they're small and fuzzy and lime green. They're absolutely adorable, when they are little. But when they grow up and get older, their hair turns white and they can get really mean. It seems like he was guarding the crystals and became enraged when he realized we were removing some of them from the cave.

"How did he attack you?" asked Anzu.

"He attacked us out of the dark. We tried to fight our way back to the front of the cave, but he caught us before we reached the underground river. Our Tasers didn't work underground; I think he disabled them somehow electronically, so we used rocks and clubs and our fists. When the Puckster slipped back into the dark, I realized Martinez was cut up more severely than I was, and I helped him across the river, but he bled to death before we could reach the front of the cave. I buried him there, just inside the opening, to the right under a pile of white rock."

"Anything else we should know about this Puckster?" inquired Anzu.

"Yes, he can see in the dark and you might smell him before you see him."

"Smell him?" Cadence asked.

"Yes. As you know, us Pleiadians lost our sense of smell centuries ago, but Martinez told me right before the attack, he smelled a strange odor like radishes."

"Radishes!" Arjun blurted out. "Why did it have to be radishes? I knew there was a reason I don't like radishes." The crew laughed at Arjun's comments, and then grew serious again thinking about the challenges of their mission at hand.

"Well, at least we know what we're going up against," ZacBox said then added, "Here's what I'm thinking. Tomorrow morning Anzu, Arjun, Cadence and I will head to Olaf Peak to harvest purple crystals. Maybe we'll get lucky and this Puckster will be sleeping in. John Paul, you stay here with Jorvik and start repairing the maglev. If everything goes well, when Zhorban and his alien invaders arrive on orbit around Jupiter, we will have two flying saucers waiting for him instead of just one. That might give us an edge."

All of the Electra's crew voiced their agreement with ZacBox's plan; however, Jorvik remained quiet for several minutes before he spoke. "There's one more thing you should know."

"What's that?" ZacBox asked.

"I set a self-destruct timer on one of Sterope's neutrino torpedoes. It is set to detonate in 72 hours unless the deactivation code is entered. I didn't want to run the risk of the Sterope or me falling into enemy hands."

"A wise precaution," ZacBox said, "so can't you simply deactivate it now?"

"I could try," Jorvik replied, "but I think it might be best to wait until the four of you are deep underground tomorrow morning. These weapons are hundreds, possibly even thousands of years old, and I don't think they're very stable."

"Captain," Anzu said, "I advise you and the rest of our crew fly the Electra out of range before any attempt is made to deactivate the self-destruct timer. I will go to the cave and collect the crystals while Jorvik deactivates the torpedo."

"A wise precaution, and brave offer, Chief Gozen," Captain ZacBox said. "But as you taught us from Sun Tzu's wisdom, we must 'Be positive at all times. If you expect to fail, you will. Before the battle begins, make sure you expect to win.' In the morning, Jorvik and John Paul will deactivate the self-destruct timer on the neutrino torpedo and repair the Sterope maglev system so she can fly again. You, Arjun, Cadence and I will find the purple crystals necessary to make her space-worthy once more. When Zhorban the Merciless enters orbit around Jupiter, he's going to have his hands full with two saucers instead of one. Now I suggest we all retire to our cabins and try to get a good night's sleep. Tomorrow looks like it might be another busy day."

✧ ✧ ✧

November 16th 08:33 hours UTC Astradate 11111.6
Propulsion Room, Saucer Sterope, Surface of Europa,
Moon of Jupiter

"If anything goes wrong," Jorvik said as he turned to face John Paul, "we will only have 90 seconds before the neutrino torpedo detonates."

"Why did you set it for just 90 seconds?" John Paul asked as he tested the electric screwdriver he held in his right hand to make sure it was fully charged.

"From the day we were shot down, I worried the Centaurians would come to salvage the crash site, searching for information on our weapons systems or to interrogate any survivors, trying to gain a tactical advantage for when they invaded Earth. So, every day since 1843, my crew or I would reset the self-destruct timer for another 72 hours, allowing our team an extra 48-hour safety buffer should one of us not be here to manually reset the timer on the torpedo. As I said yesterday, the weapons aboard this saucer are hundreds of years old, and I'm not at all certain how stable they are; plus, this is the first time in over a century we are trying to shut it down rather than to just reset the timer. I'm not certain how this timer is going to react."

"ZacBox, Arjun, Cadence and Anzu should be well inside the cave now," John Paul said noticing each of their tracking sensors had blinked off from his laptop's screen. "I'm ready if you are. Let's do this."

John Paul watched the digital timer counting down as Jorvik entered the password and hit deactivate. Suddenly they heard a buzzing noise, followed by an electrical zapping sound, and then John Paul smelled a faint odor of smoke being emitted from inside the torpedo housing.

"Do you smell that?" John Paul asked.

"I don't smell anything! Remember we Pleiadians lost our sense of smell years ago."

"I think it short-circuited," John Paul said as he began to un-screw the eight screws holding the torpedo housing cover in place.

"It's booby-trapped to keep it from being disarmed by the wrong people. As soon as the housing cover is removed, the tim-er will drop to 90 seconds," Jorvik warned.

"Then what?" John Paul asked as he prepared to separate the housing cover from the torpedo and noticed the blue Bot had waddled over and was looking over his shoulder.

"Then boom," Jorvik replied. They both noticed the blue Bot wince and cover his ears.

"Let's try to avoid that," John Paul said as he lifted the housing cover and watched the red numbers on the digital countdown clock start reversing from 90 seconds. "There, that's the problem, that gold wire is melted in half. Quick, we need to find some-thing two inches long, thin and narrow and gold or gold plated."

"I'll go below and grab another torpedo," Jorvik said as he stood up and saw the countdown clock go from 68 to 67 seconds. "Maybe we can cannibalize one of the other torpedoes for a part. What do you think?"

"Not enough time," John Paul said as he watched the timer drop from 54 seconds to 53. Both of them began searching frantically through cabinets and drawers in the propulsion room, dumping the contents onto the floor. John Paul glanced at the countdown clock, 34 seconds, 33. Then he looked around the room again and spotted his great-grandfather's briefcase standing open. "There," he said to Jorvik pointing to the briefcase, "hand me that gold-plated paperclip!"

Jorvik quickly snatched the paperclip from inside the briefcase and tossed it to John Paul. John Paul caught the paperclip midair, straightened it, and then, while holding it between his right thumb and index finger, lowered the gold-plated paperclip into the housing area where the golden wire had melted away from the torpedo's metal frame. As soon as both ends touched the metal frame, a flash of hot yellowish-blue light shot out from the inside of the torpedo and knocked John Paul backwards, where he landed hard on the floor. Jorvik quickly reentered the disarming code, stopping the countdown, and then turned to help John Paul.

"Ouch! That hurts," John Paul said as he looked at the red electrical blisters on his thumb and index finger where he had been holding the wire. "I felt that shock all the way down to my toes and up into my teeth!"

Jorvik helped John Paul to his feet and then pointed to the countdown clock; it had stopped at 6 seconds. "But it worked!" Both of them saw the gold-plated paperclip had been fused to both ends of the metal frame replacing the metal wire that had burnt in half. "Sorry about your golden paperclip," Jorvik said. "I understand it was an important family keepsake."

"That's okay," John Paul said as he carefully tested the paperclip to ensure it had been firmly welded to the metal frame. "I'm sure Great-grandpa von Braun and President Kennedy would have approved."

"Let's screw the cover plate back on, and then I'll put the torpedo back into the top of the magazine. If we run into this Centaurian who calls himself Zhorban the Merciless, your great-grandfather's gold-plated paperclip might save our butts once more. Right now, we better get to work on repairing the maglev."

"I am keeping my fingers crossed that I calculated the volume of mercury we'll need to pump out of the magnet coil tubing correctly," John Paul said as he held up the white ceramic vessel he had constructed using the Electra's 3D printer. "I was mostly guessing when I entered the data last night. I hope ZacBox, Arjun, Cadence and Anzu are having less of an exciting time than what we just experienced."

November 16th 08:35 hours UTC Astradate 11111.6
Cave beneath Olaf Peak, Tidal Face Europa, Moon of Jupiter

"Do you smell that?" Arjun whispered as he sniffed the air coming from the back of the cave.

"What?" Anzu asked as she stepped out of her space suit and pointed the blade of her naginata toward the narrowing cave.

Arjun sniffed the breeze coming from the back of the cave. "It smells like radishes. I hate radishes!"

"Quiet," Captain ZacBox said as he stepped out of his space suit and held his index finger up to his lips. Somehow, he knew instinctively their approach to the innermost cave had been way too easy.

"Over there," Anzu pointed. "Those white rocks have been stacked; that may have been where Jorvik buried Major Martinez.

"We must be getting close," Cadence said

"I hear water running; must be the river Jorvik described," said Arjun.

Approaching the bank of the underground river, the crew could see a faint purple light escaping from the small openings in the rock wall on the other side of the water. "We'll have to swim across," ZacBox said as he removed his flight suit and stripped down to his underwear. The underwear the crew wore consisted of black shorts and the women also wore black sports bras. They were used to seeing one another aboard the Electra in their crew underwear, which looked more like athletic clothing or swimsuits than underwear.

Anzu pointed her naginata ahead and walked to the edge of the water. "I'll go first," she said to ZacBox, and then stopped and handed him her weapon. "Wait until I'm on the other side; then toss the naginata over to me."

ZacBox, Arjun and Cadence watched as Anzu dove effortlessly into the water and swam easily to the other side. When she emerged on the other bank, she looked around briefly and then signaled for ZacBox to throw her the naginata. ZacBox tossed her the weapon, blade first over the water, but his aim was slightly off. The weapon would have gone over Anzu's head, but with the lighter gravity on Europa, she was able to jump six feet off the ground, catch the naginata in midair and do a summersault on the way down.

ZacBox dove into the water next. He was grateful for the swimming lessons Professor Fibonacci had given him and swam quickly to the other side. When he pulled himself up on the opposite bank he turned back and saw Arjun and Cadence were already half way across. They both crossed the water and climbed up the opposite bank. Arjun had held the drawstrings for a waterproof bag in his teeth when he swam. After he had crawled up out of the water he removed a small electronic instrument from the bag, which he activated and began scanning the chambers at the back of the cave.

"Over there," Arjun said as he approached one of the small round vent tubes leading to a small chamber emitting a faint purple light. "These readings indicate this is the type of crystal we need to get the Sterope flying again. Here," he said handing the instrument to ZacBox. Then he crawled in head first on his hands and knees. "The shaft is not big enough for both of us. I'll go and find one. You test it. See if it vibrates at 110 hertz, like the one on Electra."

Within minutes Arjun had located a beautiful purple crystal, the same size as the cracked one on Sterope, and handed it out to ZacBox. Anzu stood guard as ZacBox tapped the crystal lightly against Anzu's naginata then held it under Arjun's instrument. It registered 110 hertz indicating it would be a good replacement for Sterope's fractured crystal. Then he handed the crystal to Cadence, "Can you tuck this someplace where it will be safe? I'm a little short on pockets. We don't want to lose it and I don't want to come back here if we don't have to."

Cadence tucked the crystal into the front of her sports bra and then bent down to peer into the small chamber. "Come on Arjun, hurry up, I feel we shouldn't be here."

"Cadence is right," Anzu said in agreement. "The longer we're in here the greater the risk we'll be discovered by this Puckster. I advise we head back to the ship immediately, Captain."

"Agreed," ZacBox said and then whispered into the cave, "We're good Arjun, 110 hertz. Let's go."

"Just give me one minute, Captain," Arjun pleaded. "This cavern is full of hundreds of crystals and gemstones. These have been here for millions, maybe billions of years and have never seen the light of day. I think they are unknown to anyone back on Earth! This discovery will rewrite all the geological textbooks ever written. Just give me another minute, please!"

"You have thirty seconds," ZacBox replied as he peered into the darkness around them searching for any movement. He could hear Arjun scurrying around inside the small chamber, talking excitedly to himself, "this one's for mom, here's one to name after father, and this one's for Indu."

ZacBox was relieved when he finally heard Arjun scooting forward on the ground.

"Here, take these," Arjun said as he handed the bag full of gemstones and crystals to ZacBox. "These will be worth a fortune back on Earth. I got one for you too. It's a beautiful ruby-red heart-shaped diamond. Maybe you can buy that new sports car you want when we get back home."

ZacBox took the heavy bag and helped Arjun out of the chamber opening. "Come on, we gotta get out of here," he said as he handed the bag back to Arjun. "I'll feel better when we're all back across the river. How are you going to get these across? They're too heavy to swim with; you'll drown."

"You and Cadence go first," Arjun said to ZacBox. "When you get across I'll empty the bag except for these smaller gemstones and one of the heavier crystals to use as a weight. Then I'll throw the bag over to you and toss the other larger crystals across and you can catch them and fill the bag up again on the other side."

"I'll wait on this side until you and the crystals get across," Anzu offered as she stayed behind to protect her team from any approaching danger.

ZacBox and Cadence swam across the water first. Then Arjun threw the bag with a few gemstones across the river to ZacBox. As soon as ZacBox had caught the bag, Arjun began carefully tossing the other gemstones and crystals across to ZacBox, who caught them one at a time and then filled the bag back up on the other side. Then Arjun swam across the river. As he emerged from the water, he took a deep breath of air and that's when he noticed it.

"There it is again," Arjun said.

"What," Cadence asked.

"That odor of radishes, only it's stronger now; whatever it is it must be getting closer."

Anzu turned and peered into the darkness behind her, but without her helmet with the night vision lenses, she couldn't see it coming toward her out of the back of the cave until it was too late. The hairy white Puckster had been well concealed in the darkness until it opened its mouth and gnashed out at Anzu with its gleaming white teeth. It was huge, easily twice the size of Jorvik. It was covered with long white hair and had purple gleaming eyes. Its razor-sharp claws ripped through the air toward Anzu. But she was too quick and moved with the grace of a ballerina, evading its attempts to eviscerate her with its claws. With the lighter gravity, Anzu jumped eight feet into the air and twirled acrobatically across the cave. She fought back bravely and skillfully defended herself with her naginata, managing to slice a deep cut across the monster's lower leg. Blood spurted out as the animal screeched a mournful howl, "OUUHAA!"

Anzu tried to get around the Puckster as it limped on one good leg and bellowed with its head tilted back toward the ceiling. The loud roar echoed across the interior of the innermost cave. Then the crewmates spotted more gleaming purple eyes emerging out of the darkness—two, then three, then six pairs of eyes blinking at them from out of the darkness. There were big Pucksters and smaller ones, judging from their height and distance between their eyes.

As a half dozen Pucksters slowly closed in on Anzu, she assumed a defensive position at the water's edge and courageously shouted to her crewmates, "I'll hold them off as long as I can, you get back to the ship!"

Things had suddenly turned from bad to worse. For just a second Captain ZacBox felt conflicted and wasn't sure what to do. He turned his head back and looked into the faces of Cadence and Arjun, who were looking to him for guidance. ZacBox would have willingly given his own life to save anyone of his crew, but now he questioned if it was ethical for him to risk the lives of two of his crew to save the life of one crewmember? He turned his head back quickly to see how Anzu was doing fending off the advancing Pucksters and felt his St. Michael medallion brush across his neck.

He touched the medallion and recalled the oath the PJs always swear before each mission to leave no one behind.

"We're not leaving without you," ZacBox said, standing on the edge of the water opposite Anzu. He looked around for any weapon to give them a fighting chance to survive, and when he looked back up, that's when it happened. The wounded Puckster lashed out angrily with its long claws and sliced a deep gash across Anzu's midsection. She grabbed her ribs, took a step back, doubled over in pain and fell backwards into the water. ZacBox dove into the water after her, kicking his feet and diving deeper towards the bottom of the river to rescue Anzu.

ZacBox saw Anzu was drifting downstream and grabbed the end of her naginata. He felt her gripping the other end of the long pole. She was hanging on for dear life. He began pulling her to the surface. He looked back to see she was leaving a stream of crimson blood in the water behind them, flowing from her open wound. He wondered if there were any predators in the water, like a shark on Earth, that might smell the blood in the water and attack them before they reached the shore.

"No time to worry about what might be," ZacBox recalled White Elk's words of wisdom. "The list is endless and unimportant." ZacBox focused all his energy on solving one problem at a time; right now, he had to get Anzu to the surface while she was still holding her breath. When they broke the surface of the water, ZacBox was relieved to hear Anzu take a deep breath; she was still alive. ZacBox started pulling her toward the bank where Cadence and Arjun knelt, ready to help them out of the water.

Cadence laid Anzu back softly on the ground and began to inspect and bandage her cuts to stop the bleeding. "This is really bad," she mouthed to ZacBox. "We have to get her back to the ship immediately."

Arjun picked up Anzu's naginata, the crew's only weapon, and stood bravely at the water's edge to defend his shipmates. "I don't think they can swim, but we had better get out of here; there might be a back door!"

ZacBox saw the blood streaming down from Anzu's wound and admired how she never once cried or complained about the pain. He saw the worried look on Cadence's face, as she applied what first aid she could from her field medical bag.

"She's losing a lot of blood. I'm going to need to start an IV as soon as were back on the ship," Cadence said to ZacBox. "She can't walk. We'll have to carry her back to the Electra. We need a stretcher."

"Hand me the naginata," ZacBox said to Arjun, pointing to the six-foot-long pole weapon. Then he tied his and Arjun's flight suits around the long shaft of Anzu's naginata creating a sling below to use as a stretcher. Arjun helped Cadence lift her patient into the makeshift litter. When ZacBox and Arjun lifted her up, they put the two ends of the naginata over their shoulders and started toward their space suits waiting at the entrance. Cadence carried her medical bag and hoisted the bag of precious minerals over her left shoulder.

After taking only a few steps it was obvious the bag containing the priceless crystals and gemstones was slowing Cadence down. She was very strong, but the extra weight was taking its toll. The light grew brighter as they approached the opening for the cave. ZacBox admired how Cadence didn't complain as she struggled with everything she was carrying, and still managed to talk to Anzu to keep her from going into shock.

"We're almost there," Cadence said to Anzu, "Hang in there, girl! Stay with me! I'll have you back on your feet and dancing in no time." In the light, Cadence could see Anzu was in great pain and admired her grit as she held the bandage in place over her wound and bit her lower lip.

Now they were at the rim of the cave opening, where they thought they were safe, but then they saw him—the injured Puckster had somehow gotten ahead of them and was blocking their exit from the cave. His lower body was covered in blood and he was mad with rage.

"GRRRR!" the hairy Puckster bellowed as he beat his chest with his fists.

"Here," ZacBox shouted to Cadence, "you'll have to put on your space suits and carry her back from here. I'll distract him and give you as much time as I can to get her back to the ship." ZacBox said as he handed Cadence his end of the stretcher, "Do you still have the purple crystal we came for?"

Cadence patted the front of the sports bra, "Right here."

"I'm sorry Arjun," ZacBox said as he removed the bag from Cadence's shoulder and dropped the precious gemstones and crystals on the ground.

"It's okay. They're an impediment to us now!" Arjun shouted as he put on his space suite and helped Cadence tuck Anzu into her space suit. "They're worthless compared to Anzu's life. Let's go Cadence, we gotta get her back to the Electra. You be careful ZacBox!"

ZacBox stood between his friends and the huge hairy white Puckster. ZacBox looked into the monster's purple glowing eyes and raised both his arms above his head and gave a fierce roar. The monster turned its attention away from Anzu and started after ZacBox who was now running back into the cave. ZacBox had always been fast, but with Europa's lighter gravity, he could take long strides of twelve to fifteen feet at a time. He knew he couldn't keep up this pace forever. Within a half-minute he had reached the underground river and thought briefly about diving in, since the Pucksters didn't seem able to swim. ZacBox's fear was in not knowing how far the underground river would carry him. Would he surface again or be trapped underground?

ZacBox decided not to chance diving into the water and climbed instead atop of a large red rock where he could catch his breath. Regrettably, he found Pucksters were far better at rock climbing than he was, so he jumped down and started running toward the opening of the cave.

When ZacBox reached Major Martinez's grave near the cave entrance, he was relieved to see Cadence, Arjun and Anzu's spacesuits were gone. He heard the Puckster breathing heavily behind him and turned back to see the monster had stopped. The wound on the Puckster's leg was taking its toll. This was his chance! ZacBox quickly put on his space suit but when he turned back toward the entrance he saw five more Pucksters step forward blocking his exit. Two of the Pucksters were as big as the one that had been chasing him; he thought they were males. Two were smaller, and he thought they might be female. Then he saw a smaller one, about his height, or maybe an inch or two taller than him. It was covered with long, lime green-colored hair.

ZacBox remembered Jorvik had told them that these animals were darker green when they were born and their hair turned white as they got older. The smaller green Puckster was watching him with his purple glowing eyes and started toward him slowly as the older ones watched. ZacBox backed up to the pile of white rocks and looked for one to throw at the little green menace when it attacked. As the smaller Puckster crept forward slowly, the pungent odor of radishes grew stronger. For a fleeting moment ZacBox hoped the monsters were vegetarians. It was a funny thought, ZacBox admitted. He did not object to giving his life to save the lives of his friends, but for some reason, even though he'd be dead, he didn't like the thought of being eaten.

It had been at least twenty minutes since Cadence and Arjun had left to carry Anzu back to the ship. ZacBox hoped he had bought them enough time and felt at peace. He accepted his fate; this is where he would die. ZacBox felt comforted knowing he would soon be in the presence of his mother again. Most Utes believe a spiritual guide will be waiting for you at the moment of your death. White Elk taught him the role of their spiritual guide was to take you to Creator, to make sure you don't wander off or get lost. They serve as your ambassador when you stand in front of Him. If you have led a good life, you will be rewarded by spending eternity with Creator in the afterlife. ZacBox hoped he had led a good life; his one regret was it had been far too short.

ZacBox moved closer to the white rock pile and looked down to find one he could throw; he wasn't going down without a fight. Then he spotted it—his drum! What was it doing here? How did it get here? But this was without a doubt his drum. The one White Elk had made for him, right here sitting on a rock. ZacBox picked it up and turned it over to see White Elk's writing, hoping there was a weapon inside. The only thing he found was the drum stick.

"Oh grandfather," ZacBox said mournfully, as he sat down on his haunches and placed the elk hide covered drum on the ground in front of him. "Oh grandfather," he picked up the wooden drum stick mindlessly and repeatedly said aloud, "I needed a gun and you sent me a drum. I needed a gun and you sent me a…"

"Play for him," a voice from behind him said softly breaking the silence in the cave. ZacBox glanced over his shoulder but didn't see anyone. Then the familiar male voice repeated, "Play your drum for him."

ZacBox tapped the drumstick lightly on the drum. Then again. And again. He noticed the little green Puckster had sat down on his haunches in front of him, mimicking his position. When ZacBox beat the drum in rhythm, the little Puckster cocked its head to the side and perked up his ears. ZacBox held the wooden drum between his knees and beat the drum in rhythm, softly. Boom. Boom. It is said that the prayers of the ancestors contained in the prayer tree are released when the drum is played. The Puckster scooted forward and listened intently.

ZacBox beat the drum a little louder and began to sing the words to the only song that popped into his mind, Little Drummer Boy. "Come they told me, Pa rum pum pum pum. A new born king to see, Pa rumpa pum pum. Our finest gifts we bring…I'm sorry little buddy, I didn't bring any gifts."

The little Puckster seemed fascinated with the beat of the drum. He scooted closer to within three feet of ZacBox as he played. ZacBox handed him the drumstick and watched as he tapped lightly on the drum. The little Puckster's face broke into a smile as he played the drum.

ZacBox sensed the presence of his great-grandfather and looked around, noticing for the first time there were trees growing inside the cave. He was puzzled how trees could grow without sunlight; then he saw that the bag containing the crystals and gemstones lying on the ground nearby was partially open, and light was glowing from inside. ZacBox noticed the light of the purple crystals was the same color as the purple light in the little Puckster's eyes. The little green Puckster reached out toward ZacBox's neck and extended a hairy finger with a razor-sharp claw at the end. ZacBox looked down and watched as the hairy green finger touched the shiny St. Michael medallion ZacBox wore around his neck. ZacBox stood up and removed the gold chain with the medallion. The little Puckster stood up too and bent forward as ZacBox placed the chain with the St. Michael medal around its neck.

When the little Puckster turned back to look at two of the adult

Pucksters, they too seemed happy. Then they bowed their heads and stepped away from the cave opening. ZacBox recalled the Pleiadians could communicate telepathically and wondered if these creatures could as well. ZacBox watched as the little green Puckster picked up the bag of crystals and gemstones and draped it over his shoulder. ZacBox put on the helmet of his space suit and started toward the cave entrance. The little green Puckster followed, carrying the bag. Evidently, he didn't need a space suit. ZacBox carried his drum and together they stopped at the cave entrance and looked back at the other Pucksters.

One of the adult female Pucksters came forward, bent down and kissed the little green Puckster affectionately on the forehead. An older male Puckster came forward as well and hugged the little one for a moment in a warm embrace, and then let him go. ZacBox guessed they were his parents and it appeared that they were saying goodbye.

ZacBox still wasn't sure what was happening, but this appeared to be his best chance to escape. He took several steps past the cave entrance and looked back. Sure enough, the little Puckster was walking beside him, still carrying the bag of gemstones and crystals. When ZacBox stopped walking, the little guy stopped. As ZacBox took several more steps forward, he turned around again to make sure none of the other Pucksters were following. He saw the other Pucksters standing at the cave entrance waving goodbye. The scene reminded him of the morning he and his crew said goodbye to their loved ones and lifted off aboard the Electra. Evidently they had gained a new crewmate.

ZacBox and the Puckster ran toward the two awaiting saucers. As they ran, ZacBox noticed the strength of the muscles in the little guy's legs, arms and chest and felt this undeniable sense of loyalty and a bond began growing between them. They reached the

Electra, and ZacBox climbed aboard the spacecraft first, followed closely by the hairy green Puckster. After hanging up his space suit, and clearing the scan of their bodies before entering the bridge, ZacBox saw Cadence, Arjun, John Paul and Jorvik were gathered aboard the Electra.

"How's Anzu?" ZacBox asked of Cadence, "is she…"

"She's going to be okay," Cadence said with a nod of her head. "She's resting comfortably in our quarters, so let's keep our voices down."

"Who's this?" Arjun said, trying not to stare at the green hairy creature ZacBox had brought onboard.

"I don't know his name," ZacBox said, and then added, "but he's one of us now."

The Puckster stepped forward and handed Arjun the bag of precious gemstones and crystals. Arjun opened the bag and looked inside. "I think they're all here," he said as Cadence handed the large purple gemstone that she had brought back from the cave to Jorvik. He held it up to the light, and everyone watched as it sparkled brilliantly in the light.

"That looks like it should fit. What is it?" John Paul asked.

"I don't know for sure, but it looks like Alexandrite," Arjun replied. "Their color on Earth ranges from purple to raspberry to deep green. The ones on Earth were discovered in the Ural Mountains of Russia during the early 19th Century. Legend says a local peasant discovered them in the roots of a fallen tree."

"Then that's his name," Cadence said, "Alexander, it's easier to say than Alexandrite."

The crew watched as the Puckster stood up and patted his chest and let out a soft growl that sounded a little like a bear cub, "Der."

"Alexander the Great," ZacBox said, "I think he approves."

"Der," Alexander said again, patting himself on the chest.

"He likes the name Alexander," Cadence explained, "but I think he wants his friends to call him, Der."

"Der it is, then," ZacBox said as the crew laughed. Then their blue BeeBot entered the crew cockpit area followed by a second identical looking blue BeeBot. "Who's the twin?" ZacBox asked.

"This is my BeeBot," Jorvik explained. "Evidently your BeeBot was able to clone himself using the broken pieces of my BeeBot that he had stuffed into his pouch. The light that flashed between our two orbs somehow infused them with sufficient energy to create a new AI."

"How is the Sterope?" ZacBox asked of Jorvik and John Paul, "Were you able to repair the mercury leak in the maglev?"

"The maglev is fully functional," Jorvik replied, as he handed John Paul the purple crystal. "I think this is going to work. Come on, John Paul, let's go give it a try."

"Any trouble disarming the neutrino torpedo?" ZacBox asked as John Paul and Jorvik started toward the airlock to put on their space suits.

"No," John Paul replied. "Just another day at the office," he said as he winked at Jorvik.

"Then I suggest we get off this rock before Zhorban and his thugs catch us down here on the ground," ZacBox said turning toward his First Officer. "Arjun, if you don't mind, I would like you and John Paul to transfer to Jorvik's crew until we reach the Pleiades Star Cluster. I'm thinking there's a lot you two can learn from him that you will be able to teach the rest of us on our return flight to Earth. Cadence will remain here to take care of Anzu. Alexander, Der, you're my First Officer now, until they return. That's your seat over there, next to me." The crew watched as Alexander the Great, wearing the St. Michael medallion around his neck, took his seat as one of the blue BeeBots showed him how to buckle the seatbelt.

"Once we're underway," ZacBox said to the two crews before they split up, "I will work up a battle plan and transmit it to the Sterope for everyone to improve upon. We will almost certainly be outnumbered, but we have two tactical advantages. First, we have an advantage in knowing where they're going—to where Captain Coda's ship was last reported and destroyed. Secondly, they are expecting only one Electra-class flying saucer, not two. I have no illusions this Zhorban the Merciless will accept my invitation to leave our solar system, but if or when they attack us, they're going to have a fight on their hands."

 Ganymede or Bust

"This is Captain ZacBox, commanding officer of the starship Electra, hailing the commanding officer of the starship fleet approaching the large gas ball planet," ZacBox said as he watched the main view screen for any course adjustment of the alien flight path. The inbound alien fleet consisted of one very large spacecraft, about the size of a U.S. aircraft carrier, accompanied by twenty-seven smaller vessels arranged in a defensive formation around the larger vessel, which ZacBox took to be Zhorban's flagship.

The Electra was still too distant to scan the alien ships for lifeforms effectively. ZacBox had estimated each of the smaller spacecraft held maybe seven crew members, similar to what Captain Coda's vessel was confirmed to have held. ZacBox did the math in his head, 7 x 27 = 189, and he guessed the flagship might hold at least twice the number of crew as the support vessels, bringing the total number of aliens they were facing to roughly four hundred.

The total number of Earthlings aboard the two flying saucers was five, supported by a Pleiadian, who was dead set on revenge, two blue BeeBots, plus a teenage Puckster who had developed a taste for vegetarian pizza topped with extra radish flavoring.

Captain ZacBox had informed both crews in advance that he had planned to make initial contact with the invading fleet while they were still beyond the alien's effective firing range, but before they entered the stealth space minefield the Electra and the Sterope had planted using their neutrino torpedoes. Within a few seconds of his hailing the alien commander, the view on their main display switched to show the inside of the alien's spacecraft.

"This is Zhorban, Admiral of the Centaurian fleet," the menacing figure on the view screen replied impatiently. He was dressed in a similar black uniform as Captain Coda, only the red hourglass insignia of the black widow spider on his chest was much larger.

"Admiral, I ask you to state your intentions in this solar system," ZacBox said calmly as he sipped a cup of hot tea.

"My intentions are to destroy you and anyone else from your pathetic little planet that stands in my way," Zhorban threatened. "You may have gotten lucky shooting down one lone spacecraft with an inept commander, but now you face a far more superior foe, led by a far less merciful commander."

ZacBox watched his monitor as the alien fleet adjusted its heading to intercept the Electra in orbit around Jupiter, just as they had anticipated. "Admiral, I must warn you there is a stealth minefield all around your fleet. I ask you to halt your aggression and invite you to leave this solar system at once."

"HA! You little earthcrawler! Who do you think you are! You are one lonely ship against a mighty Centaurian armada. I decline your invitation and invite you to go straight to hell!"

ZacBox watched as the alien ships accelerated and shifted formation, sending nine smaller ships to the front of Zhorban's flagship as they entered the space minefield laced with stealth neutrino torpedoes. Within seconds the lead spacecraft began exploding as they impacted the torpedoes, clearing the way for the larger vessel to follow. Seven of the escort vessels broke formation and turned away. Zhorban's flagship fired on them as they fled. Five escort vessels were destroyed but two managed to get away.

"Grrr," Der growled from the first officer's seat to the left of the captain. He pointed his index finger excitedly at the main view screen and shook his head.

"What a waste, he's killing his own people!" Cadence said as they watched the drama unfold on the screen before them.

"Now we know why they call him Zhorban the Merciless," Anzu said as she entered the bridge from the hallway and slipped into her seat. "Permission to join you on the bridge, Captain."

ZacBox noticed Anzu was wearing her black sports bra and had a white bandage wrapped around her ribcage. He looked from Anzu to Cadence, seated to the right of him. Cadence looked at Anzu as she started bringing her cockpit to life. Cadence turned back to ZacBox and nodded her head in approval.

"Permission granted, Officer Gozen; your warrior skills may soon be required."

Der leaned forward and patted Anzu lightly on the shoulder, welcoming her to the fight.

"Anzu, how many stealth torpedoes remain active in the minefield?" ZacBox asked.

"Three, Captain."

"Prepare to blow all three sequentially on my command," ZacBox said waiting for the last of the escort vessels to enter the minefield box. "Three, two, one. Fire. Fire. Fire."

Three explosions appeared on the main screen. Anzu refreshed her monitor then turned to ZacBox, "Five escort vessels destroyed Captain. Their flagship appears undamaged."

"Understood," ZacBox said as he downed the last of his tea and handed his cup to the blue bot, "Bot, would you please stow this in the galley? We have some unfinished business to attend to." The bot accepted the cup and waddled toward the galley in the back of the ship. ZacBox pulled back on the yoke, turned the Electra to the right and pushed the throttle forward to F3. He aimed the Electra toward Ganymede, the largest of Jupiter's 79 moons. It was fascinating for ZacBox to learn that Ganymede is the ninth largest object in the Solar System. It is Jupiter's only moon known to have a magnetic field, making its orbit an ideal battlefield environment for flying saucers powered by a maglev propulsion system.

ZacBox's plan was to lure Zhorban into following him as close to the surface of Ganymede as possible, where he knew Captain Jorvik and his crew would be waiting to fire upon Zhorban's flag ship as it flew past. ZacBox had also picked Ganymede since it has no atmosphere to slow down the Electra or the Sterope, or their neutrino torpedoes. ZacBox hoped that with two flying saucers and having a better situational awareness of the battlespace, they would have gained the tactical advantage over Zhorban from changing the battle conditions he could not have factored into his plan of attack.

"Battle stations in fifteen seconds," ZacBox commanded as he fastened his shoulder harness around him and glanced at the faces of his crewmates. "This we do so that others may live," ZacBox said, repeating the PJ's oath, as he pushed the throttle to F5 and dove toward the dark side of Ganymede. As ZacBox pulled the Electra out of the bottom of the Leilani Loop, he slowed to F3 and leveled out at a thousand feet above the surface. He aimed for the saddle between two mountain peaks, where he knew Jorvik and the Sterope would be waiting on the other side.

"Meet your fate!" Zhorban shouted as he fired an impressive barrage of missiles from the flagship. Two of the escort ships also fired upon the Electra.

Using the maglev propulsion, Captain ZacBox evaded the enemy inbound missiles. As if leading the fox to the hounds, the saucer Electra slowed then slipped between the two mountain peaks, giving a perfect firing solution to the crew aboard the Sterope.

Onboard the Sterope, John Paul skillfully locked the crosshairs of the saucer's weapon system aimed tightly on the rear of Zhorban's flagship as it sped overhead. "The shot is yours Captain Jorvik," John Paul said.

"Torpedo away," Jorvik said as he pushed the fire button on the yoke with his thumb. They watched as the neutrino torpedo pierced the rear hull of the alien ship. After a split-second delay, the weapon reached the center of the vessel and exploded with extraordinary outward energy. Secondary explosions could be seen coming from within the vessel, now emitting fireballs as the weapons, fuel and oxygen ignited. Since Ganymede had no atmosphere, each of the fireballs had to have been created by whatever the alien ship was carrying; deadly weapons no doubt intended to have been used during the invasion of Earth.

"John Paul?" Jorvik said to the young Earthling seated in the Chief Engineer's seat.

"Yes, Captain?" the young man answered as he turned back to face the Pleiadian.

"Was that the torpedo you repaired with the gold-plated paperclip from your great-grandfather and President Kennedy?"

"It was," John Paul said with a knowing smile.

"Then that was the second time that tiny piece of gold-plated metal saved us and your planet from unimaginable consequences."

The Electra had also fired two more neutrino torpedoes at the exposed rear of the escort spacecraft and had unleashed her ion cannons on the few remaining escort ships within range. The crew aboard the Electra watched their monitors as Zhorban's flagship, and all but one of the smaller escort ships, exploded in a blinding light, sending countless pieces of debris showering down onto the surface of Ganymede.

ZacBox turned the Electra back around and switched the main view screen to a split screen, bringing up an image of the one remaining alien spacecraft surveying the wreckage on the surface of Ganymede. On the left screen ZacBox closely watched for enemy activity and on the right screen the interior of the Sterope. "Do you detect any survivors on the lunar surface?" ZacBox asked the somber crew aboard the Sterope.

Both crews watched their monitors for several seconds as their infrared cameras scanned the wreckage below. Two heat signatures aboard one of the smaller vessels flicked for a few seconds and then blinked off as if someone had blown out a candle.

"Other than the seven souls aboard that one lone escort vessel searching the wreckage," Arjun replied, "there are no survivors."

"It is unfortunate so many souls were sacrificed by such an evil leader," Jorvik said.

Cadence said, "But everyone on Earth is safe once again."

Both crews sat quietly watching the tragic scene playing out below, as the one surviving vessel hovered slowly over the vast debris field, searching for survivors and finding none. It was almost beyond comprehension that in less than fifteen seconds the mighty Centaurian armada had been reduced to lifeless scattered wreckage strewn across the surface of this moon of Jupiter.

Anzu finally broke the silence, "When I whet my flashing sword, and my hand takes hold on judgement, I will take vengeance upon mine enemies, and I will repay those who haze me."

"Sun Tzu?" Cadence asked softly.

"Alexander the Great," Arjun answered from the bridge of Electra's sister ship. "That is what he vowed, more than two thousand years ago, when he invaded my homeland, India, where he was ultimately defeated and sent home in disgrace."

"Grrr," Der growled and nodded his head in agreement.

"Finally," Jorvik said, "after all these years, I feel the deaths of my crewmates have now been vindicated. I suppose it may be true what you Earthlings say, 'revenge is a dish best served cold,' but I feel my Pleiadian heart, that is supposed to be seeking love, peace and spirituality, may need more than a little redemption when we eventually reach the Pleiades Star Cluster."

"Look! That last one's getting away," John Paul said, pointing to the one remaining escort vessel abandoning its search and rescue mission and making a break in the opposite direction. "Shouldn't we pursue it and finish the job?"

Without speaking, Captains ZacBox and Jorvik turned their saucers in pursuit of the lone escaping alien vessel. Leaving the magnetic field of Ganymede behind, both captains switched to ZPE drive, creating a space vacuum around both ships, shielding them from the shots fired at them from the alien spacecraft. Several cannon shots and two missiles were fired, but all were easily deflected. The saucers closed the distance on the enemy ship as it stopped firing. The vacuum shields wrapped around the Electra and Sterope protecting the two flying saucers. No doubt the alien crews had accepted the fact that they were defenseless.

Captains ZacBox and Jorvik did not know if the enemy vessel ran out of ammunition or its captain simply gave up on trying, but no other shots were fired. They watched as the Centaurian captain tried desperately to outrun the two flying saucers. After a few minutes the short space pursuit came to an end. The enemy vessel slowed and then coasted to a stop and turned to face the Electra and Sterope, accepting the fact their adversary held every superior tactical advantage.

"Jorvik?" Captain ZacBox said deferring the decision to shoot down the enemy vessel to the captain of the Sterope.

"Put them on the main view screen," Jorvik directed and then turned his attention to the captain of the fleeing spacecraft. "Hailing the commanding officer of the Centaurian starship, this is Captain Jorvik, Pleiadian commander of the starship Sterope. Do you read me?"

"This is Princess Ula de Orange from the Omega Centauri Star Cluster; I read you," a female voice said as the monitor screens of the Sterope and Electra displayed the young captain sitting in her captain's seat on the darkened bridge of the alien spacecraft.

"You are of a ruling class?" Jorvik asked, after thinking through how she identified herself.

"Yes, I am," Princess Ula replied, as she removed her helmet, and then turned up the interior lighting and looked bravely into the monitor. "Captain Coda was my uncle. His mother, my grandmother, is queen of what you know as the Omega Centauri, NGC 5139. What are your intentions for my ship and crew?" She wore a black uniform, also with the red hour-glass image on the front. Without her helmet she appeared far less menacing. In fact, ZacBox thought she was quite beautiful. She had copper colored skin, yellowish-brown eyes and long black hair. Except for the yellow tint of her eyes, ZacBox thought she looked somewhat like the people on his great-grandfather's Reservation or from the island people of Hawaii or Japan. Two of Princess Ula's crewmates came to stand behind her and removed their helmets as well. Evidently this gesture was a sign of surrender.

"I am your prisoner and will accept whatever fate you choose,"

Princess Ula said as she dropped her helmet to the floor, stood and stepped forward. "I ask only that my ship and crew be allowed to return to Omega Centauri as they were simply following my orders. As captain, I surrender myself to you and will come aboard your vessel as your prisoner or will end my life here if a death sentence is what you demand."

Both the crews of the Electra and Sterope watched as the young captain withdrew a ten-inch knife from her belt and held it to her heart. Her actions reminded Anzu of the Samurai warriors' willingness to sacrifice their own lives in defeat. Now, this noble Centaurian captain was willing to take her own life in order to save her ship and her crew.

"We no longer perceive you as a threat," Jorvik said. "You and your crew may return to your Star Cluster."

"You are most kind Captain," Princess Ula said, visibly moved by Jorvik's kindness. Then she replied, "I thank you for sparing our lives."

"You are welcome. It is my hope that in sparing your lives, you and your crew will one day prove my decision was not simply in your best interest, but in the best interest of all who share this universe," Jorvik replied. "I understand the purpose of your mission was the extraction of fossil fuels from the planet known as Earth."

"Yes, you are well informed. Our fossil fuels are on the brink of depletion. At the current rate of consumption our oil and gas reserves will be completely exhausted within the next two generations. Our political and military leaders ordered the invasion of the blue planet you call Earth, as the only means they could foresee to ensure the survival of future generations of Centaurians."

"It is unfortunate they were so shortsighted," Jorvik replied.

"How so?" she asked.

"There are many in the universe, including my people the Pleiadians, who are willing to share their talents and technology for the betterment of others."

"I will remember your words," Princess Ula said. "May we leave now? There are many death notifications to be delivered to Omega Centaurian families back home."

"There is one other message I would encourage you to carry as well, Princess Ula."

"Yes, what is that?"

"I want you to know that I speak now from personal experience, Princess Ula, when I respectfully suggest that after you return home, you and your crew carry a message not of defeat and revenge, but one of conservation for your scarce natural resources. Return with a message of hope from your neighbors in the Pleiades Star Cluster, for we as a people remain committed to sharing our renewable energy technologies with all those who seek harmony in the universe."

"We will share your message of hope," Princess Ula said, "Captain Jorvik and Captain…?"

"ZacBox," Zac replied, "Captain ZacBox, Princess Ula. We wish you and your crew safe interstellar travels and hope we meet again in space and in peace."

"By your leave Captains," Princess Ula said as she resumed her position at the helm. The crews of the Electra and Sterope watched as the Centaurian spacecraft slowly turned, then disappeared into the vastness of space.

"Jorvik?" Cadence said from the bridge of the Electra to the Captain of the Sterope as it pulled up beside her sister ship, leaving Ganymede in the distance behind them.

"Yes, Cadence," Jorvik answered.

"I don't think there's anything wrong with your big Pleiadian heart."

"Is that your medical opinion, Dr. Bahar?" Jorvik asked with a slight grin forming on his lips.

"More of a personal observation," Cadence replied softly.

"Chief Engineer von Braun?" ZacBox asked of John Paul. "I would be most interested in your professional opinion as our Chief Engineer; are both ships prepared to accelerate to a ZPE speed of F13?"

"Both ships are right as rain, Captain," John Paul said proudly.

"Very well," ZacBox said, "Captain Jorvik, please lock the Sterope onto my starboard wing. I will take command of both ships as we begin our search for the nearest wormhole."

"Done," Jorvik replied, "you have our helm. Might I ask if you intend to drop through the Einstein-Rosen Bridge directly to the Pleiades or take the closest wormhole to Orion and then find a second wormhole from there to the Pleiades Star Cluster?"

"I'm leaning toward going to Orion first, then immediately going on to Pleiades from Orion's Belt," ZacBox said, "but I'm open to suggestions."

"It's your call Captain ZacBox," Arjun said, "and we will follow you anywhere, so I don't mean this to sound like I am questioning your authority, but since you are asking for inputs, I question if navigating two wormholes, instead of just the one, might be doubling our risk. My biggest concern is that we have no way of knowing what's waiting for us on the other side. Either way, a decision has to be made; I'm just glad it's you and not me making it."

"Good inputs. Thank you Arjun," ZacBox said, "There is a risk the Rainbow Bridge, as some of our ancient people knew it, could close before we can get through it; so, I sense it would take more time to slip through a longer Einstein-Rosen Bridge, giving it more time to collapse. Navigating two bridges might take more time, but I think it's maybe safer. I don't plan on us spending much time in the Orion Constellation. Anyone else have anything to add?"

"I might have something to add Captain," Anzu said, as she got up slowly and started back to her cabin holding her left side.

"Anzu are you bleeding again?" Cadence asked, getting up from her seat and walking toward Anzu to inspect her bandages.

"The bleeding has stopped. Please give me a moment," Anzu said as she left the bridge.

Cadence returned to her seat next to ZacBox and whispered, "I think she is in considerably more pain than she lets on. With our limited onboard medical instruments, I have not been able to diagnose what's wrong internally, so therefore, I am limited on what I can to do medically. I am trusting that we will find better medical care for Anzu once we arrive in the Pleiades."

"Then let's not waste any time. We'll head to Orion's Belt and then as soon as we drop out of the wormhole, we'll start our search to find a second bridge to the Pleiades," Captain ZacBox replied confidently. "We don't know what or who might be waiting for us on the other side of either wormhole, but I feel two shorter wormholes might be safer than one longer wormhole."

"May I quote you on that observation Captain?" Arjun asked teasingly.

"Structurally speaking, he might be correct," John Paul said. "Two shorter Einstein-Rosen Bridges might be stronger structurally then one longer Bridge."

"Captain Jorvik," ZacBox asked, "do you agree with us making a quick stop in the Orion Constellation before plotting a second course to your star cluster?"

"Agreed," Jorvik said, and then asked, "But I am curious. You sense this is the correct decision, yet the Milky Way is such a huge galaxy, how can anyone be certain of our path ahead?"

"I'm not certain," ZacBox said.

"This might help," Anzu said, as she returned to the bridge and handed ZacBox a small cream-colored envelope.

ZacBox looked at the embossed seal on the envelope and asked Anzu, "Is this from the Vatican?"

"It is. One of the Swiss Guard delivered it to Julian, the evening before we left Earth."

"What does it say?" John Paul asked.

ZacBox removed a small matching notecard from the envelope and read the handwritten message aloud to both crews, "Seek Him who made the Pleiades and Orion, and turns deep darkness into the morning, and darkens the day into night; who calls for the waters of the sea and pours them out upon the surface of the earth: The Lord is his name. Amos 5:8"

"Amen," the crew of both ships whispered.

"That settles it," ZacBox said. "Next stop, the constellation Orion."

"But where are we going to find the entrance to the wormhole?" Arjun asked.

Captain ZacBox pushed the T-shaped chrome throttle on his right armrest to F5 and pulled back on the yoke, pointing the nose of both flying saucers toward the distant stars. "There," he said pointing both starships toward the two tiny stars nearly lost in space. "I can't say how I know, but I know it's there." Recalling the words his mother whispered in his ear as she kissed him on the forehead goodnight, ZacBox repeated the quote from the immortal Peter Pan, "Second star on the right and straight on till morning."

November 18th 13:32 hours UTC Astradate 11111.8
Starships Electra and Sterope, Einstein-Rosen Bridge, Orion Portal, Taurus Constellation

"Wendy was right; mapping wormholes is very complicated; all the conditions in spacetime seem very fluid," Captain ZacBox admitted as he lined the Electra and Sterope up on the outer rim of the Orion Portal. "I don't know that we would have ever discovered the entrance had it not been for our little Bot here," ZacBox said as he glanced over to his left where blue Bot sat in his favorite place, on the lap of Alexander the Great.

"BeeBot, Bot, Bot," the AI purred as he pointed excitedly to the main screen displaying the opening of the wormhole.

"He's the only one of us who's been to Pleiades, so I suppose it stands to reason he might know the way back," Cadence commented as she leaned forward in her seat to look past ZacBox at the little blue Bot. "Captain?"

"Yes Cadence?" ZacBox replied.

"Do you suppose SETI could pick up a digital signal if we were to send a short message back to earth letting them know we're okay?"

"I suppose so," ZacBox said.

"SETI was monitoring this region of space before we left. But what should we say?" Anzu asked.

"I've got it," ZacBox said as he transmitted a short message.

Cadence read the words on the main screen aloud, "Tell Boson, the Eagle has lifted off." She turned to ZacBox with an inquiring look on her face, "Boson…as in Satyendra Nath Bose?"

"Yes, and Dr. Brondsted will let Professor Fibonacci know we're not under duress and that we've been paying attention to our STEM courses," ZacBox replied, then turned to Jorvik's image visible on one of the monitors, "Everyone ready on the Sterope saucer?"

"Ready here," Captain Jorvik replied and gave a thumbs-up signal from the bridge of the Sterope.

"Let's see where this space tube leads," ZacBox said as he guided the two saucers into the maw of the wormhole. The two spacecraft began accelerating through the portal, using their ZPE engines for propulsion and hydrogen thrusters for steering. The stars and bright lights around them began racing past at blinding speed, as he accelerated to F13. Instinctively, ZacBox rolled both ships slowly to the left inside the wormhole then he saw it materialize in front of him, the Fibonacci Spiral, just as he had seen in Santa Fe, laying on his back with Professor Fibonacci, staring up the Miraculous Staircase to the Heavens. He pushed back in his seat to enjoy the ride.

Although it was undetectable to the crew, they knew time was slowing down for them, while it remained constant for everyone on Earth. They calculated their flight time through the wormhole to reach Orion would require less than two hours, but knew that several more months would have passed on Earth. To remain calibrated to their families and friends on Earth, where they hoped to return someday, the crew aboard the Electra had programmed their atomic clocks and Astradate calendars to be synchronized with those on Earth.

February 25th 15:21 hours UTC Astradate 11012.5
Starship Electra, Exit Orion's Belt Portal, Orion, Taurus Constellation

"What the heck? Where did all these spaceships come from?" John Paul asked as the Electra and Sterope dropped out of the wormhole to find a large cluster of spacecraft gathered around the exit of the Orion Einstein-Rosen Bridge.

"They don't act very friendly, Captain," Anzu said as she watched the icons of the alien ships on the screen forming up into an attack formation and start moving toward the Electra and Sterope's position. "I advise we go to battle stations Captain."

"Stand by," ZacBox said, as he opened a communications channel to the alien fleet. "This is Captain ZacBox, commanding officer of the starship Electra, hailing the commander of the fleet headed our direction. Please state your intentions."

"Well now, Captain ZacBox," a voice replied as the figure of an alien came into view on the main screen in front of both flying saucers. "My intentions are to unwrap these two little gifts the space gods have dropped in my lap. Heave to and prepare to be boarded."

When the crews aboard the Electra and Sterope got a close-up view of the alien, ZacBox thought he looked like a huge praying mantis. He had an elongated body, a large head adorned with two long antennas and big black almond-shaped eyes. His body was covered with green scales and he had two large pincers attached to his jaws. When he spoke, a long pink tongue curled in and out of his mouth.

ZacBox closed the comms channel and asked, "Why is everyone always trying to board us?" Then he turned toward Anzu, "What is the count on the enemy vessels and our weapons status?"

"Thirty-six enemy spacecraft," Anzu replied calmly, and then added, as she looked up from her computer terminal to face her captain, "Three neutrino torpedoes remain in the magazine and all ion cannons are fully charged and at the ready. It appears to be a target-rich environment, Sir."

"Agreed," Captain ZacBox replied, appreciating Anzu's warrior ethos and self-confidence. "Captain Jorvik? What does your weapons count look like?"

Jorvik replied, "One neutrino torpedo remaining, ion cannons fully charged and we stand by at the ready Captain." ZacBox looked at John Paul to confirm he agreed with their total torpedo count of four correct, both wishing they had a full magazine. John Paul held up one finger and nodded his head as he requested more time to scan the enemy vessels to assess their strengths and probe for any vulnerability.

ZacBox tapped the button on his lapel pin twice to open the channel to the commander of the alien fleet. "I'm afraid we don't have time to have you aboard this visit captain—I'm sorry I don't believe I caught your name?"

"This is Captain Houkie," the reptilian looking alien on their view-screen said as he slammed his fist on the table in front of him. "I am the commanding officer of the M-54 Force in front of you; heave to now or you will be fired upon!"

ZacBox switched off the open mic, and then said, "John Paul, anything yet on their weapons capabilities?"

"Judging from the particles left in their wake, their propulsion system is nuclear; therefore, we must assume their weapons systems may be nuclear as well. Since we are not at ZPE, we won't have the space vacuum shielding us and I don't know if our outer hulls can withstand a nuclear explosion, but I suggest we avoid trying to find out if we can."

"Thank you John Paul. Keep probing," ZacBox said as he opened the channel once again to the alien commander becoming visibly outraged on the screen. "Captain Houkie," ZacBox said calmly, "I'm sure you can appreciate our position; we are on a rather tight time schedule here, but perhaps we can have you aboard for a visit at some other time."

"Why you impudent little pissarie! Ours is not a social visit!" Captain Houkie shouted as he jumped out of his seat with rage, shook his clawed fist toward the camera and began shouting commands to his crew.

"John Paul?" ZacBox asked, over their secure comms channel, "I think we're running out of time here."

"Ten more seconds?" John Paul asked.

"Can someone please tell me what a pissarie is?" ZacBox asked over his secure ship to ship comms.

"You don't want to know," Jorvik replied with a smile on his face.

"Captains," Anzu said, "I suggest we go to battle stations."

"Agreed," ZacBox ordered, "Battle stations everyone; stand-by for a quark jump to port. John Paul?"

"Two seconds!" John Paul pleaded, as he entered the final command on his keyboard.

"FIRE!" the alien commander shouted as he ordered the attack on the Electra and Sterope.

"I'm in!" John Paul said excitedly, as his fingers raced across his keyboard. "I've taken control of their computer systems. I shut down their weapons systems and disabled their navigation system."

On the view screens aboard the Electra and Sterope they could see surprise, confusion, and then anger growing on the face of the alien captain as he stormed across the bridge trying to find out why their weapons no longer functioned. He walked up behind a subordinate, slapped him across the back of the head and then pushed him out of his seat. The captain grabbed another subordinate, threw him into the seat and shouted something as he pointed excitedly to a monitor evidently showing their weapons system frozen on the screen.

"You took over the computer systems on all thirty-six ships?" Arjun asked as the crews of the Electra and Sterope watched in amazement as the alien ships on their view screens came to a full stop.

"Yes," John Paul confirmed, "now I am slowing shutting down their onboard life support systems."

"John Paul, are any of these thirty-six ships unmanned?" ZacBox asked.

"Yes, Captain, six are unmanned."

"Are any of those six armed?"

"Yes, four of the unmanned ships are armed, the other two appear to be carrying cargo as supply ships."

"See if you can direct one of their armed-probes to take out the nearest supply ship, and then have all four armed-probes fire on one another at the same time."

The crews aboard the Electra, Sterope and the alien ship watched their monitors as the unmanned probes came to full stop. John Paul sat back in his seat; then armed with simply one joy stick, he turned an unmanned spacecraft toward the nearest unmanned supply vessel and then fired. A huge fireball erupted. "That one must have been carrying oxygen and fuel of some sort," John Paul said as he maneuvered the four armed-unmanned spacecraft into a firing position, where each unmanned ship was aimed to fire at another. Then he pressed the red button on his joystick. The four huge explosions in space rocked the nearest enemy vessels.

"How did you do this?" Arjun asked in disbelief.

"I used a honeypot," John Paul said as he hit enter on his keyboard and turned to face Arjun and Jorvik. "I can't believe they left the back door on their firewall open," John Paul said shaking his head from side to side in disbelief.

"I'm not following you, John Paul," ZacBox asked, "Can you put that in terms a tenth grader like me might understand?"

"Sure, I saw they had launched a cyberattack on our computers, so I diverted their cyber probe to an enticing set of false data I had compartmentalized weeks ago. Then when they began extracting data from our computer to theirs, I embedded a hidden code in the dummy data set that would allow me to remote into an attacker's computer system and seize control."

"Why is it called a honeypot?" Anzu asked.

"It's a naval term Saint Michael taught me," John Paul explained.

"In the old days naval warships kept only small amounts of gunpowder near their cannons or on their decks to minimize the damage if they exploded. Most of their powder was cached below decks in separate compartments. Warships carried small boys with them when they went to sea and when the fighting began, the little boys, called powder monkeys, would scurry below deck and carry up powder in small amounts to be loaded into the cannons. When they were not in battle, which was most of the time when they were at sea, another job the powder monkeys had was to empty the ship's many chamber pots, which they called honeypots because of the smell."

"I see," Anzu replied with a knowing smile, "that sounds like a Saint Michael story."

"Cybersecurity experts back on Earth have used this counter technique for years," John Paul explained. "I am just surprised it worked as well as it did on these Reptilian spacecraft."

"They underestimated their adversary," Anzu commented. "Sun Tzu would not have approved."

"Well, let's not wait around for them to figure out a counter defense," ZacBox said as he opened a hailing frequency to the alien vessel. "Captain Houkie, this is Captain ZacBox again, I hate to impose, but before we leave this star cluster for our next appointment, I want to explain something."

ZacBox watched the view screen as Captain Houkie struggled to breathe. "I'll kill you! If…if… it's the last thing I do!" ZacBox watched as Captain Houkie clutched his throat and shook his fist. Then he saw two pairs of hands reach up and grab the alien captain around the throat and drag him kicking and screaming away from the bridge.

"Captain ZacBox," another uniformed Reptilian officer said as he stepped in front of the monitor and unbuttoned the top button of his uniform tunic. "This is First Officer del Rouscia," he said calmly. He straightened his uniform jacket, while a dozen uniformed Reptilians formed behind him in support. "It appears there has been a slight mutiny aboard our ship, and I have just recently been promoted."

"We watched your change of command ceremony," ZacBox said. "Congratulations on your promotion."

"Thank you Captain ZacBox," del Rouscia replied, as he struggled to breathe. "Would you be open to discussing the terms of surrender?"

"I would indeed," ZacBox replied as he motioned John Paul to reactive the life support systems on the Reptilian spacecraft.

"Thank you Captain," del Rouscia said as he found it becoming easier to breathe aboard his ship.

"I assume your terms are for unconditional surrender?" del Rouscia acknowledged.

"I have but one condition," ZacBox replied.

"What is your condition?" del Rouscia replied, seeing his life support and navigation systems being restored.

"When you return to M-54, you, Captain del Rouscia, will personally lead a campaign to denuclearize all energy and weapons systems across your galaxy. In return, I will ask your neighbors in the Pleiades Star Cluster to consider sharing their renewable energy technologies."

"Your confidence in my abilities is very much appreciated Captain ZacBox," del Rouscia said as the two large Reptilians who had subdued Captain Houkie returned and stood beside del Rouscia. The crews of the Electra and Sterope watched as the two large Reptilians began to replace del Rouscia's rank insignia with that of a higher rank.

"It would appear I am not the only one who has confidence in your leadership abilities Captain del Rouscia. I am reminded of something my great-grandfather told me the last time we spoke. He said some people get to choose their fate, others find their fate has been chosen for them."

"I will remember and share your words and those of your great-grandfather. By your leave Captain ZacBox," Captain del Rouscia said as he assumed the captain's seat and turned the Reptilian fleet back toward their home galaxy.

The crews of the Electra and Sterope waited two Earth hours to make sure the Reptilian Fleet had left the three-star constellation that makes up Orion's Belt. Then they slowly made their way toward Mintaka, the dim star to their right-most edge of Orion's Belt, while preparing to depart Orion for the Pleiades.

"Captain," John Paul said excitedly, cupping his hands around his headphone so he could hear better. "We're being hailed. It's a faint signal coming from a small planet in orbit around Mintaka."

"Put them on the main view screen," ZacBox instructed.

"It's audio only, their technology is analogue and doesn't appear to be advanced enough to give us both audio and visual this far out in space," John Paul explained as he boosted the signal and piped it across the sound system of both saucers. They waited five seconds for the universal translator to select a common language.

"Squeak, squawk…Are they gone? Are they really gone?" a voice from Mintaka asked.

"Are who gone?" ZacBox asked.

"The Reptilians, from Messier 54?" another voice asked.

"Yes, the Reptilians are gone. They are headed home to the constellation Sagittarius."

The crews of the Electra and Sterope heard a loud cheer, and then a third voice asked, "Who is this? Where are you from?"

"This is Captain ZacBox, commanding officer of the starship

Electra being accompanied by the starship Sterope commanded by Captain Jorvik. We are from planet Earth."

"What do you want from us?" the first voice asked.

"Why, nothing," ZacBox said, "we are on a brief stopover on our way to the Pleiades."

"Pleiades?" the second voice asked, "you know the Pleiadians?"

"Why yes," ZacBox replied, "Captain Jorvik in our sister ship is a Pleiadian."

"The Pleiadians are our friends," the third voice said.

"But the Pleiadians did not intervene to help us when the Reptilians came to steal our water," the first voice argued.

"But the Pleiadians were kind enough to take the Belt of Orion to a place where it would be safe," the third voice added.

"I do not understand," Captain Jorvik said, breaking in on the argument. "The three bright stars known as Orion's Belt are still here."

"That's Orion's Belt, we're talking about the Belt of Orion, the jeweled Belt of Orion…" the second voice replied, before being interrupted by the third voice.

"You two shut up; how do we know these people are who they say they are, and this is not some kind of trap? You want our water, don't you? Is that what you're after?"

"No, we have plenty of water," ZacBox explained. "Is that what the Reptilians wanted, your water?"

"Yes," the third voice replied. "They have been stealing our water for centuries, ever since they contaminated their own water on M-54 with nuclear waste. If you have plenty of water, and don't even know what the Belt of Orion is, what is it you want from us?"

"Nothing," ZacBox replied, "I told you we are on our way to the Pleiades Star Cluster and are just passing through your constellation."

"Then tell Queen Sophia the Mintakians send their respects," the first voice replied, before being interrupted by the third voice.

"I told you two to stop talking! I am the one who contacted the Warm Springs Guards. You two don't know what you're talking about…" —then the analogue signal went blank.

"Well, let's leave them to sort things out," ZacBox said as he turned the Electra and Sterope toward the Pleiades. "Prepare for ZPE drive," he said as he watched the little blue AI crawl up onto the lap of the Puckster and buckle himself in. "Bot, would you be so kind as to point the way to the nearest Einstein-Rosen Bridge to the Pleiades?"

The blue bot extended a chubby blue finger toward the black void between the stars visible on the bridge's main view screen. "Beeee," he purred and settled back into Der's hairy green arms.

"Engage the ZPE drives," ZacBox said as he pulled the Electra's yoke back and pointed her and the Sterope toward the blackness between the encircling stars.

 A Puckster's Paradise

As the saucers Electra and Sterope dropped out of the Einstein-Rosen Bridge wormhole into the brilliant Pleiades Star Cluster in the Taurus Constellation, the crews aboard both starships were aware that time for them had slowed down again, while it had remained constant for everyone on Earth. Their flight time through the wormhole to reach the Pleiades Star Cluster had taken only two and a half hours in spacetime; however, when the crews looked at their digital clocks synchronized with Earth time, another two months had passed back on Earth. Both starship crews found the Taurus Constellation incredibly beautiful.

"Well done, Captain. There's Merope, off our starboard side," John Paul said pointing to the star ahead of them on the right. Merope was noticeably less bright than the other six stars of the Pleiades Star Cluster. "How do we know where to go from here?"

"I think this might help," Jorvik said as he removed the chain from around his neck and handed the Pendant of Pleiades to his Chief Engineer.

"Ah, I forgot about the Pendant," John Paul said, as he examined the blue metal Pendant hanging from the silver chain. He felt the weight of the heavy rectangular-shaped Pendant with the seven pearls embedded in a dark blue field and held it up to the overhead light.

"The red diamond in the Pendant of Pleiades is our destination," Jorvik explained, as he steered the Sterope on a heading to Merope. ZacBox followed in the Electra. "My grandfather, Erik the Red, gave this to my father who gave it to me before we left Earth. My father placed it around my neck and whispered in my ear, 'may it give you and your crew inspiration.' I didn't know what he meant until now. If you hold it up to the light you will notice we're on a heading toward the lower star—that's Merope. The star Electra is above and to the right, and Sterope is directly overhead. The one small red diamond appears to be in orbit around Merope; that's where we're going, Cumorah, Inspiration Point. That's where we'll find inspiration for our mission, the Pleiadian pursuit of love, peace and spirituality—universal solace."

"Lead the way Jorvik; we'll follow you," Captain ZacBox said from the bridge of the Electra.

Seven hours later, as both saucers assumed an orbit around Cumorah, John Paul handed the Pendant of Pleiades back to Jorvik and asked, "Where to now?"

"I don't know," Jorvik replied.

"If I remember my history," Cadence said, "Cumorah is a hillside, shaped like an inverted spoon, in New York where Joseph Smith was said to have found a set of golden plates, which he translated into English and published as the Book of Mormon."

"Yes, that was in 1841, two years before my crew and I left Earth," Jorvik said, "and I remember it took us about two years to get the Sterope and crew ready for space travel. There has to be a connection; it can't be a coincidence."

"I remember my great-grandfather saying there are no coincidences in life," ZacBox said, "and the Mormons and the Ute shared a common connection with the Pleiades."

"Once we arrive, I can put us on an orbital course to generate a 3D map of the planet, plotting out any hillsides shaped like an inverted spoon," John Paul offered, and then added, "but it would still take us weeks or months to decide where to search first."

Then the strangest thing happened. Der, the hairy green Puckster stood up and approached the main screen. He stood there quietly for a moment, studying the image carefully, and then pointed to a hillside with three rock outcroppings on the surface. "Grrrr," he growled softly as if he had recognized a familiar face in a crowd or in this case a landmark on a distant planet. The little blue bot waddled over and hugged Der's hairy leg, as if saying goodbye. Evidently these two knew something the rest of the crew did not.

"We might as well start there," ZacBox said as they descended toward the surface of Cumorah. "We'll drop over that mountain peak ahead there and search for a place to land on the other side."

"Captain," Cadence said as she studied the image of the mountain below them, "that's not a mountain. It's a pyramid! I recognize it from the dimensions of the seven pyramids back home at Tikal."

"She's right," John Paul said from the Sterope. "That structure was definitely built by someone with an understanding of advanced engineering and it's really old."

"How old?" Anzu asked.

"It's hard to say for certain from just this initial scan of the ruin," John Paul said, and then added, "but I'd say it's clearly hundreds, if not thousands of years old."

"It feels like it might be a tomb," Cadence said, and then cautioned, "We should proceed reverently."

"Very well," ZacBox acknowledged, "a wise precaution. We'll land over there, in that clearing."

"There's an abundance of vegetation and high humidity," Cadence said as she scanned her sensor readings while the two saucers descended slowly toward the surface. "I expect we will find a wide assortment of birds and insects, perhaps even a variety of animals."

By the time the Electra and Sterope set down, Anzu had already completed a security scan and did not detect any immediate threats.

"Cadence, are we going to need our space suits?" ZacBox asked.

"No, I think we should be fine down there; the atmosphere and gravity seem very similar to what we encountered under the ice cap of Europa. Conditions seem remarkably similar to what we experience back on Earth, but someone should remain behind to monitor our progress from the bridge."

"John Paul, would you mind staying with the Sterope and Electra?" Jorvik asked.

"No problem," John Paul said, and then reminded everyone to check in on their comms system. "But remember my scan for any life forms was only good on the surface, if you go below ground I'm not sure what you may find down there and I may not be able to track you."

"Got it," ZacBox said as he, Cadence and Anzu lined up in the airlock beside the green Puckster. "Der, you've grown a couple inches, and put on a few pounds, since we left Europa."

"More than a few pounds," Anzu said as she struggled to find room to stand next to Der in the airlock. "Too much pizza and ice cream I'd say, and I think he's reached puberty."

"What makes you say that?" ZacBox asked. Anzu just turned toward her captain and looked at him without saying anything. "Oh," ZacBox said, as they stepped out of the airlock into the natural light, noticing for the first time a patch of Der's green hair around his ears and on his chest was starting to turn white. When they met up with Arjun and Jorvik, ZacBox pointed out that the top of Der's head was nearly level with Jorvik's shoulders. "If he keeps growing at this rate, I'm not sure he'll fit through the saucer's airlocks."

Der ignored their conversation and began searching for some familiar reference.

"Now where do we go?" Arjun asked looking for a trail.

"I guess we follow him," ZacBox said as Der started off on a trail leading to the nearby pyramid they thought might be Cumorah.

After a few hundred meters' hike, Jorvik looked up at the ancient stone ruins and said, "This must be Inspiration Point." As they approached the stone steps leading up to the summit, they paused to catch their breath and looked back at the two flying saucers parked below.

Der continued climbing the stone stairs and waited on a platform near the top until the others had caught up. Then he walked between two large stone pillars marking an opening.

"Those stones have definitely been stacked," Arjun commented and then pointed to the large stone archway. "That's a keystone," he said pointing to the central stone at the top of the arch, locking the ancient stones in place. "This must be the entrance."

Der walked up to the stone wall and felt across the surface of several rocks and then pushed on one large rectangular-shaped stone. They watched as a stone wall swung open. Der stepped inside followed by ZacBox, Jorvik, Arjun, Cadence and Anzu. They walked down the shaft to where they noticed a soft yellow-green light shining and entered a large cavern.

"Cadence was right," Arjun said, "this does feel like a tomb."

They followed Der further into the pyramid. Within a hundred meters Der stopped at the entrance of the large cavern and cocked his head to the side. They stood behind him and watched as the young Puckster beat both fists on his chest, tilted his head back and let out a mighty roar, "ARUGH!"

"What's he doing?" Arjun asked quietly.

"Announcing his presence," Anzu replied.

They heard what ZacBox at first thought was an echo. Then he pointed to a pair of purple colored eyes glowing from an opening on the other side of the cavern. "We're not alone."

"Arugh!" came the reply, and Der stepped forward. The crew watched as another much older white Puckster emerged from the back of the cave and stepped into the yellow and greenish-colored light.

Der stepped into the light and faced the older Puckster. ZacBox, Jorvik, Anzu, Cadence and Arjun followed him to the center of the cavern but remained at a respectful distance back as the two Pucksters exchanged some sort of formal greeting. They embraced, and then the older Puckster began what appeared to be a short ceremony, concluding with what they thought was a tour of the cave.

"What are they doing?" Arjun whispered.

"I think we may be witnessing a changing of the guards," Anzu replied.

"Look over there," Arjun said pointing to four large oyster shells sitting on a rock; one was half open exposing a pearl orb. "Those are identical to the orbs on the Sterope and Electra. If they could generate the same amount of energy we could power four more flying saucers!"

"Back there, in that cave," Anzu said, pointing to a smaller cave, "it looks like an old bronze helmet like what the Greek warriors once wore."

"It's got to be the Helm of Darkness," ZacBox said, and then pointed to the small cave opening next to it. "In there must be the Wand of Cerci; Professor Brondsted told me about them, and I'll bet the Ring of Odin and maybe even the Belt of Orion is hidden in there as well."

"Someone must have brought these things here for safekeeping," Jorvik said.

"It looks like they've been here for hundreds of years," Anzu acknowledged. "I think Der came here to help guard these artifacts and relieve the aging Puckster."

"This must be why Der came with us," ZacBox said in agreement.

"Look at this," Arjun said, motioning for the others to come see two gold discs mounted on the cave wall. "These must be two of the four Voyager Golden Records. They were aboard both Voyager spacecraft when they launched in 1977. They contain the recorded sounds and images intended to introduce extraterrestrial life forms to humans on Earth. But why are they here?"

"Evidently somebody thought these needed to be kept safe from someone," Arjun replied. "Someone must believe this is the safest place in the universe."

"My people may have intercepted Voyager and thought this was a safer place for the gold discs than traveling through space, where they might fall into the hands of someone like Zhorban the Merciless," Jorvik said.

"But these priceless relics are being guarded by just one Puckster. Is that wise?" ZacBox asked.

"I wouldn't want to tangle with one again," Anzu replied rubbing her side where her injuries were not yet healed from the fight she had back on Europa. "If you built a large fortification, and surrounded it with weapons and soldiers, someone sooner or later is going to wonder what you are trying to protect. This might be the safest place for them, hidden from view and guarded with a minimum of protection."

"Over here," Arjun said, "this stone has been engraved with what looks like an interstellar map. Here's the Seven Sisters, Pleiades, and there's a black pearl embedded here where Merope is located. Does that mean she's about to become a dead star?"

"I don't know, but John Paul's earlier scans of the planet's surface suggested this place is no longer inhabited," Cadence said. "There's another engraving on the backside. I can't make out these hieroglyphics, but this is definitely an image of a tree and this must be a map of the interior of this pyramid. What do you suppose it means?"

"Maybe we're supposed to find this tree," Anzu suggested. "It must be important."

"But this place is huge," Arjun said. "It would take us weeks to explore it all."

"Let's split up in teams," ZacBox suggested. "Let's meet back here in two hours. Arjun, you and Cadence take the lower level. Jorvik, you and Anzu search this level. I'll climb up those stone stairs over there to search the upper level."

"Be careful," Anzu cautioned the others as she and Jorvik walked further down the dimly lit stone hallway.

ZacBox climbed the stone staircase, glanced down at the center of the cavern below and waived at Arjun and Cadence. He didn't mind exploring the interior of the pyramid alone, even though Cadence's comment about the possibility of this structure serving as a tomb was something he had sensed as well. Her suggestion of proceeding reverently was a precaution he took to heart, as he stepped into a large chamber containing two large crypts. Approaching the crypts silently he tried to read the inscriptions, but was unable to decipher the meaning. From the length, height and width, he guessed each stone crypt might contain the large body of a Pleiadian, or four people his size.

Then ZacBox heard a noise behind and spun around. "Who's there?" he said, trying not to sound as frightened as he felt. He heard it again, coming from a chamber beyond the crypts. The noise sounded like tiny footsteps, retreating down the corridor. He followed and in thirty meters he came to a T-intersection. The lighting to the right was fairly dark, but still brighter than the hallway to his left, so he turned right, trying to memorize the turns he was taking so he could find his way back out. Then he heard the faint click of a stone being kicked ahead in the darkened cavern and saw a small shadow running ahead.

ZacBox followed the shadow, made another right turn and came to a set of stone stairs leading down to an opening below. There, at the bottom of the stairs, he saw it—the most majestic tree he had ever seen. It was four stories tall, with a massive orange trunk, beautiful multicolored leaves and huge branches that seemed to welcome him. As he descended the stairs and approached the tree, he saw a brown furry animal climb up the tree. It looked like a cross between a bunny and a monkey. It chattered as it climbed up the tree and looked back at him.

Then another small furry animal came scurrying in and climbed up the tree, while a third came up a stairway and also scampered up the tree at the center of what ZacBox realized was a huge stone courtyard. It was lit from above and the tree seemed to radiate light. As he moved closer to inspect the tree, three shimmering figures appeared to be standing beneath the tree. The figures were transparent, but the one on the left appeared to be male and looked to be wearing a feathered headdress. The one on the right he thought was female, and she seemed to be wearing a long gown. But the figure in the middle appeared to be larger, maybe seven to eight feet in height, and also appeared to be male. No words were spoken; none were required. The Pleiadian message of love, peace and spirituality was self-evident.

Just then ZacBox heard footsteps coming toward him and turned to see Jorvik and Anzu jogging up the hallway toward him. When they entered the courtyard they stopped to stare up at the beautiful tree. Then more footsteps could be heard approaching the courtyard. They turned to see Cadence and Arjun bounding up the stairs. They stopped in the center of the courtyard and stared up at the magnificent tree as well. When ZacBox looked back to where he had seen the three shimmering images, they were gone.

"I guess it didn't matter which path we took," ZacBox said as he looked into the faces of his friends. "We were all destined to meet here. What do you suppose it is?"

"I think this must be the Tree of Life," Cadence said respectfully.

"You might be right," Arjun said in agreement. "All the great religions on Earth, and possibly across the universe, have some reference to the Tree of Life."

"So, this was our final destination?" Anzu asked.

"I don't think so," Jorvik replied, "I still have the Pendant of Pleiades that I am supposed to hang around the neck of my aunt or someone in a position of authority in this star cluster."

"Well, there is no one here," Cadence commented, adding, "other than the one Puckster, this place appears to have been abandoned centuries ago."

"This pyramid is an engineering marvel and had to have taken great effort to construct. But why would they abandon this place?" Arjun asked.

"Perhaps the planet became unstable," Anzu suggested.

"I am reminded of a quote Professor Brondsted shared with me," ZacBox said. "It was from the author Gene Roddenberry. He said, 'Earth is the nest, the cradle, and we'll move out of it.'"

As ZacBox spoke, a pinecone fell from the tree and landed at his feet. He picked it up and turned it over. "Look he said," holding it up so the others could see the spiral pattern on the bottom. "It's the Fibonacci Spiral."

"It's a gift," Cadence said to ZacBox, "a very special gift."

"Do you think the seeds will grow back on Earth?" Anzu asked.

"I wouldn't bet against it," Arjun replied.

"I will take it back to Earth and ask Dr. Brondsted and Professor Fibonacci where the seeds should be planted, but my great-grand-father always told me, if we take something, we must leave something in return," ZacBox said. "What do you suppose we should leave behind?"

Suddenly they heard a familiar growl, "Drrr," coming toward them from an entrance to the courtyard. They looked up to see Der and the old Puckster joining them underneath the Tree of Life.

"I think we have our answer; this must be where Der's destiny lies," ZacBox said as he watched Der nodding his head in agreement. "But our destinies lie elsewhere. It is time for us to go."

"But where do we go from here?" Jorvik asked, holding up the Pendant of Pleiades on the chain he wore around his neck.

The older Puckster saw the Pendant and walked toward Jorvik. Then, clutching the Pendant of Pleiades in the palm of his hand, pointed the tip of a sharp claw to the pearl positioned furthest to the right in the constellation.

"Celaeno?" Jorvik asked and watched as the old Puckster nodded his head. "It looks like we're going to Celaeno."

"Let's go," ZacBox said, adding, "Daylight's a burning. That's what White Elk always said."

As they made their way back toward the main entrance of the pyramid, they paused at the center cavern containing the ancient alien technologies, including the Pearls of Pleiades, Wand of Cerci, Belt of Orion, Helm of Darkness, Ring of Odin and the Voyager's two golden records. They gave Alexander the Great one last farewell hug. "Till we meet again my friend," ZacBox said. "Grrr," Der growled softly as he held up the Saint Michael's medallion he had worn around his neck since ZacBox had given it to him on Europa.

As ZacBox, Jorvik, Anzu, Cadence and Arjun turned to leave, the older Puckster held up his hand to wait and then walked over to the rock at the center of the cave where the four large oyster shells where located, each containing a pearl orb. He touched the top of one of the open shells and they watched as it slowly closed, securing the pearl orb safely inside. The older Puckster picked up the oyster shell, carried it over to where they were standing and handed it to ZacBox.

"What are we supposed to do with it?" Arjun asked.

"I think it might be meant to power another saucer," ZacBox said as he accepted the gift with both hands and held it tightly against his chest. "Is this for one of the other flying saucers?"

They watched as the older Puckster nodded his head in agreement.

"Imagine what good could be accomplished in the universe with three Electra-class flying saucers," Cadence said. "It is an important gift."

"It's not a gift," Anzu suggested. "I think it is meant as a reward. You weren't given this pearl orb, Captain ZacBox, you earned it."

"We all earned it," ZacBox said humbly. "Both saucers' crews and our ground teams back on Earth, together we earned this reward." ZacBox nodded his head in appreciation to the old Puckster. "It is our responsibility to ensure it is put to good use."

The older Puckster patted ZacBox on the shoulder and turned him toward the entrance to the pyramid. As they reached the entrance, Anzu, Arjun, Jorvik, Cadence and ZacBox turned back one last time to wave farewell to their friend.

"So, was he just a passenger then and not a member of our crew?" Cadence asked trying to understand why it was so hard to leave Der behind.

As they waved goodbye to their friend, Der held up the St. Michael medallion with one hand, beat his chest with the other, and let out one last enormous, "GRRRRR!"

"Alexander the Great will always be one of us," ZacBox said as they waved farewell and turned away.

 **Pinned by the Queen**

"I'm going to miss not having that hairy green Puckster sitting be-hind me," Anzu said to ZacBox and Cadence as the Electra and Sterope accelerated away from the gravitational pull of Merope and headed toward the bright star known as Celaeno.

"Me too," ZacBox said as he transferred the digital image of Sterope's bridge onto the Electra's main view screen. "The Electra feels a little empty without Der onboard. I will miss not hearing his growl in the morning or having him sitting here next to me during our travels."

"Alexander is where he needs to be, at least for now," Cadence said, sipping a cup of hot green tea. "I trust our paths will meet again."

Cadence, Anzu and ZacBox watched the main monitor on their bridge as Arjun, John Paul and Jorvik slowly took their seats on the Sterope's bridge.

"Good morning Captain Jorvik, I hope we didn't wake you," ZacBox said watching the large Pleiadian yawn as he assumed the helm of the Sterope saucer.

"Not at all, we've been up for, well, minutes," Jorvik teased back as he disengaged the autopilot for his spacecraft.

"The question is—are we where we need to be?" ZacBox asked as he disengaged the Electra's autopilot navigation system and checked to make sure the digital readouts on his dashboard were all in the green.

"Yes, this is the proper heading," Jorvik replied. "The telepathic messages I have been receiving from my people in orbit around Celaeno have gotten stronger throughout the night. They are happy we made it this far and will be sending a team of three escort spacecraft to guide us to our landing zone and docking towers. The rest of the official greeting party will meet us in the Pleiadian Capital City of Moroni around mid-day."

"Very well," ZacBox said as he switched the view on their main screen to display the overhead image of the three stars in the upper right quadrant of the Pleiades Star Cluster. Sterope was positioned at the very top, with Taygeta just below and to the right, and further below and to the right sits Celaeno. ZacBox pointed to their final destination before returning to Earth and said, "There it is—second star to the right and straight on 'til morning."

An hour and fifteen minutes later, the Sterope and Electra reduced their FTL speed from F8 to F5, as they approached Celaeno. "There's our escorts!" John Paul announced as he pointed to the three dots on their long-range radar screen, the tiny images of the spacecraft forming the shape of a triangle.

"We are to pull in behind the lead spacecraft," Jorvik said to ZacBox. "I am receiving a strong telepathic signal from the commander of the escort team; the other two ships will come in behind us on our right and left flanks."

"They're fighters," Anzu acknowledged as they approached their positions in the formation.

"Are we in any danger out here?" Cadence asked.

"No, they are simply acknowledging the importance of our visit," Anzu explained.

"Two life forms aboard each ship Captains," John Paul acknowledged.

"They are beautiful," Cadence said as the sleek space craft pulled within view.

"The ships or the lifeforms?" John Paul asked jokingly.

"Both," Cadence replied as the two saucers settled into formation and began the last leg of their journey.

"Up ahead, we're approaching a constellation of smaller satellites and a larger number of unmanned spacecraft in orbit around Moroni," Arjun said as he studied the main view screen from the bridge of the Sterope. "They are configured in concentric rings, almost like the rings of Saturn. I think they may have been clustered together like this purposely to avoid accidental impacts with spacecraft entering or exiting the capital city of Moroni."

"We're going to be making a close flyby of that one gigantic spacecraft ahead," Anzu said.

"It looks like a floating cruise ship," ZacBox said as they approached the brightly lit spacecraft. "It's beautiful! Look at the fireworks! How do they do that in space?"

"They must be electric fireworks with an internal fuel and oxygen mixture," John Paul said.

"Everyone seems excited to see us," Cadence added as they slowed down and flew close enough to see figures in the windows waving at them as they passed.

"Pleiadians on vacation," Jorvik explained. "Space is a very popular tourist destination here in this star cluster. Zero gravity can be a lot of fun, as we know, plus the manufacturing advantages in space can be transformational. There are dozens of these larger ships in orbit around Celaeno and the other six brightest Pleiadian stars at any one time. I understand Moroni is a dome-covered floating city out here in space and serves as a very popular travel destination for business, pleasure or spiritual enlightenment. By not having their entire population located all on one planet, like you do on your planet, if there were a disaster at least most of our people would survive. Here in the Pleiades Star Cluster, there is no need for politics or a monetary system, so there is a lot more vacation time and time for spiritual enlightenment, as well as cultural pursuits, such as art and music."

"We are starting our descent," ZacBox said as he slowed the Electra down from F3 and then to F1, matching the deceleration rate of the escort ships. "There's Moroni; what a spectacular city. It's huge! Much bigger than I ever could have imagined and look, down there, there are trees and grass and water and a beach! I've never been to a beach."

"They have opened a portal for us through the city's transparent protective dome," John Paul said. "Stay the course. Follow our escorts."

"And look, more fireworks!" Cadence said enjoying the celebration.

"There," Jorvik said pointing downward, "there's our docking stations."

The five spacecraft slowed to a stop and then hovered above the seven docking towers. Captains ZacBox and Jorvik switched their camera views to display the images a hundred meters beneath their flying saucers. They could see six of the towers were brightly lit, while the seventh tower, at the bottom of the circular formation, where Merope would have docked, was dimly lit. Intermittent blue and red lights began flashing up two of the towers guiding the Sterope and Electra saucers to their respective towers and then down toward their moorings.

The crews felt and heard a distinctive "clunk" as the three mooring claws secured the saucers to the towers, clamping their spacecraft down securely into the docking stations. "Whoosh," came the sound of the airlock being connected to the elevator shaft.

"Environmental conditions are nearly identical to what we experienced on Cumorah and grew up with on Earth," Cadence said as she scanned her instrument cluster. "We're here."

Both crews were quiet for a moment, reflecting on the obstacles they had overcome to reach their final destination. ZacBox was the first to break their silence, "Now what, Jorvik?"

"I'll go first," Jorvik said. "They are my people; let me make first contact. I'll come back to fill you in on what lies ahead. From what I have gathered telepathically we're in for a royal reception. It should be an interesting few days ahead. Evidently the Pleiadians on Moroni view our arrival here as a rather historic moment. You are the first Earthlings to have ever made a return trip to Pleiades. Arjun and John Paul, before I leave, I want to thank you for serving under my command on the Sterope. You are relieved of your positions here and may rejoin Captain ZacBox and the rest of your crew aboard the Electra. I am not sure when the Sterope will fly again, or if I will have the honor of being her Captain when she does, but it has been one of the greatest honors of my life to have flown in space beside all of you."

"Arjun and John Paul, we'll wait here until you're back aboard," ZacBox said. "I'm thinking we may want to wear our cultural clothing to meet the official party."

As Jorvik stood and started for the airlock, he stopped and

looked down at his dirty and tattered flight suit, wishing he had something better to wear. Then turned back to face Arjun, John Paul and the monitor screen showing the Electra's crew. "I have been hoping for this moment every day of my life since 1843. I just wish Morgan and Steve Martinez and the other two members of my original crew were here to share this moment with me, with us. Thank you for risking your lives to rescue me. I and my people will be forever grateful."

"Hey, we're PJ's," ZacBox said. "That's what we do—we bring our warrior home to fight another day. Welcome home, Jorvik."

"Thank you," Jorvik said as he, Arjun, John Paul and the Sterope's little blue BeeBot made their way from Sterope's bridge to the airlock and glanced around the bridge one last time as they departed their ship.

Two hours later an open-air hovercraft approached the base of Electra's tower, and Jorvik and another Pleiadian stepped down. Jorvik motioned for the Electra's crew to join him below. He was wearing a new flight suit and a huge smile across his face. He had obviously had a bath and a haircut. Although nourishment had been offered, Jorvik had declined to eat anything until the rest of his team was with him and they had greeted the official party. Captain ZacBox walked away from the Electra's docking tower with First Officer Arjun Basu on his left shoulder and Medical Officer Cadence Bahar on his right, headed toward the waiting hovercraft.

They were followed closely behind by Chief Engineer John Paul von Braun and Security Officer Anzu Gozen, wearing her fierce-looking Samurai armor and helmet. She carried her naginata upright. Two pearl orbs floated above them while the two blue Bots waddled happily behind them; apparently these two AI were happy to be home.

"I see you managed to retain your position as Captain of the Sterope," ZacBox said nodding at the gold rank insignia Jorvik wore on the collar of his new flight suit. The small collar insignia was in the shape of the Pleiades Star Cluster. At the top right of the star cluster was Sterope, with a red diamond at the center.

"Evidently, I have an advocate somewhere who had convinced my superiors my being shot down by a Centaurian spacecraft was more of a 'hard landing' made during a heroic intergalactic peace-keeping mission," Jorvik said as he observed his friends for the first time wearing their cultural clothing. "I see you have all managed to find something suitable to wear."

ZacBox had shaved his head, leaving a traditional two-inch Mohawk down the center. He was wearing his feathered Native American Fancy Dance regalia, consisting of the twin bustles adorned with brightly colored feathers. Under the crook of his arm he was carrying the small wooden drum White Elk had given him, trimmed in the traditional colors of the Ute Nation. The white, black, red and yellow colors representing the four primary colors of all The People who live on Mother Earth. ZacBox also wore his beaded headband and beaded cuffs, with the blue beads intended to honor Father Sky and green beads to honor the trees.

Arjun was dressed in his white Sherwani, the traditional clothing for men from India, consisting of a long jacket with exposed buttons running down the length of the garment. Around his waist he wore a deep purple pagri with a matching purple silk scarf tucked into his breast pocket.

"You clean up rather nicely, Mr. Basu," Cadence said to Arjun.

"As do you, Dr. Bahar," Arjun said admiring the purple sash she wore around her beautiful ivory colored Aztec blouse and her long skirt. In keeping with her Aztec traditions, Cadence wore gold jewelry; including bangles, earrings and necklaces; adorned with seashells, bone, and wood, along with stones of various types, including green jade, blue topaz and black obsidian.

"I hope this isn't over the top," Cadence said as she adjusted her headgear laced with jaguar and crocodile teeth, jaguar claws and brilliant blue-green feathers. She carried her medical bag which was made of crocodile hide.

"It's perfect, you look beautiful," Arjun said, as he reached over and squeezed her hand. "You a little nervous?"

"A little," Cadence admitted, and squeezed his hand back then added, "But not nearly as much as when we met up with the Centaurians. As long as we stick together, I know we'll be fine."

John Paul had chosen to wear his blue and green tartan kilt with his dark blue cap to match his short jacket, tartan vest, a white shirt, and navy-blue bow tie. His black-handled dirk was tucked into the top of his white woolen knee-high sock. John Paul also carried his great-grandfather's burgundy leather briefcase, which he used to hold his custom-built laptop.

Jorvik stepped closer to the Electra crew and then turned to introduce the Pleiadian standing next to him, "This is Prince Borghild; it turns out we're distant cousins."

Prince Borghild stepped forward to officially welcome Jorvik's friends. He was every bit as tall and broad-shouldered as Jorvik, with long braided red hair and a bushy red beard. He was also dressed in a kilt similar to the one John Paul was wearing. "Evidently our ancient ancestors used the same tailor," he said to John Paul with a hearty laugh.

Prince Borghild then walked up to ZacBox, gave him a crisp salute and shook hands, "Welcome Captain ZacBox. We sincerely appreciate you and your crew rescuing my wayward cousin here," he said with a twinkle in his eye, adding, "had I known he was there I'd of dropped by and picked him up myself." Arjun and Cadence were next and were also warmly welcomed. Then he walked up to Anzu, took full measure of her Samurai armor, helmet and weapon and then said, "Your name must be Brynjar, meaning warrior in-armor."

"I am Anzu Gozen," Anzu replied, as she removed her helmet. "I am Samurai, which means, 'those who serve in close attendance to nobility.' What does Borghild mean?"

"Defense in battle," he replied.

"Always wise precaution," Anzu said.

"Come," Borghild said as he motioned toward the awaiting hovercraft being driven by a gleaming white AI. "There are many Pleiadians anxious to greet you, most especially my mother Queen Sophia; she was born there on your planet Earth you know, in Venice, Italy. She always teased everyone that she held dual-citizenship, as a Venetian and a Moronian."

As the hovercraft pulled away from the docking towers, ZacBox looked back over his shoulder and noticed a Pleiadian, three blue bots and two other white robots, similar to the one driving their hovercraft, entering the docking towers. "Don't worry, Captain ZacBox," Borghild said, noticing the worried look on the young captain's face, "They are just running a preliminary diagnostic analysis of both ships so they can be serviced and rearmed. They are highly trained and well supervised by one of our chief engineers." ZacBox nodded his head and turned back toward the front of the hovercraft just as they entered the city gates.

Crowds of Pleiadians gathered along both sides of the tree-lined avenue as the hovercraft carried Electra's crew deeper into the center of the shining city. More Pleiadians stood on the balconies and waved as they passed below. Eventually the hovercraft slowed as they entered the gates of a large stone courtyard. At the far end of a reflective pool stood a stone pyramid.

"That looks like the Mayan pyramids in my homeland," Cadence said as the hovercraft glided to a stop in front of stone stairs leading up to the flat top of the pyramid.

"There are more pyramids on the other side," Arjun said.

"Seven in total," Borghild said, "arranged in the configuration of the Pleiades Star Cluster."

"Just like ours are back on Earth at Tikal," Cadence said.

"Who are those uniformed guards?" John Paul asked pointing to two rows of guards wearing uniforms with silver metal breastplates and helmets identical to the one Julian had worn in honor of their launch day back on Earth.

"They are the Queen's Guards," Borghild explained, as the guards came to attention. "This is an elite attachment known as the Warm Springs Guards; they accompany the queen whenever she is in residence here in the capital city or wherever she travels."

"Their uniforms look exactly like those of the Swiss Guards, who guard the Vatican and the Pope back on Earth," Anzu said.

"There must be a connection," Cadence said.

"The Vatican has acknowledged the existence of extraterrestrial life somewhere in the universe," ZacBox acknowledged. "I'm guessing they may have based their opinion on some solid body of evidence they came across somewhere in the past."

"Come," Borghild said, as they stepped down from the hovercraft and started to climb up the seven stories of stairs to reach the platform near the top of the pyramid.

When they reached the top platform, they took in the surroundings below and admired the six other pyramids in the distance. "Breathtaking view," Cadence said.

"And a breathtaking climb," John Paul added.

"But worth every step," ZacBox said as he admired the view.

"This way," Borghild said, directing them to a large stone throne. "I want you to meet my mother, Queen Sophia, Woman of Wisdom."

"Welcome," Queen Sophia said as she stood and stepped forward to greet them; she was very tall and graceful. She bent forward at the waist and then stood and spread her arms outward, "We have been looking forward to this day." Then she stroked the Pendant of Pleiades around her neck. "Thank you for returning my pendant. It proves you are the first of your people from Earth to return to the Pleiades. We have anxiously monitored your progress for the past twelve centuries. I must confess there were times when we wondered if the people of Earth would ever be able to evolve beyond their violent tendencies, but here you five young people stand. You have demonstrated great courage and wisdom beyond your years. I believe each of you carry within you a promise for all mankind to eventually ascend and proclaim your rightful place in the universe. While this is a path you, as a people, must follow on your own, we Pleiadians believe it is our obligation to help guide a few of you as you mature your natural talents and advance your technologies."

Queen Sophia stepped forward and bent down to embrace ZacBox, "Captain ZacBox, you have proven yourself a noble spacecraft commander. On behalf of a grateful people for returning the starships Electra and Sterope to their home ports, and for your leadership and bravery, I award you the Pleiadian rank of Commander of the starship Electra." She pinned the gold rank insignia of captain on his collar and kissed him on both cheeks."

"Thank you, Queen Sophia," ZacBox said as he looked up into her eyes. Although she towered above him, ZacBox never felt she was looking down on him. Rather he felt the warmth of her embrace linger after she stepped back from him and admired his feathered regalia. He also found her smile mesmerizing, reminding him of Professor Fibonacci's smile back home. ZacBox said, "My crew and I will make sure your trust and confidence are not misplaced."

"I see from your tribal regalia, and the drum you carry, you are a dancer."

"I am," ZacBox replied proudly, "my great-grandfather made this drum for me. He carved it from the trunk of a prayer tree and stretched the hide of a white elk across the top. He played this hand drum during the sacred bear dance on his Reservation."

"What do these seven feathers represent in your culture?"

"My great-grandfather, White Elk, taught me they represent the Seven Teachings, of truth, love, respect, courage, honesty, humility and..."

"Wisdom?" Queen Sophia said, finishing the meaning of the Seven Teachings.

"Yes, how did you know?"

"They are the same Seven Teachings we cherish here in Pleiades. One sacred teaching represents each of the Seven Sisters, the seven brightest stars of the Pleiades Star Cluster."

"My great-grandfather told me the Creation Story teaches the Ute that they were brought to Earth from the Pleiades by Creator."

"Yes, you were, but there are others on the Earth and elsewhere throughout the universe."

"Many people on Earth have felt we were not alone. It is good to know they were correct."

"We will speak more of this, before you return to your planet, but this evening we will enjoy a feast under the Tree of Life. It is intended to be a celebration of your people returning to Pleiades," Queen Sophia explained, and then asked, "Will you dance for us after dinner?"

"It would be my honor," ZacBox said humbly.

Queen Sophia then turned to Jorvik, "You have your grandfather's eyes."

"You knew my grandfather, Erik the Red?"

"Yes, of course, we played together as children. His brother, Yesfir, is my father's father."

"I have heard my father speak the name, Yesfir, many times, but did not know this was his uncle. Please tell me what does it mean?"

"It translates to star-like," said Queen Sophia. "Like you and your friends, Yesfir travels among the stars; some say he is more star-like than Pleiadian. It was he who recommended you for your rank of captain of the starship Sterope."

"Will I meet him?"

"He is not here, in this star cluster, but I believe your paths will cross one day; it's a small universe after all," Queen Sophia said as she kissed him on both cheeks.

Queen Sophia then moved to Arjun, "I understand you are a scientist, a geologist?" She said as she pinned the rank of First Officer on the collar of his white jacket.

"I am," Arjun said, "I have been fascinated by crystals and gemstones for as long as I can remember. I am looking forward to helping my people back on Earth unlock the secrets of the gemstones and crystals we discovered in the cave on Europa."

"Perhaps we can help a little with your desire and maybe add a new crystal or two from other distant places," Queen Sophia said as she kissed Arjun on both cheeks and moved to face John Paul. "And is this the young engineer I have heard so much about? You come from a very famous family. The name von Braun is well-known in our star system."

"It is?" John Paul asked.

"Your great-grandfather was well traveled on Earth and well respected among the stars," Queen Sophia explained as she fastened the rank of First Lieutenant on John Paul's collar. "We have much to share with you, things which might advance your engineering skills back on Earth or wherever your space travels might take you."

"Thank you," John Paul said and blushed as Queen Sophia kissed him on both cheeks.

Then she moved to Anzu. "Security Officer Gozen, I hear you have the heart of a lion," Queen Sophia said as she stood in front of Anzu and pinned the rank insignia of Chief Security Officer on her collar. Anzu stood as straight and tall as she could before the queen, but like her fellow crewmates, she was still several feet shorter than the noble Pleiadian woman before her. Anzu tucked her helmet beneath her left arm as Queen Sophia put her hands on Anzu's shoulders and looked into her eyes. "You are in pain my dear, what is it? Have you been hurt?"

"Yes, I was injured on Europa. Our ship's medical doctor, Dr. Bahar here," Anzu said as she nodded her head toward Cadence, "saved my life, and I will be forever grateful, but there is a burning sensation deep inside me that grows more intense with the passing of each day."

Queen Sophia placed the inside of her wrist across Anzu's forehead for a moment and then said, "You have an infection my dear, and we can fix that, but there is something else I see in your eyes, a flicker of light. There is something there behind the warrior's spirit burning in your eyes. Tell me, my dear, what is it your heart burns for; what is it that you most desire?"

"What I desire most," Anzu said softly and then looked toward the ground before adding, "is to paint the perfect butterfly."

"Ah, that's it," Queen Sophia said as she lifted Anzu's chin up with the palm of her hand. She kissed her on both cheeks and looked her in the eyes. "Then my dear we must start with you painting the perfect caterpillar. But first, for you to concentrate fully on your art, we must tend to your medical needs. Tonight, after our celebration, you and your doctor will accompany me to our infirmary. We will have you painting butterflies within a day or two."

Queen Sophia then turned to Cadence. "From your medicine bag I could see you are a doctor and from your dress I see your family descends from the ancient Aztecans," Queen Sophia said as she pinned the rank insignia of a medical doctor on Cadence's medical bag. "I don't want this to clash with your beautiful outfit my dear. As to your name, Cadence, it infers a rhythmic flow of words or music. Are you perhaps a poet or do you play musical instrument?"

"Yes, I do play several stringed instruments," Cadence replied.

"Do you play the lyre by any chance?"

"Yes, I love to play the lyre. It is one of my favorite instruments."

"Have you heard of the Lyre of Ur?"

"Why yes, of course. If I recall my history correctly, the Lyre of Ur was recovered during an excavation of the Royal Cemetery of Ur. The Lyre of Ur is considered to be the oldest stringed instrument on Earth, dating back in antiquity some 4,500 years. It was recovered among the bodies of ten women. One of the bodies was found with her skeletal hand placed on a Lyre where the strings would have been had they not rotted away. I understand there are three Lyres of Ur."

"There is a fourth, a second Golden Lyre of Ur," Queen Sophia said, as she kissed Cadence on both cheeks. "It is here, in the city of Moroni. Would you consider playing it for us this evening during dinner?"

"Why yes! Indeed! I would be honored."

"Good, then it's settled; tonight's celebration will be long remembered," Queen Sophia said as she turned back and held out one elbow toward ZacBox and the other toward Jorvik, inviting the two saucer Captains to escort her, and the others, down the stairs to where the celebration was beginning in the large courtyard beneath the sacred Tree of Life. "Tell me Captain ZacBox, you and your intrepid crew must be exhausted after your long and arduous journey. I'm sure you noticed the large luxury cruise spacecraft on your way to the city; what would you and your crew say to two weeks' vacation while the Electra is being serviced and prepared for your return trip home?"

ZacBox stopped on the steps as Queen Sophia and Jorvik stepped down two more steps. The two Pleiadians then stopped on the steps below him and turned back to face ZacBox, now almost standing eye to eye. Next to ZacBox, stood Arjun, Cadence, John Paul and Anzu, who had also stopped on the same step, almost as if the five of them had been frozen in place.

Queen Sophia smiled and waited patiently for one of the young people standing on the step before her to speak.

Cadence was the first to break the awkward silence, "Queen Sophia I, we, sincerely appreciate your kindness, but there is still much pain and suffering on my planet. So, if it's agreeable to you, and Captains ZacBox and Jorvik, I would rather spend the next two weeks learning how I might help improve the health and wellness of my people back on Earth from your medical staff."

Queen Sophia smiled, nodded her head and waited for Captain ZacBox to speak.

Before ZacBox could speak, Arjun spoke up, "Sir," he said to ZacBox, "if it's all the same to you I would rather spend the next two weeks learning more about the crystals and gemstones from the experts here in this star cluster. You, Anzu and John Paul can go on without me if you want; I just wouldn't feel right relaxing on a cruise ship when there is so much to learn about the crystals and gemstones before we return home."

"And before I can try to paint the perfect butterfly," Anzu said, "I feel I must first paint forty-nine imperfect butterflies and one perfect caterpillar. From these beautiful flower gardens here, I see there is an amazing assortment of beautiful butterflies in the floating city. If it's all the same to you Captain, I would prefer to stay with Cadence and Arjun. You and John Paul can go."

John Paul spoke up next, "Not me! No way. If there's a chance for me to stay here in the capital city, I would much rather spend the next two weeks studying the advanced technologies all around us from the engineers of this city. That's my idea of having fun. I have so many questions. How is this place powered? How do you keep it floating above the surface of the planet? How do you provide the renewable energy, clean water and food? Those answers and more are what are important to me, learning about the things to make our world a better place when we return. I want to fulfill my great-grandfather's dream of helping build the spacecraft that will allow us to explore the universe. Thank you, Queen Sophia, but with all due respect, I think there is nothing I would rather do than spend the next two weeks crawling through your engine rooms and your power plants with your engineers."

Queen Sophia smiled, admiring the maturity of the four young ambassadors from planet Earth.

Lastly, ZacBox spoke. "Personally, there's nothing I would rather do than spend the next two weeks flying aboard your other spacecraft with their captains. I've got to get a better handle on navigating the ins and outs of these Einstein-Rosen Bridge wormholes, or I'll never get home in time to graduate high school. I hope you're not offended if we don't accept your kind invitation."

"Not at all," Queen Sophia said. "It is what I expected you to say. When Leonardo de Vinci visited us he wouldn't take any time away from his engineering pursuits, unless it was to draw or sculpt or paint. Even then much of his artistic talents were still focused on engineering and advanced technologies. He felt studying art helped advanced his engineering skills and innovative military technologies." Then she turned to Anzu and added with a warm smile, "But instead of painting the perfect butterfly, Leonardo always seemed possessed with painting the perfect smile."

 Homeward Bound

June 19th 10:00 hours UTC Astradate 11061.9
Yellow Star, Outer Arm of Orion, Outskirts of Virgo Super-
cluster, Milky Way Galaxy

"Nicely done captain," Cadence said to ZacBox, from her seat to
the right of the captain's seat.

"That was smooth as silk," Arjun said from his first officer's
seat to the left of the young captain.

"Thank you," ZacBox said, as he relaxed his grip on the steering yoke. "Navigating wormholes with the Pleiadian starship
commanders for the past two weeks evidently paid off."

"You brought us out of that last portal exactly on course to
where we need to be, Captain," John Paul said, adding, "The
Rings of Saturn are just off our port bow. You are lined up to
begin your run home anytime you want."

"Very good," Captain ZacBox said, and then looked down and
to his left where Anzu was seated in the Security Officer's seat.
"Anzu, do you detect any alien vessels or other possible threats
on our horizon?"

"Negative, captain," Anzu replied, "I'm not detecting anything between the Kuiper Belt behind us and Earth's moon in front of us. You're green for go."

"Very good," ZacBox said as he pushed the chrome throttle lever on his armrest forward and aimed the Electra to the space just beyond Saturn's outer ring. "ZPE at FTL F13," ZacBox read aloud as they accelerated steadily around the outer ring and increased their speed incrementally. "Once we come out of this last quarter turn, we should have sufficient speed to reach F21. Then I'll break us out of Saturn's orbit and we'll head for home."

"Sounds good to me," Cadence said as she pushed herself back in her seat and braced for the increase in speed, an unnecessary precaution since the ECU minimized all the g-forces they would have felt by their ECU being parked for a nanosecond in a parallel universe. To lessen the effects of spacetime, Cadence had previously set the saucer's ECU to Earth's gravity and adjusted the artificial environmental conditions to help the crew adapt back to conditions back on Earth. Since the time to reach their destination was short, she adjusted the gravity replicator to 108% of Earth's gravity to help the crew adjust more quickly to the gravity on their home planet.

"Once we approach the Earth's moon I will slow us down to F3 and attempt radio contact with Earth. I'm thinking it would be good to let them know we're inbound," ZacBox said.

"Good idea captain," Anzu said. "We don't want to surprise anyone."

"Agreed, we wouldn't want them to think they're under attack," Cadence said.

"Their deep space radar antennas should pick us up well beyond the lunar surface, but we will probably just show up as an unidentified bogie on their radar scopes," John Paul said. "I concur with letting everyone know we're coming home."

"Once we get within range of our moon," ZacBox said as he slowed the Electra to F3, "I will attempt contact with our command center. Then I think it might be a good idea for each of us to make radio contact with our families personally to let them know we'll be landing in Colorado Springs the day after tomorrow, they will want to be there to greet us at the docking tower."

June 21ˢᵗ 16:43 hours MDST Astradate 11062.1 Summer Solstice
CAT² Electra Docking Tower, Colorado Springs, CO USA Planet Earth

"ZacBox1 to Earth, do you read?" ZacBox said into the headset clipped to his ear. Silence. "This is ZacBox1, captain of the flying saucer Electra, inbound to planet Earth. Do you copy?"

More silence, then static. Then a familiar female voice broke through the static and spoke, "ZacBox1 we read you, this is Chief Mission Officer Wendy Hubble. Welcome home Electra!"

This far out in space, Electra's crew estimated there would be an eight second delay in their radio signals reaching Earth, but soon they heard cheering in the background, as a sense of pride rushed over the crew of the saucer in space and the ground crew in the Ops Center.

"It's nice to be home Dr. Hubble," ZacBox said, "We bring warm greetings from the Pleiades."

"Is Jorvik with you?" asked Wendy, "There's an anxious father here in the command center."

"Jorvik is well and sends his father his respects, as does Queen Sophia," ZacBox said. "However, the Sterope was in need of extensive repairs after its hard landing on Europa. The Captain of the

Sterope thought it best if he stayed behind with his ship for a few more months until she is space-worthy again."

"Understood, I will let Mr. Eriksson know," Wendy said. "I am sure the rest of your families are looking forward to hearing from you, so I will let you go here in a moment, but for planning purposes we have been tracking your progress and are anticipating your landing here at the Electra tower at 10:00 hours tomorrow morning. Does that time frame sync up with your flight plan, Captain ZacBox?"

"Sounds wonderful to us," ZacBox said looking around at the smiling faces of his four crewmates. "We are looking forward to being back on the ground."

After dinner that evening ZacBox went to his cabin and closed the door so he could call his father. "Hi Dad, it's me. Last night in space, I should be home tomorrow morning around 10am."

"Hi Zac, it will be good to have you home, Son."

"It's good to hear your voice, Dad."

"Same here Zac. Everyone is looking forward to greeting you and your four friends when you touch down in the morning."

"I can't wait to see everyone. Will White Elk be there?"

"No, Son, I'm afraid I have some bad news; your great-grandfather walked on two years ago. He died of a heart attack while working in his garden."

"I felt he might have walked on," ZacBox said, as a tear formed in the corner of his eye. "I sensed his presence and thought I heard his voice when I was kind of in a bad way. I was in this cave on Europa, and I remember thinking at the time that the only way his spirit could have reached me was if he was no longer physically back on Earth."

"He lived a long life Zac. He is with his Creator now, but I know you will miss him as much as I do."

"He will be missed on the Ute Mountain Ute Reservation as well. Do you think Alicia Many Horses will be coming up from the Reservation tomorrow?"

"No, I don't expect we'll see her or her family."

"Why not?"

"Well, Zac, Alicia's married now and expecting her second baby in the next few months."

"Married! She said she'd wait for me."

"I wouldn't be too hard on her Zac. I know it's been not quite a year for you since you've been gone, but three years have passed here on Earth since you left, and none of us knew for certain if you would even be coming home. And if you did and were still planning on attending the Air Force Academy, well that would mean four more years she'd have to wait."

ZacBox was quiet for a moment, trying to visualize Alicia being married with a baby and another on the way. "I guess it's probably for the best. Most of Alicia's family lives on the Ute Mountain Ute Reservation and I know she would never have wanted to move away from her family. Without great-grandfather being there, well, I don't know that I would have wanted to spend the rest of my life on the Reservation. I think maybe her mother knew that all along. Will Professor Fibonacci and Dr. Brondsted be at the docking tower in the morning when we land?"

"Yes, I know neither of them would miss your homecoming. In fact, you will be seeing much more of Dr. Brondsted from now on; he and Professor Fibonacci got married last year on a deserted island in the Caribbean. Jorvik's father, Olaf, was best man and I walked Lisa down the aisle. She insisted they get married barefoot on the beach rather than in a chapel."

"Wish I could have been there!"

"It was memorable; have you ever seen a Pleiadian wearing a Hawaiian shirt or in a bathing suit?"

"HA! That would be memorable!"

"Saint Michael told me to let you know the Air Force Academy is holding five slots for you and your crewmembers, if any of you still want to go to the Academy."

"Anzu and I definitely want to go, and we both passed our GEDs; so we're prepared academically. John Paul is pretty excited about starting next week as well, but he wants to weigh his offers from MIT, Harvard and Oxford. Cadence will be doing a residency at the Cleveland Clinic in Abu Dhabi; she wants to specialize in emergency medicine. She'll be staying with Arjun's parents and his little sister, Indu, while she's studying in the UAE. Arjun wants to finish his doctorate degree at the School of Mines in Golden and keeps talking about teaching geology somewhere. He's really excited over a quasicrystal Queen Sophia gave him. He says it will levitate when it's electrified. Maybe he could be a professor at the Air Force Academy one day. But first he wants to publish his research findings on the orbs, crystals and gemstones we are bringing back with us. I can't wait to be home."

"Chef Reggie asked me to find out what you want for dinner on your first night home."

"Anything but pizza!" ZacBox said with a laugh. "I think we've eaten pizza or spaghetti and vegetarian meatballs for breakfast, lunch or dinner almost every day since we've been gone. I'm craving a cheeseburger and French fries and a real milk shake! Please tell Reggie I'm ready for anything other than Italian!"

"Okay, will do, Zac. Be safe. It will be nice having you home tomorrow night."

"I'm looking forward to being home and seeing you and Bo

and sleeping in my own bed."

"Mr. Bojangles is full grown now, but I'm sure he'll recognize you. He still sleeps on your bed every night, unless it's thundering and lightning outside; then he sleeps under your bed. I've taken some time off from the Fire Department; is there's anything you need me to help you with before you start basic training next week at the Academy?"

"Yes, I have been training on our treadmill to run the Pikes Peak Ascent next weekend and wanted to ask if you can drive me to the start line for the race and wait for me up on top."

"I can do that Zac, no problem, anything else?"

"Yes, one more thing, Dad?"

"Yes, Son, what is it?"

"Tomorrow, could you please drive me to the DMV, so I can get my drivers' license?"

June 22nd 10:00 hours MDST Astradate 11062.2
CAT² Electra Docking Tower, Colorado Springs, CO USA Planet Earth

Three F-35 Lightning jetfighters escorted the Electra slowly over the U.S. Air Force Academy football stadium. They flew at 500 feet above ground level, from south to north, and then circled around to the east and approached the Electra docking tower. "Wow!" ZacBox said, as he brought the flying saucer to a halt above the tower. "Everything has really built up down there since we left."

"I spoke with Julian last night," Anzu said. "He said the Center for the Advancement of Talent and Technologies, CAT², has representatives from 11 different countries working here now."

"Something tells me it's about to get even bigger," John Paul said as ZacBox began their descent to the docking tower and lightly touched down.

"Clunk," came the familiar sound as the docking claws locked onto the hull of the flying saucer. That noise was followed by a hissing "whoosh" sound as the airlock connected to the docking station and depressurized the interior of the flying saucer. As ZacBox spooled down the powerplant to zero RPMs, the crew sat in complete silence for a moment.

"Before we leave to go meet our families," ZacBox said as he unstrapped his shoulder harness, "I want you all to know how appreciative I am, as Captain of the Electra, of your service and dedication to our mission. Thank you."

"Captain ZacBox," Arjun said, "I know I speak for the entire crew when I say it has been one of the greatest honors of our lives to have served under your command. None of us knows for certain where our paths will lead us once we step away from this ship, but one thing will forever remain certain, we are PJs and will always do whatever is required to deny the enemy a victory and bring our warrior home to fight another day."

"URRAH!" the crew shouted, pumping their fists in the air, just as the elevator door opened and Saint Michael burst onto the bridge. "What is this? A party or something? Come on you Guardian Angels, there's a bunch of excited folks down there waiting to welcome you home!"

The rest of the day was a bit of a blur for ZacBox and the rest of the crew. After being reunited with their families, they were brought into a large conference room for a twenty-minute debriefing, followed by a luncheon, catered by Chef Reggie from Fibonacci's Diner. Several military and political dignitaries greeted them and asked a lot of questions informally over lunch. After lunch the crew appeared together on camera in front of dozens of international news sources. The crew had been made aware that more in-depth debriefings and other television appearances would take place in the days ahead. John Paul announced during a press conference that he had decided to commit to the Air Force Academy, and was excited to be joining ZacBox and Anzu as incoming freshmen. As expected, Cadence announced she would continue her medical pursuits in the UAE, following a short stay back home in South America. Arjun announced he would be returning to the School of Mines in Golden to complete his Ph.D. The Superintendent of the Air Force Academy offered Arjun an adjunct professorship at the Academy; the position could become full-time once his Ph.D. had been awarded.

Later that afternoon each of the crew were given a short medical exam, followed by another twenty-minute individual debriefing focusing on their designated positions aboard the Electra. At 4:30pm the crew met aboard the Electra one last time to pack their belongings and clean out their cabins. Julian and two members of his security team came aboard and took possession of the orb, crystals and gemstones they had collected on Europa. By 5:15pm ZacBox was standing on the bridge, next to BeeBot, to give his final farewell as the crew left the ship. BeeBot would remain onboard, but as captain, ZacBox made sure he was the last to leave the ship.

When ZacBox finally stepped off the elevator into the underground chamber below the launch tower, he saw Dr. Brondsted standing next to Professor Fibonacci's red Tesla convertible waiting with the passenger door open. "Give you a lift home? Your dad had an errand to run and Reggie and Lisa are fixing dinner. You and your dad are expected next door at our place at 6:30 for dinner. Saint Michael will be there, along with Julian, but the rest of your crew will be having dinner with their families."

"Yes sir, a ride home sounds great Professor Brondsted!"

ZacBox said as he put his flight bag and other personal belongings behind the front seats. "I am happy for you and Professor Fibonacci getting married. It will be great having you both next door, at least for the next week until I report to the Academy."

"Getting back together with Lisa is the best thing that could have ever happened to me. I should have asked her to marry me years ago," Professor Brondsted said as they drove up the ramp, into the sunlight.

A few minutes later they pulled into their neighborhood at Flying Horse. ZacBox looked down the street to where he once rode his bike to school. It felt strange, like it was only yesterday, but at the same time, it seemed so long ago. It was odd knowing everyone he went to school with had graduated and most of his classmates would be starting college in the fall. Maybe he would see a few of his friends at the Academy next week.

As Professor Brondsted turned the red Tesla into his cul-de-sac, ZacBox noticed there were a lot more cars parked on their street than he had expected to see, including his dad's black Chevy pickup, which he always parked in the garage. Dr. Brondsted pulled into ZacBox's driveway and honked the horn. ZacBox got out of the car and watched as the garage door slowly began to open. When the garage door was three feet above the ground, he saw Bo sitting on the floor in the garage. Then Bo spotted ZacBox and came racing out of the garage to greet him.

"Hey Bo!" ZacBox said as he knelt down and gave the three-year-old black lab a big hug. "Look at you! You're a big dog now! Boy have we got some catching up to do."

ZacBox stood up just as the garage door stopped opening. There parked in the middle of the two car garage, was a beautiful black customized '49 Chevy 5-Window pickup. "Wow!" ZacBox said as he stepped inside the garage. "It's just like the one grandfather used to drive!"

"It is the one your great-grandfather used to drive," ZacBox's dad said as he stepped forward and tossed ZacBox the keys. "Grandpa wanted you to have it," he said with a smile on his face. "Did you notice the personalized license plates?"

ZacBox looked down at the front license plate and read aloud, "ZACBOX1, Dad! This is so cool!" Then he looked past the pickup and noticed Professor Fibonacci and Reggie and Saint Michael and Julian were all standing in the garage, along with a half dozen of his father's friends from the fire station, lined up behind the pickup.

"I had to do something with my spare time while you were gone. We did a complete body-off restoration," his dad explained. "I never could have done this by myself," nodding at his six firefighter friends standing behind ZacBox's new truck.

ZacBox's dad opened the driver's door, showing ZacBox the customized tuck and roll black leather interior. "Come on, get in and fire her up," Zeke said as ZacBox got in behind the steering wheel, put the key in the ignition and listened as the engine roared to life.

"That's so awesome," ZacBox said as he turned the engine off, got out of the cab and hugged his dad. Then he went around to each of the firefighters and shook their hands and thanked them for what they had done.

"I can't wait to drive it!" ZacBox said excitedly.

"Well, you better wait at least one more day," ZacBox's dad said. "First thing in the morning I'll drive you down to the DMV and you can get your driver's license."

"I hope you can pass the driving part of the test," Saint Michael teased as everyone laughed. The thought of ZacBox failing his driver's license test, after flying a starship to the Pleiades and back, was quite humorous.

"Who's hungry?" Reggie shouted, "BBQ's ready in the backyard!"

June 24th 08:53 hours MDST Astradate 11062.4
Barr Camp, Pikes Peak, Colorado Springs, CO USA Planet
Earth

As ZacBox ran past Barr Camp, he overtook several other runners. He focused on keeping three elite marathon runners in sight, hoping he might have a shot at winning the Pikes Peak Ascent. The 13.3 mile race had begun below, in Manitou Springs, at an elevation of 7,815 feet above sea level. The finish line was at the summit of the 14,115-foot peak towering above him. He had given some thought to running both the Pikes Peak Ascent and Marathon, racing up to the summit and back down to Manitou Springs, but he was reporting into the Air Force Academy in the morning and that was something he wasn't going to miss. ZacBox's dad had driven him to the start line that morning and promised he would be waiting for him on the summit to take him home. ZacBox wanted to win the race, not just to make his father proud, but to honor his great-grandfather and his people who had made vision quests to the top of Sun Mountain for hundreds if not thousands of years.

Since arriving home from space, four days ago, ZacBox's busy schedule had only allowed him one marathon practice run. He was pleased with his time, 3 hours 43 minutes. Depending on the competition and race conditions, ZacBox felt he had a good shot at the record. In fact he had never felt stronger in his life, thanks to the ECU onboard the Electra and the physical fitness routine Cadence had implemented to keep the crew in shape while in space. He had grown a full inch in space, but was still just 5'-5" tall, an average height for a Ute, but he had added 8 pounds to his previous 120-pound frame and it was all muscle, mostly in his legs. With Electra's ECU being set at 108% of Earth's gravity ZacBox was able to more than compensate for the effects of zero gravity. He noticed his endurance was dramatically improved and was able to sprint past several previous Ascent and Marathon winners as they approached timberline, where the air had thinned even more. When they reached the Golden Staircase, he planned to make his move.

Only three runners were ahead of him: Marc Miyahara from Japan, Allen Nicholson from the U.S. and Ricardo Rodriguez from Mexico. Allen Nicholson was a previous winner, and the one runner everyone had their eye on to win. But Marc Miyahara had been training on Mount Fuji and although its elevation of 12,388 was below that of Pikes Peak, he held the lead as they approached the Golden Staircase. This rugged part of the course is well above timberline and within a quarter-mile of the finish line. The Golden Staircase got its name from the many large boulders the runners had to climb to reach the top. As ZacBox increased his speed, he began to leap from one boulder up to the next. His legs burned, and he could feel his heart pound in his chest, but he pushed past the pain. The finish line was in sight above him. The other three runners also sensed it was now or never to take the lead.

Marc Miyahara was breathing hard when Allen Nicholson passed him, but Ricardo Rodriguez showed he had a lot of heart and picked up his pace. ZacBox glanced up to the summit, just 150 meters away, to see if he could spot his dad, but there were too many other spectators crowding the finish line, so he concentrated on passing Rodriguez now just six feet in front of him. ZacBox matched his stride and looked past him to the rocky trail ahead where he thought he might be able to make his move, that's when he knew he could win this race, but a strange thought came over him. He began to realize the Electra's ECU had given him an unfair competitive advantage over the other runners. For a second, he was conflicted and wasn't sure what to do, but then suddenly it happened. Rodriguez's left foot slipped off the edge of a rock and he rolled his ankle.

"Ouch!" Rodriguez shouted, as he limped out of the way, hopping off the trail on one foot.

"Here," ZacBox said, "putting Rodriguez's arm over his shoulder to support his weight, "come on, we can finish this."

"No, you go on," Rodriguez said, looking back down the trail at the group of racers fighting for third place, "you can still finish in the top three. Leave me!"

"No. It doesn't matter now," ZacBox said, "I am not leaving you behind."

"You're crazy," Rodriguez said as he leaned on ZacBox and struggled toward the finish line being passed by five more runners.

"Come on Ricardo, we're almost there."

"How do you know my name?"

"Everyone up here knows the name Ricardo Rodriguez, you're famous on this mountain.

"What's your name?"

"I'm Zac, ZacBox."

"Wait, you're that ZacBox, you're famous on this mountain or just about anywhere else on this planet or the next."

"Come on, Ricardo, you can do it, just ten more meters, five, three—YEAH! We made it!" ZacBox said as they hobbled passed the finish line and waited as a race official approached them to record their times and remove the tags from their racing bibs.

ZacBox supported Rodriguez as the race official removed his tag, then he looked at ZacBox who was holding his hand over this racing bib. "I'm good," ZacBox said politely to the race official who smiled back at him and then turned to record the time on the next runner.

"How old are you?" Rodriguez asked.

"I'm sixteen," ZacBox said proudly, "You?"

"I'm seventeen, ouch! OUCH!" Rodriguez said as he removed his shoe and sock and tried to put weight on his now swollen ankle. "Guess we'll have to wait till next year to break any records."

"Let's get your ankle checked out, make sure you didn't break something this year."

"Thank you, you might have won this race if you would have just left me on the trail."

"That's just not me. There's my dad over there, he'll know where the first aid station is."

"Hey Dad," ZacBox said as his father put Ricardo's other arm around his shoulder and headed them toward the first aid station, "meet Ricardo Rodriguez. Could you help him get checked out at the first aid station? There's something I have to do."

"Sure thing, Zac," Zeke Box said, "I'm parked over there; I'll meet you at the truck when you're ready to head down."

ZacBox walked over to the west face of the summit of Pikes Peak, the mountain the Ute people knew as Tava. He took in the view of many other 14,000-foot mountain peaks standing off in the distance. He bent over, untied his shoe and removed a small elk hide pouch tied to his shoestring. He opened the leather pouch and emptied its only content out into the palm of his hand. It was the red heart-shaped diamond Arjun had collected for him from the cave on Europa. Then ZacBox whispered a silent prayer and tossed the priceless diamond down the side of the mountain as an offering to Creator.

ZacBox's dad insisted on driving Ricardo back down the mountain and lent him his cellphone so he could call his parents waiting for him in Manitou Springs. On the way down, ZacBox shared the meaning of a vision quest in the Ute culture with Ricardo, including the importance of leaving Creator an offering in gratitude. Before he got out of the truck, ZacBox invited Ricardo to stay at his house for a few weeks next summer, so he could train at altitude before next year's ascent on the Peak.

"You can have my bed," ZacBox said to Ricardo, "if things go well I'll be sleeping in the woods and going through survival training with the incoming freshman cadets next summer."

June 24th 21:38 hours MDST Astradate 11062.4
Flying Horse, Colorado Springs, CO USA Planet Earth

ZacBox's dad came outside the house and found his son and Bo lying in a lounge chair in their backyard staring up at the stars. "Hey, Dad?" ZacBox said quietly as his dad settled in the reclining lawn chair next to him.

"Yes, Zac?"

"Do you think mom and grandpa are up there together right now looking down at us?"

"I'd like to think so, but there's no doubt in my mind that wherever they are, both of them are just as proud of you as I am," ZacBox's father said as he handed him a wooden flute. "This was grandpa's flute, he wanted you to have it."

"Thanks, Dad, I remember Grandfather playing this early in the mornings when he took me fishing on the back slope of Sleeping Ute Mountain," ZacBox said as he cradled his great-grandfather's flute in his arms. "I always wanted Grandpa to teach me how to play his flute. Have you ever tried to play it?"

"No, it wouldn't be proper," ZacBox's dad explained. "A musical instrument is a very personal thing; he never invited me, and it would not have been right for me to play his flute without his permission. The last time I saw White Elk on the Reservation he was insistent I take the flute home with me and give it to you when the time was right. I told him he should wait until you were home and give it to you himself. I think he knew he would not see you again, not in this life anyway. Go on, try it."

ZacBox held the flute up to his lips and blew. Nothing happened. He tried again. Nothing. No sounds at all came out of the flute.

"Maybe it's broken," ZacBox's dad suggested.

ZacBox inspected the flute carefully and tried again. He wasn't sure what he was looking for, but it appeared to be intact. Then he held his palm against the opening and blew into the mouthpiece again. "There's no air coming out, it's like its blocked or something."

ZacBox separated the mouthpiece from the flute stem and looked inside. "There's something in here," he said as he shook the flute and a piece of rolled up paper slid out into his hand. ZacBox set the pipe in his lap and carefully unrolled a piece of old parchment paper and held it up to the light. "There's a map drawn on it, and it's in grandpa's handwriting, I recognize his writing from all the birthday cards he sent me. I think this map is showing the entrance to a cave and a tunnel under Sleeping Ute Mountain. Look! Down here in the corner, there are seven stars drawn in the shape of the Pleiades! And the second star from the right, just above Electra, that's Celaeno, I've been there! It has a circle around it! I think Grandpa knew where there's another flying saucer."

"Must be; is there anything written on the back?" ZacBox's dad asked.

"Yes," ZacBox said, "but it's not Grandfather's handwriting; I think it's written in a foreign language, I can't read it."

"Let me see. I can't read it either but the lights are still on next door at the Brondsted's. Come on, let's go knock on their patio door; between them they speak at least seven different languages. One of them might be able to read this and tell us what is says."

A kitchen light flicked on when ZacBox knocked on the Brondsted's patio door. Professor Brondsted, along with his Cocker Spaniel, Persephone, greeted them at the sliding glass door. "Hey Zac, Zeke, come on in," Professor Brondsted said as he slid open the door."

"Sorry to bother you so late Professor," ZacBox said as he handed him the note. "We're hoping maybe you or Dr. Fibonacci can translate the writing on the back of this map for us."

"Let me see," Dr. Brondsted said as he held the map up to the light. The professor adjusted his glasses and examined the paper. "It's really old, I can tell you that much, maybe 15th century, judging from the parchment and ink. It might be Italian, which has always been a bit of a challenge for me. Lisa, could you please slip on a robe and join us in the kitchen?"

When Professor Fibonacci stepped into the kitchen, Dr. Brondsted handed her the paper. "Could you please read this for us; my Italian is a little rusty."

Professor Fibonacci stood in her kitchen examining the note, wearing a pair of fuzzy slippers and pink bathrobe instead of a white lab coat. ZacBox thought she still looked scholarly.

"Sorry to bother you this late, Lisa," Zeke said as everyone waited for her to translate the handwritten message on the back of the map.

"Quite alright, dear," Professor Fibonacci said as she looked at the map and then turned it over to read the other side. "This inscription is written in Italian, but it was written backward; we need a mirror. Come follow me," she said as she led the way to the guest bathroom, flipped on the light above the sink and held the old parchment paper up to the mirror.

"Who would write Italian backward?" ZacBox asked.

"There's only one person I can think of, and he lived in Italy during the 15th Century," Professor Fibonacci said as she, ZacBox, Zeke, Dr. Brondsted, Persephone and Bo all huddled together in the bathroom. Professor Fibonacci read the quote on the back of the map, "It's dated 1492 and signed," and then she gasped and said, "I can't believe this!"

"What? Who? Was it him?" Professor Brondsted asked excitedly.

Professor Fibonacci looked at the signature one more time in the mirror and then said, "Yes! This map was signed by Leonardo da Vinci over five centuries ago."

"What does it say?" ZacBox asked Professor Fibonacci as she held it up to the light.

"When once you have tasted flight, you will forever walk the earth with your eyes turned skyward, for there you have been, and there you will always long to return."

Author Biography

John Wesley Anderson, MBA, is a published author, artist and TEDx speaker. John spent ten years in the aerospace business and retired from Lockheed Martin in 2012 to launch a consulting firm allowing him the freedom to pursue his love of writing, history, and the arts. Prior to working in the corporate world, John enjoyed a 30-year law enforcement career including being twice elected to serve as the Sheriff for El Paso County, Colorado (he was term-limited in 2003). His nonfiction book, *Rankin Scott Kelly, First Sheriff El Paso County, Colorado Territory 1861–1867*, received a 2017 Literary Award from the Historical Preservation Alliance of Colorado Springs. Most of John's books, including *Native American Prayer Trees of Colorado* are available online at Amazon.com. Although John has traveled around the world, including five adventures on a catamaran sailing the Caribbean, three corporate assignments into a combat zone on the Horn of Africa and landed on an aircraft carrier at sea, he remains most fascinated by the rich history and art found in his own back yard in the American Southwest.

To learn more about John Wesley Anderson and his books: Visit www.jwander.com

Acknowledgments

A special thank you goes to three author friends: Bill Scott, Steve Coonts and Tony Kern. My friend William B. Scott, retired Rocky Mountain Bureau Chief for Aviation Week & Space Technology, helped shape this story early on saying, "ZacBox would make a great call sign and instead of having him find a flying saucer, how about having a flying saucer find him?" Stephen Coonts, New York Times bestselling author, an inspiration for me since his first novel, *Flight of the Intruder*, to his three-book series: *The Saucer Novels*. Dr. Tony Kern, U.S. Air Force pilot and B-1B flight examiner, thank you for sharing your military experience.

Much gratitude goes to Southern Ute tribal elder, Dr. James Jefferson, Bob Chapoose, Austin Box, and Irwin Taylor and my other Ute friends and elders from all three Ute Reservations, for sharing their stories and rich culture. My hope is that what I have written here honors your ancestors and inspires the children of the Seventh Generation; Towaoc. I also wish to express my sincere appreciation to Dr. Gary Ziegler, for sharing his passion for archaeology and to Jon and Eileen Koenigsberg for sharing their sacred land.

To my wife Brenda and daughter Laynie, thank you for your continued love and support for me as an author. A warm thank you goes out as well to all my other family; including Haley and Taylor Kline, Jordan and Yousef Shakhsheer, my Aunt Betty Davis, cousins Sheila Lockwood and John Davis. Thank you all for your continued support and engaging conversations.

A special thank you goes to Elizabeth Taylor, Gayle Krzemien, and Karen Rhodes who did a wonderful job editing and fact-checking my draft manuscript. To retired Physics Professor Richard Cook, Ph.D., Professor Emeritus USAFA, for his unending patience in trying to teach a street cop a little physics during our multi-day road trip to the top of Sleeping Ute Mountain. Richard, your careful line-by-line review of my draft manuscript to make sure I hadn't violated any major laws of physics was very much appreciated. To Chris Day, US Coast Guard Commander (ret.), thank you for reviewing my manuscript and sharing your experience as a helicopter pilot.

To special friends Ginger and Skee Hipsky, Tim Hayden, fellow retired Lockheed Martin engineers and science fiction enthusiasts Vern Kuykendall, Phil Tinsley, Heidi Wigand-Nicely, and to Bruce and Cree Clark, I thank you for your engaging discussions. Thank you to my friends Brandon Sutherlin, for introducing me to a hero with a thousand faces and Janet Sellers, for sharing her talents and experience in Japan. To my writing coach Toni Robino, the publisher of my first three books, Susie Schorsch and Don Kallaus with Rhyolite Press, a huge thank you to each of you for seeing promise in my writing. Your continued commitment to help me evolve as a writer is very much appreciated.

Lastly, I want to thank Major Jason Furcron, USAFA Class of 2003, for being such an important part of our family. It was our good fortune to have had the privilege of being your cadet sponsor family during your four years at the Air Force Academy. I appreciated you sharing your experience as a cadet and insights as a pilot in helping shape this novel. Watching you grow from your first days at the Academy, to becoming the military officer you are today, has been one of the greatest pleasures of our lives. Whenever I hear the mighty roar of the C-130 Hercules engines, and look aloft to see the distinctive profile of the powerful Lockheed Martin aircraft pass overhead, I always think warmly of you and appreciate your service to our country. Thank you.